Secret Life

Jeff VanderMeer

With an Introduction by Jeffrey Ford

GOLDEN GRYPHON PRESS • 2004

Edited by Marty Halpern

LIBRARY OF CONGRESS CATALOGUING–IN–PUBLICATION DATA

VanderMeer, Jeff
    Secret Life / by Jeff VanderMeer ; with an introduction by Jeffrey
Ford. — 1st ed.
        p.   cm.
    ISBN 1-930846-27-4 (alk. paper)
        1. Fantasy fiction, American.   I. Title.
PS3572.A4284   S43   2004
813'.54—dc22   2003027519

"Learning to Leave the Flesh," first published in *Dreams from the Strangers' Café*, no. 5, January 1996.

"London Burning," first published in *Worlds of Fantasy & Horror* (formerly *Weird Tales*), no. 1, Summer 1994.

"The Machine," first published in *Strangewood Tales*, edited by Jack Fisher, Eraserhead Press, 2001.

"Mahout," first published in *Asimov's Science Fiction*, mid-December 1992.

"The Mansions of the Moon (A Cautionary Tale)," first published in *Nemonymous*, no. 1, November 2001.

"The Sea, Mendeho, and Moonlight," first published in India in a very different form in *2001: The Future Perfect*, November 1989; and in the United States in *Visions*, Spring 1990.

"Secret Life," first published by Hoegbotton & Sons, December 2002, in a 100-copy chapbook edition for the author's personal distribution.

Contents

For Ann

Acknowledgments: Thanks to all of the editors who have published my work over the years. Thanks to my parents, Penelope Miller and Robert K. VanderMeer, for instilling in me not only a love for art and for creativity, but also a good work ethic and a sense of purpose. Thanks to my sister Elizabeth for inspiration and for laughter. Thanks to Duane Bray for reading all of those early stories back in high school. Thanks to Denise Standiford, my creative writing teacher at Buchholz High School (Gainesville, Florida), Jane Stuart, Enid Shomer, and Meredith Ann Pierce for their early guidance and example. Thanks to everyone who has helped form these stories with their incisive comments and their generous readings. Specific thanks to James Patrick Kelly and Wade Tarzia for their comments on "Balzac's War," and to Alan DeNiro for comments on "The City." Thanks to Michael Moorcock for . . . well, everything: Even before I knew you, you were there in spirit. Thanks for acts of kindness early in my career to Dean Wesley Smith and Ann Kennedy—if you hadn't advanced me money on stories you'd bought, it would have been difficult to continue. Thanks to *Fantastic Metropolis* and *Storyville* for friendships and for good writing. Thanks to Mark and Cindy Ziesing for their support over the years—you guys are just the best. Thanks to everyone associated with this project for making it a pleasant and aesthetically pleasing experience: Jeffrey Ford, Scott Eagle, and Gary Turner, with special thanks to Marty Halpern for his meticulous care in editing these stories. Thanks to my wife's children, Jason and Erin, whose creativity inspires and instructs. But most of all, thanks to my wife, Ann, who through the years believed in me more than I did, has been my first reader for every work of fiction I have ever written, and without whom these stories would not have been possible.

Introduction:
The Secrets of
VanderMeer

SINCE THE LATTER HALF OF 2002 AND EVEN MORE so in 2003, the tourist population in the city of Ambergris has risen exponentially. Have you been? For the modest price of a hard-cover book, or, for those of lesser means, a paperback, one can embark on a journey of the imagination to a locale that has few equals in this world, or that of fantastic fiction.

If you need testimony from satisfied customers read the reviews, there are many online, or consider the plethora of "year's best" lists that this tour, in the name of *City of Saints and Madmen*, appeared on. The highlights of the trip have nothing to do with something so mundane as magic, so hackneyed as dragons, or as threadbare as wizards and elves. In Ambergris the wonder arises from the Baroque complexity of its design and the unusual social structure and rituals of its inhabitants. There is nothing supernatural about this city, but the intricate detail with which it has been conceived and the depth of portrayal of the lives of some of its more noted personalities makes it more uniquely memorable than fantasy cities of less realistic constraint. When you have finished the tour, closed the book, and Ambergris has become part of you and you part of it, you will have the persistent sense that for all its strangeness it lies in a geographical, intellectual, and emotional location overlapping that of your own life.

Jeff VanderMeer, the architect of Ambergris, has been writing fiction of a speculative/surrealist/fantastic nature for decades. For many readers, it must have seemed that he had just appeared out of thin air in 2001 with the paperback publication of *City of Saints and Madmen*. Granted, he did win a World Fantasy Award in 2000 for the novella "The Transformation of Martin Lake," but few readers are aware of this. If you look at the venues in which the different stories in this collection, *Secret Life*, were published, you will note that most appeared in publications and from publishers who operate independently, outside the realm of media conglomerates or corporations, relying on personal funding and limited to smaller print runs. For those not in the know, it might seem that these fictions could be lacking in the vision and craft necessary to be worthy of publication by more prominent venues and publishers, but after reading a few selections here it will be easy to recognize that this is not the case, for what VanderMeer represents, at least on one level, is the triumph of the independents. When I say "triumph," I do not mean triumph *over* well-funded, larger publishers, but a triumph in their own right. Their dedication to quality and idiosyncratic vision over commerce is beginning to resonate within the greater book-buying public.

In speaking with Jeff VanderMeer, I know that, at first, it wasn't that he did not want to see his work published in more prominent venues. He did and does, but what he found was that his personal vision was not concurrent with theirs. Instead of making the fatal mistake of changing his style, diluting his vision, as so many newer writers do in order to find a home with an established publisher or magazine, he trusted explicitly in his own imagination. In doing so, he chose another path, and eventually found that there was a whole community of like-minded writers and publishers. It was here, among the independents, that the sea change that speculative fiction is undergoing today started. VanderMeer played a sizeable role in it with his own press, Ministry of Whimsy, publishing works by wonderful writers like Jeffrey Thomas, Stepan Chapman, the authors in his *Leviathan* anthology series, and by contributing his own fiction to magazines whose interests lay more with original voice and vision, the hybridization of genre, exploration of character, "experimental" technique, than with the tried and tired tropes that dominated the bestseller lists. Today, all one has to do is be slightly aware of the goings-on in the realm of speculative fiction to see that independent presses like Ministry of Whimsy, Small Beer, Night Shade, and Golden Gryphon (the publisher of this book you now hold) are increasingly competing for awards, "best of" lists, and, in some cases, even sales, with corporate publishers, and they've done it without compromising their own directives.

Now, here is where all this comes back to *Secret Life*. As well-received and lauded as *City of Saints and Madmen* was, and as much as readers and reviewers enjoyed it, the book did not appear without a great deal of writing experience. VanderMeer did not become an interesting and excellent writer when he sat down to create *City of Saints and Madmen*. It was more that the field and its readership, through the influence of the independents, widened its scope to allow this remarkable writer a place on its radar. What *Secret Life* represents is the best of his fictional output that existed prior to a more general recognition of his work. What this also represents for the reader who enjoyed *City* is the discovery of a secret treasury of stories that contains all of the best elements of that larger work. These stories are at times exotic, surreal, lush in their description, philosophical, humorous, romantic, and always eminently readable.

I think readers who have not yet had the pleasure of reading *City* but have merely read its reviews, will be pleasantly surprised by this collection. A good portion of those reviews focused merely on the intricacy of the construction of that book, the reflexivity, the mock scholarship and literary gamesmanship. Rightly so, to some extent, for the encoded story and the complex connections between stories and the *fictions* that explained the fictions were enjoyable aspects of it and reviewers made a strong point of noting these "novelties." What I think was often missed, though, was a discussion of VanderMeer's strengths as a storyteller, his command of style and his craft. I think reviewer Nick Gevers was correct, when compiling his list that appeared in 2001 on *Locus online*, in choosing Jeff VanderMeer as one of the top ten short-fiction writers in the field of fantastic fiction.

One thing that will be very evident in *Secret Life* to both his new and long-time readers is the range of VanderMeer's interests and abilities. The settings of these pieces are as varied as Cambodia, Tennessee, Central America, Florida, nightmare cities of the imagination, an alien world, Veniss (the city featured in his novel *Veniss Underground*), and, of course, Ambergris (for those who have been longing for another visit). They are rendered with great attention to detail and an understanding of the local culture and landscape, giving us a sense that we are there with the characters. The characters, again expertly drawn to the point where we are convinced of their existence and care about their outcomes, cover a wide spectrum—a soldier, a god, a harried office worker, a corpse, an elephant, an artist, even you yourself. There are pieces here that will leave you with a sense of existential angst, your head swimming, like "Experiment #25 from the Book of Winter: The Croc and You," or through their fabulation perhaps call into question some aspect of your own life, as in "The Mansions of the Moon" and "Secret Life," or return you to some point in history, as in "Mahout" and "London Burning," or offer a science lesson derived from VanderMeer's vast knowledge of the freshwater squid, or leave you on the verge of tears, like in "Balzac's War" or "The Bone Carver's Tale."

You can sense traces of a great pedigree in VanderMeer's fiction, leading back to the very finest writers of the literature of the fantastic—Jorge Luis Borges, Franz Kafka, Angela Carter, Italo Calvino, Vladimir Nabokov. At the same time, because of the visual nature of the reading experience, I was aware of the influence of films like *Invasion of the Body Snatchers* and John Carpenter's remake of *The Thing*, and both of these in just one story. There is an obvious connection in other stories to the films of Svankmejer and to *The City of Lost Children*. Certain other fictions reminded me of the artwork of Max Ernst, di Chirico, Rousseau, and Cornell. All of these varied influences are recombined and filtered through the original voice of this author. Unlike much writing in the fantasy "genre" with little memory beyond the history of "genre," VanderMeer's writing harkens back to a time when fantastic literature was "literature" and did not deny character development or fine writing or complexity of plot for the sake of a cardboard character's single-minded drive toward the culmination of an adventure. This said, it must also be understood that there is a wicked sense of humor that often undercuts the "literary" gravity of these stories, not obliterating it but melding with it so that the piece can both engage your intelligence and emotions and leave you laughing. For an example of this type of thoughtful satire, see the title story of this volume.

When reading the stories in *Secret Life*, you might wonder what type of person could have written them. Here I can be of some help, for I have spent quite a bit of time corresponding with Jeff VanderMeer through e-mail and have actually been in his presence on more than one occasion. The first time I met him face to face was at a poolside bar in Ft. Lauderdale, Florida, while attending the International Conference on the Fantastic in the Arts. He was dressed like a Xerox copier repairman, with rumpled, short-sleeved white shirt and necktie. His image didn't exactly jive with my knowledge of his writing or his correspondence, but he struck me as a very earnest individual, and yet his sense of humor, which was quick to show itself, belied a sardonic wit. There was a certain buttoned-down eccentricity to him I couldn't precisely put my finger on, but his conversation was very interesting and we laughed a lot.

His mind must constantly be racing because he usually has about a dozen irons in the fire at one time—fiction writing projects, publishing projects, reviews, critical essays, obscure books he is trying to find. There is something of the perfectionist in him that occasionally drives him to the brink of neurosis, and he is blatantly honest, occasionally getting himself in trouble with even his friends. If you *are* his friend, you can expect to be included in projects like *The Thackery T. Lambshead Pocket Guide to Eccentric & Discredited Diseases* and find yourself trying to fit into a two-sizes-too-small lab coat a few seconds before participating in a panel discussion during which you are expected to pretend to be an insane physician. Or you might get the mail one day and find there a box filled to the brim with dried mushrooms to protect a little box within, containing a small book, a letter printed with golden ink, which carries a beautiful image of a giant squid, and a Porfal Memory Capsule. A few weeks ago, I received a chapbook from VanderMeer in the mail, printed in a language I had never before seen.

Most importantly, he is the facilitator of a kind of loose community of writers and illustrators and publishers who share his love of the art of the fantastic. Acting like a switchboard, he freely distributes e-mail addresses, puts people in touch with one another, distributes word of editors looking for submissions to anthologies and magazines. Through knowing Jeff VanderMeer, I have met many interesting people and been exposed to ideas and books I would otherwise not have ever heard of.

Still, with all my testimony, what makes VanderMeer tick is a secret, and though I can name writers and artists who have influenced his fiction and can describe some of its wonderful qualities, how that fiction conveys its powerful ideas and images and emotions is also a secret that can only be plumbed by your choosing a story within this volume and beginning to read.

Jeffrey Ford
June 2003

Secret Life

Secret Life

Legion

A VISION OF THE BUILDING FROM ON HIGH: FIVE glittering floors surrounded by a dull concrete parking lot. To the west lay a forest. To the east, the glint of a shopping mall, substantial as a mirage. To the north, highways and fast-food restaurants. To the south, a perpetual gloom through which could be seen only more shadow.

The building housed hundreds of people. They worked day and night, as relentless and constant as the seasons. The first four stories lay open to all, but no one could visit the fifth floor without a special key. Few had ever seen the roof.

The stairs were used for emergencies only. Some of the elevators clanked and groaned. Some of the elevators, quiet and smooth as ghosts, rose and fell with limitless grace.

Most inhabitants of the building, even the janitors in the basement, it was rumored, preferred the noisy elevators. When the quiet elevators reached the first floor, a scream could sometimes be heard, as of an animal trapped and then crushed beneath their feet. The screams might continue for several minutes. No one knew what kind of animal it was, or how it came to be trapped there.

Here Be Dragons

Over time, the inhabitants of the third floor grew to despise the inhabitants of the second floor. "They cannot see what we see," the people of the third floor would say to themselves. Sometimes, they would put an ear to the carpet and listen to the people on the second floor as they performed their empty rituals.

"They are no more intelligent than bees or ants," the people of the third floor would say, and smile. Yet they still visited the second floor, often for no particular reason, and would talk to the blank-eyed people they found there. After all, they too had once lived on the second floor, before the growth of the company.

Over time, language fell away from the people of the second floor, as if words had been something gifted to them by those on the third floor. Over time, the words of those on the second floor came to seem like the hum of busy wasps, or the sound wind makes through corn not yet ready to be harvested. Over time, the people of the third floor grew afraid, for reasons they did not understand.

The Pen

How did it get there, he wondered as he stared at it. The pen held in his manager's right hand had, only an hour ago, been on *his* desk. With that pen—extinct, no longer made, refills imported from a foreign land—he had signed important documents, written condolences, drafted memos. The pen had a black obsidian exoskeleton, a fine, sleek body. Strange symbols had been carved into its surface. The point rode across the page as effortlessly as his fingers rubbing his wife's back.

Might the pen be as responsible for his success as any other factor?

The manager walked across his field of vision again. Behind the manager, conveyed by a film projector, images flashed across a screen: of badgers killing moles, of men in trench coats, of complex diagrams, of open briefcases like wings. The manager continued his singsong chanting of the training mission as the twenty-five trainees, one penless, watched him.

Could he be certain a signed contract was binding without that pen? Could he be certain his good fortune would continue? And did his manager know what he had done by taking the pen? Looking at the smooth smiling face of the manager, he realized he could not be certain of anything. Images of falling bombs painted the manager's face gray and black. Anger began to glimmer inside the man, like moonlight reflected in a dark pool. He began to sweat, to fidget. His hand was empty; he could feel the phantom presence of the pen as if he had lost a finger.

The manager continued to pace and smile as he talked, sometimes pointing with the pen for emphasis. Behind him, the bombs had stopped falling and a man in a raincoat was walking slowly up the side of a barren hill, above him an observatory. Could the manager have taken the pen by mistake? No. Everyone knew what the pen meant to him. No one could take it from him "accidentally."

Sweat flecked the man's forehead. He could not keep still.

The pen had been a birthday gift from his wife five years ago. She had given him the pen by hiding it between her breasts. She had made him hunt for it with his mouth, his tongue. After he had found it, they had made love for hours, urgently. He could not think of the pen without thinking of her soft, hot skin. He could not think of the pen without remembering her nakedness, shining in the dark room.

Overcome, he rose.

The manager stopped pacing.

"Is there a problem?" the manager asked, his eyes cold. Steam seemed to rise off the top of his head, but it was only the screen behind him.

"Is there a problem?" he repeated when the man said nothing, all of the man's will focused on the pen.

With a shudder, a sigh, the man shook his head and sat down.

The manager gave him a sharp look, then resumed his lecture.

Behind the manager, the walker had reached the observatory, which had turned into a museum, which had become a library, and then was gone, replaced by the V of geese migrating across thin, light-blue air . . . and the time between the manager's curt words and the man's realization that he was capable of killing the manager yawned across that expanse of sky like the slow curve of his own signature.

Sometimes

Sometimes, sitting in the basement, staring at dim green light through a murky portal, the janitor-in-training had a strange longing for another life, a life he received an inkling of in the small hours of the night, in a stray sentence of conversation curling away from him around a corner of the office. A chance meeting on a crowded elevator. A life he knew he would never find, too enraptured by or entangled in the life he had already chosen. Each day he eyed the back of his trainer with suspicion and found less logic in the speeches of the Head Janitor.

Conquest

At dusk one day, the company that had colonized the second and third floors conquered the first and fourth floors as well. For months, they had sent their employees to work on one or four. For months, these new employees had infiltrated the first and fourth floors. The liquidation, when it came, was swift and brutal. Cruel smiles. Locked doors. Blood sprayed across walls, carpet, ceiling. No one on the outside heard the shouts and screams. No one came to help. The janitors in the basement, balanced teetering on their chairs as they watched television screens filled with snow, paid no heed, even to the muffled echoes that descended to them from the air ducts.

For a time, all was still. All was quiet. The outside of the building glimmered with patchwork lights. The sounds of traffic dulled into silence. A wind came up and the nearby forest rustled with the music of leaves. To the east, the shopping mall lost the glister of its neon signs. To the north, the highways slowed to a sometimes car, flaring like the tip of a cigarette. To the south, the sudden stars cut off abruptly, victims of the gloom that hid the south from all but the most piercing gaze.

The moon, like a cross section of rounded bone, rose into a deep blue-black sky. Crickets broke into song. The quick brown shadows of nighthawks began to glide over the building. Then, faintly, quiet and yet so clear, a sound came from the top of the building. A knife against a glass. A pen against a coffee mug. An exhalation of breath. A softly muttered curse. The scuffle of feet—a lunge, a thrust.

On the roof, the owners of the victorious and vanquished companies met in hand-to-hand combat: two identical fat men in dark suits. They sweated as they swore and swung at each other. Grappled. Gouged. Bit. Their ever-more-numerous wounds did not seem a part of them—caused by the other and thus somehow part of the other, each wound hurting the giver.

The morning would find them huddled together on the roof, as peaceful as if they had died in their sleep, conquest finally complete.

Interlude #1

The company that occupies the first through fourth floors of the building has a secret name. This name is never spoken aloud and almost never written down. A few people have seen its syllables, at night, in confidence. The name glows a fiery gold when looked upon. Those who see it are said to be changed forever. Some leave the building immediately. Others rise so fast in the company that they ascend to the fifth floor and few ever see them again. The secret name of the company is older than the company itself. It will remain long after the company is gone.

The Vine

The office building was a long rectangular box with miserly vents and faulty air conditioning. The inhabitants of the building breathed air that their predecessors had breathed years ago. Some argued that breathing this air perpetuated a sense of tradition in all employees. Most said it made them ill.

One day a woman on the fourth floor began to grow a vine in her office. At first, she feared the cutting, taken from a patch of soil near the great gloom of the south, would not grow for her. But she so hated the austere look of her office—the gray-white ceiling tiles, the brown, worn carpet, the pale gray desk and old brown chair. The instant she placed the vine in a corner, on top of a filing cabinet, she felt better, as if she could breathe again.

Her boyfriend laughed when he saw the vine. "Like a pig with pockets," he said, looking around her office.

They were having lunch. He worked across the street as the assistant manager at a bookstore. He always smelled of lighter fluid for some reason. She liked his looks but not his manner.

"I think it's a breath of fresh air," she said, determined to fight cliché with cliché.

In the silence that followed, they ate their sandwiches and stared at one another. She thought about the shopping she had to do after work.

Something mournful had entered the room.

At first, the vine blanched and would not bloom. Even with the support of a trellis, even with enough potted soil and the direct light filtered through the murky glass of her window. She felt guilty, gave it more soil, added fertilizer, bought shades for the window so she could regulate the sunlight that fell upon its leaves.

For months the vine refused to grow, or die. The woman forgot about the vine. She watered it automatically, in much the same way she stapled papers together or answered the telephone or had lunch with her boyfriend. Her boyfriend ignored the vine, his disregard a palpable presence in the room.

But one day, in the spring, she entered her office to a new smell, a fragrance unfamiliar to her. Perfume? Air freshener? No. It smelled vaguely of honeysuckle, of fresh berries, of vanilla, but wilder, more pungent.

She turned toward the window—and gasped, almost dropped her purse. The vine had turned a dark, healthy green, racing up the trellis, muscular and thick. It had blossomed: large, fluted flowers, a bright yellow that had transformed it into a fountain of color.

The plant brought her great happiness after that. People complimented her on it. She felt better because the air smelled like a garden all the time. The vine outgrew her small trellis. It outgrew the medium-sized trellis she brought in to replace the old one. At first, she had clipped its offshoots, but found she did not have the heart to prune it. It was too beautiful to contain.

Oddly enough, her boyfriend now liked the vine. This change of heart irritated her and she soon stopped seeing him.

When the vine outgrew even the large trellis, she faced a decision: cut it back or give it some new outlet. The flowers were huge now, as large as any she had ever seen, and a pure yellow that gleamed like gold even in the gloom. The vine was taking over the office, but she still could not bring herself to cut into such a healthy plant.

So one morning, she shut her office door, pulled her chair over to the vine, and carefully climbed up onto the seat. Using a ruler, she pried up a ceiling tile. The top of the vine unfurled itself and sprang upward as if it had been waiting for just that moment. It disappeared into the space she had created between the tiles.

From then on, her problem was solved and she did not think about the vine for many months. The curl of vines as they reached the ceiling concealed the gap in the tiles. No one noticed. Her vine had become such a part of the office décor that few visitors ever commented on the tangled explosion of green and gold in the corner.

Home

They found the manager after many years, finally. He had not quit without notice. He had not gotten trapped on the forbidden fifth floor without a key and died of starvation. Neither had he flung himself off the roof and landed in a drainage sluice. Nor had the large billboard visible from his office, the one advertising island holidays, been too great a temptation.

No, they found him inside his own desk. A night janitor had triggered the secret latch under the right-hand filing cabinet, revealing the secret compartment, revealing the manager.

He lay curled up inside, a man in a business suit, the skull now buried in the jacket, the leg bones loose in the slacks. He lay upon a simple bed, a pillow at one end, a tiny television at the other, a bottle of good brandy tucked into the corner.

They found a peephole in the front of the desk. They found a toothbrush. Floss. Towels. A jug of water. Snacks. Cans of tuna fish. A can opener. Several people wondered if he had ever left the office. The night janitor remembered him staying late to compile reports or edit the next training film. Some said that the images from those films had affected him, had seared themselves onto his skin, these ghostly tattoos only seen when the lights were off. In all ways, he had made his own coffin.

It seemed only incidental when the company coroner discovered that someone had broken the manager's neck and shoved a very cheap ballpoint pen between the manager's teeth. No one knew why this should be so. Nor could anyone recall a moment when the manager had ever been truly happy.

Interlude #2

Some say that more people travel up to the fifth floor than ever come down. Others, that more come down than go up. Those on the first floor say the fifth floor is empty, while those on the fourth floor say it is full, but will not say full of what. A few have speculated that a vast ossuary fills up the space—a plateau of bones and skulls receding off into the distance. That no manager is ever buried outside the building. That this field of bones, if measured, is longer than the building could logically contain. The janitors laugh at such speculation. They like to say, "Wiser to ask: What is in the basement?" But this only the janitors know.

"Down There"

"We rule from the bottom up," the janitors say from their basement stronghold, knowing in their hearts that they could as well survive without the floors above as a turtle can survive without its shell.

There exist two types of janitor in the office building: night janitors and day janitors. They can be distinguished by how they manifest themselves. The night janitors rest in closets during the day, among the brooms and mops, and do not emerge until dusk. The day janitors leave the building at twilight in large, unsmiling groups. The two types of janitor never meet—know each other only by their handiwork, the signs left in the patterns of swept floors, polished hallway lamps, changed light bulbs. They are as ghosts to one another. Each has created a mythology for the other—an act of faith. On the rare occasions when they by accident meet, they stare at each other as if seeing a stranger in the mirror, and to as much effect.

Only one janitor travels between the two worlds of night and day: the Head Janitor, he who works during both light and dark and rarely sleeps. It is the Head Janitor, bulked and bulky, tall and thick, who growls out orders in a gravelly baritone from between moistened lips, as much despot as cleaning agent. They listen as if to a force of nature; during the day, he comes to the night janitors in their closets as a premonition of darkness and they smile in their twisted sleep, dancing through the halls with mop and broom.

He it is who gives voice to their thoughts, their desires, as he paces up and down the basement hallway, neither cleaned nor cleaner.

"You shall not think of them as your masters," he says to them. "You shall not think of them at all. Your work exists independent of them, without them. They are as wraiths to you. Our faith has to do with honest labor, with the purification of the inanimate. This is how we pray and how we do our jobs. Remember that. They are nothing: a scrap of cloud, a hint of a breeze."

"We empty their trash," the janitors intone. "We straighten up their messes. We complete their very thoughts. They can as well survive without us as without the very air."

Their philosophy has descended to them through long years from the floors above—from crumpled pages saved, from the backs of notepads casually scribbled upon and tossed aside. They are as likely to divine wisdom from a discarded sentence passed down from generation to generation as from any reputable source. Theirs is a philosophy of scraps and fragments, the punctured code of incomplete memos and torn note cards. What words were meant as flotsam, they regain as compost for their ways.

The Head Janitor cannot remember a time when he was not alive. He looks out sometimes through the ground-floor window that faces the south and grumbles about the gray, the gloom. "Clean," he mumbles. "Cleaner." His bloodshot eyes widen and he trembles, in the grip of some secret emotion.

Infiltration

. . . and the vine continued to grow, twisting its way across the inside of the ceiling tiles, winding its way past layers of insulation, found the air ducts, and began to colonize the building's arteries, harming no one, so that even the strange people of the second floor, with their clicking beetle speech, noticed that the air had become fresher, while in the basement the janitors grumbled and jabbed their mops into the air, for they had grown to like the stifling mustiness above the basement, the vine still crawling and pushing its way through the building, filling every hidden corner, allowing mice to crawl over it and chew on its blossoms, their droppings over time creating a thin layer of soil from which it grew stronger still, the infiltration continuing . . .

The Shadow Cabinet

Every second week of the month, on a Thursday, the Shadow Cabinet meets, all twelve men and women in black suits rising frictionless and fast via the glistening silver elevator.

On the fifth floor, the doors open with precision and out walks: the Shadow Cabinet. Eyes hidden by black shades. Faces unsmiling. Smoke-gray briefcases caught in vicelike grips at their side. Silver cufflinks. Black shoes so shiny the ceiling reflects in them.

As they pass through the sliding glass doors to the receptionist's outpost, the Shadow Cabinet seems to flow or glide, their steps so smooth and controlled that they might as well be moving forward on an escalator.

In neat rows of two, they wordlessly pass by the receptionist—she scrunched low in her chair, making herself as small as possible; mouse to their collective snake—and ripple into the fifth-floor conference room: a wide space without windows. The last two in line always stare back at her, nod once, and close the door.

Outside the conference room an hour passes. No one knows

how much time passes inside. No one has ever discovered the purpose of these meetings. No sound comes from behind the closed doors. Ever.

The receptionist's part in the ritual is, by tradition, limited. After an hour, she will enter the now-empty room, gather up the twelve empty, open briefcases—resembling the discarded exoskeletons of thick gray beetles—and toss them into the incinerator at the end of the hall. The briefcases feel hot to the touch long before she reaches the incinerator. Any curiosity this phenomenon might arouse in her, she quells immediately. It is not her job she fears for.

One week, she entered the room as usual and was gathering up the briefcases when she felt an odd prickle on her neck. Turning, she looked up—and screamed, dropping the briefcases. There, on the ceiling, clung a man in a black business suit. His pale hands were splayed flat against the ceiling tiles. His eyes were large and luminous. When he saw the receptionist staring at him, he let out a soft moan, a shuddering shiver. Then he scuttled across the ceiling in a series of quick-darting movements, crossed over to the sidewall, and disappeared out the door, taking a route as far away from the incinerator as possible.

Since that moment, there has been no curiosity so great the receptionist could not ignore it.

Unexpected . . .

A green tendril of vine curled out from under one of the ceiling tiles. The janitor-in-training was certain it had not been there a moment before. It seemed to form a finger, beckoning to him.

For a minute or two, he did nothing, dark eyebrows scrunched together. He looked around. Was this, perhaps, a test of his integrity concocted by the Head Janitor? Should he investigate or not? He put down his pencil. The Head Janitor had assigned him the dull duty of requisitioning supplies. He had been writing down numbers in columns and then crossing them out, a scowling smile on his face. His parents had been artists. His grandparents had been circus acrobats. Yet he sat in the basement of an office building and created strings of numbers. If only he could lose the ability to write them—if only the numbers would, like leaves carried by the breeze, fly off the page and fall to the floor . . .

The young man contemplated the curling tendril above him. It was not in his nature to ignore it. He could not ignore it. So he stood on top of his desk and peeled aside the ceiling tile, revealing

insulation, the hollow area between the tile and the next floor—
and a tangled welter of green vines and giant yellow blossoms. The
sweet, sweet smell of the flowers overwhelmed him; he almost fell,
just from the memories they brought back to him. They smelled
like the perfume worn by his first lover. They smelled of even earlier memories, too, like firewood burning in the fireplace of his
childhood home, or the spices his father had used to season the pot
roast for Sunday dinner.

The young man breathed in deeply and saw new numbers in
his head: the chances of the Head Janitor noticing his absence; the
chances of finding the source of the vine; the chances he might die
of boredom while sorting through the inventory. Nothing added
up. Nothing made complete sense.

An image floated into his mind: him, at the same desk for another fifty years, his lithe, muscular body, seemingly made for
climbing in tunnels, slowly turned to fat and defeat. He leapt off the
chair, found some sticky notes and a pen in a desk drawer, then took
a big bag of change over to the vending machines and bought as
many bottled waters and snacks as he could shove into his pockets.

Standing again beneath the tendril, he hesitated, staring up at it
for a long time.

Interlude #3

The smell on the third floor did not come from someone's rotted lunch, but from an executive vice president
who, having lost a spoon behind the lunchroom refrigerator late one night, fell during his efforts to retrieve it,
was knocked unconscious, and died without a murmur
in that small space, victim of the diet that had allowed
him to fit, not found for three weeks, the whole episode
distasteful to his wife and four children, not to mention
the day janitor who found the body and almost left it
there, hopeful that at some later date the white of
picked-at bones might be more easily cleaned up.

. . . Beauty

It was a form of release, an escape, for the janitor-in-training to pull
himself up into the air ducts using the vine for support. As soon as
he replaced the tile behind him, the young man felt lighter and
happier. He almost laughed aloud. In the darkness ahead, the

yellow blossoms glowed a friendly phosphorescent yellow, giving him enough light to see by. Like a lithe and clever lizard, he crawled forward, first through one corridor and then the next, always leaving a trail of sticky notes behind him.

The tendrils of the vine brushed against his face. The flowers bumped against his nose. His eyelashes became dusted with pollen. I'm a bee, he thought to himself, not unhappily. I'm a humming-bird. Below his hummingbird self, through minute openings, he could hear the buzz of conversation, the reverberation of people walking just a few feet below him. Something about the secret life he had entered gave him a deep sense of satisfaction.

Hours later, the young man had still not found the source of the vine. With astonishment, as he rested, the water bottles weighing him down, he realized that the vines had taken over every secret part of every floor. It might take a day or more to find the source. He could either turn back now or continue the search until he was successful. It did not seem like a true choice to him.

Minutes passed or days, hours or months—he could not tell. As he gave himself up to the search, he also gave up time. There was only the vine, the blossoms, his need. When hungry, he ate the sweet fruit of the vine, with its lingering aftertaste of regret. When thirsty, he licked moisture off the vines or sucked water from the blossoms. After a while, he could hear the vine—a soft undercur-rent of sound, a hum that matched its glow of good health. He would fall asleep entangled in the vines, wake refreshed, and continue on. Below him, at times, he thought he could hear the janitors grumbling among themselves in their own language, and he would laugh silently because now he knew more than even the Head Janitor.

The vines, the floors, the confined labyrinthine ecosystem that had come to life in the air ducts amidst the insulation, had its own rhythms and patterns. At regular intervals, for example, which he somehow equated with morning, a phalanx of mice would stam-pede down the vine—running right over him, their feet cold and tiny, their speech a deep chittering that he could swear sometimes held hints of human language. At other times, biting flies would assail him. Dragonflies and frogs. Dust and rivulets of water. Once, at the end of a long passageway, an animal with pale eyes stared at him before vanishing into darkness.

He felt himself twisting into the vine itself, so surrounded by leaves and flowers that surely they must sprout from him. At some point, his clothing fell away from him, no longer necessary. He did not pine for the sun or for any other living thing. Once, following a stray tendril of the vine, he burst from darkness into light—the vine having found its way out through a crack in the side of the building —and looked out into blue sky and gulls wheeling over the parking lot, four or five stories up. The light disturbed him. To the new senses he had developed, the light felt wrong. True light could only come from the source of the vine. He dove back into the darkness without regret.

Finally, when he had reached a place that suggested there might be no separation between himself and the vine, he found the source. It started as a sudden stubbornness on the vine's part—a thickening that resisted his progress. He had to suck in his breath and flatten his stomach to wriggle forward. The vine grew bigger still, muscular and gnarled. It cut into his skin, bruised him. He would have stopped and turned back, but a mote of light in the semidarkness ahead caught his eye. As he grunted and groaned his way toward the light, the mote became a gash, and the gash turned into a gap in the tiles, smothered with leaves.

His breath caught in his throat. Somehow he had forgotten that his journey might have an ending. What if this was the source? What would he do?

Slowly, heart pounding, he wriggled into position and pried the tile open. Light flooded the space around him. He stared down. Below, the vine burrowed down into a large pot. To the right of the pot, a woman sat at a desk. She had brown hair, and small hands that found their way over the keyboard of her computer by degrees —hunting for each key as if for the first time. Her face, as her gaze shifted from the computer screen to her window and back again, became now young, now older, sometimes tired, sometimes lively, but always anchored by the deep eyes, the stare neither stern nor gentle.

The smell of blossoms in his nostrils, the young man could not separate the vine from the woman. A feeling the young man had never before experienced flooded over him. He did not know what he had expected of the source—salvation? revelation?—but she seemed as miraculous as anything in his imagination. A vision formed in his head of the two of them covered in the vines, making love, their limbs rapturous with blossom and with root, the imprint of her hands burning into his skin.

As if awakening from dream, the young man pulled aside two tiles and lowered his head and chest down into the room below.

The woman looked up, gasped, pulled back in her chair.

"Oh!" she said, her voice surprised but melodious.

"So you—" he said, in a cracking voice unused to speech, and grinned. "So you're the source," he said.

And wept, for the face she turned up toward him was the most beautiful he had ever seen.

A Confusion of Tongues

Once, through a glitch in the system, an employee on the fifth floor was forgotten but remained on the payroll. She had only one task: to stamp APPROVED on various documents. Several years before, this job had required a full-time employee because so many documents had to be approved. However, that time had passed long ago. Now, in an office on the opposite side of the building, another employee rushed to stamp REJECTED on a mountain of documents. The order of such things might again reverse itself, but for now the woman spent her days in languid anticipation of the next document, which might not arrive for several hours.

The woman did not even have a window to distract her. A rare storm from the south had broken the window and the janitors had replaced it with planks of wood. Sometimes, she would peer through the cracks of light in the wood, but all that lay beyond was the sky. Had she expected anything different? Yes. Yes, she had.

Mostly, the woman read or listened to the radio. Late in the day, she might dance or even drink whiskey from a flask. She did these things at home in her tiny apartment, too, but they felt more daring at work.

Tiny gray mice that poked their heads out of cracks at the base of the wall near her desk provided the only break in the monotony of her routine. The first time she saw a mouse, she gasped and lifted the receiver of her telephone. The janitorial staff did not like mice. But as the mouse wrinkled its nose, scenting, and sidled out into the office, she put the receiver down. There was no reason to call—she had been acting out the role of someone who was not her.

Instead, she took out the whiskey and poured herself a shot. It tasted crisp and burned her throat. Nothing this exciting had happened to her all day. As a child, she had spent summers on her grandparents' farm. She used to sleep outside, smelling clover, grass, and the thick earth as she stared up at the sky. She would ride her horse for hours over the lush green countryside. Much to her grandfather's bewilderment, she had also tried to save mice from the half-feral farm cats.

The next day, the woman began to bring breadcrumbs, seeds, and other scraps from her apartment. She even went to the store to buy cheese. As many as ten scruffy, nervous mice feasted on what she had brought in with her. Their quick, hesitant movements amused her. Their psychic abilities impressed her as well; they always disappeared at least fifteen minutes before the courier arrived with the latest document to enjoy the stamp of approval.

She found herself trying out names for the mice on a pad of paper: Charles, Leisa, Paul, Zeb, Gwen, Jonathan, Diana, Bob . . .

After a while, as she sat in her office without windows, waiting for the next document, she found herself listening to the chirping language of the mice as they bickered over a biscuit or a rind of cheese. The more she watched them as they spoke to each other, the more she began to understand the nuances of their speech. Once or twice, she lay on the floor and covered her arms with bits of cracker and seeds. The bristly feel of their whiskers, the softness of their noses, the delicate touch of their paws—all of this helped her to understand them.

Several years passed. The woman's hair became flecked with gray. Her father and mother both died within a year of each other. The number of documents to be stamped never increased or decreased. Her entwined states of being friendless and alone were broken by all-too-infrequent periods of happiness that only made her feel worse when they ended, abruptly.

But she did learn the language of the mice. So well did she learn their language that she was able to teach them elements of her own language. This happened slowly and steadily, so that she almost did not notice the change, how the mice became her eyes and ears in other parts of the building. How they reported back to her on events and people that fascinated her. And because the viewpoint of a mouse is rather like that of a child—different and new and sparkling around the edges—their accounts were all the more entertaining and insightful.

The woman let her hair grow long and did not bother to dye the gray out of it. She wore long patchwork skirts and slippers. She stopped drinking whiskey. She no longer even bothered to say hello to the infrequent courier.

Instead, she found herself speaking more and more often through her mice, the voices of the mice become her voice. They spoke out in rustles and murmurs and chirps from the air ducts and the little holes in the vents and pipes: a dusty whisper that filled the building little by little until the janitors would look up from their jaded contemplation of the newspaper, struck by what seemed like a tongue of air in a place where no breeze ever blew.

At least, this is the story some inhabitants of the building tell to explain why, at odd times—on elevators, in an empty hallway— voices can be heard, speaking through the walls.

The Mimic

Dressed in a black business suit, a mimic appeared among the office workers on the third floor. He set up his computer in a just-abandoned cubicle. The dull hiss of his gray-spackled monitor reflected ghoulishly off his chalky face. He had an odd way of staring at the monitor, with his head cocked to the side. He had wrists and hands pale as the underbelly of a toad. He did not talk much.

"He is not natural to this place," some said.

"None of us are," others said.

If there had been fewer employees, perhaps the mimic would have been found out sooner. But the inhabitants of the third floor now numbered in the hundreds. They pressed down into the emergency stairwells, where middle managers sat in bewildered little groups, laptops balanced on their crossed legs. Everyone had to take lunch in shifts, for otherwise the elevators would groan with the weight for hours. Even a half-desk of space was coveted as a promotion.

Perhaps it was strange enough for the mimic to have taken a cubicle for himself, but stranger things soon occurred on the third floor. When the mimic began to pluck bugs from the stalks of his neighbor's hydrangea—the long, pink tongue erupting from the pale, calm face—everyone pretended not to notice. His neighbor told herself that it was nothing really, nothing important; after all, hadn't they acclimated themselves to the strange customs of the people who lived on the second floor?

Gradually, they noticed several other strange things about their new coworker. For example, despite the dress code, he did not actually wear shoes; his feet just resembled shoes. And when he ate his open-faced sandwiches of thick green paste, he swallowed in such a way that his large eyes receded into the back of his head, as if pushing his food down like a frog. He wept almost continuously as well, which was disconcerting if poignant, although one coworker remarked in a whisper that since the new employee's face never changed expression, it might just have been rheum, not tears at all.

The mimic smelled of cardamom and mango, sometimes of pears, sometimes of fresh rain on newly tilled soil. Sometimes he smelled like a thunderstorm come up from the south.

The mimic had violet eyes. "Violet, sad, soulful eyes," as someone said, sarcastically.

Anyone who looked into those eyes found themselves falling. They would remember events or people they had not thought of in years. They would feel a sudden compulsion to leave the building. They would feel an ache, a yearning for something they could not quite name.

For this reason, most people avoided looking at the mimic directly. Shaking hands was also not recommended because his oddly curled fingers were always damp. The pads of both his hands and his feet were sticky, and festooned with natural suction cups, although they did not learn this until later.

At meetings, the mimic would imitate the chatter around him, but afterward no one could remember exactly what he might have said, if anything. They just remembered it had sounded good at the time.

The woman who shared the cubicle to his left often defended him. "He's quiet," she would say. "His lunch doesn't smell. He's polite. He's considerate of other people's privacy."

For long hours, the mimic stared out the window toward the south, and wept the tears that might not be tears at all.

It was not until the night the mimic was discovered scuttling across the ceiling tiles in a twitching frenzy of movement, sucking insects and spiders into his mouth, that the people of the third floor turned against him. The sight was too strange for them. It did not mimic them at all.

He mewled as they bound his limbs. He made a soundless scream as they kicked him. He mumbled to himself as they hauled him into the elevator.

By the time the elevator doors opened on the second floor, he had gone limp, staring hopelessly off into the distance as they roughly dropped him in the second floor lobby and brushed at their clothes in distaste.

The mimic stared at them as they left. As the doors slid over their solemn, disgusted faces, they distinctly heard him speak to them. But each heard something different—reassurance, admonishment, joy, grief.

When the elevator doors opened at the third floor, they had all become very different people.

Interlude #4

As for the darkness to the south, it never advanced or retreated, but, like a perpetual thunder cloud threatening rain, remained in position: a wall of gray to block all traffic, all commerce, all thought. There were those who had passed on into the south, but no one ever saw them again. Some nights, lights would be seen in the southern darkness and in the morning strange creatures found dead at its perimeter. But over time it became as much a part of the landscape as the shopping mall and the fast-food restaurants. No one remarked upon it. No one cared. No one spared it a second thought.

Liberation

From floor to floor, the vine began to know its own deep green strength. The woman who had brought it to the building had left long ago with the young janitor, but it no longer needed her. Tendrils of an advance guard of triumphant yellow blossoms had found the outside of the building and begun to discreetly colonize cracks and indentations. Water coolers had been suborned to feed it. Any plant on any floor rooted in any kind of soil found a sly invader in its midst: a little curling vine exploring that soil with it.

The plant began to thicken and mature within its hidden passageways. The blossoms hardened into fruit, blackened, and fell off. The seeds sprouted in the most unexpected places, rattling through filters and vents to fall on desks and floors. The plant grew brown and tough. It could feel the sun all around it but not upon it, except in that niggling place where it had reached the outside. That tiny scout sent back the most pleasurable of sensations. The vine flexed and pulled and writhed. Ceiling tiles popped in remote corridors. Walls bulged. The Head Janitor muttered darkly to himself about the end of the world.

The people of the second floor embraced the change. They opened up their air system by order of their new leader, a pale man dressed in a black business suit who liked to climb across the ceiling. Great draping vines fell out of the ceiling, trailed across the floor. Soon a dense forest covered the second floor, and the people of the second floor lived among it in solitude and peace.

The vine grew stronger still.

Until one day, it filled every crack, every crevice, every secret area of the building. It had reached as far as it could go. And still the sun maddened and teased it.

The building began to crumble from the pressure, the stone and metal subverted, infiltrated, by vegetation, compromised beyond repair. The cascade of ruin moved inward and outward, everywhere revealing the miracle of green: a slow avalanche that took many weeks.

First to leave were the people of the second floor. The vine rent a gaping hole in the side of the building, the vine feeling for the earth. They crawled down the vine, still buzzing their fey speech, their possessions strapped to their backs. Led by the mimic, they disappeared into the southern gloom, never to be seen again. It is said that when they reached the perimeter of that melancholy place, the mimic gave out a great cry, raised his arms, smiled widely.

Others tried to fight back, enlisting the help of the janitors, but it was no use: cracks had appeared in the very foundation, and the sweet nectar smell of the vine was everywhere. The edifice began to crumble. The fifth floor, long since abandoned except by the Shadow Cabinet, fell to the street in an almost silent collapse in the middle of a cloudless day. Empty briefcases shattered on the pavement below. Now the building wore a cascading green fountain of vines down its sides.

After a while, all was still. The company was no longer really a company anymore. Half had fled. Most of the rest had been drawn back by the sheer rote power of routine, but this did not hold them for long. In pairs and packs, they drifted away. Gradually, the parking lot became empty in the middle of the day. The offices nearby became abandoned, bereft.

The vine kept growing—under the pavement, under the topsoil, coming up in odd and unexpected places, always seeking the light.

Soon, even the strip mall lay abandoned. Birds flew overhead in thick flocks. The fruit of the vine fell where it would and took root everywhere. Stone and vine and steel, the slumped ruins of the building stood guard over squirrels and trees.

Beneath the ground, the Head Janitor railed and shouted at his staff. They had successfully sealed off the basement from the vine, but now found their philosophy as useless as a basement without a building.

Lighthouse

One woman remained in the building, even after silence had fallen over it, even after the janitors had given up their struggle. Every afternoon she would walk from her apartment and climb through the rubble to her office with its ever-empty APPROVED box. The mice had long since left. She didn't mind—she was happy for them. They would send her words throughout the world and one day they would come back and tell her tales of where they had been.

She had long gray hair now, but her stance remained straight as she stood by the cracked window, framed by the hissing half-light of tentative fluorescent lamps powered by a failing emergency generator.

The woman neither lamented nor welcomed the death of the building. It was unimportant to her. She came back because there was nowhere else to go and nothing else to do. Her check, issued by some central location, was hiccupped out to her at irregular intervals by some bureaucracy that had not heard of the building's fate.

Nothing ever changed.

In a way, she found it peaceful looking out across the green, watching the way the clouds sped across the sky. Through the broken glass, the wind sometimes leapt into her office and she would close her eyes and enjoy the sensation of it against her face. She had lost her voice, but felt she did not need it anymore.

Sometimes she would walk through the crumpled passageways, the corridors that led to unexpected light, and wonder about her coworkers. She had never really known them before. Now, though, by the things they had left behind, she knew them well. She had found love letters buried in the rubble once. Another time, a wrapped present. Fingerprints on a windowpane had caused her to stop and examine them, wondering who they had belonged to, why they had felt the need to place their entire hand against the glass . . .

Every night she would let the emergency generator sleep, turning out the lights on her floor. The stars would come out all at once, soft and glistening. The world would be reduced to a shadow, a coolness. At such times, she would wrap her shawl more tightly around her and look back over her life—at the spaces in her life, the gaps—and she would be only a little sad.

After a while, she would take out her flashlight and shine it into the darkness, slowly turning and turning. The darkness ate the light. She couldn't really see anything clearly—just the outlines of shapes, of the vine, of the dull, reflective chrome of a distant car, approaching the gloom of the southern border.

She did this for many nights. She didn't know what she expected to find, or why she had decided to shine the light. She only knew that the ruination of the building had released something within her. So she held the light and flashed it out into the darkness.

Then one night, from the deepest part of the southern gloom, a light shone back at her: a violet light, small but intense.

She almost dropped her flashlight in surprise.

Some say it was only the mimic, mimicking her from the safety of the southern gloom. Others, that it was just a reflection in a pool of water. Still others say it was her one true love, created from need and darkness.

"Is it you?" she might have said. "Are you the one?" she might have said. She might have said nothing at all.

But come morning, she was gone, never to return, her flashlight dropped on the floor of the office, and all across the world there were only the sounds of the vine: the bees upon its blossoms, the ants collecting drops of moisture from its leaves, and its own distant hum, vibrating against the earth.

Notes on
Secret Life

*In 2001, the company I work for moved into a new office
building: five gleaming stories of glass and metal. As soon
as we got settled in on the second floor, I sent a short-
short story called "Here Be Dragons" around to some
of my coworkers. That story made us out to be old-time
explorers plunged into a new environment. Then, my
company took over part of the third floor and I wrote the
short-short that now comprises the section "Here Be
Dragons" in "Secret Life." After that, I just kept adding
to it, mythologizing the office. A lot of it is pure invention. Other parts, like the mimic, came to me because one
of the graphic designers had a habit of dressing all in
black and working in an office with the lights off.*

*A shameful confession regarding "Secret Life": I wrote
part of it because I thought, for a split second, that
writer Andy Duncan had stolen my pen. When my
wife Ann and I attended the 2002 Slipstream Conference
in LaGrange, Georgia, I was deep into the writing of
"Secret Life," to the point that whatever entered my environment became fodder for the story. During Andy
Duncan's reading, I suddenly realized my pen was missing. All these ideas were boiling up in my brain, and I
had nothing to write them down with. (During prior
readings, I'd tried to listen to the speaker and write notes,
making it look as if the notes had something to do with
the reading. I don't know how successful this ruse was . . .
I suspect not very.)*

*So I looked up, grieving over my penless existence . . .
and there was Andy, fiddling with a pen as he read. A
pen that looked suspiciously like my own. A pen that — I
had this sudden paranoid insight — was my own. Andy
Duncan, sly, clever crocodile that he was, had stolen my
pen! On purpose! So I couldn't write my story!*

*Sanity washed over me a second later, but it was too
late: I had an idea for a new section of "Secret Life." And,
right after Andy's reading, I pounced on the pen where
he had left it on the podium and used it to write the rest
of the first draft.*

Flight Is for Those Who Have Not Yet Crossed Over

THE ONLY SOUNDS INSIDE THE PRISON ARE THE drip of water, the weeping of prisoners, and the *chink-chink* of keys on Gabriel de Anda's belt as he limps through his 2:00 A.M. rounds of the third floor. The prison walls glow with green phosphorescence and, from far below, Gabriel can hear the ocean crashing against the rocks. A storm builds out in the Gulf, where sargasso clings to drowned sailors and does not allow them to sink into the formless dark of deep waters. Gabriel feels the storm in the pressure of air pushing against his face and it makes him wary.

He has been a guard at the prison for so long that he can see it in his mind like a slowly turning, dark-glittering jewel. The Indians call the prison "Where Death Walks Blind of Justice." It is a block of badly mortared concrete, surrounded by barbed wire, electric fences, and jungle. Resembling nothing less than the head of a tortured, anguished beast at sleep, a twenty-four-hour lamp at the front entrance its solitary eye, it hunkers three stories tall, with tiny barred windows checkering a brackish, badly lit interior where bare bulbs shine down on graffiti, guard, and prisoner alike. No one has ever escaped, for the prison, its foundations rotting, dominates the top of a cliff on the eastern coast of that country known more for its general, El Toreador, than for its given name, a name once Indian, then Spanish, but now forgotten.

Gabriel's rumpled uniform scratches his back and fits poorly at the crotch. He shuffles over the filthy catwalk that leads from one side of the third floor to the other. Muttering to himself, he fights the urge to spit over the side into the central courtyard, where the secret police hose down the violent prisoners. His gimp leg throbs.

When only twenty-two, Gabriel was visiting Merida, Mexico, his brother Pedro driving and jabbering about some girl he knew in Mexico City "with thighs like heaven; no, better than heaven." Enraptured, Pedro took a curve too quickly and careened into oncoming traffic. Gabriel remembers only a high-pitched scream and the pain that shattered his left leg, the bone breaking in two places.

It gave him a limp. It gave him grist to chew as he navigates the catwalk. The janitors haven't cleaned the catwalk from the last food riot. Dark, scattered lumps form an obstacle course, exude the stench of rotted fruit and flesh. What sweet relief it would be to press his face up to one of the outer windows; then he would see, framed by moonlight, the breakers far below tumbling against a black sand beach. The first refreshing hint of summer gales might touch his face in forgiveness, but afterward, he would only have to return to the catwalk and the last prisoner, Roberto D'Souza.

Roberto D'Souza has been held for five days and nights, charged with aiding the guerrillas who live in the northern mountains and call themselves Zapata. Gabriel has nothing but contempt for the rebels. If not for them, rationing would be less severe and goods would be more plentiful in the stores.

Gabriel's pace quickens, for he can leave once he has checked on D'Souza. He can drive the twenty miles to his small house outside Carbajal, the capital, and to his wife Sessina. She has worked late hours setting up window displays and may still be awake, perhaps even have supper waiting for him: huevos rancheros with hot tamales. His stomach rumbles thinking about it.

But first, D'Souza.

D'Souza sits in the corner farthest from the bars and the only window, his knees drawn up tight against his chest. Gabriel sneezes from the stench of shit and piss, wonders yet again if it is necessary to deny political prisoners a chamber pot. Why haven't the janitors at least hosed down the cell?

None of the cells have their own illumination and so Gabriel shines his flashlight on D'Souza. D'Souza's back is crisscrossed with red and black. Where whole, the skin appears yellow. The spine juts, each bone distinct, below a ragged mop of black hair.

As the light hits him, D'Souza flinches, hides his head, and tries to disappear into a wall pitted from years of abuse. Gabriel flinches too, despite himself. He must remember that this man is an enemy of the state, a guerilla, a terrorist.

"Number 255," Gabriel says, to confirm and then leave, limping, for home.

No answer.

"Your name, please," Gabriel says.

D'Souza does not stir, but when his voice comes, it has a wiry strength, a determination ill matched to the wasted body.

"Roberto Almada D'Souza."

"Good evening to you, Roberto."

"Is it? A good evening?"

"The sky is clear outside, as you could see if you looked. The waves are still low. Tomorrow, though . . ."

"I don't need to see. I can smell it. I can taste it. Rotted wood and salt and the last breaths of lost lovers. Can't you feel it?

Unfolding his long arms and legs, D'Souza rises with gangly imprecision. He is shrouded in shadow shot through with flashes of skin as he turns toward Gabriel, who cannot see his eyes.

D'Souza says, "I have children. A father who is blind. How can I feed them from in here?"

"My father is dead."

In the coffin, his father still wore the shabby black blazer and gray trousers from his days in prison, looking like an actor trapped in an old black-and-white movie.

"Should I feel sorry for you?" D'Souza says after a swift scrutiny of Gabriel's face.

"Tell them what they need to know and they will let you go."

A frustrated sigh. "I cannot tell them what I do not know."

"Everyone is innocent here," Gabriel says.

"Everyone except for you."

"It's a living."

"Is it?"

"Good night," Gabriel says and turns to leave.

"Would you take a message to my wife?" The faltering timbre of D'Souza's voice, the anticipation, the hope, sends a tremor down Gabriel's spine, even as he faces the prisoner.

"What?"

"My wife's name is Maria. Maria D'Souza. She lives in Carbajal, in the projects. Please. It is not very far. She is tall and thin and has hair as long and thick as the silk of angels. Please. Her name is Maria. Tell her where I am. Tell her I think of her. Tell her to visit my father and let him know where I am. Her name is Maria."

Inside of Gabriel, something comes loose. A lurching nausea, a dislocation. It will pass, he tells himself. It has always passed before, no matter how they plead—which is not often because most times they just sit and stare at the walls.

But he says only, "No. I cannot."

"Please?"

"No."

D'Souza comes swiftly to the front of the cell, silent, his white, white skin stretched over his scarecrow frame, mottled by moonlight and shadow. His hands around the bars are gray and splashed with a violet color that would be red by any other light. D'Souza has burning pink flesh instead of fingernails. His face is a welter of dried blood and yellowing bruises. An apparition from the Night of All Saints, a carnival figure, but too grim for a clown. D'Souza stares at Gabriel, and Gabriel, transfixed, stares back, wondering at the passing resemblance to his brother Pedro, the drawn cheekbones, the fiery black eyes, the anger that pins him, helpless: a priest hearing a confession, a vessel to be filled.

"Do you know what they have done to me?"

"I don't know what you mean."

Gabriel is not a member of the secret police, but he has at times come to a cell at the wrong time and seen things that have made him retrace his steps while thinking desperately about the current football scores and his country's chances of making it to the World Cup. *A door left open. A shriek, abruptly cut off. Blood under the fingernails.*

D'Souza's hand snakes out from between the bars. He clutches Gabriel's wrist so hard it throbs. Gabriel smells the blood and filth on D'Souza, feels the sticky cool softness of D'Souza's nail-less thumb against his palm. He struggles, wrenches away from that touch, backpedals out of reach, confronted with a rage accumulated not over years but days.

"I must shit where I eat and I eat nothing because what they feed me is less than nothing. They come at all hours, without warning, with electric cattle prods. They beat me. They have torn my fingernails out. They have attached electric wires—"

"Shut up!"

"—to my scrotum and stuck needles up my penis. They have tried to make me confess to crimes I haven't committed, never committed. . . . They are tireless and well fed and confident, and I am none of these things. I was a painter before they took me. Now I am nothing."

"I said to shut up!"

But Gabriel does not pull out his nightstick or walk away from the cell. His lack of action mystifies him. He cannot understand why he finds it so difficult to breathe.

D'Souza loses his balance, slides slowly down the bars, into the darkness of the floor.

"Take a message to my wife or do not take a message to my wife . . ."

And then, in a self-mocking tone: "It truly does not matter. I have dreamed of flying to her myself, you know. Flying over this country of El Toreador. My arms are like wings and I can feel the wind cool against my face. All the stars are out and there are no clouds. Such a clear, clean darkness. It seems almost a miracle, such clarity . . . Below me I can make out the shapes of banana plantations and textile factories. I can tell the green of the rainforest from that of the pampas. I see the ruins of the Maya and the shapes of mountains, distant . . . and yet when I wake I am still here, in my cell, and I know I am lost."

D'Souza looks up at Gabriel, the whites of his eyes gleaming through the broken mask of his face and says, "My wife's name is Maria D'Souza. When I have died, you must tell her so she can come for my body."

By the time Gabriel has stumbled back along the third-floor catwalk, ducking the swinging light bulbs, and down to the second floor and finally the first; by the time he has passed through the endless security checkpoints in the first floor administrative offices where the secret police lounge, still wearing sunglasses; by the time he has lit a cigarette and limped through the rain-slicked parking lot to his beat-up VW, he has managed to distance himself from D'Souza and think of other things. The car, for instance, which was a present from Pedro, now a used-car salesman in Mexico City, perhaps not where he wanted to be at fifty, but happy. It is like the shedding of some insidious skin, this thinking of other things.

The car crankily shifts into gear and Gabriel turns on the headlights. He backs out under the glare of the moth-smothered lamppost and drives past the outer ring of guard stations, waving at his friend Alberto, who is good for a game of pool or poker on the weekends.

The road is bumpy and ill marked, but as Gabriel speeds down it he reaches an exhausted calm; his shoulders relax and he slides back in the seat, slouching but comfortable. Mottled shadows broken by glints of water reflect the stars. There is no traffic at this hour, the bright murals and billboards depicting El Toreador muted, rendered indistinct by a night littered with broken street lamps.

Magnified by the hush of surrounding trees, the silence is unbroken, except for the chugging huff of Gabriel's VW, the even sound of which reminds him of an old Mickey Mouse alarm clock; the ticking had more than once lulled him to sleep, wedged between three brothers on a small bed. His father had been alive then, and they had been poor, although well-off compared to some families, until he'd been caught selling drugs to supplement their income. A thin, short man in a shabby black blazer and gray trousers too baggy for his legs; eyes that had once reflected laughter become as flat and gray as slate; shoeless feet a flurry of scars from working hard labor in the quarries. Mother had had to find work in a clothes factory, making bright cotton designer shirts that would be shipped off to the United States, to be sold in shopping malls with names like "Oaks" and "Shady Brook."

The silence, then, and the space, which allows Gabriel to pretend that nothing surrounds him, that the road passes through an infinite bubble encompassing the sky, and within that bubble he is the only person alive; that once he passes through the silence and space, washed clean by it, when he is home, he enters his second life.

Glancing at the stars, Gabriel gets a crumpled feeling in his chest. Once, he had dreamed of flying as a career: a commercial pilot or a member of the air force, like his grandfather. His grandfather—Ricardo Jesus de Anda—whose hands were so soft and supple it was difficult to remember that he was a hard man who had spent many nights in his MiG defending the country's borders from attack. Before the coup, his grandfather shot down three F–15s in four hours over Honduras and they gave him a medal. The next day he was at Gabriel's house, laughing, holding a beer, and looking at the ground in embarrassment while Gabriel's mother detailed his exploits. And Gabriel had thought, What could it possibly be like to fly at such a speed, no longer bound by the earth, curving the air with the violence of your passage?

Gabriel's leg begins to throb and he remembers D'Souza saying, "When I have died . . ."

He stops thinking and stares ahead at the road. Soon he pulls into the gravel driveway of his four-room house. It forms part of a state-sponsored housing project, not much different from the relocation sites made available to Indian tribes uprooted from the mountains. His house is constructed of unpainted concrete, single-story, with the gracelessness of a building block. As the VW comes to a stop, Gabriel blinks his headlights three times before turning them off, so that if Sessina is awake she will not mistake him for the police.

Gabriel knocks on the front door and then unlocks it, certain she is in the kitchen preparing his meal. Inside, Gabriel can smell rice, beans, and eggs. Sessina has turned off the lights to conserve electricity and he has to orient himself by the glow of the kitchen and the television in the living room. The bedroom is off to the left. They share an outdoor bathroom with the couple in the house next door. The living room wall is half wallpapered, half rude concrete.

"Sessina?" he says. "Are you in the kitchen?"

"Yes," comes the muffled reply. "You are late."

Gabriel unbuttons his shirt, places his guard's cap on the baroque iron hat rack. Another present from Pedro.

"A little trouble with a prisoner," Gabriel says. "Nothing to worry about."

"What?" she says as he walks into the living room. A replay of the football game is still on and the national team is up three to two, with thirty minutes to play. The green sofa calls to him, but he disciplines himself and walks into the kitchen, shielding his eyes from the angry white light of the naked bulb that hangs there.

"I said I had a little trouble with a prisoner."

Sessina stands before the stove, spatula in hand. The light illuminates her face in such a way that her beauty is almost painful to him. Her hair is black and shines a faint metallic blue, her eyes large, her nose small and slightly upturned. She still wears the dress she wore to Garcia's Department Store in downtown Carbajal, but she has taken off her black pumps. The grace of her small feet, their contours clearly visible through her pantyhose, makes him smile. He comes close to her and touches her lightly on the shoulder.

She smiles a tired smile and says, "It was a long day at the store, too. I had three window displays to set up. We finished very late; I got home after eleven. Sit down and watch the game. I'll bring you your dinner."

A peck on the cheek and back to her skillet.

Although Gabriel wants to linger, wants to say how good she looks to him, he walks into the living room. The sofa springs are old and he sinks into the cushions with a grateful sigh. His back muscles untense and only now does he really feel sleepy, lazy, relaxed. He lets the low hum of the announcer's voice, broken by moments of excitement, lead him into a half-doze.

After eighteen years, Gabriel is still bewildered that Sessina agreed to marry him, although at the time he must have appeared to be a man who would make something of his life. But then had come the leg injury, Pedro having whisked him away for a "little bachelor fun" a month before the marriage. While Gabriel was still in Mexico, El Toreador staged his successful coup and Gabriel's grandfather was stripped of his rank, forced to retire because he had refused to join El Toreador.

"Stay in Mexico," Pedro pleaded. "Don't go back. I'm not going back. No one can make me go back. It will be Guatemala all over again. *Don't go back.*"

But he had gone back. He remembered getting off the plane and walking onto the escalators at the airport and, seeing the black-red banners of El Toreador, realizing it was not his country anymore. Until he saw Sessina waiting for him. And then it didn't matter.

"Here you are," Sessina says, and hands Gabriel a steaming plate of rice, beans, and eggs. From beside him, Sessina kneads his back in just the right spot while the game drones on.

"Thank you," he says, and begins to eat.

"What was the trouble with the prisoner?"

"He wanted me to get a message to his wife," he says between bites of food.

"And what did you say?"

"No, of course."

"Did you have to say no?"

"He's a prisoner, Sessina."

"What did he do to get put into prison?"

"Traitorous things. A traitor to the country. An enemy of the state."

"Oh. That explains why your back is so tight. Was it difficult to say no?"

Gabriel shrugs, then shouts, "Yes!" when the national team scores again. The television blips to a news brief: more bad news about the economy, three murders in the southern city of Baijala were still unsolved, and a boy had poured a pot of boiling water over a puppy and felt no guilt. The last item makes Gabriel feel sick inside.

"How terrible."

"People are terrible," murmurs his wife. "You could find another job."

They have discussed this before, it is old news, and Gabriel does not answer.

Sessina's hands draw larger and slower circles across his back. Soon the hands stop moving altogether.

"Sessina?"

Gabriel finishes his meal and puts his plate next to him on the sofa. He carefully lifts Sessina's arms away from him and sets them down in her lap. He turns off the television and walks into the kitchen holding the dishes, puts them in the sink.

A rosary hangs on the wall over the faucet, on a nail, and next to that, a photograph of his grandfather beside his MiG, smiling with his wide mouth so that his tan, leathery forehead crinkles up even further. Sunglasses hide his eyes.

Gabriel turns away and comes back to the couch. Sessina still lies there, her mouth half-open, her breaths shallow, the top two buttons of her wrinkled white blouse unbuttoned.

When they married, Sessina had aspirations of a modeling career. Now she dresses up the mannequins that decorate the window displays of Garcia's Department Store. In the bustle and fatigue of day-to-day living, the dream had slipped away from her, fragment by fragment, until she must have forgotten, or believed she had never dreamt of such a thing.

And does she, Gabriel asks himself, stare into my eyes and think the same thoughts, and there we both are, caught in moments that trickle away endlessly, lost in the repetition of doing the same things over and over?

Looking down at Sessina, her beauty remote from him, a movie image, not flesh and blood, Gabriel knows he still loves her—a sudden intake of breath when he sees her at night, a palpitation of his heart, the sense that even caught in the morass of daily life she makes it worthwhile. Yet there is such distance, as if, were he to reach out and touch her, he would find that she is really miles away.

D'Souza, pressed up against the bars of his prison cell. Might Sessina have met his wife in Garcia's shopping for clothes or perfume? How difficult would it be to simply whisper, *"Your husband is in prison."*

Gabriel gathers Sessina up, a feather weight in his arms, and she locks her arms around his neck and, half-asleep, nuzzles up against him. Not bothering to turn on the light, Gabriel takes her into their bedroom, past the chest of drawers with the photographs of her mother and father, Pedro, and Gabriel's mother; another of his grandfather, months before his death. He lays Sessina on the bed and undresses her. Instead of turning the covers down, he slips out of his shoes, sheds his trousers and unbuttons three buttons on his shirt. He pulls it over his head and drops it onto the floor to join the pants.

Sessina has curled up on her side and so he slowly gets into bed opposite her, slowly makes his body fit the contours of her body. He puts a hand on her breasts and kisses her freckled back. Her skin feels warm to his touch. She makes a purring sound and reaches out with one hand to stroke his hair. He runs a hand along the side of her hips and she arches her back until his thighs come to rest against her buttocks. She is very hot; he wonders if she is a fallen angel, come streaking down from the sky, to be so hot. Such a beautiful stranger in his bed.

As he is about to fall asleep, Gabriel hears the sudden whisper of rain, and then an echo, and then a thousand voices, a speechless, rumbling patter. The storm will come in the morning, he knows, and he cocks his head to one side, as if listening beyond the sound of falling water for some other sound entirely.

Waking to the patter of rain against the roof, Gabriel looks groggily at the clock, which blinks "1:04 P.M." Sessina left for her job at the department store hours ago. The bedroom window has fogged over and he smells the rising sweetness of orchids laden with moisture, bromeliads nearly choked with it. Drains gurgle with water.

Gabriel rises with a half-groan, half-yawn, his neck muscles aching. His mouth is dry; he feels parched, weak. Eyes blurry with sleep, he trudges out to the communal bathroom to take a shower, then dresses and eats a quick lunch. At three o'clock he leaves the house, hurrying to the car under the shelter of a tattered gray umbrella. His shoes are soaked by the time he closes the VW's door. The engine starts reluctantly when he turns the key, then growls, as if the rain has done it good.

The drive to the prison takes no time at all under the gray-black sky, blurred further by his faulty wipers, so that the concrete blocks of houses, the shiny metal of cars, and the sharp straightness of trees become patternless streaks of green and brown.

As Gabriel passes through the prison gates, he begins to discard thoughts of Sessina, Pedro, the news on the television. He begins to think of his rounds, the fifteen-minute breaks he will have as the night progresses, how he will have to speak with the janitors about cleaning the third-floor catwalk. He knows that the ceiling leaks and that moisture will bleed through the walls, bringing with it lizards and cockroaches.

In the administrative offices, Gabriel passes the secret policemen. They are frozen in the same positions as the night before, only now three of them smoke and one man gazes out a window at the cliff face and the downpour falling onto the black sand beach below. The sea bellows and shrieks against the rock.

These men always look the same—outwardly relaxed, but posed so exactly that Gabriel believes them guilty of a hidden tension, as if, full to bursting with secrets and mystery, they must sit just so, their clothes pressed perfectly so they resemble figures in a wax museum.

What new secrets do they possess that they did not know yesterday? Gabriel thinks as he checks in at the front desk.

Administrative work awaits Gabriel and he spends six hours sorting and filing various forms in a ten-by-ten room with flickering fluorescent lights. He can feel the pressure of the sea colliding against the impervious rock: the crunch of waves, maddened beyond reason, so compressed and thick that something, somewhere, must *give way*, the entire world unmoored.

His friend Alberto—short and swarthy and enjoyably foulmouthed—enters three or four times to share a joke and a cigarette, but for the most part Gabriel is alone with his aching leg and the red tape of El Toreador's bureaucracy. As Gabriel places one file atop the next, one piece of paper atop another, he thinks of D'Souza's face pressed up against the bars, and then of his father's face.

Gabriel cannot remember many times that his father was not in prison, pressed up against those bars. The wane smile. The sad eyes. Gabriel can remember the feel of his mother's hand in his during those visits, the hand progressively thinner and more bony, until it seemed she was only made of bone, and then even less substantial: a gossamer strand, a dress blowing, empty, in the wind. She had survived her husband by less than three months and Gabriel knew that his father's incarceration, his death in jail, had diminished her, so that she had died not so much from a broken heart as from a sense of shame that burrowed beneath the skin and poisoned her every action.

The sheets of paper he collates seem as thin as his family history, the only depth provided by Pedro, who once caroused with him around a Merida traffic circle and crashed joyously into on-coming cars. Lucky Pedro, well fed in Mexico.

At last, Gabriel has filed the last file and he begins his rounds with the common prisoners on the first and second floors: the murderers and rapists and bank robbers.

The wind buffets the prison walls; Gabriel thinks he can almost feel the floor shift beneath his feet as if moved by that wind. Or perhaps he is just tired and afraid. Afraid of what?

Lightning strikes nearby, followed by thunder, and the lights flutter violently. The beach will be drowning in water soon and only the cliff will stop the water from rising farther and flooding the interior. The rush of water is almost a second pulse.

When Gabriel reaches the third floor, he is out of breath, in darkness lit by the bare bulbs. They swing like low-strung stars, blinding him with their glare. The janitors have yet to clean the mess and he moves through it cautiously.

The guard at the entrance to the political prisoners' section is not on his stool.

The hairs on Gabriel's arms rise in apprehension. Has the man abandoned his duties or gone to the bathroom? Gabriel hesitates. Perhaps he should return to the first floor?

Instead, ignoring his fear, he moves to the first cell. He shines his flashlight on the bed. He shines his flashlight in the corners and under the bed. The prisoner is gone.

The flashlight shakes in Gabriel's hand. He feels nauseous. Perhaps the secret police have taken the prisoner for questioning and not bothered to inform the guards. Perhaps the third-floor guard accompanied the secret policemen.

But when he comes to the next cell, it too is empty. The next cell is also empty, and the next, and as each new cell is revealed to be empty, Gabriel walks faster and faster, until he jogs and then runs, sweeping the flashlight over each bunk as he passes it. No one. No one at all. They are all gone.

Panting, sweating, Gabriel comes to the last cell: Roberto D'Souza's cell. The cell is lit by the moon shining into the window: a huge burning white globe shrouded by the torn ends of purpling storm clouds. Gabriel drops his flashlight to the floor. His mouth opens and closes. He does not even know what he is trying to say.

D'Souza floats next to the window that faces the sea, his eyes tightly shut and his arms outstretched like wings.

There is a raw churning in Gabriel's stomach. He wonders if, perhaps, he is still lying next to Sessina in their bed.

He pulls out his nightstick. He takes the cell key from his belt ring and unlocks the door.

D'Souza continues to float next to the window. The wind sends his long hair streaming out behind him.

"Come down!" Gabriel shouts. And, in a lower voice, *"Come down."*

D'Souza does not open his eyes. His body is still scarred and pitted with the excesses of his torturers, but the wounds are clean and unmarked by red or black. D'Souza floats toward the window until his head is pressed up against it.

D'Souza *melts* or wriggles through the window. It happens so slowly that Gabriel should be able to tell what has occurred, but he can't; it is as if he blinked and missed it. Gabriel runs to the window.

In the light of the moon, he sees D'Souza and dozens of other prisoners, washed clean by the bracing wind, the stinging rain. As they dip, gyrate, and glide through the sky, Gabriel can hear distant laughter, faint and fading. As they fly farther away, they appear as swathes and strips and rags of darkness swimming against the silvery white of the moon. He stares until he cannot see D'Souza, just the shapes of bodies moving like dolphins through water.

Watching their flight, Gabriel feels a weight in his heart, an emptiness, a loss, and a yearning. He shuts his eyes so tightly they hurt and wills that his spirit too should fly up into the moonlight, into the clouds, the torrential rain, and the wind. But as he wills this, as his body starts to become lighter than air, than life, he sees the images he has sought to block out: the scalpels edged with blood, the secret police gathered around their victims, the rubber gloves and the wires.

When Gabriel opens his eyes, he is still on the ground, in the empty cell, with the door open.

Gabriel stands there for a long time before he takes off his guard's cap and lets it fall from his hands to the floor. He walks downstairs to the first floor, where the secret police no longer lounge, but instead run back and forth, scream, shout, and gesticulate wildly. This secret is too big for their minds to hold. Boots clatter against cement runways. Automatic rifles are loaded with a desperate *chut-chut.*

Gabriel walks past them and out into the rain. The rain feels good against his face. It dribbles into the corners of his mouth and he tastes its sweetness. Above, the prisoners, and ahead, from the parking lot, guards and secret police, soaking wet and strangely silent, shoot at the prisoners as if their sanity depends on it.

Ignoring them, Gabriel gets into his car and drives off, past the empty observation posts, past the twenty-four-hour light, past the useless barbed wire, past the ludicrous outer fences, and onto the twenty-mile stretch of road that leads home. He shivers as his shirt sticks to his skin, but he feels the cold only as a numbness that has no temperature. The night along the roadside no longer feels like an infinite bubble; it is static, dead.

Finally, he drives past his neighbors' ugly concrete houses and into the driveway of his own home. He gets out of the car and stands in the rain, but it no longer invigorates him. It makes him tired and old. He walks to the door, opens it, and shuts it behind him almost as an afterthought.

"Sessina?" he says, expecting no reply and hearing none.

He walks into the kitchen. Beside the stove he finds a message: "Dinner is in the refrigerator." He does not look in the refrigerator.

Instead, he unbuttons his shirt and takes it off, letting it fall to the floor and, as he makes his way into the bedroom, he frees himself from shoes, socks, pants, underwear, so that when he enters he is naked. He does not bother to towel himself dry before he gets under the covers with Sessina. Ignoring the photograph of his grandfather that stares accusingly in his direction, he snuggles up next to her and finds that he trembles against her skin, his heartbeat as rapid as if he had just run three miles. Clutching her to him, he is relieved to hear her pulse slow and even beneath the pressure of his hands, having feared in some irrational way that she might prove to be a phantom. But she is here, and she is real.

Sessina stirs in her sleep and murmurs, "Gabriel."

"Yes."

"How was the prison?"

Gabriel's mouth curls into a smile and a frown at the same time.

"I . . . I saw a miracle. A miracle," he whispers, and now the tears come softly as he holds her. "He flew. He flew . . . *and I could not follow him.*"

But she is asleep again, lost in her own dreams, and does not seem to hear him. No matter. Soon he too is drifting off to sleep, so tired and confused that he cannot think of anything and yet is thinking of everything, all at once, for the first time.

Notes on
Flight Is for Those Who Have Not Yet
Crossed Over

A song by Freedy Johnson called "Can You Fly?" pro-vided the inspiration for this story. It sparked a mental image of a political prisoner floating in his prison cell in a small Latin American country. But somehow writing the story from the political prisoner's point of view just didn't interest me. That seemed like the typical approach. So I switched to the viewpoint of a guard caught up in the maze of repression and lies that dictatorships en-gender. I found him a much more interesting character because he is morally ambiguous.

I'm proud of the small details of Gabriel's life in this story. I also like that the reader must absorb a miracle to enjoy "Flight."

The Bone Carver's Tale

ONE NIGHT, SOME MONTHS BEFORE THE MON-soons, the bone carver Sajit Xuan-Ti left his house, made from the whittled ribcage of a whale, and walked down to the black sand beach which had been his, and his alone, for six years. He had awakened from dreams of Angkor Thom, the great religious city to the North, and had seen the visages of its rulers broken along the boundaries of the land of Kampuchea, where the Mekong River flows into the China Sea.

The weather was hot and dry, and even under the cooling glance of the moon he felt restless. During the day, the sails of junks at sea had seemed to droop. Now his sarong stuck to his skin as he paced the beach, hoping for a flash of bone amid the shells and seaweed. Often, he would find crocodile skulls, or the stream-lined spines of dolphins. These he would gather, bring back to his house, and treat with a distillation of ginseng root, camphor oil, and dried copra.

Increasingly, he spent his days receiving nobles and holy men who admired his carvings. Within a Xuan-Ti carving, it was said, one could find the souls of one's ancestors; within the eyes of a Xuan-Ti figurine lay the mystery of death. But Sajit ignored such speculation. He saw only the bone, which was smooth to the touch and smelled, in its purest form, like water, like air.

"*Namo kuanshiyihuan Bodhisattva mahasattva,*" he chanted over the hiss of the surf, remembering the *scree* and *clack* of the bone as he worked on it, more pleasant than the laughter of women or the clatter of dice against a gambling board. Sometimes he closed his eyes, his hands knowing the way more readily than his eyes, and he would listen to the tempo, the rhythm, of *scree* (a narrow, blade edge stroke) and *clack* (the flat of the blade), to tell if the work went well or poorly.

He spotted the delicate bones of a scorpion fish splayed out in the sand. It could become a mask, perhaps, with the bones worked into a tangle of feathers.

As he stooped over the fish, the fluid trill of a *serunai* rose above the crackle of waves and his fingers trailed in the sand. Never had he heard the instrument played with such precision. The music spoke of the coming of the mountains to the sea: liquid sound with the power of swells and breakers. As a child in his father's butcher shop, he had made a *serunai* from the bones of a pig, but the sounds he had forced from the long stem, the five holes, had mocked the caw of crows.

Sajit stood up, the scorpion fish forgotten. For, in the sound of the *serunai*, he heard the familiar blindness that struck him every so often—a fumbling in the dark for form and content and style. In his fumbling, his hand would become firm, his knife strokes sharp and purposeful. The feeling that welled up inside him at such discovery made him shiver, as if the energy of the Gods had entered into him.

The music came from the direction of the village of Go Oc Eo, and he turned that way, head held high as if to sniff out a new and unknown scent. The wind no longer felt hot. The smell of bone, salty with the sea and the acidic bite of the liquids he used to preserve it, rose in his nostrils. The music played on, rising and falling in tempo, drawing him close and then setting him free, before imprisoning him once more.

The smell of bone brought back the feel of bone, the roughness where it had snapped to a will greater than itself and then the smoothness after he had shined it with an extract of mango and water chestnut, the smoothness that excited his nerves, made his fingers capable of ever grander, more daring designs.

The *serunai* drew so many feelings out of him that he wondered, fleetingly, if he was in love. He could not tell. He had never been in love before.

✳　　✳　　✳

"Who plays the *serunai* at night in the village of Go Oc Eo?" he asked Jen Jen the next morning. Jen Jen was his housekeeper, an older woman from Go Oc Eo, who had fine black hair, a small nose, and often leered mischievously. He thought she must be an incarnation of the Naga Queen, and more menacing. Yet without her, he could barely remember to feed or clothe himself, so intent was he on the work. The plates from breakfast—rice and eel curry —would lie scattered on his table until she removed them.

"Prei Chen plays the *serunai*," Jen Jen replied as she wove a tiger-orange sarong upon her shuttle. "The Four Fishers for Gossip tell me she is the most accomplished master since Ty Som. She has played at the Khmer court in Angkor Thom."

"Hmm," Sajit said. "I believe I shall use the water buffalo jaw to depict Hanuman—this flaw, here, resembles his body. I need only accentuate the lines."

It did not matter to him that he had no living model to work from. When he had lived in the Khmer court, he had rarely glanced at a woman or lain with the prostitutes of the Avenue of a Thousand Pleasures, and yet from the haunch of a snow leopard, he had created a sensuous scene depicting a courtesan, her lover, and the kinsman to whom she had been pledged.

Jen Jen slapped her thigh, her hand leaving an imprint of white against the smooth brown of her skin. "You work much too hard, Sajit Xuan-Ti! You work so hard you see monkey gods in a water buffalo's jaw! If your parents were alive today, Sajit, they would see that you are still a child to live in such bliss."

"Hmm," said Sajit. "Why is she in Go Oc Eo?"

Jen Jen took up her shuttle. "Why do you wish to know?" She snorted. "Perhaps she has come for you?"

Bones, hardened and bleached to an unbearable white hue, awaited his knife two days later, on a morning when the sky was lay-ered like rice paper and the wind sputtered and spun against the surf.

In the Khmer court, at the University of Yasoharapura, Sajit had studied the anatomy and physiology of mammals, fish, and birds— and under his ministrations, some bones had already taken on new life: ape skulls became flasks for plum wine, for the apes of the northern Sukhothai Jungle often competed with An tribesmen for plums; thigh bones from the striped tapir became matching oars carved with scenes from the Sanskrit epic *The Ramayana*.

He was etching the eyes of the Goddess Kali into a fruit bat's wing bone when music washed over him like a summer gale, treacherous, but possessed of a freshness and vitality that overwhelmed the musk of dead fish, the bitterness of sea salt. It cried out above the wind that stung the palm trees on the shore, shook the sand, scattered the fiddler crabs.

A *serunai*, played by a master.

He did not move. He did not blink. Surely Prei Chen had not come here?

Jen Jen ran through the open door and crouched in front of him, spilling words like dried rice, scattered almost to senselessness: "Prei Chen begs to speak with Sajit Xuan-Ti, master carver. She has seen your work. She has seen your work in the courts of the Khmer rulers—and the Thai. She wishes to visit the illustrious man behind such art."

He did not move. He did not blink.

"Well, come on! Get up! Get out there!" Jen Jen tugged his arm until he rose from his seat. She straightened his sarong, and, chuckling, shoved him out the door.

A woman waited for him in the antechamber, her legs crossed beneath her on the prayer rug. She cradled a *serunai* in her arms.

When she saw Sajit, she bowed; a smile creased her face as she looked up at him.

"I am honored," she said, "to be in the presence of such a man."

He bowed. "And I in the presence of such a woman."

But the woman, he saw, with his bone carver's eye, was merely pretty. Her legs resembled the stocky legs of a water buffalo, muscled but not graceful. A mole marred her right cheek and her sarong was clumsily tied. Her smile framed a mouth much too wide to be seductive. The kohl around her eyes was too dark a shade.

Nevertheless, his pulse quickened, and his own movement to sit, the way he crossed his legs, seemed awkward, ugly. Jen Jen had disappeared.

"What has brought you here?" he asked, ignoring the tension in his body when Prei Chen caressed her *serunai*.

Her stare seemed to split him open. "I came to see you. I have admired your work in many courts."

He thought he heard the rattling of bones in his workshop, but it was only his heart. She had anointed herself with the scent of franjipani, a sweet smell which announced her suitability for marriage. Arabic and Sanskrit words were woven into her sarong, all of which spoke of union and commitment.

Her eyes were an unreflecting black, and her hair as flowing and shimmering as the mountain streams.

When he did not reply, she said, "I have followed your work to you, to see if the artist is as beautiful and worthy." She reached over and placed a hand on his shoulder. The touch scorched his nerve ends. Fear, he told himself. It was fear and the temptation of the woman before him.

He fingered a bone sculpture on the table next to them.

"I shall play for you," she said, and put the *serunai* to her lips.

She played the sensual music of the Mekong, music which followed the river's sinuous curves, lined its banks with treble notes and deep clefts. She played of the fisher folk and the clay silt which enriched the farmers' fields. She played of the mongoose and tiger, come to the water's edge to drink, and to stare. Then the music changed, became slower, more thoughtful: soft, introspective notes that told Sajit Xuan-Ti, *I saw your work in the courts and I followed the trail left by your work—the scenes of love and of hate, the perfection and the artful lines—until I could see only that the man who produced such work must be a great lover, a wise man, a man with whom I could join.*

The *serunai* spoke of her craft's loneliness, how for her craft to have meaning, she must have union with another. She sang of the wonder of the conjoining of the two crafts, the *serunai* and the bone carving. How, together, they could make art more powerful, more elegant, than any before or since.

Sajit heard all of these things in the gentle pressure of her mouth on the *serunai*. His ears buzzed and his mouth felt dry. Sajit stared into the eyes of his bone sculpture, an elegant woman with willowy legs, and could not meet Prei Chen's gaze.

"Sajit Xuan-Ti?" Prei Chen's voice quavered. "Sajit Xuan-Ti, look at me."

His name, said with such hope. Fear settled over him.

"You are not beautiful," he said, staring at his bone maiden. "You are not beautiful as this sculpture is beautiful. You are not as beautiful as the bones." His heart clattered and his hands felt icy and his breath came shallow and quick, as if he were dying then, there, in that place.

When he looked into her face, drawn by his own awful curiosity, he saw that her eyes were like dead stars, all the energy coiled within, but not a mote of brightness escaping. Her body had become rigid and her mouth had drawn tight, the lips trembling only slightly.

"You are not as beautiful as your art, Sajit Xuan-Ti," she said, and turned and ran to the door. "You are ugly."

The monsoons came, and with them moist, orange skies. The Mekong overflowed its banks, disgorging yellow silt from upriver and, for those who drank from it, the yellow-green sores of the sleeping disease. The Khmer Emperors grew desperate in their struggle against the Kings of Siam and did not wait out the rains. Battles raged on ground that had turned to mud.

But Sajit Xuan-Ti continued in his work. He loved the monsoons, for he could remain in his workshop for many hours, the air cool and the rain a reminder of the creativity which fueled his efforts. Raindrops needled his rooftop, fell upon the small bones of otter and deer, which filled the gaps in the whale's rib cage. The voices of the animals rose in a hush-hush-susurrus in his awareness.

His bone carvings were now so beautiful that they no longer took the form of people or animals, but only suggested the lines of people or animals, so that the purchaser must guess the meaning behind each sculpture.

Jen Jen teased him (or taunted—he could not tell which) with updates on Prei Chen gleaned from the Four Fishers for Gossip, but only when she was mad at him, if he had failed to comment on the sarong she had woven, or the splendid meal of prawns she had prepared.

"In the courts of the Thai vassals, Prei Chen plays the song of a young woman rejected by a man she loved."

"Hmm," he would reply, pretending not to hear her. "The prawns were delicious, Jen Jen."

"Thank you, Sajit," she would say, and he would hear disappointment in her voice, as if he had missed something—a subtle inference, perhaps, a nuance of speech that had proven quite beyond him.

This game continued until the day, two months after the monsoons had begun, when Jen Jen came to his house crying, dressed in the stark white of mourning. The stark white of bone, he could not help thinking.

"What is wrong?" He took Jen Jen by the arm and led her to a chair. "What is the matter?"

"Prei Chen is dead."

"Dead?"

He sat down in his chair, hands upturned in his lap, eyes staring at the floor. He felt as though his bones had been ripped out of him, that he was a body without a skeleton.

"How?" he asked, not daring to look into her eyes, afraid that if he did he might lose control, his mask of a face crumble. Why couldn't he breathe?

"There was a battle at Angkor Thom, near—"

"I know what it is near."

"—a battle at Angkor Thom. The Khmer and the Thai fought for three days and three nights until finally, finally . . ."

His vision blurred.

"Jen Jen," he said, and held her hand. "Tell me. Simply and slowly."

"Finally, the Khmer killed the Thai king and the Thai fled the battlefield. Prei Chen and several other artisans are among the bodies of the slain. She had been entertaining at the Thai court. All of Go Oc Eo is mourning her death."

His hands and legs shook and his mouth kept trying to widen in a rictus of grief, but he would not let it. He felt Jen Jen's eyes upon him then, and set his jaw and clenched his hands against what he felt inside.

"Can you say nothing, Sajit? Can you say nothing at all? Do you feel for anything except your precious bones?"

The tightness in his body became unbearable and in one furious, desperate motion he rose to his feet and shouted at her, "Get out! Get out! Leave me be! I have work to finish . . . "

Jen Jen's mouth quivered. She looked at him strangely, hesitated, then bowed and said, "I am gone, Sajit Xuan-Ti. I am leaving."

The rains tapped and tormented Sajit's roof ever more and he would stir restlessly in his sleep, hearing the whisper of the *serunai*, hearing the ghosts of the bones. Wake up, they insisted. No. Wake up. No. But, finally, when they said to him, in Prei Chen's voice, "You are ugly," he would wake, drenched in sweat and swatting at mosquitoes. "Jen Jen?" His voice sounded fragile in the dark. "Jen Jen, are you there?"

Every night now, Sajit walked the black sand beach. The music of Prei Chen's *serunai* filled his ears, so he could not hear the rush and withdrawal of the waves as they plunged against the coast. He envisioned her bones buried in a grave in the God-city of Angkor Thom and sometimes he would wake from the thought to find himself thrashing in the surf, spittle clinging to his lips.

The bones he worked with became unfamiliar to him—vaguely

threatening, the skulls those of gibbering beasts, the claws and the fangs out of some harrowing Hindu demonology. It seemed that his hands were lending themselves to his own destruction.

He thought often, as he had not thought for years, of his father's butcher shop and his youth spent toiling behind the counter, amongst the blood and the offal and the shards of bone. How the carcasses, dangling from the roof beams, bled onto the floor. There was such calm on his father's creased face as he gutted them, slowly, methodically. At night, the green light from the lanterns turned the blood dark, almost purple, and his father's knees, whorled with wrinkles, took on that same sheen.

The towering height of the counter, the light beyond, and the customers' faces, looming. The *scree* and *clack* of another time and place.

Once, deep in his heart, he had wondered if there could be anything else to the world beyond blood and bone and lantern light.

Then, one evening, the moon spoke to him. He looked up at its shining face and his father stared down at him.

The moon said, *Sajit Xuan-Ti, think of the bones lying wasted in Angkor Thom. Think of the bones of the finest serunai player in the land. The delicacy, the lightness of them. Would they not be more perfect, more pure, more beautiful than anything you have ever carved before? Do they not tempt you more than the woman tempted you in life? Do you not long for the bones of Prei Chen, lying buried under the eyes of the Gods in Angkor Thom?* The question curled in his mind like a finger, beckoning him into the heartlands of war.

"Yes," Sajit said. "Yes."

There was no reply.

Just the moon, bright as a perfectly rounded and smoothed bone. Just the waves that lashed the beach, and the sky, already dark, becoming black: a squall, blowing across the peninsula.

"The bones," he muttered, looking at his hands as if for the first time. His fingers were thin and long, but rough, calloused: the hands of a bone carver and nothing else.

Relentlessly, night after night, in a torrent, the moon voice spoke to him—in the whisper of the webs the *gonchai* spider wove to catch its prey, through the chorus of the barking tree frog, through the slats in his house, the flashes and scintillations of the sea forming Sanskrit before his eyes. "*The bones*," the moon said. "*Think of the bones . . .*"

When the rains were at their most ferocious, the encroaching jungle a wall of green which seemed to have no end, Sajit slipped out from between the leviathan's ribs, taking only a sack of carvings with him, and disappeared from the sight of Go Oc Eo forever.

Sajit Xuan-Ti traveled by night and hid by day. In the darkness, he could gauge the direction and distance of the warring armies: where they fought, the sky erupted in funnels of fire, watchtowers ablaze. The horizon was a red scar that bled into the darkness. He could hear the screams of wounded battle elephants and he thought of the hundreds of Buddhas he might still carve from their bones.

Refugees fled from the lights. They brushed against him moth-like in their rags, their shoeless feet churning the mud, their progress pitifully slow. When they saw him, walking toward Angkor Thom, they often stared at him blankly, the joke taking time to settle into the mud, and through the mud into their souls. Then: laughter. As if he were a clown. Or mad.

"Look! Look!" an old man shouted. And: "Look!" again, as if moved by the absurdity of Sajit's destination to repeat no other word, but to announce the bone carver's presence with the insistence of a mynah bird.

He did not reply to such taunts. Surely, he told himself, it was not so bad. Surely not. He ignored the tangled limbs of corpses, their slack mouths, the way shadow traced their faces as if with charcoal.

But he could not ignore the ground under his feet. A hole had opened in his left sandal and through this hole came all the mud, the water, the blood, the excrement, upon which he walked. Slowly, his left leg became sensitized to the hole, until he trembled with each step, for each step brought with it a premonition of the land's pain. The pain spread through his bones until each seemed alive with agony. He felt his face twisting in discomfort, so that his grin was like the cockeyed reflection of a slit moon in the sea— curving up one side and down the other. The refugees began to run from the man he knew he had become: emaciated and rag-clad, with a leer that leapt across his face in time to the flinching limp with which he negotiated the ground. His hands dangled from the soaked cuffs of his shirt like the roots of a long-dead ginger plant.

In places where the armies had not slashed and burned, the road reverted to jungle, for without the civil authorities to cut it back, the trees spread where they pleased, their roots firmly entrenched, even in the mud. The constant rain—which, like a ringing in his ears, became an annoyance, then a presence to be ignored, and finally a dismal fact he could not escape and therefore resigned himself to—this rain fed the roots, the branches, the leaves, until by the seventh day, he could see only a wall of trees ahead, broken by a few scattered tiles.

On the ninth day, the skies were clear and, early in the morning, an enormous face stared down at Sajit through the wall of green: the visage of Emperor Jayavarman, carved into the sharply triangular temple tops of Angkor Thom. Under the gaze of Jayavarman's languorous eyes, the firm but caring mouth, Sajit should have felt at ease, protected, but the sweetness of corrupted flesh and the brusque, choking sour of burning bones dispelled any such illusion. He came out from the forest onto a wide plain, upon which lay the city-shrine Angkor Thom. Ahead of him, two lines of statues, cut from solid stone and connected at the arms and legs, formed a passage to the gateway, which rose one hundred fifty meters high. From every tower, Jayavarman's visage peered down, until it seemed to Sajit that a giant audience had gathered to watch him.

He shuddered, whispered *"Namo kuanshiyihuan Bodhisattva mahasattva."* Jen Jen had said he knew nothing except his art, but here that would help him, for the corpses would not bother him if he could think of them as bone.

It was not until he had almost passed by the rows of fire-blackened statues that he felt, from his left, the eyes of one following him.

Sajit stopped walking. The silence of the city struck him then and fear twisted in his belly. He did not turn to face his watcher. That a statue should watch him seemed almost normal, for hadn't the moon with his father's face spoken to him?

No, he avoided the statue's eyes because he feared he would find reflected there the same fascination and the same laughter he had seen in the refugees' faces. Instead, he looked at the bodies sprawled across the entrance. Most were soldiers, dressed in the uniforms of a half-dozen armies. To the left, they had been stacked in patterns like lotus flower petals. The smoldering corpses sent plumes of smoke into the air; the smoke covered the face of the south tower, distorting Jayavarman's lips into a frown. The smell filled Sajit's nostrils and he felt a lightness in his stomach. With revulsion, he realized he was hungry.

He turned to face the statue. A dwarf had taken the place of the stonework; some machinery of war had dislodged the statuary, leaving only the base upon which sat the dwarf, who stared neither left nor right, but straight ahead. The left eye had given Sajit the illusion that someone watched him; made of glass, it seemed to stare directly at Sajit no matter how he moved in relation to it. He had believed the dwarf to be a statue because the man's skin matched the fire-washed stone: a pure black sheen that marked him as South Indian.

Sajit smiled, nodded, bowed, but the dwarf stared straight ahead. Gathering his courage, Sajit put down his bag of carvings. He stepped close enough to touch the man's shoulder. The eyes stared straight ahead.

The dwarf's features itched to be carved into bone; he resembled a gnarled banyan root dark with rot. Jowls hung below his chin and folds of skin drooped over the eyes. Wrinkles creased the forehead, hidden by the same blackness that had masked him among the real statues.

The dwarf wore a gray tunic and a matching dhoti. A karta, his only weapon, was stuck through his sash, and lying beside him on the stone were a necklace of silver bells, a mask of the monkey god Hanuman, and a staff carved from sandalwood, its musk overlaying the rancid odor of flesh.

"A jester!" Sajit exclaimed.

Blood began to trickle from the right eye, following a set course amid the wrinkles, which were marked by a dark line where blood had dried days before.

Sajit wiped at the blood with the hem of his sarong.

"How long have you been sitting here?" he asked, not expecting a reply.

"Four days," the dwarf said, the good eye locking onto Sajit so swiftly that the bone carver snatched his hand away from the tears of blood and stuttered an incoherent reply.

"Four days," the dwarf repeated, and smiled. Yellow teeth shone against the absolute dark of his face. "Three nights. No one has approached me until now nor could I, it seemed, move in all that time, until you touched the blood upon my face."

"You hid from the soldiers?'

The dwarf shrugged. "I sat here and pretended indifference to their battles. Before, when I ran, it seemed that the very act of flight made them pursue me. So I took up my post here, in the way of the Buddha, and have watched the blood sport of the Khmer and the Thai and their allies, as they stalk the same ground over and over. I have opened my mouth to the sky and survived on rain water . . . Who are you to walk beneath the shadow of these gates?"

"I am Sajit Xuan-Ti, the bone carver."

The dwarf began to laugh, but put off Sajit's questions with, "You are not he. I know Sajit Xuan-Ti well. I have bought some of his carvings and stolen more from the Khmer court, and you are not he. Everyone knows he resides in the village of Go Oc Eo where he works at his craft by the sea and knows nothing of the world."

"And yet, I am Sajit."

The dwarf grunted, looked away. "I would rather you had stayed home and carved for the rest of us, who are more world weary than you ever need be — if indeed you are Sajit. My name is Tien Tievar — a jester, a clown in the court of the Khmer."

"Did you know the *serunai* player, Prei Chen? Do you know how she died?"

The words came out swiftly, clattering one on top of the other, and he lowered his head in frustration, cupped his face with his hands.

"Forgive me, Tievar. I have not eaten in three days. My hands shake. I cannot remember the simplest rules of bone carving. The moon has told me to seek out the bones of Prei Chen and carve them into something wondrous, something with as much beauty as her music."

"The moon is deceitful, Sajit," the dwarf said, his blind eye looking out toward the horizon. He was silent for a long time. Finally, when it seemed he might never speak again, he said, "I knew of Prei Chen. I heard her play many times in the court. How she died, I cannot tell you. I do not know. No living person knows."

"Where is she buried?"

Tievar shrugged. "In Angkor Thom. Under the shadow of the Naga Queen, but where within the tangle of bodies?"

"Will you show me?"

Tievar smiled. "I am afraid my position here is too comfortable. If I should force my palms to remain upward in my lap, toward Heaven, then, like the Buddha, I shall go there when I die."

Sajit nodded, turned toward the gates of Angkor Thom.

". . . but if you could do me one kindness. I cannot move my arms. Could you place the smiling mask of Hanuman upon my face? Thus I may sleep behind the mask yet have the appearance of watchfulness should the armies return."

"Of course."

When Sajit leaned over the dwarf to attach the mask, he saw the blood that had gathered in a pool behind Tievar, caused by a gash in his back that had paralyzed him.

"I shall leave a carving of the Buddha beside you, for safety and luck," Sajit said, hoping Tievar could not see his hands tremble as he swung the sack of bones back over his shoulder.

The dwarf only smiled.

Sajit Xuan-Ti entered Angkor Thom, the eyes of kings above him, a man weeping blood behind, the sun just another eye—jaundiced yellow, with a spirit of evil within its corona that made him want to lie down and weep; to put aside his bag of carvings and hug the loamy ground to him.

But the bones in his legs held him upright. The bones in his legs continued to lift his feet and let them fall.

They fell now upon bodies, the hole in his sandal driving him past madness with the feel of flesh beneath his own flesh. Soldiers by the hundreds littered the interior—dragged over walls, battlements, and each other. The battles had raged for months so that the dead were layered three deep, a light green moss coating the most recently fallen, a yaw of bones sticking up from the earth the only marker for those who had died months before. The smell hit Sajit at the gateway: mingled blood and rot and earth and flesh. It scoured his clothes, curled into his nostrils, made him feel faint. He half fell, put out a hand to balance himself, and splashed his thumb into the water-filled pool of an eye socket, scattering mosquito larvae.

Strangest of all to Sajit were the fresh wounds he saw as he wandered toward the central courtyard. These bodies—like those of the animals in his father's butcher shop—still had moist flesh upon them, some bloated with the rains. Beneath the pale flesh, the slashing yellow-red of unclean wounds, he could see the startling white riddle of bone, a purity at odds with the surrounding offal. The flesh disturbed him. It frightened him, and he hurried past the bodies. Here was a substance he could not make beautiful or carve to his own desires.

The sky had turned a blue shot through with amber. There was no sound. Even the birds were silent: enormous Malay vultures that moved with a slow respect for the dead, a daintiness which spoke of morticians more than grave robbers.

*   *   *

He found Prei Chen where Tievar had told him to look—beneath the shadow of the Naga Queen, whose nine stone heads reared skyward in denial of the death beneath her coils.

Beside the grave, an elephant had died, falling onto its side. Four men lay within the caved-in flesh, and this puzzled Sajit until he realized that the men had died atop the elephant and had fallen through to rest among the beast's organs once the flesh had grown too infirm to support them.

Somehow, the sight of the elephant calmed him. Perhaps it was the peaceful way the four men seemed to sleep within its womb, or the white tusk that reminded him of the god Ganesha.

All such speculation left him when he saw Prei Chen, lying half-in, half-out of a shallow grave, flesh still clinging to her body. Her face had disassembled itself until he barely recognized her, could not even catalog the bones that stuck through to ruin her beauty. Someone had placed her *serunai* within her encircling arms. He approached on hands and knees until he had crept to her side. The earth covered her torso, but her arms lay free. He put down his sack and took her hand in his. The flesh had dried so that he could feel the bones beneath. Her skin was warm, but so was the earth beneath her.

He tugged at her arm, but she would not move; there was too much dirt and he was too weak. The Malay vultures watched him with idle interest from atop the elephant's skull.

He tugged again.

"Prei Chen," he said, speaking to her as he tugged a third time. "Prei Chen."

But she would not move from beneath the Naga Queen.

When he tried one last, desperate time, her arm came off in his grasp and he sprawled, panting, against the side of the elephant, looking into the faces of the four men it had swallowed after its death. The dirt of the grave stung his chin. The taste of the grave coated his tongue. He looked at Prei Chen's arm, which he still held in his left hand; yellow bone stuck out from the end, but he felt no desire to carve it. Instead, he shuddered and tears came to his eyes, though he could not pin a reason to them. He could not remember the features of Jen Jen's face. He could not even remember the first rule of bone carving. His craft seemed to him no art at all, but artifice and deception. There was nothing except flesh, and there never had been, and he had forgotten more than he learned when he carved the bone.

He crawled up from the elephant, until he came again to Prei

Chen's corpse. He looked full into her rotting face and covered her body with his, caressed her hair with his calloused, bone-carver hands and said, "Prei Chen, Prei Chen," until it became a meaningless chant, a ritual to hold off despair that even Tievar eventually heard, sitting in his tears of blood, among the visages of the Kings of Angkor Thom, in the land of Kampuchea, where the Mekong River flows into the China Sea.

Notes on
The Bone Carver's Tale

In addition to my travels as a child with my Peace Corps parents, I was exposed to Southeast Asian art and culture because of my mother's graduate studies. I felt very comfortable, for example, with the idea of portraying a mixture of Buddhism and Hinduism in the story. In that part of the world, the demarcation between one religion and another is not always clear.

Other influences included the modern carnage inflicted on Cambodia by the United States and then, as Kampuchea, by its own Pol Pot regime. However, a story I had heard about Hemingway was a more important influence. According to this story, Hemingway witnessed the goring of a matador by a bull at a bullfight in Spain. From his seat, Hemingway could see the white of bone winking out from the red of the wound. Instead of going along with other spectators to help, Hemingway scribbled down notes about the event to use in his fiction.

As a twenty-something writer, who had been perhaps overly serious about my Art, it seemed very important to say, in a way that would convince me, that choosing writing should not mean denying life. I also like the way the fairy tale veneer of the story gives way to a horrific reality by story's end.

Whenever I read the story, I am also reminded of the circumstances under which I wrote it. I had just been fired from my job working for the remainder store Book Warehouse (I'd complained about my crappy salary). I remember I experienced this terrible clarity born from not knowing what I was going to do, whether I could find another job, or if I even wanted to find one. In my six weeks of unemployment, I wrote "The Bone Carver's Tale." I experienced a weird kind of freedom. There was nothing I could do, so I just wrote.

The Sea, Mendeho, and Moonlight

ABOVE MENDEHO OBREGON AN INCANDESCENT moon shone, eclipsed from time to time by the lumbering shadows of interstellar freighters as they took the I-wire up and down from Veniss. Always, they headed for the city whose lights curved away from him down the almost silent beach.

Mendeho listened only to the call of gull and lurcher, the strangled choke of meerkat at its kill. Saw only the vermilion sea, studded with tiny glints, glares, ripples, and the strobes of squid. He blinked away a tear as he watched, the moisture collecting in the wrinkles of his face. It was forty years since he had last seen the ocean at night.

Mendeho had his eccentricities—the cane he used to conquer his rheumatism, for example, when a simple y-scan could have nipped it without so much as an operation. When pressed, he told his cousin, "I want to remember pain, to know I am alive." His cousin, an I-wire tech named Onry, had stared blankly at him, keeping his own opinions to himself and his link.

A rustle caught Mendeho's ear: the sound of tiny scuttling feet. He squinted against the moonlight, finally saw that thousands of fiddlers were scouring the beach in a living wave of carapace and claw. Whatever dead tissue had washed up during the day would be devoured.

Mendeho smiled. The bioneers had not yet reconstructed the fiddlers. He was glad. Once, long ago, his great-great ancestors had stood offshore and cast nets to catch such creatures. For the raw protein. At least, the family records told him so.

A rare in-system shuttle rumbled into view, a clot of lights soon swallowed by the city's intense glow. It would land in one of the cool-down canals that had given Dayton Central the nickname "Veniss."

The thunder scattered fiddlers, sent night waders up in a flurry of leathery wings. Waves died at the shoreline and a weak bluster of wind whipped Mendeho's unfashionably high collar against his neck. Already, he had defied the curfew for service citizens; the double placed in his bed would not fool the solimind forever.

And for what? He laughed, kicked at the sand with his good leg, leaning on his cane. A midnight skinny dip? He squared his shoulders, assumed the straight-backed posture that had aided his swimming stroke and, later, helped him survive two sections at the academy years and years ago.

Mendeho's grip on his cane tightened, fingers clenched. The sea—the color of the sea—was so dark tonight, despite the occasional flash and sparkle. The fiddlers had returned and, beyond them, bathed in moonglow and wave, dolsynths slid through the water as smoothly as a solimind shuttle. The wind felt good now, having picked up (probably at the solimind's request), and he took halting steps down from the dunes, silhouetted against the city's continual splendor. The fiddlers froze, not knowing what to make of him.

Perhaps poor Julia had been right, he thought, breathing faster than he would have liked. Perhaps defying the solimind would have been too dangerous, but he had been willing to try . . . Later, he saw Julia for what she was—a component in the system, chip-simple. Meanwhile, his approved wife bore and bored him with four children, as requisitioned. All four were linked before their first birthdays. What use for a father then? Onry told him he was lucky. Since the Diaspora Plague, some had had to bear the burden of five or six children.

And all the while Mendeho diligently oversaw the production of shuttle emulsifiers and clogshop units, choking on the taste of dust-dull work.

The fiddlers compromised, clearing a space around him, perhaps hoping he would die and leave plenty of protein for their eager mouths. He shooed them back. Then, staring at the sea,

Mendeho let his cane fall to the sand with a soft *scrunch*. The buttons of his gray shirt and pants popped free as he undressed himself. His shoes with their sticky adhesive had already been discarded and soon he wore only a pair of jet-black briefs. He took a deep breath through his nose, swiveling his shoulders. For a man of sixty-seven, he had a firm body, with white hair that crawled across his chest like stringy seaweed. Mendeho smelled the salt spray and smiled, content with his decision.

Often he had swum when he was younger, in the old days when the restriction of a triplehand badge was unnecessary. The rule took all the fun out of it—exactly the solimind's intent. "Safety first," it proclaimed on vidolos where it paraded and pouted, taking on the disguise of mother, father. The worst irony? Life *was* ordered, everyone richer, more comfortable than before. The freighters docked graceful as ballerinas under I-wire control and the clockwork universe humankind had created for itself out of chaos ticked on oblivious to strife.

But Mendeho Caranza Obregon, son of Juan Carlos VII, son of Juan Carlos VI, could not marry whom he wanted, could not set his own job requirements, and—most important at that moment—could not even swim in the ocean. And this thing he was determined to do before his death. If they would not let him swim at Dayton Central, then he would swim here, where Earth regained some guise of the natural, where the meerkat could play amongst the dunes, and out at sea dolsynths romped through deep water.

Mendeho Obregon told himself he was stubborn, and found that he was stubborn. A light shone from his eyes, in the set of his mouth, the outward thrust of his chin. He limped toward the surf, fiddlers skittering from his path. The city lights shrank and the sound of airborne traffic became muffled. There was only the sea in front of him, the living carpet of arthropods, and the rising wind. And, above all, the gutted and pockmarked moon, still transcendent on a night like this one.

Mendeho had a foot in the water when a warning sounded from the link lodged in his ear. He stopped, hands at his sides.

Citizen, it whispered, *turn back. Turn back. You have broken curfew to swim. You cannot swim. The waves are too dangerous and you have no triplehand badge to keep you safe . . . You are old . . .* The whisper took on a placatory tone. *Turn back, citizen, and all will be forgiven.*

"You are the Devil! The physician was mistaken—I am fit. And

I am going into the sea!" His second foot hit the water with a satisfying splash. "I am going to swim!" He smiled, saw his crankiness as
a gift, a weapon.

Your wife worries. The voice in his ear oozed sympathy.

Mendeho stopped short. "Julia's been dead for a year," he said.
"A year ago today, and I am going to swim."

Your wife's name is Carlina, not Julia, chided the voice. *She is
alive and so are your four lovely children, and all five are worried.*

"They are *your* children. Shut off!"

The line of his mouth quivered before blossoming into a grin. A
certain exultation rose within him. They could not stop him now,
no matter what the danger. He walked farther into the water. Back
on shore, the fiddlers had disappeared, alarmed by the spectacle of
an old man talking to ghosts. Out in the ocean's deepest waves, a
pseudowhale breached, humming songs for its forgotten dead. The
songs reminded Mendeho of the doomed starship *Tai-keegi*'s high-
speed transmissions—sonorous and tragic—for even he had never
seen a whale.

You will see sense, said the solimind, and left him.

Was that it? A warning and they would leave him alone?

He plunged forward, the water splashing up to his knees, and
yelled for joy. Now, indeed, the fiddlers knew him to be insane . . .
But then, just as he prepared to jump into the water and really
swim, the waves swirled in on themselves. While he watched with
disbelief, sinking to his knees, one hand to his mouth, the sea
pulled back from him, washed itself away. It slid back and back
until the shoreline lay new and shimmering some forty meters
ahead, held in check by an invisible dam or blockade. Mendeho
cursed and wept, fish flopping and dying in the dryness before him.
Under the moon, the expanse of sand was filled with the living
debris left by too swift an ebb tide.

You cannot come to harm, old man, said the calm, patient solimind. *All citizens must obey the rules. You cannot swim, old man
—come back . . .*

An anger as surging and powerful as the sea built inside
Mendeho until his hands clenched and unclenched fitfully.
Ignoring the solimind, he wiped his brow, hoisted himself to his
feet with a grunt, and said, "If the sea will not come to me, I shall
come to it."

He took a slow breath, exhaled, and began a stumbling run, feet
slapping against the wet sand. A graveyard surrounded him, many
of the creatures out-system forms restructured by the bioneers. He

passed dying catechetans, their oar-shaped tusks hopelessly siphoning the air for moisture. Octopoids, too, wriggled and squirmed in the briny mire, tentacles clutching at him. Fish gasped for breath like living slates of ore, glimmering in the moonlight, some striped and smaller than Mendeho's finger, others solid purple and almost as large as a pleasure yacht.

Mendeho ignored everything but the line of waves and water ahead. He could not say he did this for Julia, but he was stubborn even with himself and could not have told a psychewitch his motivation.

The thing in his ear came alive. *It is no use, Mendeho. Come back. The sea is beyond your grasp. We will always control the tides. Turn back.*

Mendeho tried to tear the metal from his ear, gasping at the ragged pain. Blood trickled from the wound, but it would not come free.

Still he ran and still the waves retreated as if alive and wary. Sweat stung his eyes and his heart sent flames shooting through his body until he moved with both hands clutched to his chest. His legs were giving out; his left leg felt wooden. Perhaps the physician had been correct. He shook his head, though his entire being felt slump-heavy. He stumbled over the carcass of a saylber, a rancid stench already issuing from its blowholes. A dozen phosphorescent creatures ate at the slippery flesh.

He crawled now, body threatening to quit completely, mind near blackout. The waves, he craned to see, were still distant. The bitter taste of failure coated his tongue like tyrol. Arm shaking, he fingered the wound where the link still clung.

"Solimind," he rasped. "You bring me to death this way. The waves are out of reach and there are bodies of creatures greater than I already stiffening." A flash of intuition struck him, a loophole of logic he could exploit only once. "It is killing me not to swim. My health is threatened. My wife will be worried. Help me . . ."

Hesitation, then the whisper, accompanied by what he thought was a sigh: *Swim, Mendeho . . .*

Even exhausted, lying with his face against the sand, Mendeho felt elation.

Soon water licked at his feet, an insistent touch that strengthened under the solimind's ministrations and then buoyed him up. The body of the saylber drifted past him and he was floating, grasping seaweed, gulping air. Too tired to swim, to do anything except lie there in the water, Mendeho looked up at the moon and stars and clusters of light that were spacecraft. The waves rolled over and through him, enveloped him in their cool richness. Creatures nudged him but did not bite, tentacles wet and smooth. Bathed in the sea, he turned his head to catch a glimpse of the city. It still sparkled, but not, Mendeho decided, with the overwhelming light of the moon. His ear throbbed, his leg ached, and the pains in his chest intensified, but he floated in a weightless world, sensation deadened. And everywhere: the sibilant sound of moving water.

Slowly, the solimind's treacherous current carried Mendeho Caranza Obregon away from land, until he was far from the minds of men, the city a dot, and only the moon looked large enough to touch with an outstretched hand.

In Veniss, there is told a tale called "The Sea, Mendeho, and Moonlight," bootdisked from Filecomp. The sailors of space hear it in the telemar saloons and soon it is "The Vacuum, Mendeho, and Starlight." In the free-triad markets, farmers hear it and soon it is "The Land, Mendeho, and Sunlight." The story has become a legend of Dayton Central.

And the solimind approves, within limits. According to the legions of psychewitches, nominal dissent can be healthy for a frustrated I-wire tech. Yes, the solimind has decided, myths can be useful things. For in all the tales the old man Mendeho drifts out to sea, space, or pasture on a destiny of the solimind's making and is never seen again.

Notes on
The Sea, Mendeho, and Moonlight

I wrote this story when I was seventeen, and it is not only one of my earliest stories but one of the earliest chronologically in the Veniss cycle. As with "A Heart for Lucretia," also in this collection, I was interested in mythologizing science fiction.

Some readers might think "The Sea, Mendeho, and Moonlight" is very static: an old man standing on a beach, about to perform an act of civil disobedience. Such readers would be right. When you're learning to write, many of your characters stand around for obscenely long amounts of time while the author figures out what to do with them. By the time I wrote another Veniss story, "Detectives and Cadavers," I knew damn well you couldn't just stand around on a beach—you had to at least be investigating something *to earn the right to stand there.*

The Festival of the Freshwater Squid

An Article by Harry Flack

First published in *The Orlando Sentinel*, June 3, 2001

EARLY RISERS

EVERY SECOND WEEKEND IN MAY, THE MAYOR and other municipal officials of Sebring, Florida, rise well before dawn to kick off the annual Festival of the Freshwater Squid. From the lichen-mottled steps of the Old Town Hall, the mayor addresses a crowd that has, in recent years, risen to more than 20,000 (5,000 local residents and 15,000 tourists). The hotels have been booked for months and the town has been preparing for the influx of festival-goers since the end of the last festival. A recent building boom means that hundreds of little red surveyor flags dot otherwise abandoned lots. Meanwhile, swarms of sterile mosquitoes released as an experiment by the University of South Florida fill the cool predawn air, but the spectators and I don't mind— we're all too excited about observing another of the state's exotic species, the mayfly squid.

After a short speech, mayor Frank Lewden cuts the green-and-silver ribbons held across the parade route by two cheerleaders from nearby Highlands High School. The mayor's brother, town sheriff Eric Lewden, signals for the first parade floats to glide into position. As night begins to give way to dawn, we surge ahead of the parade, eager to be the first to the boats that will take us to the middle of Lake Jackson and the freshwater squid's traditional mating grounds.

FLAGLER'S FIND

In July 1894, during the construction of Standard Oil magnate Henry Flagler's East Coast Railway, railroad workers discovered the remains of several small "silver and green octopi with ten arms" stranded in the shallow pools left behind by dynamiting and draining. Perplexed, the workers brought the "octopi" to their foreman. The foreman showed them to the chief engineer, who, on the advice of his wife, sent the specimens, already rapidly decaying, to marine biologist Raymond Furness at the University of Florida.

Furness examined them, consulted his reference books, classified the creature as the squid *Fons floridanius* (later changed to *Fons volatilis*), and promptly turned his attentions back to his first love, the Florida scrub jay. Given that even Seminole Indian records and accounts by early naturalists do not mention the squid, the 1894 Flagler railroad specimens constitute the first sightings of what would come to be known as the "Florida freshwater squid" or the "mayfly squid." The most plausible theory for how the mayfly squid reached Florida's lakes and rivers is that juveniles of the Brazilian freshwater squid (*Fons brasiliensis*) arrived in Miami or Tampa accidentally via ships of South American registry.

ORIGINS OF THE FESTIVAL

Sebring, Florida, is perhaps the perfect setting for a freshwater squid festival. Situated amid 15 kilometers of lakes that lie along the south end of the Lake Wales Ridge, Sebring is a popular location for water sports and boat trips. Although Lake Jackson, Sebring's largest lake, does not contain Florida's highest concentration of mayfly squid, it is the most accessible of the squid's breeding grounds—and once featured the first attempt to harvest the squid commercially. (Mayfly squid are more plentiful in the boggy cypress habitat of the northern Wacissa River, but the area is off-limits to all boats except canoes.)

Sebring needs a festival in the summer, since the town is otherwise moribund until the autumn racing season brings the Grand Prix Raceway alive for the American Le Mans Series. In May, Panacea's Blue Crab Festival and Fernandina Beach's Isle of Eight

Flags Shrimp Festival are the only competition. The event closest in spirit to the Festival of the Freshwater Squid, the Sea Turtle Watch held in Jensen Beach on the Atlantic coast, does not occur until June. Sebring's only other festival of note, the Great Sebring Mushroom Hunt, has declined in popularity in recent years due to low attendance and a poisoning incident.

The Festival of the Freshwater Squid began 12 years ago as the brainchild of local writer Fred Mednock, a 46-year-old print shop manager who at first "just saw it as a good excuse for a summer party, and to sell some of my books. I never thought the town would actually sponsor it. And I never thought we'd ever see thousands of people coming down here for it."

The books, self-published through Mednock's print shop, are very popular at the festival. They relate the adventures of a talking squid named Hellatose. "They're for children and adults," Mednock says. "Children like the plots and pictures. Adults like the subtext. It's all in good fun."

As for the thousands of tourists, most of them are from in-state, brought by word of mouth, newspaper articles, and the guidebooks. A few, like a German family I met on the parade route—sweaty and pink and slightly dazed from all the noise and color—come out of curiosity.

"We were on vacation in Orlando," the father told me, "and wanted to see part of the real Florida."

They seem satisfied that they have, one of the daughters even waving an uprooted red surveyor flag, seemingly ignorant of its real meaning.

THE SQUID IN FLORIDA

Festival-goers can learn quite a bit about the squid from the helpful laminated exhibit occupying one corner of the aging Sebring History Museum. However, it would be best to visit the exhibit soon. The building that houses the museum is rotting away from a combination of termites and purple fungus that has infiltrated the wood.

"No one cares about anything but the squid," says curator Janet Sheik, a hint of sadness in her voice. Sheik has seen tourist traffic to her museum fall sharply over the last ten years, due in part to the popularity of events like the festival. "I'm afraid we're coming to value the details about a particular animal over our local history. But I can't deny that the squid is a fascinating creature."

As the exhibit shows, once the mayfly squid became established in Florida, a number of factors allowed it to expand its range to such areas as the lakes around Sebring. Studies have shown that squid larvae can survive for weeks surrounded by only a thin protective bubble of water. In such circumstances, the squid's normal growth cycle slows or halts altogether until the squid finds a larger water source. Florida's May-to-September hurricane season has helped spread the mayfly squid from south to north Florida and beyond. The heavy rains also clarify the Brazil-Florida link and explain the temporary hook found on the juvenile's mantle.

Whenever possible, the Brazilian freshwater squid attempts to lay its eggs on or near the Giant Amazonian Catfish (*Pseudoplatistoma tigriinum*). The catfish will eat some of the young squid, but most use their hooks to find safety on the sides of the catfish. Over the next four to six weeks, they scrounge scraps left over from the catfish's own scavenging and reward its host by eating any parasites that settle on the catfish's skin. Sheik has set up some really first-rate diagrams showing this process.

In Florida, the walking catfish (*Clarias batrachus*), another intruder, serves a similar purpose for the squid. After periods of heavy rain, the catfish lives up to its name by using its pectoral fins as crutches, wriggling its tail like a propeller to move from pond to pond. Paula Leepin, a University of Miami professor of ecology in the 1950s, soon noticed that many of the walking catfish she tagged after thunderstorms had masses of insect larvae clinging to their sides. Further investigation revealed that these "insect larvae" were actually mayfly squid juveniles. In a remarkable instance of instinctive adaptation to a new environment, the female mayfly squid had recognized a variation on an old theme and proceeded to take advantage of the situation.

However, unlike the walking catfish—considered a pest—the mayfly squid has settled into its Florida environment with ease. Because it does not displace native species, form parasitic relationships, or cause damage to crops, the mayfly squid has never appeared on a Florida Department of Agriculture and Consumer Services pest report. And, a study conducted by the Florida Department of Environmental Protection in 1985 concluded, in a typically laconic statement, that "the mayfly squid neither requires protection nor containment." The lack of good general information has been compounded by inaccuracies published in Florida travel guides. Two recent mentions of Sebring's festival, for example, describe it as "a celebration of squid worldwide" and "a parade centered around the annual auto racing competitions."

As Sheik says, "It is difficult to organize a local history museum around NASCAR events and squid."

THE PARADE

Despite the fact that the mayfly squid is neither endangered nor particularly edible, an entire subculture, largely unknown to the outside world and adhering to its own set of rituals, has grown up around this small invertebrate.

The parade represents the first of these rituals, a preliminary event that most locals participate in even if they don't take to the water later. It constitutes a uniquely Floridian oxymoron of sincerity and tackiness, part of a town that, by virtue of its strip malls, old abandoned Art Deco hotels from Sebring's boom period of the 1950s, and falsely antique Historic District, epitomizes the Florida impulse to meld pristine landscapes with facades of authentic human habitation.

The parade winds its way through the three blocks of quaint white-washed wooden houses that comprise the Historic District, past such institutions as the Inn on the Lakes, and then onto Sebring's main drag, Albion Boulevard. The path is lined with crepe paper lanterns in the mayfly squid's most common strobing colors: vibrant shades of purple, green, and silver. The candles inside the lanterns make the crepe paper shimmer with light. The usual cavalcade of high school bands, ROTC units, clowns, and Shriners in tiny red cars is supplemented by six or seven squid floats mounted on rusting Ford pickup trucks. Most of the floats are made of crepe paper as well, although a couple have been painstakingly woven together from honeysuckle and green ivy, the pungent scent of the flowers taking the edge off the ever-present marsh smell from Lake Jackson.

Meanwhile, the parade-goers have begun to don their squid masks and take out their squid noisemakers. Any chance the high school bands had of impressing the tourists is soon lost in the clacking and croaking of the noisemakers. Small boys always feel the need to set off caps and the resulting gunpowder smell gives the scene a slightly anarchic flavor. As I follow the festival crowds, the fake squid formed by the floats seem to waver and disintegrate in the early morning light. Excitement builds as we all realize we will soon be seeing the freshwater squid itself.

EARLY SQUID SIGHTINGS

Of course, I will just be replicating an experience shared with thousands of people over the past few years. And, my encounter with the squid will in no way compete with the encounters of the earliest scientists who studied the squid. Foremost among these was Edna Flocke (1879–1937), a protégé of the great Florida ecologist John Kunkel Small (1869–1938). In the early 1900s, while still a graduate student at Florida State University, Flocke made her initial reputation by publishing a dozen monographs on the symbiotic relationship between certain types of flowers, fungi, and the ruby-throated hummingbird (which proved to be a reproduction vector not just for the flowers, but for the fungi).

Flocke might have continued to study hummingbirds for many years, if not for an expedition to Lake Jackson in May of 1915, during which she observed telltale "flashes of green." Upon further investigation, Flocke was able to document the aftermath of a squid mating frenzy. Intrigued, Flocke decided to take a brief sabbatical from her bird studies to study the squid. Her sabbatical would eventually turn into ten uninterrupted years of squid research.

What attracted Flocke to the mayfly squid? Biologist Richard Smythe, Flocke's contemporary, believed she had intuited superficial similarities between the squid and her hummingbirds: both have high metabolic rates, short life spans, and delicate bodies. Both are highly maneuverable creatures built for sudden, extreme changes of direction. As Smythe remarked in 1923, "Dr. Flocke must have thought she was just changing environments, water for air, rather than making a radical leap."

Unfortunately, this change in environments led Flocke astray. Modern readers of her two books on the mayfly squid, *The Strange World of the Freshwater Squid* (1920) and *Mysteries of the Freshwater Squid Revealed* (1923), quickly become exasperated by the lack of specific detail and, more importantly, her blindness to the subject of silt. (The latter title was partially composed while staying in Sebring, which may account for its popularity in local bookstores.)

Silt would form the main stumbling block to acceptance of Flocke's theories because she had chosen to base her research on a stretch of the Ichnetucknee River that had become the most polluted in Florida, primarily due to runoff from nearby paper mills. A 1920 U.S. Army Corps of Engineers study, for example, showed a 300 percent increase in the Ichnetucknee's silt level between 1916 and 1918. The added silt made the river murky and slow-moving. Yet Flocke claimed to have "observed the squid in the water at some length while wearing snorkeling equipment," a claim that is difficult to take seriously. Any swimmer in those waters, in addition to imbibing possible carcinogens, would have been unable to see well enough to document the more than one hundred complex mating rituals, color fluctuations, and feeding habits set out in Flocke's books.

Some experts believe that photographs from the period showing Flocke in an old-fashioned bathing suit also undermine her claims. The cut and design of this suit, combined with the pale quality of Flocke's skin, would have made her similar in outline and color patterns to a large predator fish of the Toxicana family, thus increasing the likelihood of squid flight upon her approach.

With the exception of her monographs on the squid's life span, in which she coined the term "mayfly squid," Flocke's work is today considered primarily of historical importance. However, much to the irritation of many naturalists, the Florida Department of Education persists in renewing approval for a high school textbook called *Fundamentals of Biology.* This book uses quotes and excerpts from Flocke's work to blatantly impart erroneous information on the life cycle of the freshwater squid. A spurious third book, planned but never published, intended to report a symbiotic relationship between local Sebring varieties of fungi and the squid—a claim that, if made public, would only have further sullied Flocke's reputation.

Regardless, Flocke has become one of the Sebring festival's unofficial patron saints.

THE MATING GROUNDS

Eventually, packed tightly together, the crowds lurch within sight of Lake Jackson. The floats, bands, and other parade participants march off into a side alley while we tourists head for the water. The near side of the lake teems with waiting boats. Most of the vessels have been chartered weeks in advance and I hear a few unlucky tourists asking if anyone has a seat available. (All lake traffic, whether rusted fishing boat or two-deck yacht, must adhere to the city council mandated speed of 5 mph, "so as to facilitate," according to Sebring City Ordinance No. 93-0053A, "an atmosphere conducive to the squid's habits while also reducing the possibility of boating accidents.")

Among the lines of tourists are a few trained cephalopod biologists like myself, eager to record what they can of the mayfly squid's mating habits, even in such congested conditions.

However, some local biologists do not think much of the festival, considering it a hazard to the squid. Verna Bender, a marine ecologist who has worked for the Florida Department of Environmental Protection for 20 years, told me that the festival "disturbs the mating cycle. It also disturbs the ecosystem. Most of the tourists are pretty indifferent about tossing their trash in the water. Every year, the town has to hire people to clean up afterward. The degradation of the lake also tends to perpetuate the buildup of harmful lichen and fungi along its banks."

Nevertheless, after we get on board and the boats begin to move slowly forward toward the center of the lake, everyone quiets down. When the telltale silver-green glow begins to cut through the nascent sunlight, it is clear that the squid have once again congregated in great numbers. (Bender estimates the lake contains more than 2,000 squid.) Excitement gives way to a kind of anticipatory awe. I look around and find that the squid have everyone's full attention, even the attention of the children. The old man to my right takes off his baseball cap and shoves it into the pocket of his Bermuda shorts. A college student stops writing in her journal.

Then the engines cut off and the silence really encroaches upon us, the only sound a quiet ripple of waves against the prow. Everyone gathers along the railing, staring down into the water. They're looking for the squid and, out here in the center of the lake, with the silt and hydrilla almost completely absent, you can really see into the water. On the far side of the lake, the last remnants of the squid mills popular here in the 1950s bob like the tangible ghosts of another era.

For a moment, though, I don't see anything in the water. Then, a boy reaches out between the railing bars and points at something. Everyone leans in the direction of that pointing finger—and there they are, the squid, in numbers, sleek and small and incredibly fast, looking for all the world like Florida naturalist Edna Flocke's hummingbirds retrofitted for the water. They pulse with an emerald light that ripples up and down their silvery bodies. Despite the fact I've seen them up close and at a distance, in the wild and in the laboratory, so many times, my breath catches in my throat.

Still no one says anything. I have the feeling I'm not the only one holding my breath. The quick scooting and sliding through the water of these squid, their third eye blinking on and off on the underside of their mantels, at first seems random, chaotic, without purpose . . . but on second and third glances, I can tell that they've already entered the final stages of a complex series of maneuvers that should end in a successful mating.

The male squid actually initiates the mating rituals two or three days before the events we're now witnessing from the boat. On the first day, the male squid anchors itself amid the dead leaves and aquatic plants on the lake or river bed. Once firmly secured to the bottom, the squid uses its pistolaro and beak to secrete a series of clear bubbles that it then gently sticks to its skin using its tentacles. After covering its mantle, head, and arms, the squid will hide its tentacles beneath whatever debris is handy, leaving only its eyes free of bubbles. The male squid then puts on a kind of light show to attract the female, skillfully manipulating its colors and patterns to shine refracted bioluminescence through the bubbles. From a distance, a bubbled male squid resembles an exotic gemstone with a thousand perfectly cut facets.

Within 24 hours of the male constructing its "bubble tent," a female squid will appear, circling in the water over the male for several minutes before either investigating further or swimming off into the distance. (At any stage of the mating rituals, up to and including mating, the female may break off the engagement and swim away.) If the female investigates further, she will first hover directly over the male and then gently rub off the bubbles on its mantle and head. As soon as she does so, the male squid's light show ends and he begins to pulse a deep, rich green. The female, silver rippling up and down her body, then presses up against the male's mantle and head, wriggling the fins of her mantle as if to tickle the male squid. Less than a minute later, she places her arms and tentacles over the arms and tentacles of the male. They both change color to pure silver. This color change concludes the first phase of the mating ritual—and is followed by what the festival-goers have come to see: the mating itself.

Below us, dozens of squid riddle the water, and yet, through an ingenious recognition mechanism, no mating pair becomes separated in the process.

This intense level of activity continues for about an hour, until the sun has completely risen, casting a glow on the water that hampers visibility. Then the moment I have been waiting for, the moment I'm not sure my fellow watchers expected, occurs: the activity ceases all across the lake and each mating pair in the water below us lies perfectly still, the male atop the female, the tiny eyes of each seemingly turned up to watch us. With the flashing of colors abruptly ended, the water is dull with our own reflected faces. Several minutes pass. No one speaks. No one moves. Then, all at once, the lake erupts with streaks of emerald—a deep, bright green that suffuses the sides of the white-hulled boats. A gasp rises up all around me. This synchronization of mating and color display may be one of the most beautiful yet mysterious events in the natural world. Despite 20 years of study, no one, from cephalopod experts at Harvard to researchers in the Everglades, has been able to pinpoint the exact how's and why's of this phenomenon.

After a few minutes, the display subsides, the squid disappear into the depths of the lake, and everyone begins chattering happily, as if to confirm that it really happened by replaying it again and again in words.

The unhappy epilogue to the event, which most of my companions on the boat probably do not realize, is that almost immediately after mating the male squid will die of fatigue and old age. The female will survive only long enough to ensure the successful birth of her young. The mayfly squid does, in fact, live up to its namesake.

SQUID MILLS

Oddly enough, the period of most excitement about the mayfly squid predates the festival by a few decades. As described in the Sebring History Museum exhibit, the brothers Richard and Roger Mann stole a page from the already booming Florida fish farms and built the first squid mills on the banks of Lake Jackson in 1948. Like many Florida entrepreneurs before and since (for example, George Morel and his sink hole mushroom farms), the Manns believed that exotica could be turned into a profitable replacement for more traditional meats. The enterprise was funded with money from their inheritance; their father Bill Mann, recently deceased, had been a real estate developer and politician.

The Mann's risky scheme called for construction of squid mills and a cannery without first testing a squid mill prototype or acquiring a nationwide distributor. For the squid mill design, they secured the services of the inventor Thomas Porfal. Porfal had previously obtained patents for an automated dog kennel, a self-cleaning cat carrier, and several other animal-confinement devices. Wealthy retirees in West Palm Beach had bought his more domestic inventions by the score. As he wrote in a May 1948 letter to the Mann brothers, "It is time to work my magic on a more commercial scale."

Porfal eventually delivered a contraption on pontoons that combined elements of a lobster trap with his earlier inventions. Made of wire mesh, the squid mill's several compartments could be lowered by a winch until they touched bottom and closed off a portion of the lake. Lures popular in squid jigging (along with live bait) would be placed on the inner "gate" of the squid mill, with access controlled through a series of latches. The latches would be easy for "wild" mayfly squid to open, but would be alligator-, fish-, and turtle-proof. Once inside, the wild squid would eventually find their way to the central pen that housed the domesticated squid, adding to the potential meat harvest. Several squid mills could be set side by side, or they could be placed at a distance from each other. The center pens could be subdivided or enlarged as necessary.

The Manns ordered 30 units of Porfal's invention. They then hired men with fish farming experience and set up operations on the south shore of Lake Jackson. By the summer of 1949, the first canned squid were rolling off the assembly line and into grocery stores across Florida. A distribution contract with the Publix Supermarket chain helped fund an advertising campaign in a few Florida newspapers. One ad in the *St. Petersburg Times* showed a classic clip art '50s dad sharing a can of squid with his son over the tag line "Mann Bros. Canned Freshwater Squid: As Pure As the Best Things in Life. Buy Some at Your Local Grocer's Today!"

Based on their initial success—third-quarter sales of $10,000— Richard Mann wrote to his mother-in-law in November 1949 that "It's official! They can't keep our product on the shelf! We'll be rich in under a year." Unfortunately, due to certain limitations of the mayfly squid, success was even then slipping away from the Mann brothers.

First, the squid did not do well in captivity, even though the pens were immersed in the lake. The Manns' domesticated squid stock suffered a 60 percent mortality rate in the initial nine months, which not only cut into the amount of product—many of the carcasses rotted before they could be retrieved from the bottom of the mazelike squid mills— but also reduced the breeding stock. Jigging large numbers of wild squid provided a temporary boost in meat quantity but did nothing to help the decimated breeding stock.

Second, as mentioned previously, mayfly squid do not taste as good as other types of squid. In the interests of research, I have eaten over 20 different species of squid. Although edible, the mayfly squid is at the rubbery end of the spectrum, and tasteless. The Manns had reduced the rubbery quality by immersion in salt and dealt with the taste issue by adding cheap watered-down soy sauce. Even so, the novelty had worn off and, by the end of 1951, Mann Bros. Canned Freshwater Squid, the "Distinctly Floridian Treat," no longer leapt off the shelves and into consumers' shopping carts.

To compound the brothers' problems, Publix failed to renew its contract at the beginning of 1952. By July of that year, desperate for revenue, the Manns set up a tour of the mills. This was the first time anyone had attempted to use the mayfly squid to attract tourists. Photographs in the Sebring History Museum show the two smiling brothers in dapper suits welcoming crowds to the opening of the tour. However, records show that the Mann brothers only sold 300 tickets between July 1952 and July 1953.

By April of 1954, the squid mills served merely as holding tanks for wild squid. All but seven of the original 35 employees had been laid off.

The Manns took out a loan in August of 1953 to buy large quantities of squid directly from the West Coast and Japan, only to find most of the meat in rotted condition upon its arrival. The brothers hung on for the rest of the year, but in mid-1954 Richard Mann left the business, signing over his half of the company to his brother. Roger continued on for 18 months, despite mounting debts, but in 1956 sold the business to a local developer and moved to Cincinnati, Ohio, to work as a clerk in his father-in-law's bank. (Richard met a different fate, trying to establish himself as a landscape artist overseas. He eventually died in poverty in Central Asia, of malaria.)

Thomas Porfal's abandoned squid mills survived longer than their creators. As late as 1975, birders walking along the shore of Lake Jackson could inspect the pontoons and rusted wire cages. In 1976, tropical storm Ada dislodged the squid mills from the shore and since then they have floated around the lake, a source of irritation for fishermen and other locals.

DISTINCTLY FLORIDIAN FESTIVAL RITUALS

After watching the ritual, we return to the dock and climb out of the boat. There's nothing left to do but "party," as several teenagers loudly announce as they brush past me to get off first—and they are essentially correct. The mayfly squid has played its part in the festival and will not be seen again in the flesh. However, the iconography of the squid, its role as a motif in the Sebring subculture, is just beginning as festival-goers head back to the Historic District.

The full gamut of Florida tourism ingenuity is on display here, from plastic squid and squidsicles to glow-in-the-dark squid rings and a few tattered plush squid. Squid hats proliferate to such an extent that for long hours it appears that a sea of squid has left the lake to stroll around on land atop pale mannequins. Balloon squid with tentacle tassels are a favorite among the children, who run up and down the increasingly sizzling sidewalks in bare feet. Delicacies such as squid ink ice cream are hawked by vendors who seem unsure of the tastiness of what they're offering to the public. Vendors pace back and forth, selling T-shirts that read "Squid for a Day," "Experience the Festival," and, criminally, "I Like to See Squid, Mate."

The farmer's market set up opposite the Old Town Hall features a squid chili contest in the midafternoon, proceeds going to the charity Habitat for Humanity. Squid chili event organizer Sarah Higgenbottom, also the town's treasurer and inheritor of an ancient export/import business, offers passersby sample cups of chili. Higgenbottom is, I have been told, a festival fixture, and not only at the chili contest. Higgenbottom wears a squid costume that glows green with silver running lights but she also, in special translucent pouches affixed to her costume, carries live mayfly squid with her along the parade route. Every year, Higgenbottom is sent off in the first boat launched, balanced on the prow like a figurehead, the other boats, by established tradition, made to follow the light of her squidlike luminescence to the breeding waters. Once there, in a dramatic ceremony that I did not get to see because other boats blocked my view, she releases her pouched squid into the waters of Lake Jackson while reading a poem written for the occasion by local balladeer Carlton Signal. (The one irony of this gesture is that by holding the pouched squid back until this time, she almost certainly prevents them from mating and thus they die without propagating.)

"It's important," she tells a local television reporter for the six o'clock news. "It's true that some of this is tacky, but you have to be sincere about the squid on some level. Otherwise, how can it be fun?"

THE MAYFLY SQUID'S FUTURE

That the squid will be around to delight visitors to Sebring for many years to come is a near certainty.

Says Sheik, "For the exhibit, we did some research and found that most biologists estimate Florida's freshwater squid population at from 150,000 to 400,000, but all researchers agree that the squid's population is increasing almost as dramatically as its range."

Considering the dynamic nature of Florida's environment, subject to ever increasing pollution and loss of wetlands, it is remarkable that the mayfly squid continues to thrive. (Recent research indicates that one reason may be the ability of the squid's nerve ends to neutralize the harmful effects of such substances as mercury.) In 1997, researchers confirmed the presence of mayfly squid in Georgia. By 1999, mayfly squid had been reported as far west as Louisiana's Mississippi River Delta.

The mayfly squid could become a pest species due to overpopulation or, in its new range, encounter a native species on which it has a negative impact, but no hard evidence exists to indicate that it will do anything more or less than continue to adapt unobtrusively to its environment. As Edna Flocke once wrote, "The squid is most memorable for its subtlety."

THE END OF THE FESTIVAL

The late afternoon, punctuated by suffocating heat, proves to be little more than an opportunity to catalogue more squid-related phenomena. Many of the locals, preparing to turn their attention to televised racing events, have already changed into racing T-shirts and NASCAR caps. This leaves the tourists free to browse through the festival crafts show. More than 100 artists attend, some traveling from as far away as Alabama and Mississippi. Squid-specific objects are, of course, showcased, from paintings of squid (usually anatomically incorrect) to abstract sculptures of squidlike objects locked in an embrace. One participant from Boaz, Alabama, water color specialist Marsha Lake, admits that the squid festival is part of a longer Florida summer circuit: "If it was just this festival down here, I wouldn't make the trip. I make money, but not enough to justify the expenses."

At the center of the crafts show, the Lake Wales Little Theater and the Highlands Little Theater have joined forces to put on a production of Mednock's "Dr. Flocke, I Presume," a play in three acts that dramatizes important scenes from Edna Flocke's life, including her first encounter with the mayfly squid. In Sebring, naturalist Flocke has become something of a martyr to the squid. The tourist shops sell postcards of Flocke in her distinctive bathing suit alongside images of the Kraken, squid mills, and Elvis. T-shirts of Flocke are also sold, as are bumper stickers.

The pleasantly bohemian feel of outdoor theater permeates even the impromptu book stall, Borgess Book Corner, wedged between a jeweler and a wood carver. It features Mednock's stories for children, in bright, glossy covers, along with such staples of the squid book trade as Clyde Aldrich's overrated *The Search for the Giant Squid.* A few Dover editions of old marine biology studies round out the selection.

When I emerge from the narrow alleys formed by the crafts show stands, I am confronted by a ten-armed whirling dervish, a squid-themed amusement park ride borrowed by the town council from the county fair. The arm spokes end in carriages for the many tourists who like to be turned into centrifugal jelly.

Supersaturated with squid images, I retire to the Mayfly Saloon for a beer. The saloon is just beginning to fill up with festival memorabilia, from photographs to flags to bumper stickers. The walls are painted in the kind of palm tree mural motif more appropriate for a Jimmy Buffet concert, but you get the sense that in another 20 years the Mayfly Saloon will be as much a shrine to the squid as a passable eatery and bar.

As I sit there, I marvel at the level of identification with the squid displayed by many of the festival attendees throughout the day. There is no Florida Manatee Festival, no Florida Scrub Jay Festival, no Florida Panther Festival, even though these animals, on the verge of extinction, deserve the attention. Yet the mayfly squid has its own festival. Perhaps helped along by the beer, I am tempted to attribute this sense of community to the squid's own sense of community, or to the way its short life cycle forces us to contemplate our own mortality, but I think the real answer is much more cynical: someone found a clever way to promote a summer party for in-state tourists, achieving a level of success in popularizing the squid that the Mann brothers and their squid mills could not.

Outside, as the long afternoon shadows fade into dusk, the day concludes much as it began for mayor Lewden and the other town officials: they are performing an official act, this time bringing the festival to a close. Lewden and about 50 stalwarts, including Higgenbottom and balladeer Signal, have gathered lakeside to sing songs and light candles. Janet Sheik and the Sebring History Museum, the official sponsors of the sing-along, have thoughtfully provided both a DJ and a banjo player. The air is again cooler and full of mosquitoes. The lake is dark and still, aglow with the phosphorescence along its banks, either vestiges of the squid or the ever-present fungi. In the morning, the first of the dead mayfly squid males will wash up on the very shore that the mayor now solemnly presides over.

Notes on
The Festival of the Freshwater Squid

My family moved to Florida when I was ten. We lived in Gainesville, near the middle of the state. Every year, especially during the summer, we would pile into the family car and go to various local arts fairs and festivals so my mother could sell her artwork. The car didn't have air conditioning, so we'd be sweating long before we reached our destination. Tarpon Springs, St. Augustine, Jupiter Beach, Cedar Key, Daytona—the towns and cities blur in my memory. My father had built a display for mom's paintings and we'd spend the first hour placing the paintings on it, followed by a long weekend of watching anxiously as tourists and locals walked by. Which ones were the judges? Was mom going to get a ribbon? How many paintings would sell?

At some point, my sister Elizabeth and I would go off exploring, taking in the local atmosphere. I still remember the visit to the emergency room for the fish bones caught in my throat in Tarpon Springs. The thick, wonderfully greasy smell of Seminole bread cooking at a stand in St. Augustine. Not to mention the insane mix of talent and bizarre non-talent on display in the art shows.

In "The Festival of the Freshwater Squid," I wanted to capture that atmosphere—the mix of the earnest and the silly, the familiar and the surreal. I hope to write more stories set in Florida, now that I've found the right tone, the right distance.

The General Who
Is Dead

MY NAME IS STEPHEN BARROW AND I SERVED IN the Korean War, under the auspices of the 52nd Battalion. You would not have heard about the 52nd Battalion on the news-reels, for all we did was defend a city of the dead from the dead without, and the city held us in its thrall. From afar, it appeared as a glittering white crown of pagodas and snow, undisturbed and pris-tine. The walled kingdom of an ice witch, something right out of C. S. Lewis' *The Lion, the Witch and the Wardrobe*, perhaps.

Our mission was morbid and macabre and we loved it fiercely, for it kept us from the front lines. The city had been abandoned for over a year. Within its walls, the U.S. High Command had decided to house, catalog, and prepare for shipment stateside the bodies of the soldiers who had died at the front in our stead. We also housed, cataloged, and prepared (for cremation) the remains of South Korean civilians who had been caught in the crossfire. At times, the city streets were littered with the dead, all formally laid out, limbs no longer akimbo from bomb or mine blast, faces much more serene since their grimaces had been crafted into the artifice of smiles. Perhaps they merely slept, I would joke with my fellow soldiers, usually Nate Burlow, a muscle-bound lunk from New Jersey, and Tom Waters, a slender willow with hair so black it was almost blue and pale green eyes that stared out unblinking from beneath a helmet too big for his head. Nate was garrulous and Tom silent to a fault, calm as ice in a Rusty Nail. Between the two of them, I came very close to keeping my sanity amongst the dead.

All of us doubled up on our duties to conserve manpower, and so I became, much against my will, a writer of press releases for the army, under the supervision of Colonel X. It was easy work and I did it at my desk on the fourth floor of headquarters, which had been set up in the Buddhist temple at the city's center. The temple was the tallest structure in a place where the buildings seemed to genuflect and make themselves as small against the earth as possible.

I would sit with the snow-white pieces of paper in front of me and, when the pens were not frozen, I would write about the death of General So-and-So, the bravery of Corporal What's-His-Name. It gave me a lot of time to think. Perhaps too much time. My past did not bear up under close scrutiny and if, in describing what I am about to describe I am indirect about my own life — if, to be blunt, I discard bland fact in favor of hard truth — forgive me.

Suffice it to say, the war had passed us by in more ways than one. By the time I came into the middle of it, my landing at Inchon had none of the biting melodrama of MacArthur's initial beachhead. Colonel B. Powell had urinated proudly in the Yalu River more than six months before, doing several "takes" for the *Stars and Stripes* boys, blissfully ignorant of the fact that no American soldier after him would advance so far to demonstrate his backwardness. U.S. General Smith, a marine, had already declared, "Retreat, Hell! We're not retreating! We're just advancing in a different direction!" All the photo ops and all the best lines had been taken. By the time I came to Korea, the war had bogged down to a slow, futile, and bloody shifting of the lines along barren fields of snow, advance and retreat along the 38th Parallel, like the ebb and flow of some Ice Age tide.

All I had were dead bodies to take care of and paper to write on and my buddies to shoot the shit with. And, of course, the dead Chinese soldiers outside the city's walls.

When I came to the city, along with Nate and Tom, the dead Chinese soldiers were the first things we saw. You couldn't miss them. Over forty thousand of them on the plain outside the city's walls. The sergeant at arms had made sure the chopper let us off in the middle of the plain so that we had to walk through the dead to reach the city. What the man was trying to prove, I have no idea.

There were thirty of us new boys and we said nothing to each other at the time — out of nervousness or sympathy or respect, I don't know which. All I know is we were so quiet you could hear the crunch of our boots in the snow. The sunlight suffused the snow and bled through the Chinese soldiers, turning them crystalline and divine and pathetic all at once. As you can see through the skins of certain fish to their internal organs, so you could see through the ice and know the shapes, the contours, of the dead men on the frozen field. Some knelt and some stood and some huddled in clumps seeking a warmth that had long since left them. Forty thousand dead Chinese soldiers sprawled along a snowy plain. There were forty thousand stories in those lives, for they had all died in subtlely unique ways, and those ways had lent all of their faces a fierce individuality that would mark them even when spring came and thawed them out.

They had called themselves "The Army Which Casts No Shadow" because they had marched by night and lay camouflaged from reconnaissance planes by day. United Nations forces had not spotted them until they crossed the 38th Parallel. They had outrun their own supply lines out of Manchuria in an attempt to cut off U.S. forces from Inchon. They had no choice but to march forward and assault the U.S. perimeter at Pusan. They never made it. Our forces just kept retreating, left no supplies behind, and their progress slowed as they grew hungry, and then a blizzard caught them out in the open. They had already eaten their boots; almost none of them that I could see had shoes on their feet.

Parodies of statues in Pompeii.

The ice that had hardened around their bodies had also hardened their features, disguised their uniforms and weaponry, so that indeed it was a plain of statuary, ethereal, ghostly, and mocking. No one would have guessed they were once an army, or that they had marched anywhere, that once they had been alive. Walking among them I felt a crawling sensation across my spine—a helplessness and a despair that I did not know could live within me. I had a sudden frantic urge to write it down, to write about their deaths. I could not tell whether the impulse was ghoulish or commemorative, so I let it pass.

"Come spring," muttered Tom.

"Come spring what?" said Nate.

"Come spring, they'll thaw and then there'll just be forty thousand stinking dead people here for the vultures to feast on."

It was about the longest sentence Tom ever said, and when I got to know him better, I knew it meant those dead soldiers had really gotten to him, under his skin.

But they looked curiously at peace out in the snow, the longer I stared at them—as if they waited for someone or something to resurrect them. Or perhaps I read that into them and I was waiting for someone to resurrect me. I had a sudden memory of making snow angels in the front yard of our house, my Dad at six-six spread out ridiculously, making giant angels, while my own had been much smaller divinities.

We walked among the dead men for nearly an hour that first, most important, time, although the walls of the city were near. We did not feel, not having seen the indignities of war first hand, that we could leave without paying our respects, if that is the correct term. It was like walking among gravestones, only these men needed no such symbolism. They stood staunchly for themselves. Seeing them so vulnerable, waiting for the thaw that would make them fully human again, my imagination began to unfetter itself from the cold and the company of my fellow soldiers. Something churned in my stomach and up, into my heart. What if these men, these soldiers, really were waiting for someone? As if they had been enchanted, put under a spell? Who were they waiting for?

"Who are they waiting for?" I said it aloud.

"General who?" Tom said, as if reading my mind.

"General Who," I said. Inside, the churning stopped and I thought, yes, it was General Who who led them. General Who who would come back for them. He could protect them, much as my father had often wrapped his arms around me in the snow and held me against his chest, warm and secure.

As we finally left the field, I saw a Chinese woman who had frozen to death along with the soldiers, a look of divinity upon her face. As if she could see something magical beyond her reach. Her head was inclined upward and when I saw her, her features etched cruelly in the ice, I looked where she looked, almost expecting there to be someone in the sky, or some sign.

But this time, there was just the white. Always the white. And from then on, I could not hate our Enemy, or even think ill of Him, but thought only of when I too would be stiff, my eyes staring out into the unknown, afraid—taken away from the sudden, lacerating beauty of this world and into the cruel glacial light of the next.

"General Who is dead," I said as we left that place, and Tom and Nate nodded like they almost understood what I meant.

Notes on
The General Who Is Dead

Sometimes writers keep writing past the true ending of a story. This happened to me on "The General Who Is Dead." I thought I had a whole novel. It took another thirty pages of futile attempts at making a magical "General Who" come to life before I realized my story had ended long before. Nothing can come after that plain of frozen bodies. The story begins and ends with the bodies. Anything else is anticlimax.

Ghost Dancing with
Manco Tupac

Ghost dancing was not simply a phenomenon central to the North American Indian mythos, but also an integral part of the ritual of the indigenous South American populations, particularly to the descendants of the Incas. The primary difference between the North and South American versions of the ghost dance is that the Incas danced more for remembrance than renewal. To the Inca, the future, unknowable, was considered to be at a person's back and the past, known, opened up before a person to be seen clearly.
—Sir Richard Bambaugh, *Inca Ritual* (Harper & Row, 1986)

I

AT TIMES IT SEEMS TO THE REPORTER AS SHE scribbles notes in the dim light that this is his last breath, that the lungs will collapse in mid-sentence; the arms—hands twiglike but supple—will punctuate his stories with a flourish and then convulse, become limp, cold, languid. The eyes, shining from the sunken orbits, will dim to the color of weathered turquoise. The mouth will die a hummingbird's death, slackening in a final flutter of lips. Already a smell, old as parchment and strong as vinegar, has begun to coat the hotel room. Outside, Cuzco's moonlit streets are silent.

She can taste his death on her tongue: a bitterness softened by the sweet-sour of incense burning in a bowl. Her pen falters on the page, then hurries forward ghoulishly, to catch his essence before it vanishes into the air.

But he does not die that evening, despite the heaving of his breaths, the pauses and halts that disrupt the urbanity of his voice and its subtle hints of accent, none of which can quite break the surface of syntax.

Behind him, black machinery sputters and jerks as it feeds his lungs. At times he is lost within the machines that engulf him, their own cough-cough threatening to drown out his words, or snatch them before they can reach the reporter's ears, and by extension, her pen.

She thinks it odd that a machine, a collection of cogs and wires and bellows, should keep a man's soul in his body, the two having no natural connection, nor even a common meeting ground. Yet, when she looks up from her page, he appears to have melted into the machine, no longer a figure draped in sheets, lying placid on a wooden bed.

Then, too, she finds it odd she should be here, having closer kinship to the machinery than the man. At least she can understand the machinery. Peru stonewalls her. It has nothing to do with who she is or what she desires from life. The hotel, for example, carved into the mountainside, and the hotel room with its small window that winks from the wall opposite her chair. The window, during daylight hours, shows a cross-section of mosses and lichens, the loamy soil alive with beetles. Now it is just another shadow, rectangular amid deeper shadows.

The window reminds her of the grave and, staring again at Manco Tupac, last true descendent of the Inca Emperors, she realizes just how small, how birdlike, he is. She had expected a giant, with the sinewy, leathery health of a man who claims to have survived one hundred forty winters in a country that already has her gasping for breath, ears popping. The man lying on the bed looks as though a breeze could strip the flesh from his ribs.

Her expectations have often led her astray; her vision of New York City before she moved there from Florida was of a citadel of shining chrome and steel—evenings at the Met, operas at the Lincoln Center, walks in Central Park. Cultural Eden. It was an image that, as her editor at *Vistas: Arts and Culture Monthly* often says, "Got turned on its ass."

When her thoughts stray, as now, to home, or the hypnotic movement of his hands lulls her toward sleep, his *words*, muscular and tight, bring her back to her notes, to the physical sensation of the pen in her hand, to the nerves in her wrist that tense, untense, tense again.

Already she has been writing for an hour, her tape recorder broken and discarded an isthmus away in Mexico, her wrist ready to break on her now, with no money to replace that, either. She feels a spark of resentment toward the old man in front of her and then rebukes herself. She asked for it. It was the type of assignment her rival freelancers regularly had orgasms over as they drummed up articles from their pathetic little stomping grounds in Manhattan and Brooklyn: interviewing the last of a breed, with all the echoes of faded glory, lost triumphs, a hitherto overlooked pocket of nostalgia that readers and award judges alike could fawn over. Dramatic headlines dance through her head: BRUTAL IRONY: LAST DESCENDENT OF THE INCAS DYING OF ASTHMA; THE SECRET HISTORY OF THE 20TH CENTURY, AS REVEALED BY THE LAST OF THE INCAS. She does not know much more — yet. She knows that the old man requested the interview and that he holds an honorary degree from the National University of Lima at Cuzco. Beyond this, nothing. A void as black as the window carved into the mountainside.

"Do you think you have transcribed my words accurately thus far? It must be difficult."

His voice startles the reporter, because now it is directed at her. She squints at the page. Her eyes blur. The words become hiero-glyphics. What did it mean, really, as a whole? Where is the article she dreamed up while still in New York? The perfect story and yet, almost indefinably, she can sense it going sour, going south.

"Yes, I think so," she says, smiling, looking up at him. Even her feet and ankles ache, a healthy, well-used ache, as if she just swam ten laps at her local gym.

"Good," he says, and spins out the dry reed of his voice until it is impossibly thin, impossibly tight, tighter than the quipo knots his ancestors wove into compact messages: scrolls of knots sent across the Empire by fleet-footed men with muscles like knots beneath their skin.

She has only her pen.

II

In 1879, when I met the man who called himself Pizarro, though Pizarro had been dead for over 300 years, I knew the Inca knots better than the Español of the usurper. I had not yet left my village for renown on the Brazilian coast, nor infamy in the United States, where I would spend many years being hunted by Pancho Villa over one misunderstanding and two exaggerations. I had yet to become known by the moniker of "Jimmy Firewalker," and still relied upon my given name, Manco Tupac, which I have returned to in these later years.

And also in 1879 my mother and father were still living. My parents, my four brothers, two sisters, and I all worked the land, never owning the land, although we were allowed to plant some crops for our family's use. The hours were hard and we had few pleasures in our lives, but, for better or worse, I was always scheming to do better, to get out of our ruined hut of a house, to be *someone*. For the man you see before you is dissipated and jaded from too many years traveling this world, but in 1879 I was very, very *young* . . .

The man who would be Conquistador again entered my village, two miles from this very city, as winter began to settle over the land. The trees had lost their few leaves, the sun had a watery, distant quality, and in the far off mountains, I heard the raw sound of avalanches as falling snow dislodged packed ice.

The man who would be Conquistador again rode up the old Inca road from Cuzco. He rode a nag, was himself a nag of a man: thin to a shadow, arms like poles of balsa wood, and his age above sixty. Wedged into the wrinkles of his face, his blue eyes shone with a self-assurance that beggared the decay of his other parts. He wore a rusted helmet from the past century, such as the men of the Peruvian viceroyalty wore before Bolivar swept them into the sea. At his side hung a rusty sword in a scabbard and a flintlock rifle, aging but oiled and shiny. Supplies weighed down his horse—blankets, water skins, pots, pans—and it was the banging and clanging of these supplies that alerted me to his presence.

As this oddity approached, I sat idly in a chair outside our leaky house and pretended not to see him. Our family had just eaten our noontime meal and everyone was already in the fields, my father yelling for me to join them. I pretended not to see him as well.

The stranger's shadow fell across my body. The voice that addressed me held no trace of quaver, more akin to the Damascus steel in his eyes than the ruins that surrounded them.

"Manco Tupac?"

"Yes," I replied.

"I am called Pizarro. I require a guide."

I stared up at him, saw the yellow cast to his face, smelled the *quinoa* berries on his breath.

"Where?"

He pointed to the mountains.

"Up where Tupac Amaru used to rule. I seek the Lost Treasure of the Incas." He said this with precision, capitalizing the phrase. "In Cuzco they say you are the best guide, that your ancestors are descended from Tupac."

I nodded and folded my arms. I was not the best guide. I was cheap. I had gained my meager reputation from my name, which combined the names of the two last and greatest Incan Emperors, this an act of bravery on the part of my mother. It had been several months since anyone had requested my services due, no doubt, to the landowner wars that sputtered and flared like brushfires across most of the lower country.

"I have a map."

I stifled laughter. They all had maps in those days, whether it was black-clad Dominicans searching for treasure for a European diocese, or the newly coined "archaeologists" who dug up our graves, or common thieves from Lima and Quito. Maps on parchment, lamb's skin, papyrus, even tattooed on their skin. Never once had I heard of their quests turning up anything more profound than pottery shards, skulls, or abandoned mercury mines.

I nodded and stated my fee for such a venture.

"Of course." He inclined his head, an odd gesture of deference that almost made me forget he claimed the inheritance of Pizarro.

Our quest began amicably enough. I said goodbye to my family, my father stern, his brow furrowed with worry, as he handed me his own set of bolas, with which I could bring down wild game. My mother, feigning indifference, had already returned to the fields by the time I left with the Spaniard. I cannot pretend they did not fear for me, but the money I earned would keep us fed and clothed through the winter. All the while, Pizarro upon his nag looked neither left nor right, harmless as statuary from another age.

We set out into a morning sharp and bright enough to cut our eyes, he upon his horse, myself following on foot. We traversed the Incan highway, still intact after four hundred years, which ran from Cuzco into the mountains. The road was pockmarked with rubble, shot through with sweet-smelling grasses. We would not leave the highway until well near the end of his quest.

Every few miles my companion would point proudly to the

etched initials of a Spaniard immortalized in stone. Some of the crudest carvings dated back to Pizarro's original few score men.

As we traveled, he spoke to me of his ancestors, of what they had endured to bring my ancestors into the light of Christendom.

"It was a time of great energy! A time of great industry, unlike today, when Spain has fallen back on its haunches like a toothless lion." He grimaced at the thought, but then he brightened. "Perhaps a time will again come when . . ." He trailed off, as if realizing to whom he spoke.

"You are Christian, are you not?" he asked.

"I am not," I said.

"But you have been baptized?"

"I have not," I replied.

"Your parents?"

"They have not."

He shook his head, as if this did not make sense to him.

"There is but one true God," he said, in a lecturing tone, "and His Son, who died for our sins, is Jesus Christ. If you do not believe in Jesus Christ, you shall be eternally damned."

"What do you hope to find?" I asked. I had no religion, only a faith in the myths my mother had whispered to me even as a baby at her breast, a faith in the confident way she told them. It gave me secret pride that such tales had outlived the Spanish conquest, for the Christian god was by contrast colorless.

"What do you hope to find?"

A one word answer.

The only honest answer, ever.

"Gold."

We did not converse much after that first brittle exchange, but contented ourselves with watching the countryside unfold, always ascending along the winding road. The mountains surrounded us ever more and if we looked at them for too long, perspective seemed to place them within reach, as if we had only to clutch at the glittering domes of snow and they would be ours. But when we let our gaze drop to the ground beneath our feet—and we did this rarely—we quickly noted the precariousness of the path: our feet often came to the edge of open air, almost stepping out into a sky that could plunge us one thousand, two thousand feet to a valley floor, a river bed. Pizarro developed the habit of glancing down, then over at me, as if he wondered whether I would lead him to his death.

Near dusk of the third day, weary and ready for sleep, we came upon a troupe of Ghost Dancers. They danced around the ruined spire of an old Inca guard tower. The tooth of stone had served as a home to animals for at least three hundred years, but they danced to restore the guard tower to its former glory and purpose. The bittersweet smell of sweat and exertion was a testament to their faith, their hope—a dream I could not share, for I found it impractical at that age. It would have accomplished much more, in my view, to rebuild the tower and refit the stones into the highway.

The dancers had adorned themselves in the rags of old ceremonial dress, clothing that still glittered with iridescent reds and greens, where it was not torn and resewn. The women, stooped and folded in on themselves, stank from years of labor in the mercury mines. Miraculous that they walked at all, and they danced like scarecrows on a puppeteer's strings, their jerky strides worn down to a caricature of normal human motion. To me they appeared bewitched, their twitches and stumbles those of a people caught forever in trance.

The men blended in with the women, except for one, who looked up at Pizarro astride his horse. Age had hardened this man until his true nature had retreated into the wrinkles and taut skin around the bone: one last rear guard against death. One could not guess whether he was happy or sad or merely indifferent, for his face had become such a mask that even ennui was a carefully guarded secret. And yet, if one discounted the faded rags, the dull eyes, this man resembled Pizarro closely enough to be his brother—and Pizarro must have recognized this, for he turned quickly away and muttered to me, "Do not stop here. Do not stop. Go on. Go on!" and urged his nag forward at a pace I could hardly match.

When, after several strides, I glanced back, I saw that the man stood in the middle of the highway, staring at us. His gaze stabbed into my proud Pizarro's back like a dagger blunted by ill use, though why the similarity in their faces should frighten the Spaniard I did not know.

That night we camped in the sandy soil beside a patch of thorny yuccas. Though our clothing barely protected us from the chill, the Conquistador refused to unpack the blankets. He seemed to invite the cold, to embrace it, as if seeking penance. But for what? Because a mirror had been held up to him?

He remained awake for a long time, watching the stars glint like the eyes of gods. In his face, I still saw the ghosts of the men from the dance, and realized they haunted him. His prayers that night, conducted in a whisper I strained to understand, were for his wife and children in Spain.

Ever upward we climbed. I led now, despite his map, for the road contained treacherous potholes, overgrown with eel grass and other weeds that disguised ruts until too late. On the fifth day, I brought down a wild pig with my bolas to supplement his supplies. Always we went higher. Always higher. However we traveled—slow or fast, on foot or leading his horse—we went higher.

"The air is thinner here," he said, wheezing.

"Yes, it is."

"How much longer?"

He asked this question often and I had no ready reply. Who could predict what obstacles we might encounter? Our conversations consisted of little else, and this depressed me, for I was normally talkative and animated with my clients. But when I asked Pizarro, he had no stories, no descriptions of his country. At most he might say, "Where I live it is beautiful this time of year." Or, "Churches are the only bastions of faith left, the only strength left in Spain." Once he said, "You will never go to Spain. Why do you ask?" He said this so matter-of-factly that I determined that I would travel to Spain, if only to spite this stupid old man who really thought his map and his alone led to the lost treasure of the Incas.

Now the mists began to roll in: thick soups that our weak eyes could not penetrate. We traveled through this underworld with no anchor to secure our senses. In the absence of taste, touch, hearing, we became each a ghost to the other, a form in the mist. Only sharp sounds—the jingle of bit and harness, the creak of leather saddle—pierced the whiteness. It did not, of course, affect our camaraderie, because our camaraderie would have fit into the space between his saddle and his horse's back.

Pizarro's nose bled copiously in the thin air. He tried, and failed, to staunch the flow with his spare shirt. The white fabric was soon clotted red as if he had suffered a fatal wound.

I had many strange thoughts. Disembodied by the mist, not even able to see our own feet, I found that my imagination tried to compensate for the loss of sight. Soon, every tree root under my tread was a human bone—here a thighbone, there a spine. Helmets, too, I found aplenty with my feet, no doubt only rocks.

The only relief from the mist came in the form of lakes so blue and deep that they seemed black; so thickly placid that a skipping stone would only *plunk* and disappear, leaving no ripple to mark its entrance. The bones and treasure of many Inca lay at the bottom of such lakes, and I felt in my heart that a man would fare no better than the stones. The lakes were all graveyards without markers.

I told this to the Conquistador and he laughed.

"Think of the gold," he said. "If only we could find a way to raise the gold."

I began to fear his determination, his single-mindedness, his refusal to make camp until after the moon rose high above the mountain peaks. He was old and yet by strength of will refused to allow his body to betray him.

On the seventh day, when the silence and the mist made me both jumpy and melancholy, he asked me to tell him a story. I told him it was an odd request.

I thought I saw him shrug through the mist as he said, "My father once told me stories to pass the time when we went out into the fields—to oversee the men. This mist unsettles me." And then in a whisper, "Please." I wondered if he saw the ghost dancer in his dreams, if the man stood in the ruins of the old Incan highway and stared at Pizarro, night after night.

I thought for a moment and then said, "I shall tell you a tale from the beginning of the end of our reign."

He nodded, motioned for me to continue.

And so I launched into my tale, determined to drive away the mist that clotted my eyes and stole my breath . . .

III

They journeyed to see the toad that lived in the maggot-cleansed eye of an eagle. This eagle had died high above a granite canyon, and already on the trek all seven llamas had been lost to thirst and fatigue. The meat was rationed by the seven Quichua who walked the ancient paths. These paths had been laid down long before the Inca rulers had arrived at Machu Picchu and built the city of Vilcapampa. The paths never remained the same—carefully chosen stones led the uninitiated to ravines, or places where the earth buckled, cracked, as mountains tossed and turned in fitful sleep.

One Quichua, Melchor Arteaga, was a lunatic. He danced the dance of the Emerald Beetle, Conchame, bringer of drunkenness and shortened breath. Twelve days before, Melchor had been struck by a Spanish musket load near Vitcos, where even now refugees straggled in ahead of the conquerors. The left side of the lunatic's head had darkened; he moved jerkily. His eyes darted back and forth, perhaps following a hummingbird's frantic flight from flower to flower. By nightfall, Melchor would be dead. By nightfall, the toad would have told them what they wished to know.

Two men, nobles, had already died, but three strong men carried the corpses on shrouded litters, muscles straining, faces long since stripped of any fat. Captain Rimachi Yupanqui, oldest of them all, had suffered through Inca Atahualpa's capture by Pizarro. He of narrow eye and hawkish nose had seen the old king butchered once he filled a room with gold. Rimachi remembered the delicate butterflies, beetles, alpacas: children's toys. The metal work had bought nothing. It never would. Rimachi walked with a soldier's sense of fixed steps. His companions, Sayric Tupac and Titi Cusi, sons of the seventh man, had witnessed excesses themselves on the fields outside Cuzco; they listened with hatred when Rimachi spoke of Pizarro, the man who had robbed them of their birthright. All three carried bolas at their waists, the stones flaked with dried blood.

The seventh man was the king, Manco. His army awaited his return, bearing the oracle of the toad. The toad had always decided the punishment of the worst evildoers. Manco staggered forward, clutching his side, Rimachi supporting him at intervals. The wound would heal in time. But the king's eyes were hollow and the clear, cold air cut through his robes. He shivered.

"Treachery," Manco muttered, speaking to the sky. After raising the banner of revolt, many Quichua had joined him. But the Spanish had routed Manco near Cuzco and he had fled to the Urubamba Valley; the safety of fortress-capital Vilcapampa reassured him. Steep drops, raging rivers, and passes three miles high would hinder pursuit. But his forces needed a sign as the Spaniards approached, stripping bodies of metal, their thirst for gold unslaked. Manco made this pilgrimage because his captains had lost faith, and he himself refused to be ruler over the solitary mountain peak of Machu Picchu. Manco still hoped the toad who watched from the eagle's eye, the oracle of the Quichua, would shed some wisdom on this crisis. Certainly the resident priest could help him understand.

So, sliding and stumbling, seven men lost themselves on the paths. Squinting, Manco pressed forward in the glare of the morning sun. Melchor followed, giggling and clutching his broken head. Behind both, the king's sons and his captain dragged the dead nobles; they would be placed near the oracle, buried under rocks. No one spoke, though once or twice Rimachi would mutter a word to Titi, staring with concern at Manco. They ate as they moved, llama meat and *quinoa*, the cereal-like seeds kept in waist pouches. The sun eclipsed Melchor's face. Manco allowed himself a smile, his callused feet lifting more easily with each step. They were close. Rimachi smiled too, a guarded smile. He knew the odds, had known them since Manco had cast off the role of puppet king.

They reached the bridge that joined the two sides of the canyon. Its liana cord made it durable, but the ropes swung and groaned in the wind. Manco crossed first, bracing himself against the gusts, planting one foot in front of the other. Melchor ran across, nearly ramming a foot through the webbing. When everyone had reached the other side, Manco said, "We will cut the bridge once we cross over again. We will cut every bridge . . ." He looked to Rimachi, who nodded his approval. Manco glanced at his sons, then moved forward.

The stone hut next to the bridge was empty. The priest who had stood guard was discovered by Rimachi. He pointed downward to the base of the cliffs. The man was dead, sprawled with arms outstretched, his robes a blur of blood. Manco frowned, and said, "Leave him."

Together, they made their way to the toad's alcove, their bolas held ready. The alcove lay in a grotto which had been hollowed out at eye level above a shelf of rock. From the shelf, the men could see the stacked range of mountains fading into the distance, clouds stalking from above. The valleys beneath them were green smudges, the rivers sinuous lines broken by the white interruptions of rapids.

Although Rimachi and Titi searched, fanning out to cover the shelf's rim, no enemy could be found. A cold wind blew out of the west and Manco shivered again. He called his son and captain back and, bravely, he approached the alcove. A judgment would be passed down. Behind him, Rimachi watched, a grimace forcing its way through wrinkles; the death of the priest made him wary. Sayric and Titi stood frozen, their burdens temporarily forgotten. Melchor picked a flower from behind two stones.

Manco peered into the hole. Within lay the toad, staring out from the eagle's eye. How it sparkled in the sunlight!

Manco's shoulders slumped. He sank to his knees, a sigh and snarl of exhaustion on his lips. Rimachi cursed, kicking at the ground. Sayric and Titi dropped their burdens. The dead men tumbled over the edge of the rock shelf, falling until they disappeared from sight.

Melchor laughed, as though Conchame, the Emerald Beetle, was buzzing in his ear, and brought his musician's pipes to his mouth. Whirling, flailing, Melchor pawed at his head. A hollow sound, slow and melancholy, crept into the air, a counterpoint to his crazy dance. Manco, knowing he would never reclaim his lands no matter how hard he fought, raised his head to catch the notes. He nodded wryly as Rimachi helped him to his feet and his sons wept. A dirge. How fitting.

For the toad had turned to gold.

IV

I told this tale as a warning. If it marked centuries of slow decline and failure for the Inca, it also foretold a punishment for the Spanish: to be enraptured and consumed by their obsession with gold. Pizarro did not take it as such. He was silent for a long time, so long that I thought he had fallen asleep on his horse.

But then he said, haltingly, as if explaining to an idiot, "I studied at the military academy in Barcelona many years ago. You must understand that war is not a game for children."

"Thank you for your wisdom, but I do not see it that way," I said.

To which he replied, "That is why I am upon this horse and you are my guide."

I kicked at the skulls that must have been roots or rocks, and cursed myself for telling such a story at all. The Spaniard was without subtlety and I without patience.

The sparse yucca and scraggly herds of wild alpaca gave way to bleak ice and snow, without the mist, which we soon learned had been a blessing, for now we saw each other more clearly, and neither of us could more than tolerate the other. Myself, because the Spaniard was conservative and withdrawn. The Spaniard, because I refused to agree with him and told him stories with no useful moral.

We argued about supplies.

"Surely there is wild game about," he said when I suggested his dry beef and water skins would only last the journey if we turned back within three days.

"Look around you," I whispered, afraid of avalanche. "Look around you! Do you see any trees? Any bushes? Anything for an animal to eat? Do you?"

We were tiptoeing through a field framed by abutting mountains whose flanks raced upward toward the sun. Not a blade of grass, and no water, except in the form of ice. Beneath the ice, more ice.

"How do you know?" he said.

"Because I live here," I said.

He shivered, nudged his horse forward, its hooves making soft scrunching sounds in the snow.

An hour later, we came upon a frozen waterfall.

The Spaniard, complaining of the cold, trailed off in mid-insult, saying, "My God!" A solid wall of ice confronted us. In the center of this wall, a doorway had been covered over by water that had once flowed in a river down the mountainside and now formed a facade of ice. A man, frozen through, looked down at us from within the doorway. At first I thought he was floating in the ice, but as we moved closer I saw the frayed end of a rope. The man had been hung by the neck and the passage sealed with him inside it. The man wore a Conquistador's armor and his head lolled; his helmet had frozen to his forehead and his arms hung limply at his sides.

"An angel! It is a sign," Pizarro said. He dismounted, bent to one knee, and crossed himself.

"Just an adventurer," I said. "A plunderer, who was put here by my ancestors as a warning."

He ignored me, walked up to the frozen doorway, put out a hand to touch the ice near the dead man's head. He muttered a few words.

"A fire," he said. He turned away from the man. "We must light a fire to melt the ice. Beyond the ice lies the lost treasure of the Incas."

As the sun faded, we lit a fire. Rather, I lit a fire and Pizarro hacked at the ice with an ax. The blade was dull and made a hollow sound as it cut into the ice. Pizarro was strong for his age and his technique fluid. Soon, the dead man began to float and when Pizarro finished hacking a hole in the ice, water spilled out, more ice broke, and the man was set free. He came to a stumbly rest at our feet, face down, a sodden mass of armor and rags and flesh. The doorway was almost clear and beyond lay a passageway untouched by frost.

Then I knew that we had entered the spirit world and our minds, our wills, were not truly our own.

In one convulsive motion, the lump of flesh at our feet roused itself, bracing itself with its arms until the face, still lolling hideously against the neck, looked up at us with soggy eyes, exhaled one last breath and, shuddering, fell back to the ground. In the moment when the eyes stared at me, I swear I saw someone else looking out at me, not the dead soldier, but someone else, a god perhaps, or one aspiring to godhood. A sentry for the immortal.

I screamed and turned to run, but tripped and fell in the snow, bruising my left shoulder. Pizarro, through inertia or bravery, stood there as the corpse died a second death.

His sheer ignorance of the danger forced me to curb my instinct to flee, though my heart pounded in my chest. I remember that moment as the one time when I could have moved against my future. The moment after which I could not turn back, could never again be just a simple guide in a town outside Cuzco. If I could, would I go back to that wall of ice and tell myself to run? Perhaps.

Pizarro gently knelt and closed the corpse's eyes with a sweep of his gnarled hand. He crossed himself and laid his crucifix upon the dead Spaniard's breast. The light in his eyes as he rose frightened me. It was the light of a beatific yet cruel self-assurance. It lifted the wrinkles from the corners of his mouth, sharpened and smoothed his features.

Pizarro did not choose to break his silence now. He merely pointed toward the path cleared for us, patted me on the back, and remounted his horse. We entered the tunnel.

The tunnel was damp and cold and the sides painted with old Incan symbols, the paint faded from water erosion. Everywhere, water dripped from the ceiling, speaking to us in drips and splashes. The temperature grew warmer. Soon we saw a sharp yellow light through the dimness and the passageway opened up onto the burning orange-red of sunset.

The tunnel overlooked a shallow basin between mountains. We had come out upon a hillock that overlooked a vast city, the likes of which I had never dreamed: magnificent towers, vast palaces of stone, a courtyard we could barely discern, radiating out from a ripple of concentric walls. A *city*, whole and unplundered, lying amid thick vegetation—this is what took our breath, made us stand there gawking like the explorers we were not.

It is difficult, even now, to describe how strongly it affected me to have reached the location on the Conquistador's map and to have found the bones of my ancestors in those buildings. No longer was I a simple villager, poor and bound to the earth—here was my legacy, my birthright, and if nothing else, that knowledge gave me the confidence with which I met the world the rest of my days. Here was yet another last refuge of the Inca, another place the Spaniards had never touched, could never touch. I wept uncontrollably, wondering how long men might have lived there, how finally they must have died out, protected from everything except their own mortality. The city radiated a desolate splendor, the pristine emptiness of the abandoned, the deserted. Perhaps then I understood what Pizarro meant when he had called Spain an old lion rocking back on its haunches.

But if my reaction was violent to an extreme, then Pizarro, by virtue of his hitherto unbroken mien, had passed into madness. He wept tears, but tears of joy.

"It is truly here! I have truly found it!" He let his horse's reins fall and he embraced the ground. "Praise to God for His mercy."

To see his face shine in the faded sun and his mouth widen to smile its first smile in nine days, an observer would have believed him caught in the throes of religious ecstasy. It did not strike me until then what a betrayal it had been to guide him to that place.

"Come, Manco," he said. "Let us descend to the city center." We made our way down into the basin—along a path of red and green stones locked perfectly together, into the antique light, the legion of yellow flowers, the perfumed, blue grasses.

We could not simply press through to the center of the city, for walls and towers and crumbled stones stood in our path. But, as we progressed, gaps in the stone would allow us to glimpse the ragged flames of a bonfire near that center. A bonfire that, minutes before, had not been lit. Yet now we could feel the heat and hear the distant sound of Incan pipes: a dry reed that conveyed in its hollow and wispy sound the essence of ghosts and echoes and every living thing deadened and removed from its vitality. Behind it, as a counterpoint, a flute, twining and intertwining in plum-sweet tones, invited us to dance, to sing.

From the moment we first heard the music, we fell under its spell and could do only what its husky silken voice told us. We hurried in our quest for the center, the courtyard. We wept. We sang. We laughed. Pizarro threw his rifle to one side. It caromed off a wall and discharged into the air. I dropped my bolas to the ground, prancing around them before moving on. We were slaves to the spirit of the city, for the city was not truly dead and the life in it did not come from the wilderness beyond, nor yet from the power of its ghosts. No, these were *living* forces that had fled from Cuzco and all the lower lands.

Thus we drew near over the ancient and smoothed flagstones, luminous-eyed crocodiles lured in dance to the hunter's spear. The Conquistador was crocodile indeed with his salty tears and I, uncowed even by the myths my own mother had told me, an unbeliever at heart, was brought back into belief only by the compulsion and evidence of my own eyes.

We danced through the city until my lungs ached from laughter and my feet throbbed against the stone. Finally, we unraveled the circles of the maze and came out upon the center square. Within a blackened pit, a fire roared, muffling the music that had seemed so pure.

Around the fire danced men and women wearing the masks of gods and goddesses from the Inca faith, and from earlier, more powerful faiths. Conchame, the Emerald Beetle, bringer of drunkenness and shortened breath, danced his own mad dance, while Cupay, the amorphous God of Sin, adorned himself in cockroach carapaces of the finest black and aped their scuttling walk with a shuffle and hop, his eyes always surveying the others with suspicion. Ilapa, God of Thunder, made lightning-fast moves around the flames, letting them lick his fingers, his feet, as he twisted and turned in a blur. The hummingbird, messenger to the gods, was there too: a woman who wore thousands of feathers about her arms and legs, so that she shimmered and dazzled; even when she stood still, the movements of the others were reflected in the feathers, to give her the illusion of motion. Of them all, only her face was not hidden by a mask. She had delicate features, with high cheekbones, and lips that formed a mysterious smile. Her chest was bare, covered only by her lustrous black hair.

The rest I could not identify by name, and no doubt they came from older faiths—jaguar gods and snake gods and monkey gods— but nowhere could I see the Sun God, Inti. The smell of musky incense rose from them. The fire spewed sparks like stars. The laughter of the dancers, the chaffing of bodies moving closely together, seduced our ears with its other-worldly wonder.

From behind, wind-swift, hands guided us to positions closer to the fire. I found myself reluctant to glance back, to identify our hosts, and Pizarro, too, looked only ahead. The hands—strangely scaled and at times too heavy with hair—brought alpaca meat on golden trays and a wine that burned our throats but soon went down smoothly until it was mild as water.

Alternately, we wept and laughed, the Spaniard embracing me at one point as a brother and asking me to visit him in Barcelona. I heartily agreed and just as quickly burst into tears again.

The dancers continued in their dance, a numbing progression of feet and whirling arms. Sometimes they moved at double speed, sometimes much slower than natural. Through it all, I caught glimpses of the hummingbird woman's smooth brown legs as she made her way around the fire—or a flash of her eyes, or her breasts, the nipples barely exposed, brown and succulent. She spoke to me when she drew close, but I could not understand her above the fire's roar, the jocularity of the Conquistador and our invisible servants, the hands that offered us berries and wrens in spicy sauces. Her lips seemed to speak a different language, the effect akin to ventriloquism.

The Conquistador mumbled to himself, seeing someone or something that was not there. Even in my drunken state I could tell that he did not see the gods and goddesses. Cupay danced much too close to him and eyed him with evil intent, sprinkling him with a golden dust that melted when it touched the old man's clothes. "Yes, yes," he muttered to no one. "It is only fair," and "I, your servant, cross myself before you."

While Pizarro talked, I watched the hummingbird woman. She flitted in and out of the dance with such lascivious grace that my face reddened. A toss of black hair. A hint of her smile, with which she favored me when I looked in her direction.

I wept again, and did not know why.

Pizarro said, "To the glory of Jesus Christ!" and raised his glass high.

The heat became *cold*, a burning as of deep, deep chill.

Conchame danced a dance of desperation now, bumping into the others with a bumbling synchronicity, his laugh as bitter and wide as an avalanche. A sneer lining his mouth, Cupay no longer danced at all, but stood over the Conquistador. The jaguar god snarled and writhed beside the fire. The snake god hissed a warning in response, but discordant. The Inca pipes grew shrill, hateful. Only the hummingbird woman's dance remained innocent. The incense thickened, the sounds deepened, and my head felt heavy with drink.

The jaguar god, the snake god—all the gods—had removed their masks, and beneath the masks, their true faces shone, no different than the masks. The jaguar head blended perfectly onto the jaguar body, down to the upright back legs. The snake's scales ran all the way down its heavily muscled flanks.

They were my gods, but they frightened me; the fear came to me in pieces, slowly, for my thoughts swam in a soupy, crocodile-tear sea. They were so desperate in their dance, their very thoughts calculated *to keep them moving*, because if they ever became still they would die. The Spaniards had taught them that.

A hand grabbed mine and pulled me to my feet. The woman. She led me into the dance, my fear fading as suddenly as it had come. Calm now, I did not weep or laugh. We whirled around the heat, the sparks, growing more sweaty and breathless in each other's company. The feel of flesh and blood beneath my hands reassured me, and my desperate attempts to keep up amused her. I danced with recklessness, nothing like the formality of dances at the village.

I even began to leap over the fire, to meet her litheness on the opposite side. She laughed as I fanned mock flames. But the next time I jumped I looked down and saw in the flames a hundred eyes burnished gold and orange. They slowly blinked and focused on me with all the weight of a thousand years. After that, I simply sat with the woman as the others danced and Pizarro talked to an invisible, presumably captive, audience.

"The flames," I told her. "I saw eyes in the flames."

She laughed, but did not answer. Then she kissed me, filling my mouth with her tongue, and I forgot everything: the eyes, the Conquistador, Conchame bungling his way around the fire. Forgot everything except for her. I felt her skin beneath me, and her wetness, and my world shrank again, to the land outlined by the contours of her skin, and to the ache inside me that burned more wildly than the fire. I buried my head between her breasts, breathed in the perfume of her body and soon forgot even my name.

I believed in the old gods then. Believed in them without reservation or doubts.

When I woke, I remembered nothing. I had dirt in my mouth, an aching head, and the quickly fading image of a woman so beautiful that her beauty stung me.

I recalled walking through the city and marveling at its intricacies. I recalled the fire, and that we had met with . . . with whom? A beetle crawled past my eyes, and I remembered it was Conchame, but I did not remember seeing him the night before, bereft and sadder than a god should ever be. It would be many years before I truly remembered that night; in the meantime, it was like a reflection through shards of colored glass.

Slowly, I rose to an elbow and stared around me. The city lay like the bleached and picked-through bones of a giant, the morning light shining cold and dead upon its concentric circles. The courtyard's tile floor had been in ruins for many years. All that remained of the fire was a burnt patch of grass. Near the burn lay the Conquistador, Pizarro, his horse nibbling on a bush.

Beside Pizarro lay a pile of golden artifacts. They glittered despite the faint sun and confounded me as readily as if conjured from thin air, which indeed they had been. Children's toys and adult reliefs, all of the finest workmanship. There were delicate butterflies and birds, statues of Conchame, Cupay, Ilapa, and Inti, and a hundred smaller items.

Pizarro stirred from sleep, rose to his knees. His mouth formed an idiotic "O" as he ran his fingers through the gold.

"It was no dream, Manco," he said. "It was no dream, then." His eyes widened and his voice came out in a whisper. "Last night by the fire, I sat at the Last Supper and Our Savior hovered above me and told me to eat and drink and he said that unto me a fortune would be delivered. And he spoke truly! Truly he is the Son of Heaven!"

He kissed me on both cheeks. "I am rich! And you have served me faithfully." So saying, he took a few gold artifacts worth twice my meager fee, put them in a pouch, and gave them to me.

Pizarro was eager to leave in all haste and thus we left the ruins almost immediately, although I felt a reluctance to do so. We soon found our way back to the dead Spaniard and lower still by dusk.

That night, I fell asleep to the *clink-clink* of gold against gold as Pizarro played with his treasure.

But, come morning, I heard a curse and woke to the sight of Pizarro rummaging through his packs. "It has vanished! It is gone!" His cheeks were drawn and he seemed once more an old man. "Where has it gone? The gold has vanished from my hands, into dust."

I could not tell him. I had no clue. If he had not seen it disappear himself, he might have blamed me, but I was blameless.

We went back to the city and searched its streets for two days. We found nothing. Pizarro would have stayed there forever, but our food had begun to run out and I pleaded with him to return to Cuzco. With winter closing in, I thought it dangerous to stay.

We started down again and Pizarro seemed in better spirits, if withdrawn. But, on the fifth day, we camped by a small, deep lake and when I woke in the morning, he was gone. His nag stood by the lakeside, drinking from the dark waters. His clothes were missing. Only the map remained, black ink on orange parchment, and his sword, stuck awkwardly into the hard ground. I searched for him, but it was obvious to me that the Spaniard had been broken when the treasure turned to dust, and had drowned himself in the lake.

I continued the rest of the way down, leading the nag but not riding her, for I did not know how. I knew only that my gold had not faded. It still lay within the pouch, and it was with that gold that I would later buy my way to America.

Soon I came upon the ghost dancers again, but I did not stay long, though I wished to, for the man who resembled Pizarro stood in the highest part of the tower and for some reason he troubled me. I believe I thought it was Pizarro, gazing down on me.

Thus, rich beyond measure and fortunate to be alive, I hurried past the tower and down into the lowlands and the fields to rejoin my family.

V

The reporter doesn't know what to say at first, so she doesn't say anything. Ignore the parts that aren't possible, she tells herself. He's an old man. He's just mixing fact and fiction on you. But it's not the impossible parts that bother her.

Manco stares at the wall, as if reliving the experience, and she says, "Did you ever discover who the Conquistador was?" She could really use a smoke, but she doesn't dare light up in front of a dying asthmatic.

His gaze turns toward the darkened window, toward the movement outside that window. His eyes seem unbearably sad, though a slight smile creases his lips.

"Among his personal effects were letters written to his family and when I returned to Cuzco, the *mestizo* he had bought the horse from filled in the gaps. It is quite ironic, you see—" and he stares directly at her, as if daring her to disbelieve "—he was an immigrant, a destitute carpenter whose father had herded sheep across the Spanish plains. Had he attended the military academy in Barcelona? I do not know. But during the time of land grants, his forefathers had settled in Peru, only to come to misfortune at the hands of other fortune hunters, the survivors limping back to Spain. No doubt he had read the accounts of these pathetic men and hoped, long after it was possible or politic, to acquire his own land grant. Practically speaking, though, he chose the best route: to steal treasure."

"But where did the map come from?"

Manco shrugs, so that his shoulders bow inward, the bones stark against brown skin.

Silence, again, the reporter trying to think of what to ask next. It frustrates her that she is reduced to *reacting*. Her mind alights upon the woman dancing around the fire. An adolescent wet dream. Believable? Perhaps not in the setting he had described, but the romances in the man's life might fill up a side bar, at least.

"What happened to the woman?"

He closes his eyes so that they virtually disappear amid the wrinkles. He must have twenty wrinkles for each year of his life, she thinks.

"I forgot her. I forgot much, as if my mind had been wiped clean. Sometimes the memories would brush against my mind as I sought my fortune in America. Other women . . . other women would remind me of her, but it was as if I had dreamed the entire night."

"When did you finally regain your memory?"

"Years later, as I walked through Death Valley, dying of thirst, certain that the bandits who had stolen my horse would find me again. My eyes were drawn to the horizon and the sun. It was so hot, and the sun was like a beacon filled with blood. I stared and stared at that sun . . . and after a while it began to give off sparks and I heard myself saying 'Inti was in the fire.' I saw the bonfire then and the gods who had surrounded the bonfire, and . . . her, the woman—and I wept when I realized what I had lost when I lost my memory, for she had been human, not a goddess.

"Those memories sustained me through that dry and deadly place, as if I drank from them for strength, and when I reached California, I decided to return to the city."

"You went back to the city?" the reporter says, which vexes her even more.

"I spent a night in the ruined tower where the Ghost Dancers had once danced. I stopped by the lake where the Conquistador had drowned."

"And you found the city again?"

"I did, although it had changed. The vegetation—the path of flowers, the many trees and vines—had died away. The towers and buildings still stood, but more eaten away, in ruins. So too did I find the woman—still there, but much older. The gods had left that place, driven back into the interior, so far that I doubt even a Shining Path guerrilla could lead you to them now. But she was still there. The gods had preserved her beauty well past a natural span, so that in their absence she aged more rapidly. I spent seven years by her side and then buried her—an old woman now—in the courtyard where I had once jumped across a fire with a hundred eyes staring up at me. And then I left that place."

Manco's voice is so full of sadness that suddenly the reporter feels acutely . . . homesick? Is it homesickness? Not for New York City, not for her apartment, her cats, her friends, but for the bustling white noise of her office, the constant demands on her time which keep her busy, always at a fever pitch. Here, there is only silence and darkness and mysteries. There is too much time to think; her mind is working in the darkness, trying to reconcile the possible, the impossible.

Something dark moves against the lighter dark of the window. Something in the darkness nags at her, screams out to her, but she wants to forget it, let it slip back into the subconscious. Outside, someone shouts, "*No habla inglés! No habla! No habla!*" She can feel dust and grit on her and her muscles ache for a swimming pool. When her husband left—was it four years now?—she had swum and swum and swum until she was so tired she could only float and stare up at the gray sky . . . and suddenly, she is looking up from the water . . . into Manco Tupac's eyes.

"You changed the most important part," she says, her heart thudding in her chest. "You changed it," and as she says it, she realizes that this story, this man, will never see print, that the darkness, the shadows, the past, have changed everything. What is there left to her with this story? What is left at all? Nothing left but to go forward: "Tell me what you left out." It is one of those moments that will not last—she'll recant later, she'll publish the story, but for this moment, in this moment, she is lost, and frightened.

He is quiet for a moment, considering, then he turns his head to consider her from an angle. "Yes, I will," he says. "Yes. I'll tell you . . . What does it matter now?"

Then he is whispering, whispering the rest of the story to her, an enigmatic smile playing across his lips, as if he is enjoying himself, as if the weight of such a story, never before told, can now leave him, the machines the only weight left to keep him tied to this earth. And every word takes her further from herself, until she is outside herself, out there, in the darkness, with him.

VI

Tupac remembered precisely when he decided to kill the old man he called the Conquistador. They had stared into the dark waters of a lake above Cuzco and the Conquistador, already dismounted from his horse, had said, "This place holds a million treasures, if we could only find a means to wrest them from the hands of the dead." The lake held the bones of Tupac's ancestors as well as gold, but he did not say this, just as he had not protested when the old man's map had led them to the hidden city. He had done nothing while the Conquistador had rummaged through the graves on their last day in the city, picking through the bones for bits of jewelry to supplement the gold. How could he have done nothing?

But as they stood and looked into the dark waters, Tupac realized that the old man's death had been foretold by the lake itself: the Conquistador's reflection hardly showed in those black depths. If the Conquistador's reflection cast itself so lightly on the world, then death was already upon him. Killing this man would be like placing pennies upon the eyes of the dead.

When they came out of the hills and the fog of the highlands into the region of the deep lakes, Tupac's resolve stiffened. In the early morning light, the Conquistador's horse stepping gingerly among the ill-matched stones of the old Inca highway, Tupac had a vision: that a flock of jet-black hummingbirds encircled the Conquistador's head like his Christian god's crown of thorns.

The Conquistador had not spoken a word that morning, except to request that Tupac fold his bed roll and empty his chamber pot. The Conquistador sat his horse stiffly, clenching his legs to stay upright. Looking at the old man, Tupac felt a twinge of revulsion, at himself for serving as the old man's guide, and at the old man for his casual cruelty, his indifference, and most frustrating of all, his stifling ignorance.

At midday, the sun still hazy through the clouds, the Conquistador dismounted and stood by the edge of yet another lake. He did not stand so straight now, but hunched over, his head bent.

Tupac hesitated. The old man looked so tired. A voice deep inside him said he could not kill in cold blood, but his hand told the truth: it pulled the Conquistador's sword from its scabbard in one clean motion. The Conquistador turned and smiled when he saw that Tupac had the sword. Tupac slid the sword into the Conquistador's chest and through his spine. The Conquistador smiled more broadly then, Tupac thought, and brought close to his victim by the thrust, he could smell the sour tang of *quinoa* seeds on his breath, the musk of the Conquistador's leathers, and the faint dusty scent they had both picked up traveling the road together.

Then the old man fell, the sword still in him, Tupac's hand letting go of the hilt.

Tupac stood above the dead man for a moment, breathing heavily. An emptiness filled his mind as if he were a fish swimming blind through the black lake that shimmered before them. The sound of a chipparah bird's mating call startled him and he realized that the Conquistador had died silently, or that his own frantic heartbeat had drowned out any noise.

The Conquistador's eyes remained open and blood had begun to coat his tunic. Blood coated the sword's blade, which had been pushed upward, halfway out of the Conquistador's body when he fell to the ground. Tupac tasted salt in his mouth and brushed the tears from his eyes. He felt nothing as he rolled the Conquistador's body over and into the water. The body sank slowly, first the torso bending in on itself, then the legs, and finally the arms, the palms of the pale hands turned upward as if releasing their grip on the world.

When the hands faded from view, the emptiness spread through Tupac, from his arms to his chest and then to his legs, until it felt like a smooth, cold stone weighing down his soul. He would never forget that moment, even when he was old and bedridden. He would see the Conquistador falling, for a hundred years, and no matter how many places he visited, no matter how many adventures he had, no matter how many memories he filled his mind with, he could not stop seeing that slow fall, or stop feeling the sword, as if it had entered his body, as if *he* had fallen into the dark wet lapping of waves, into the unending dream of drowning. . . .

Notes on
Ghost Dancing with Manco Tupac

In the 1970s, my family visited Peru, including the ancient Incan ruins of Machu Picchu. We set out by train from Cuzco—chugging along tracks that hugged the sides of sheer cliffs, above ravines in which the silver-white trail of rivers shone thousands of feet below us. After the train, we took a bus that spiraled up the mountain road leading to the site. At that time, Machu Picchu was remote, with few tourists making the journey. I remember green terraces, stone houses without roofs, long curving walls, and a stunning view.

Having seen Machu Picchu, I can sympathize with archaeologist Hiram Bingham, who thought it must have been more than just an Incan garrison town—something sacred, something other. The exotic beauty of the location, and the ruins themselves, must have made it difficult to accept mundane explanations. Standing there at dusk, with remembered light striking remembered stone, I too let my imagination run away with me. And years later wrote "Ghost Dancing."

Much as with "The General Who Is Dead," another story in this collection, "Ghost Dancing" began as a novel and became something shorter. The novelette included here was always self-contained, but it originally provided the opening chapters to a novel that told the rest of the events in Manco Tupac's life. I actually might have finished the novel, except for the Coleridgean "visitor from Porlock" who knocked on my apartment door late one night when I was in the full flush of fictional discovery. And perhaps not. It's always convenient to blame the inconvenient stranger rather than your own lack of nerve. Regardless, the implosion of this novel still reverberates in my writing, as I slowly take the individual pieces and find the complete stories waiting to be rescued from among the fragments.

Learning to Leave
the Flesh

I

BROWSING THROUGH THE BORGES BOOKSTORE, on a mission for my girlfriend Emily, I am suddenly confronted by a dwarf woman. The light from the front window strikes me sideways with the heat of late afternoon and, when she upturns her palm, the light illuminates all the infinite worlds enclosed in the wrinkles: pale road lines, rivers that pass through valleys, hillocks of skin and flesh. A matrix of destinies and destinations.

Before I can react, the dwarf woman takes my hand in hers and stabs me with a thorn, sending it deep into my palm. I grunt in pain, as if a physician had just taken a blood sample. I look down into her large, dark eyes and I see such calm there that the pain winks out, only returning when she shuffles off, hunchback and all, out of the bookstore.

The walls rush away from me, the shelves so distant that I cannot even brace myself against them. I bring my hand up into the light. The thorn has worked itself beneath the surface and might even burrow deeper, if I let it. I examine the blood-blistery entrance hole. It throbs, and already a pinkish-red color spreads across my palm like a dry fire. The hole itself could be a city on a map, a citadel torn apart by the angry pulse of warfare that will soon spread into the countryside. A war within my flesh.

I leave the bookstore and walk back to my apartment. The boulevard, Albumuth, has a degree of security, but only two blocks down, on graffiti-choked overpasses, young teenage futureperfects carouse and cruise through the night-to-come, courting pleasures of the flesh, courting corruption of the soul. Albumuth is my life-line, the artery to the downtown section where I work, buy gro-ceries, and acquire books. Without it, the city would be dangerous. Without it, I might be unanchored, cast adrift.

As it is, I drag my shoes on the sidewalk, taking every opportu-nity to run my fingers along white picket fences, hunch down to pet cocker spaniels, converse with smiling apple grannies, and stare into the deep eyes of children.

Even now, so soon after, the wound has begun to change. I manage to pry out the thorn. The hole looks less and less like a city in flames and more like part of my own hand. Rarely has a portion of my anatomy so intrigued me. No doubt Emily has traced the lines between my freckles, explored the gaps between my toes, run her hands through the sprawl of hair on my chest, but I have never examined my own body in such detail. My body has never seemed relevant to who I am, except that I must keep it fit so it will not betray my mind.

But I examine my palm quite critically now. The wrinkles do not share consistency of length or width and calluses gather like barnacles or melted-down toothpaste caps. Abrasions, pinknesses, and a few tiny scars mar my palm. I conclude that my palm is ugly beyond hope of cosmetic surgery.

I reach my apartment as the sun fades into the blocky shadows of the city's rooftops and scattered chimneys. My apartment occu-pies the first floor of a two-story brownstone. The bricks are wrinkled with age and soft as wet clay in places. The anemic front lawn has been seeded with sand to keep the grass from growing.

Inside my apartment, the kitchen and living room open up onto the bedroom and bath to the left and right respectively. In my bed-room there is a window seat from which, through the triangular, plated-glass window, I can see nothing but gray asphalt and a deserted shopping mall.

In the kitchen and living room, my carefully cultivated plants behave like irrational but brilliant sentences; they crawl up walls, shoot away from trellises despite my best efforts. I have wisteria, blossoms clustered like pelican limpets, sea grapes with soft round leaves, passion fruit flowers, trumpet vines, and night-blooming jasmine, whose petals open up and smell like cotton candy melted into the brine-rich scent of the sea. Together, they perform despotic

Victorian couplings beyond the imagination of the most creative ménage à trois.

Emily hates my plants. When we make love, we go to her apartment. We make such perfect love there, in her perfectly immaculate bedroom—a mechanized grind of limbs pumping like pistons—that we come together, shower together afterward, and rarely leave a ring of hair in the bathtub.

II

I suppose I did not think much about the thorn at the time because now, as I lie in bed listening to the dullard yowls and taunts of the futureperfects riding their cars halfway across the city, the wound's pulsating, pounding rhythm leads me back to my first real memory of the world.

Orphaned very young, my parents lost at sea in a shipwreck, yet not quite a baby to be left on a doorstep, I remember only this fragment: the sea at low tide with night sliding down on the world like a black door. Water licked my feet and I felt the coolness of sand between my toes, the bite of the wind against my face. And: the *plop-plop* of tiny silver fish caught in tidal pools; the spackle of starfish trapped in seaweed and glistening troughs of sand; ghost crabs scuttling sideways on creaking joints, pieces of flesh clutched daintily in their pincers.

I do not know how old I was or how I came to be on that beach. I know only that I sat on the sand, the stars faded lights against the cerulean sweep of sky. As dusk became nightfall, hands grasped me by the shoulders and dragged me up the dunes into the stickery grass and the sea grape, the passionflower and the cactus, until I could see the ferris wheel of a seaside circus and hear the hum-and-thrum hollow acoustic sob of people laughing and shouting.

Whether this is a real place or an image from my imagination, I do not know. But it returns to center me in this world when I have no center; it gives me something beyond this city, my job, my apartment. Somewhere, magical, once upon a time, I lay under the stars at nightfall and I dreamed the fantastic.

I have few friends. Foster children who move from family to family, town to town, rarely maintain friendships. Foster parents seem now like dust shadows spread out against a windowpane. I can remember faces and names, but I feel so remote from them compared to the memory of the wheeling, open arch of horizon before and above me.

Now I have a wound in my palm. A wound that leads me back to the beach at dusk, of my grief at my parents' death, that I had not drowned with them. Living but not moving. Observing but not doing. At the center of myself I am suggestibility, not action. Never action.

My parents took actions. They *did* things. And they died.

III

Despite my wound—not a good excuse—I drive to work down Albumuth Boulevard, turning into the parking lot where tufts of grass thrust up between cracks in the red brick. The shop where I work occupies a slice of the town square. It has antique glass windows, dark green curtains to deflect the gaze of the idly or suspiciously curious, and stairs leading both up and down, to the loft and the basement.

My job is to create perfect sentences for a varied clientele. No mere journalism this, for journalism requires the clarity of glass, not a mirror, nor even a reflection. I spend hours at my cubicle in the loft, looking out over the hundreds of rooftops, surrounded by the fresh sawdust smell of words and the loamy *must* of reference text piled atop reference text.

True, I am only one among many working here. Some are not artists but technicians who gargle with pebbles to improve the imperfect diction of their perfect sentences, or casually fish for them, tugging on their lines once every long while in the hope that the sentences will surface whole, finished, and fat with meaning. Still others smoke or drink or use illicit drugs to coax the words onto the page. Many of them are quite funny in their circuitous routines. I even know their names: Wendy, Carl, Daniel, Christine, Pamela, Andrea. But we are so fixated on creating our sentences that we might well pass each other as strangers on the street.

We must remain fixated, for the Director—a vast and stealthy intelligence, a leviathan moving ponderous many miles beneath the surface—demands it. We receive several paid solicitations each day that ask for a description of a beloved husband, a dying dog, a sailor on shore leave soon to rejoin his ship, or a housewife who wishes to tell her husband how he neglects her all unknowing:

He hugs her and mumbles like a sailor in love with the sea, drowning without protest as the water takes him deeper; until her lungs are awash and he has caught her in his endless dream of drowning.

Ten years ago, we would have been writing perfect stories, but people's attention spans have become more limited in these, the last days of literacy.

Of course, we do not create *objectively* perfect sentences — sometimes our sentences are not even very good. If we could create truly perfect sentences, we would destroy the world: it would fold in on itself like a pricked hot air balloon and cease to be: poof!, undone, unmade, unlived, in the harsh glacial light of a reality more real than itself.

But I am such a perfectionist that, in the backwater stagnation of other workers' coffee breaks, in the *tapa-tap-tap* of rain trying to keep me from my work, I continue to string verbs onto pronouns, railroading those same verbs onto indirect objects, attaching modifiers like strategically placed tinsel on a Christmas tree.

By my side I keep a three-ringed, digest-sized notebook of memories to help me live the lives of our clients, to get under their skins and know them as I know myself. Only twelve pages have been filled, most of them recounting events after I reached my fifteenth birthday. Many notes are only names, like Bobby Zender, a friend and fellow orphan at the reform school. He had a gimp foot and for a year I matched my strides to his, never once broke ahead of him or ran out onto the playground to play kickball. He died of tuberculosis. Or Sarah Galindrace, with the darkest eyes and the shortest dresses and skin like silk, like porcelain, like heaven. She moved away and became an echo in my heart.

These memories often help me with the sentences, but today the wound on my hand bothers me, distracts me from the pristine longleaf sheets of paper on the drafting boards. The pen, a black quill that crisply scratches against the paper, menaces me. My fellow workers stare; their bushy black eyebrows and manes of blond hair and mad stallion eyes make me nervous. I sweat. I teeter uneasily on my high stool and try not to stare out the window at the geometrically pleasing telephone lines that slice the sky into a matrix of points of interest: church spires, flagpoles, neon billboards.

A woman who has finally found true romance needs a sentence to tell her boyfriend how much she loves him. My palm flares when I take up the pen; the pen could as well be a knife or a chisel or some object with which I am equally unfamiliar. My skin feels itchy, as if I have picked at the edges of a scab. But I write the sentence anyway:

When I see you, my heart rises like bread in an oven.

The sentence is awful. The Director leans over and concurs with a nod, a hand on my shoulder, and the gravelly murmur, "You are trying too hard. Relax. Relax."

Yes. Relax. I think of Emily and the book I was going to get for her at the Borges Bookstore: *The Refraction of Light in a Prison*. Perhaps if I can project from my relationship with Emily I can force the sentence to work. I think of her sharp cadences, the way she bites the ends off words as if snapping celery stalks in two. Or the time she tickled me senseless in the middle of her sister's wedding and I had to pretend I was drunk just to weather the embarrassment. Or this: the smooth, spoon-tight feel of her stomach against my lips, the miraculous tangle of her blond hair.

So. I try again.

When I see you, my heart rises like a flitting hummingbird to a rose.

Now I am truly hopeless. The repetition of "rises" and "rose" knifes through all alternatives and I am convinced I should have been a plumber, a dentist, a shoeshine boy. Words that should layer themselves into patterns—strike passion in the heart—become ugly and cold. The dead weight of cliché has given me a headache.

At dusk, I ask the Director for a day off. He gives it to me, orders me to do nothing but walk around the city, perhaps take in a ball game in the old historical section, perhaps a Voss Bender exhibit at the Teel Memorial Art Museum.

IV

I spend my day off contemplating my palm with my girlfriend Emily Brosewiser, she of the aforementioned blond hair, the succulent lips, the tactile smile, the moist charm. (My comparisons become so fecund I think I would rather love a fruit or vegetable.)

We sit on a lichen-encrusted bench at the San Matador Park, my arm around her shoulders, and watch the mallards siphoning through the pond scum for food. The gasoline-green grass scent and the heat of the summer sun make me sleepy. The park seems cluttered with dwarfs: litter picker-uppers armed with their steely harpoons; lobotomy patients from the nearby hospital, their stares as direct as a lover's; burly hunchbacked fellows going over the lawn with gleaming red lawnmowers. They distract me—errant punctuation scattered across a pristine page.

Emily sees them only as clowns and myself as sick. "Sick, sick, sick." How can I disagree? She smells so clean and her hair shines like spun gold.

"They were always there before, Nicholas, and you never noticed them. Why should they matter now? Don't pick at that." She slaps my hand and my palm thrums with pain. "Why must you obsess over it so? Here we are with a day off and you cannot leave it alone."

Emily works for an ad agency. She designs sentences that sell perfection to the consumer public. Before I ever met Emily, I saw her work on billboards at the outskirts of town: BUY SKUTTLES: WE EXPECT NO REBUTTALS and SOMEDAY YOU ARE GONNA DIE: IN THE MEANTIME, BUY AND BUY—AT THE CORIANDER MALL. At the bottom, in small print, the billboards read: ADS BY EMILY. At the time, I was girlfriendless so I called up the billboard makers, tracked down the ad agency, and asked her out. She liked my collection of erotic sentences and my manual dexterity. I liked the gossamer line of hair that runs down her forearms, the curves of her breasts with their tiny pink nipples.

But her sentences have become passé to me, too crude and manipulative. How can I expect more from her, given the nature of the business?

So I say, "Yes, dear," and sigh and examine my palm. She is always reasonable. Always right. But I am not sure she understands me. I wonder what she would think about my memory of the arc of sky above with night coming down and the sea rustling on the shore. She did not argue when I insisted on separate apartments.

The circle on my palm has gone from pink to white and the way the wrinkle lines careen into one another, the scars like tiny fractures, fascinate me.

Emily giggles. "Nicholas, you are so perfectly silly sitting there with that bemused look on your face. Anyone would think you'd just had a miscarriage."

I wonder if there is something wrong with our relationship; it seems as blank as my life as an orphan. Besides, "miscarriage" is not the appropriate logic leap to describe the look on my face. Granted, I cannot myself think of the appropriate hoop for this dog of syntax to leap through, but still . . .

We return to our separate apartments. All I can think about are dwarfs, hunchbacks, cripples. I sleep and dream of dwarfs, deformed and malicious, with sinister slits for smiles. But when I wake, I have the most curious of thoughts. I remember the weight of the dwarf woman's body against my side as she stuck the sliver into my palm. I remember the smell of her: sweet and sharp, like honeysuckle; the feel of her hand, the fingers lithe and slender; her body beneath the clothes, the way parts do not match and could never match, and yet have unity.

V

A most peculiar assignment lies on my desk the next morning, so peculiar that I forget my damaged palm. I am to write a sentence about a dwarf. The Director has left a note that I am to complete this sentence ASAP. He has also left me photographs, a series of newspaper articles, and photocopies from a diary. The lead paragraph of the top newspaper article, a sensational bit of work, reads:

> David "Midge" Jones, 27, a 4-foot-5 dwarf, lived for atten-
> tion, whether he ate fire at a carnival, walked barefoot on glass
> for spectators, or allowed himself to be hurled across a room
> for a dwarf-throwing contest. Jones yearned for the spotlight.
> Sunday, he died in the dark. He drank himself to death. Tests
> showed his blood alcohol level at .43, or four times the level
> at which a motorist would be charged with driving under the
> influence of alcohol.

I pick up the glossy color print atop the pile of documentation. It shows Jones at the carnival, the film overexposed, his eyes forming red dots against the curling half-smile of his mouth. At either side stand flashy showgirls with tinsel-adorned bikini tops crammed against his face. Jones stares into the camera lens, but the showgirls stare at Jones as though he were some carnival god. The light on the photograph breaks around his curly brown hair, but not his body, as if a spotlight had been trained on him. He stands on a wooden box, his arms around the showgirls.

The film's speed is not nearly fast enough to catch the ferris wheel seats spinning crazily behind him, so that light spills into the dazzle of showgirl tinsel, showgirl cleavage. Behind the ferris wheel, blurry sand dunes roll, and beyond that, in the valley between dunes, the sea, like a squinting eye.

The photograph has a sordid quality to it. When I look closer, I see the sheen of sweat on Jones's face, his flushed complexion. Sand clings to his gnarled arms and his forehead. The lines of his eyes, nose, and mouth seem charcoal pencil rough: a first, hurried sketch.

I turn the photograph over. In the upper right hand corner

someone has written: *David Jones, September 19–. The Amazing Mango Brothers Seaside Circus and Carnival Extravaganza. He cleaned out animal cages and gave 50 cent blow jobs behind the Big Top.*

Jones is a brutish man. I want nothing to do with him. Yet I must write a sentence about him for a client I will never meet. I must capture David Jones in a single sentence.

I read the rest of the article, piecemeal.

> In his most controversial job, Jones ignored criticism, strapped on a modified dog harness, and allowed burly men to hurl him across a room in a highly publicized dwarf-throwing contest at the King's Head Pub.

> "I'm a welder, which can be dangerous. But welders are frequently laid off, so I also work in a circus. I eat fire, I walk on broken glass with bare feet. I climb a ladder made of swords, I lie on a bed of nails and have tall people stand on me. This job is easy compared to what I usually do."

I spend many hours trying to form a sentence, while sweat drips down my neck despite the slow swish of fans. I work through lunch, distracted only by a dwarf juggler (plying his trade with six knives and a baby) who has wrested the traffic circle away from a group of guildless mimes and town players.

I begin simply.

The dwarf's life was tragic.

No.

David Jones' life was tragic.

No.

David's life was unnecessarily tragic.

Unnecessarily tragic? Tragedy does not waste time with the extraneous. A man's life cannot be reduced to a Latinesque, one-line, eleven-syllable haiku. How do I identify with David? Did he ever spend time in an orphanage? Did he ever find himself on a beach, his parents dead and never coming back? How hard can it have been to be an anomaly, a misfit, a mistake?

Then my imagination unlocks a phrase from some compartment of my brain:

David left the flesh in tragic fashion.

Again, my palm distracts me, but not as much. I see all the imperfections there and yet they do not seem as ugly as before. David may be ugly, but I am not ugly.

As I drive home in the sour, exhaust-choked light of dusk, I admire the oaks that line the boulevard, whorled and wind-scored and yet stronger and more soothing to the eye than the toothpick pines, the straight spruce.

VI

By now the plants have conquered my apartment in the name of CO_2, compost, and photosynthesis. I let them wander like rejects from '50s B-grade vegetable movies, ensuring that Emily will never stay for long. The purple and green passionflowers, stinking of sex, love the couch with gentle tendrils. The splash-red bougainvillea cat-cradles the kitchen table, then creeps toward the refrigerator and pulls on the door, thorns making a scratchy sound. Along with this invasion come the scavengers, the albino geckos that resemble swirls of mercury or white chocolate. I have no energy to evict them.

No, I sit in a chair, in underwear weathered pink by the whimsical permutations of the wash cycle, and read by the blue glow of the mute TV screen.

David grew up in Dalsohme, a bustling but inconsequential port town on the Gulf side of the Moth River Delta. His parents, Jemina and Simon Pultin, made their living by guiding tourists through the bayous in flatbottom boats. Simon talked about installing a glass bottom to improve business, but Jemina argued that no one would want to see the murky waters of a swamp under a microscope, so to speak. Instead, they supplemented their income by netting catfish and prawns. David was good at catching catfish, but Jemina and Simon preferred to have him work the pole on the boat because the tourists often gawked at him as much as at the scenery. It was Jemina's way of improving business without giving in to Simon's glass-bottom boat idea. Some of the documents the Director gave me suggested that Simon had adopted David precisely for the purpose of manning the boat. There is no record of what David thought of all of this, but at age fifteen he "ran away from home and joined a circus." He did whatever he had to on the carnival circuit in order to survive, including male prostitution, but apparently never saved enough money to quit, though his schemes became grander and more complex.

"Most little people think the world owes them something because they're little. Most little people got this idea they should be treated special. Well, the world doesn't owe us anything. God gave us a rough way to go, that's all."

Soon the words blur on the page. Under the flat, aqua glow, the wound in my palm seems smaller but denser, etched like a biological Rosetta Stone. The itch, though, grows daily. It grows like the plants grow. It spreads into the marrow of my bones and I can feel it infiltrating whatever part of me functions as a soul.

That night I dream that we are all "pure energy," like on those old future-imperfect cardboard-and-glue space journey episodes where the budget demanded pure energy as a substitute for makeup and genuine costumes. Just golden spheres of light communing together, mind to mind, soul to soul. A world without prejudice because we have, none of us, a body that can lie to the world about our identity.

VII

The day my parents left me for the sea, the winter sky gleamed bone-white against the gray-blue water. The cold chaffed my fingers and dried them out. My father took off one of his calfskin gloves so my hand could touch his, still sweaty from the glove. His weight, solid and warm, anchored me against the wind as we walked down to the pier and the ship. Above the ship's masts, frigate birds with throbbing red throats let the wind buffet them until they no longer seemed to fly, but to sit, stationary, in the air.

My mother walked beside me as well, holding her hat tightly to her head. The hem of her sheepskin coat swished against my jacket. A curiously fresh, clean smell, like mint or vanilla, followed her and when I breathed it in, the cold retreated for a little while.

"It won't be for long," my father said, his voice descending to me through layers of cold and wind.

I shivered, but squeezed his hand. "I know."

"Good. Be brave."

"I will."

Then my mother said, "We love you. We love you and wish you could come with us. But it's a long journey and a hard one and no place for a little boy."

My mother leaned down and kissed me, a flare of cold against my cheek. My father knelt, held both my hands, and looked me up and down with his flinty gray eyes. He hugged me against him so I was lost in his windbreaker and his chest. I could feel him trembling just as I was trembling.

"I'm scared," I said.

"Don't be. We'll be back soon. We'll come back for you. I promise."

They never did. I watched them board the ship, a smile frozen to my face. It seems as though I waited so long on the pier, watching the huge sails catch the wind as the ship slid off into the wavery horizon, that snowflakes gathered on my eyes and my clothes, the cold air biting into my shoulder blades.

I do not remember who took me from that place, nor how long I really stood there, nor even if this represents a true memory, but I hold onto it with all my strength.

Later, when I found out my parents had died at sea, when I understood what that meant, I sought out the farthest place from the sea and I settled here.

VIII

At the office, I have so much work to do that I am able to forget my palm. I stare for long minutes at the sentence I have written on my notepad:

David was leaving the flesh.

What does it mean?

I throw away the sentence, but it lingers in my mind and distracts me from my other work. Finally, I break through with a sentence describing a woman's grief that her boyfriend has left her and she is growing old:

She sobs like the endless rain of late winter, without passion or the hope of relief, just a slow drone of tears.

As I write it, I begin to cry: wrenching sobs that make my throat ache and my eyes sting. My fellow workers glance at me, shrug, and continue at their work. But I am not crying because the sentence is too perfect. I am crying because I have encapsulated something that should not be encapsulated in a sentence. How can my client want me to write this?

IX

Emily visits me at lunchtime. She visits me often during the day, but our nights have been crisscrossed, sometimes on purpose, I feel.

We go to the same park and now we feel out of place, in the minority. Everywhere I look dwarfs walk to lunch, drive cars, mend benches. All of them like individual palm prints, each one so unique that next to them Emily appears plain.

"Something has happened to you." She looks into my eyes as she says this and I read a certain vulnerability into her words.

"Something has happened to me. I have a wound in my palm."

"It's not the wound. It's the plants out of control. It's the sex. It's everything. You know it as well as me."

Emily is always right, on the mark, in the money. I am beginning to tire of such perfection. I feel a part of me break inside.

"You don't understand," I say.

"I understand that you cannot handle responsibility. I understand that you are having problems with this relationship."

"I'll talk to you later," I say, and I leave her, speechless, on the bench.

X

After lunch, I think I know where my center lies: it lies in the sentence I must create for David Jones. It is in the sentence and in me. But I don't want to write anything perfect. I don't want to. I want to work without a net. I want to write rough, with emotion that stings, the words themselves dangling off into an abyss. I want to find my way back to the sea with the darkness coming down and the briny scent in my nostrils, before I knew my parents were dead. Before I was born.

David Jones found his way. If a person drinks too much alcohol, the body forces the stomach to expel the alcohol before it can reach a lethal level. Jones never vomited. As he slept, the alcohol seeped into his bloodstream and killed him.

My shaking fingers want to perform ridiculous pratfalls, rolling over in complex loop-the-loops and cul-de-sacs of language. Or suicide sentences, mouthing sentiments from the almost dead to the definitely dead. Instead, I write:

From birth, David was learning ways to leave the flesh.

It is nothing close to layered prose. It has no subtlety to it. But now I can smell the slapping waves of the sea and the alluring stench of passionflower fruit.

Before I leave for my apartment, Emily calls me. I do not take the call. I am too busy wondering *when* my parents knew they might die, and if they thought of me as the wind and the water conspired to take them. I wish I had been with them, had gone down with them, in their arms, with the water in our mouths like ambrosia.

XI

When I open my apartment door, I hear the scuttling of a hundred sticky toes. The refrigerator's surface writhes with milk-white movement against the dark green of leaves. In another second I see that the white paint is instead the sinuous shimmer-dance of the geckos, their camouflage perfect as they scramble for cover. I open the refrigerator and take out a wine cooler; my feet crunch down on a hundred molting gecko skins, the sound like dead leaves, or brittle cicada chrysalises.

I sit in my underwear and contemplate my wound by the TV's redemptive light. It has healed itself so completely that I can barely find it. The itching, however, has intensified, until I feel it all over, inside me. Nothing holds my interest on my palm except the exquisite imperfections: the gradations of colors, the rough pliable feel of it, the scratches from Emily's cat.

I walk into the bedroom and ease myself beneath the covers of my bed. I imagine I smell the sea, a salt breeze wafting through the window. The stars seem like pieces of jagged glass ready to fall onto me. I toss in my bed and cannot sleep. I lie on my stomach. I lie on my side. The covers are too hot, but when I strip them away, my body becomes too cold. The water I drank an hour ago has settled in my stomach like a smooth, aching stone.

Finally, the cold keeps me half-awake and I prop myself sleepily against the pillow. I hear voices outside and see flashes of light from the window, like a ferris wheel rising and falling. But I do not get up.

Then he stands at the foot of my bed, staring at me. A cold blue tint dyes his flesh, as if the TV's glow has sunburned him. The marble cast of his face is as perfect as the most perfect sentence I have ever written. His eyes are so sad that I cannot meet his gaze; his face holds so many years of pain, of wanting to leave the flesh. He speaks to me and although I cannot hear him, I know what he is saying. I am crying again, but softly, softly. The voices on the street are louder and the tinkling of bells so very light.

And so I discard my big-body skin and my huge hands and my ungainly height and I walk out of my apartment with David Jones, to join the carnival under the moon, by the seashore, where none of us can hurt or be hurt anymore.

[Article excerpts taken from newspaper accounts in 1988 and 1989 by Michael Koretzky in *The Independent Florida Alligator* and by Ronald DuPont Jr. in *The Gainesville Sun.*]

Notes on
Learning to Leave the Flesh

For six months in 1991, I worked at a Book Warehouse, which is to bookstores as Denny's is to restaurants. For six months, I had to accost customers within seconds of their entering the store, always with "how" or "what" questions so they couldn't just answer "yes" or "no" and go about their business. We sold remaindered books and usually didn't have what people were looking for, so I was instructed to lead them to books "similar" to the desired book. This practice annoyed most customers.

We also had to deal with weird things like discovering that a customer had taped condoms to the inside back covers of all of our young adult romance novels. Meanwhile, I had my own problems. I once led a customer asking for information on the "Great Plains" to the airplane section. I also once led a midget who asked for the mystery section to the juvenile mysteries instead. I honestly didn't notice.

The day after leading the midget to the juvenile section, I was telling a coworker about it when I felt a presence at my back. I turned around. There, scowling up at me, was a dwarf. I felt wretched. The point of the story had been my stupidity, not any prejudice against short people. That same day, we got a shipment of books via truck. The truck driver was not the usual guy, but a dwarf. I had one of those literal "shiver down the spine" moments. Was someone trying to tell me something?

At around the same time, a dwarf who had let himself be tossed in Gainesville bars died of alcohol poisoning. Because of a quirk of their physiognomy, dwarfs can drink themselves to death—they don't necessarily black out before they imbibe enough to be lethal. By implication, the death had been intentional. This story came together shortly thereafter, when I had a strange dream in which future-perfect youths wearing anarchic face paint manned ambulances that drove out from a nameless city to *place corpses along the highway. In the dream, as they returned to cavort in the city's center, my gaze was drawn to a strange shop with words in the window that read "Sentences for sale."*

Notably, the story mentions a couple of elements from my Ambergris story cycle: Albumuth Boulevard and the River Moth. Only six months after writing "Learning," I wrote the first true Ambergris story, "Dradin, In Love." A few years later, I found another use for "Learning"—it figured prominently in an Ambergris metafiction called "The Strange Case of X."

Greensleeves

I

OUTSIDE THE SAMUEL DEVONSHIRE MEMORIAL Library that January night, birds froze in midair, skidding to emergency touchdowns at O'Hare; children, hauled inside by their parents, were thrown in fireplaces to thaw; iron horses ghosting through the city huffed and puffed, breath breaking on the tracks.

Inside, librarian Mary Colquhoun had her four stories of silence. Silence coated the aisles, the stacks, the desks. No one could shake it off. Mary had cultivated this silence over the years until she knew its every subtlety: the pitch and tone of its soundless echo, the whispery quality of the first floor compared to the musty pomp of the second, the gloom of the fourth. If clean and absolute enough, the silence could conjure up memories, coffee washing over her in sleepy brown waves. The muscles of her forty-three-year-old face would relax, wrinkles smoothing out. She could forget the few hardcore bibliophiles who still perused the pages of such classics as *Green Eggs and Ham*. She could forget that the drifters had pitched camp in a far corner of the second floor. "Shhh . . ." hissed the air ducts. "Hush," sighed the computers. "Quiet," clucked the clocks.

To the right and left of Mary's desk, the stacks rose monolithic.

Ahead, some one hundred sixty feet down the hall, the glass doors showed a welter of snow, through which Mary could just discern, with the binoculars kept for this purpose, the bright sheen of the road. Snow plows, lights shining, trudged down the street at random intervals. The front automated counter stamped its seal of approval, always burbling to itself. When someone tried to leave without checking out her books, the doors refused to open, jaws set in bulletproof glass.

The second through fourth floors were hunched against the building's sides, leaving the roof open to view three hundred feet above her. Stage lights illuminated a dome of stained glass: an eagle, its wings spread wide against an aqua sky. Under their expanse, Mary sometimes thought she saw smaller birds: finches, sparrows, and warblers. Once a week she placed seed atop the stacks.

Tonight, however, there was only the eagle, a blanket of snow darkening the glass, flakes falling into the library through a hole in its left eye. Although the thermostat read seventy-five degrees, Mary always shivered when she thought of that black hole.

Mary's concentration was broken when she heard the door open, vibrating through the stillness.

She glanced up, but the door was shut and no one in sight. Snuggling into her chair, she opened a book, Edward Whittemore's *Jerusalem Poker*. Usually she would have played poker with the library staff, but they were all at home, Mary having volunteered for single duty. The library had served as an excellent retreat from two failed marriages, better almost than a convent, though she had never meant to stay eight years, only long enough to regain her feet. Sometimes, though, thoughts rebounding in her head would escape, breaking the conundrum of silence: *Mary, Mary, quite contrary, your garden is dead; books are fine and good, but where, oh where, to rest your weary head?* Strange thoughts, fey and disconnected from her. They only served to make her remember the past. Once, she knew, she had managed a nightclub, but that had failed along with her husbands. Their faces had faded with the years, until now they might as well have been stick figures, fingers thin and brittle, but still pointed at her. *You*, they told her, *you were to blame. We only wanted what was best* . . . So now she cavorted with Lord Byron and vacationed with Don Quixote. A shelver and filer. A bespectacled terror to the children (that part she liked) and a patient custodian to the parents.

Then the door did open with a rush of cold air, and Mary looked up. In stepped a multicolored blob. Mary straightened her glasses, bringing the binoculars up to her eyes. She raised her eyebrows. *Oh, this is interesting. Very interesting. No mere bird can compare.*

The creature was a man, the man a jester. The belled cap, the striped velvet-satin tunic, the patched pantaloons, had been colored by an aficionado of urban camouflage: red graffiti rioting against cement and earth tones, the oily sheen of dirty glass. The boots, black and worn, pointed toward the eagle's eye. The air *changed* as he moved, a rising wave of . . . purity? She could not quite put a name to it. On the second floor the drifters broke into a jig.

Now Mary could see his face: a strong jaw, cheekbones ruddy with cold, softened by a well-proportioned nose, and a gaze that skipped from aisle to counter to shelf like a pebble glancing over water. His mouth curled into a perpetual smile, held in place by lines carved into the skin. The body attached to the face was strong and wiry. Mary's chest constricted and she realized she was hyperventilating. She sucked in deep breaths, tried to relax, hands aflutter. She had fallen in Intense Like.

Mary Colquhoun no longer believed in love at first sight. Both husbands had been hooked that way. No, one did not throw oneself at another human being. One did not exchange glances across crowded rooms and instantly become intimate. *Now I choose more sensible ways,* Mary reassured herself, when in fact she blocked every path. Except one: Intense Like, which could evolve into love, or more probably, mild disdain. The buzz of her former husbands' advice threatened to overwhelm her, but she shook it off. Something deep within her had been rekindled upon seeing this ridiculous jester; she could feel a quiver, a movement, in her heart.

The man stepped up to her desk. Mary put down the binoculars and closed her mouth. Swallowing, she took off her glasses, managing to fluff her hair in the same motion. She smiled.

"What can I do for you?"

His grin broadened.

"Well, Miss . . . Mrs.?"

"Oh. Miss Mary Colquhoun."

"*Miss* Mary Colquhoun, my name is Cedric Greensleeves—professional calling, you understand—and I am searching for my frog."

"Your what?"

"My frog."

"Oh?" she said.

Cedric Greensleeves' chuckle chased away her silence.

"Yes," he said, his tone teasing her. "I work for the . . . the Amazing Mango Brothers Circus, currently touring the Greater Chicago area. I provide entertainment for the children and, sometimes, for lucky parents. My familiar, so to speak, is a frog. A big one—five feet long and four wide. Stands three feet at the shoulder. Found him myself in the South American rainforests. Very rare. And smart, devious—even Machiavellian—in his intrigues."

"I see," interjected Mary, simply to catch her breath. Her heart still beat fast, but she couldn't shed her skin. She had labeled herself, she realized—the unfamiliar brushed off as petty irritation. She shivered.

On the second floor the drifters danced to slow rhythms, birthing shadows that left their masters and undulated down to the first floor, over the guardrail.

Cedric glanced up, eyes narrow: the gaze of an ancient man.

"It's just the homeless," Mary said. "I let them use the second-floor fireplace. It's electric." Her jaw unclenched somewhat.

Cedric nodded. "I know. We have always said the chosen shall dance."

Mary could have sworn she saw fire reflected in his eyes.

"What do you mean?" she asked.

"Nothing." The fire, if she had not imagined it, had vanished.

"Anyway, we were driving past here on our way to the show and the car was caught in a snow drift." He said *car* as if it were a foreign word, a word without meaning. "I opened the door, the frog made a break for it—as if I don't treat him with kid gloves already—and I've been looking for him ever since."

Cedric leaned over Mary's desk, stared at her. His eyes were cinnamon-colored, flecked with gold. "Have you seen him?"

"No. No. I haven't seen your frog. Sorry."

In her mind, a forgotten part of her past said, "Stay, stay and have a nightcap in this silly mausoleum of learning, under the eagle's eye . . . "

A vision of conquest possessed her: a way to reenter the world triumphant, on the wings of clocks and computers, with this man beside her, perhaps traveling on ghost trains, subduing misfortune through the passage of years, the green hum of television screens. A bustling consumerism, a wonderful new nightclub, perhaps, magic rising from the machinery of the Samuel Devonshire, her husbands swept away, little stick limbs and all.

But the vision faded and she was back inside her skin and she knew the library's special properties were not transferable or exportable, that it simply *was*, like—she guessed—the man who stood before her. Cedric was talking.

"—sure this was the place, but if you do see him, please give me a call."

Cedric rummaged through the many pockets on his vest.

"He can giggle and he can sing. 'Greensleeves,' of course. Rather, he can whistle it."

He picked a card from its hiding place and offered it to Mary. As he leaned toward her, the smell of salt spray and sandalwood washed over her. Mary closed her eyes to catch the scents, to never lose them. Cedric's hands touched her, shocking, burning. Vaguely, as if from a tunnel of snow, Mary heard him say, "This *was* the right place, but for now . . . goodbye."

She opened her eyes. Cedric Greensleeves had reached the doors. Mary lunged for the red button that would lock them, but her hand wavered, terrible thoughts freezing her. *He knows. He knows I'm hiding. He saw it with his own eyes.* How could she keep anything from those cinnamon eyes? The jester passed into the night, leaving jumbled impressions in her mind and a silence the color of sandalwood.

Mary's shoulders relaxed; her fists flowered into hands. *Giggles and Greensleeves*, she thought, glancing down at the card. A frog with belled cap graced the front. On the back, it read, "Greensleeves and His Magic Frog: Services of Whimsy Available at Typical Prices. Call 777-FROG for details. Or contact the Amazing Mango Brothers Circus. Humor on demand."

Probably a womanizer, she thought, but felt hollow inside as she remembered his eyes, the perpetual smile.

Mary hardly noticed the last bibliophiles shuffle off into the night.

At nine, the clocks dutifully chimed and ate their tongues for another hour. The computers amused themselves by placing obscene phone calls to the CIA, while the heated air ducts wheezed from perpetual sore pipes. An unease had stolen over Mary. The quality of silence had changed once again. It was somehow . . . *green?*

Slapslapslap! Green swathes swept by her sixth sense, wrapping themselves in her hair, hitting her face like the pages of a wind-blown newspaper. She spluttered, rose from her chair. Damn it! Something was out of synch. Straightening her skirt, she began to walk toward the entrance. A left-behind brat had probably over-turned a whole shelf of *Better Homes and Gardens*, spilling this dreadful silence from the second or third floors and down onto her.

Then a sound that was a sound began to rise and Mary stood transfixed, an expression of wonder illuminating her face. For two hundred years, the building that housed the library had played host to other institutions: banks, hotels, synagogues, post offices, but never—never!—had this sound been heard among the balconies and hallways, stacks and marble statues.

The clocks burped and hiccupped in surprise as the sound twisted its way toward the ceiling. A whistle, or brace of whistles intertwined, clear and vibrant, broke Mary's silence, unraveling thread by thread the cloak she had woven for so many years. "Greensleeves" melody filled the Samuel Devonshire Memorial Library, softly, softly, then louder and deeper, until Mary lost herself in the mournful notes. On the second floor, the drifters halted in midstep of a Caribbean mamba and bowed to their partners, now sweeping across the floor in synchronized simplicity. Their shadows stayed with them, teaching the steps, before separating to form their own company. No laughter, but the men and women facing each other stared into opposite eyes and felt the thrill of intimacy. The fireplace crackled a counterpoint.

Below, Mary stood entranced, remembering past romances and the possible one that had slipped through her clumsy fingers. Slowly, awkwardly, she began to dance, hands held as if in an invisible partner's grasp. Her high heels slid effortlessly across the floor, her moves more and more elegant as she lost herself to the music.

She spoke to her invisible partner, to her husband (was it the first, the second?): *I love you. I really love you. Yes, yes, I'll try to do better. I know I don't know the steps* . . . The fantasy soured. She shoved it away, but it shoved back. It was no use; despite her best efforts, her husbands' stick figure faces took on depth, color, substance. Now both danced with her, silent while she apologized to them: *I'm sorry. I know I don't cook what you like. I know you tell me I'm bad in bed. I know, I know. Just, please, please* . . .

Mary stopped dancing. Her shoulders slumped. Why did she always apologize? Why? It always made her feel terrible. Angrily, she brushed tears from her face; the eagle looked on without mercy. She tried to stop crying, failed. *God*, she thought, *what am I doing here?* The eagle, possessing the only eye of divinity in the cavern, did not answer. There was no need. She knew the answer, no matter how she blocked it out with silence. And still "Greensleeves" rose and fell upon her ears, breaking every covenant she had made with herself. The sound, piercing the roof through the eagle's broken eye, emerged into the cold night air to nudge the memories of passersby. Mary whispered the words, eyes shut.

The last note echoed, died away. The whistler giggled. Giggled and broke the spell. Giggled and was answered by a tentative burble from the checkout machine, only too happy to gossip. Mary's eyes blinked open. The frog! The frog *was* here, between the aisles. Her librarian instincts came to the fore. Search and destroy! Find the intruder! Return the intruder to Cedric . . .

Mary rolled up her sleeves and walked down the nearest row, shoes clicking on the marble floor. She reached the end, was faced by more stacks. A loud, obnoxious giggle sounded to her left. A solid green bullet. An emerald Volkswagen Beetle. A *whump!* and the thing she had seen bowled her over, its skin clammy, its breath damp.

Face red, Mary got up and dusted off her skirt. All thoughts of "Greensleeves" left her. For the first time in several months, Mary Colquhoun was mad. *Either that,* she thought, *or start crying again.* She stomped down the aisles. She came to the end: a wall lined with portraits. No frog. Mary started to turn around when a chorus of voices spoke up.

"He went that-a-way!"

"Divide and Conquer!"

"Up the kazoo with Tyler too!"

"He's heading North by Northwest!"

"Get a net!"

"Get a gun!"

"Get a life . . ."

She stared at the wall. A dozen pairs of eyes stared back from the paintings. Governors and hotel managers, postal generals and nouveau riche millionaires. Mary was too mad to be shocked, too wise in the library's ways.

A man with bushy eyebrows and a beard streaked white said, "Ya know, when I was in the army, we smoked 'em out. Cooked 'em real good, missee! Take my word for it."

"SHUT UP!" shouted Mary. The sound rebounded from the walls and almost knocked her off her feet. A hand went to her mouth. A garbled echo sounded: "Sush op . . ."

She, Mary Colquhoun, who had been quiet as a dust mouse, had raised her voice, broken her own silence. A ghost of a night-club owner flickered in her features. She smiled. She laughed. She chortled. Nothing was particularly funny, but she couldn't help herself. She'd call Cedric, tell him his frog was in the library. Grinning, she left the disgruntled portraits still whispering advice.

"Get it in a headlock. Get it in a headlock."

"Make it play Simon Says . . ."

"Promise it ice cream—or orange marmalade; frogs like marmalade."

She turned a corner. The voices faded.

II

"Satchmo," Mary said, the second floor electric fireplace raging behind her, "I need your help. Please?"

She spoke to the tall, grizzled black man who served as the drifters' unofficial leader. Mary had called Cedric, only to get his answering service and an extra helping of frog giggle.

Although Satchmo had lived on the second floor for almost two years, Mary did not feel comfortable speaking to him. He called himself Satchmo because he owned a saxophone, and she had observed him long enough to realize that, if eccentric, he wasn't crazy. But he *was* mute, and that created a special silence in itself. When he had first arrived, Satchmo had greeted her with a note card which read, WHY ARE YOU SO SAD? Three weeks later, it had been, YOU DON'T TALK MUCH. And still later, WERE YOU A MUTE ONCE? At which point, she had to giggle despite herself.

Gradually, he had revealed himself through the cards: I HATE VEAL. CAT FUR MAKES MY EYES WATER. MY PARENTS DIED WHEN I WAS FIVE. MY HERO IS MARCEL MARCEAU. IS THERE FUZZ IN MY BEARD? Last week the message had been more complex: MY ANCESTORS WERE BARBARY PIRATES WHO RAPED AND PILLAGED THEIR WAY DOWN THE WEST AFRICAN COAST. DO I LOOK BLOODTHIRSTY TO YOU?

She did like him, though his questions often tempted her to write back, LEAVE ME ALONE! Satchmo's music stopped her. His saxophone was a curious instrument. It had been hollowed out, keys stripped from it. But he would put the reed to his lips and the silence would ripple, dance with color. No library visitors ever heard him or saw the music, but his fellow drifters could, and so could Mary. When he played, Satchmo moved with his instrument: a stealthy, fluid grace that she admired. She felt so clumsy next to him.

"I need you to help me catch a . . . a rather *large* frog."

Satchmo grinned, revealing uneven yellow teeth. He scribbled a note, handed it to her.

WHY SHOULD I PLAY TOADY TO A FROG?

She frowned. Now was not the time for bad puns.

"Please, Satchmo. It'll ruin the books, possibly bring down the stacks, and then I'll be in real trouble."

Satchmo's eyes widened.

Scribble.

HOW BIG IS THIS FROG?

She sighed. "Big. Three or four feet at the shoulder."

Behind him, the drifters muttered darkly. They had been interrupted in the middle of a Romanian polka.

Scribble.

WILL YOU ORDER ME BOOKS ON BARBARY PIRATES?

"Anything . . ."

Satchmo motioned for her to wait, and walked over to the other drifters. He scribbled something on a card, gave it to a pale, stocky woman.

"He says," she said, "DO YOU WANT TO HELP THIS CRAZY WOMAN CATCH A FROG THE SIZE OF A LARGE DOG OR DO YOU WANT TO KEEP DANCING?"

Mary groaned. She had hoped Satchmo would give them no choice. Almost to a man, this particular group of drifters had personality disorders. Behind Satchmo were pretenders to the name of Nixon, Nader, both Shelleys, Thatcher, Kubrick, Marx, Antoinette, and many more. Visitors to the library soon learned to avoid the second floor.

Much to her amazement, after a prolonged huddle, Satchmo walked over and handed her a note which read, WE WILL HELP —EXCEPT FOR MARY SHELLEY. Mary Shelley was a tiny, birdlike woman with a stutter.

"I-I-I tthh-think we shh-should ll-ll-let it go. I-I-I like mon-mon . . . Monsters!"

Thus began the first (and last) Samuel Devonshire Memorial Library Frog Hunt. While the clocks churned out seconds like organ grinders, Satchmo and his folk spread across the first floor.

Mary watched and coordinated from the second floor. Satchmo played the sax, hoping to entice the beast with jungle-green, swamp-brown music. Thatcher tried to set an ambush. Marx formed a collective with a reluctant Marie Antoinette. Nixon built a trap with himself as bait. Kubrick sat in a corner and made psychotic faces. Nader ran around pleading for humane measures.

Mary had unleashed a monster—an ineffective monster, for the frog remained at large. Very large. The portraits were no help either. Insulted, they now screamed abuse at her.

Finally, as the scene below developed into a freeform dance experiment with Thatcher and Marx doing the tango, she heard a giggle. A suspiciously green giggle. From above her. Through an air duct. An air duct leading to the fourth floor. Aha! She would have to deal with it herself. Alerting the lunatic drifters would only result in losing the element of surprise. Quietly, she backed away from the second floor railing . . .

Mary feared the fourth floor. People disappeared while on it: spinsters or young louts, babies or dogs, it made no difference. At least three, four times a year someone made the trip up . . . and never came down. She had never called the police because the missing person always turned up at some later date . . . but she never saw them come down. Why try to understand it?

Besides, it was too late now. She was walking onto the fourth floor, brought by the pre-Civil War elevator, a clanking contraption that belched smoke and drank three cans of oil a week.

She shivered; it was colder here. And so gray. The fourth had once housed rare books, but a fire had destroyed them and the debris had never been cleared. Scarred book spines poked out from gutted shelves. She could feel a watchful silence, not at all green, as she drew her arms tightly together. Ghosts lived here. Phantom janitors with spectral mops, or perhaps the books themselves would rise, the pages flap-flapping like wings. *Get a grip*, she thought, suppressing the urge to slap herself.

She sped wraithlike through the stacks, headed for the railing which overlooked the first floor. When she reached it and stared down at the dancing drifters, she wondered if she shouldn't have told someone where she was going. The grayness, the silence, unnerved her. The frog wasn't dangerous, was it? Above her, she could see the eagle, spread continent-wide across the dome.

"Frog?" she whispered. "Greensleeves?"

No response. She sighed. The frog would not willingly give

itself up. She edged her way along the corridor formed by the railing and the nearest stacks. Alert for movement, she sensed only dust and a faint burnt smell.

Then came a rustle, a twitch, followed by a hearty belch. She caught a hint of green silence, tracked it forward. She crept toward a cubbyhole that jutted out like a balcony. Peering out from behind a column, she saw—

THE FROG! She gasped, but the creature did not hear her. It watched the drifters. The frog was larger than she remembered when it had bolted past her in the first floor stacks: huge, with pouting lips and thick, dark green skin. No wonder it didn't feel the cold. As she watched, it giggled, apparently amused by the drifters' search. (Mary had no idea what made a frog giggle.)

A thought struck her and the hairs on her neck rose. A giggling frog could mean an intelligent frog.

How much do I know about Cedric Greensleeves? she fretted. *Is it really a good idea to jump this frog? Does it bite? Whywhywhy am I doing this?*

She jumped.

The moment her feet left the ground, time seemed to slow down. She took hours, days, weeks to fall. In those weeks, the frog looked up, saw her, and—eyes wide—spit out whatever it had been chewing. Mary distinctly saw its lips move, form the word *Fuuuccckkk* with excruciating slowness.

She fell across its back legs, grabbed hold. The frog kicked out. Her grip loosened, but she recovered and grappled with it: a blur of thrashing, scrabbling frog muscles. She held on and slapped at the green flesh. But when she tried to squeeze its chest, the beast inflated its throat and, like some beach blowup toy, increased its surface area 100 percent. She spat out frog slime.

With a final frog kick, she landed on her back, the frog atop her, its head too close for comfort. The eyes winked at her, the mouth smiled, and—*whap!*

The blow which lost the battle. A tongue to the forehead. An incredibly tough, wide tongue. It felt like a battering ram. *Whap!* She flailed at it, tried to flop back onto her stomach, but *whap!* failed. She grunted in disgust, punched the frog in the head. It punched back. *Whap!* She fell, but stubbornly latched onto one slippery toe. *Whap!* Her hand fell to the floor. The frog giggled, stepped over her bruised body and, with one last *whap!* to the belly, hopped from view.

*   *   *

Mary lay there for a long time. It felt better than standing up, going back downstairs, and admitting to Satchmo that, yes, a frog had bested her in fisticuffs. Worse yet, frog saliva beaded her forehead, matted her hair. Two for the frog, zero for the librarian.

Mary glanced up at the glass eagle. It was much prettier up close, the detail of wings and talons almost lifelike.

Never mind the frog. It wasn't a fair match. It used kudzu judo on you . . .

A whisper, or perhaps an exhalation of breath. But who had spoken? She sat up, glanced around her. No one. Had she imagined it?

"What's kudzu judo?" she asked, just in case.

A complicated form named after a trailing vine that strangles and smothers forests in the South . . .

"How do you know?"

I read over people's shoulders . . .

A spark of irritation entered her voice. "So who are you, where are you, and what are you doing spying on me?"

A slow, deep chuckle.

Up here, Mary. Look up. Really look.

She looked up at . . . well, at the eagle. It filled her field of vision. Now that she examined it, she could see the burnished brown-amber wings *moving*, second hand slow, but swimming through the glass. *Alive.* She gasped. The azure eye blinked, the talons unclenched. Snow drifted through the vacant hole. She rubbed her eyes, but the stained glass still rippled.

"I'm dreaming," she said. "I'm dreaming."

The chuckle again. It sent the clocks clucking among themselves, scrambled the computers, put a hitch in the drifters' dance.

I've seen you feed the birds which enter through my eye, Mary . . .

In a subdued voice, she said, "You're the eagle? You're alive?"

I woke the morning the meteorite shattered my eye. I had been lost in dreams of sand and heat and wind. It brought me out of myself, into the world . . .

"But, but," she spluttered, "that's ridiculous!"

How curious . . . Talking portraits are not ridiculous. Frogs the size of baby elephants are not ridiculous, but somehow I am ridiculous. Surely you understand this place is special? You thought so yourself in your daydream of nightclubs and green computers. The only air of reality trickles through my broken eye . . .

"You can read my thoughts?" Mary found this rude, even peeping Tom-ish, but she suppressed the thought when she realized he might eavesdrop.

I read dreams, Mary. The sleeping city keeps me awake with its dreams. So many dreams. During the day, it is worse: childish wish fulfillment, revenge, anxiety, paranoia. It tires me, saps my will. They enter through my eye, never let me rest . . .

"You've watched me all this time?"

Yes, Mary. I have tried for so long to make you hear me. But my voice grows weaker and weaker, and you have never before been close enough to hear it . . .

"Why weaker?" she asked, concerned.

Look once again. Closer still. Truly see . . .

She looked. At first she saw nothing except the movement of his body, but then . . . the glass was moving *around* his wings, encroaching like a cancer. The glass that formed the sky was bleeding into the wings, making them lose their form. The eagle beat his wings to keep them from being pinned down and distorted.

The intact eye sparkled as it watched her, the glass liquid, color changing . . .

I need your help, Mary . . .

"How?" she said, still caught up in the dark vision of cells eaten up—eradicated and replaced with the unhealthy.

You must help release me . . .

A sudden jolt of librarian sense came over Mary. She got up, backed away from the railing.

"What, exactly, do you mean?"

A long, sorrowful sigh.

That's what they all say. All the ones who come here. And then they forget, certain that they dreamed me! Only to dream again at night—of me. What do I mean, Mary? I mean you must release me from the dome . . .

"But won't the roof cave in?" She wrung her hands. "No. No. How could I possibly do it, anyway? I'd need construction workers, city permits. Everyone would think I was crazy. Mad! Ha! I would be mad . . ."

The eye blinked, the wingtips dipped, rose again.

Please, Mary. I have watched over you for so long. I know how much this library means to you, but please, release me. If not soon, then never. The glass shifts and shifts and imprisons me, clips my wings. Ever since I woke, the glass has been closing in on me. I do not want to return to thoughtlessness. Nor can I stand the dreams. Mary . . .

She sympathized, but what could she do? Nothing. If she set him free, the dome would collapse, ruining the upper floors and destroying the first. She would lose both job and library, be kicked out into the world again.

"I will think about it," she said, avoiding his eye. "I will tell you when I have decided."

Mary's ever-so-clumsy legs led her to the elevator. Behind her, a whisper: *Please, Mary. Ask Cedric. Cedric will know what to do . . .*

III

When Mary came downstairs, she found the drifters, frog, and Cedric gathered around her desk. Cedric had changed clothes so that now he looked as though he had been painted in greens and blues and browns, camouflage more suitable for a forest. But it fit him. Cedric seemed shorter than before, less magical, but still the cinnamon eyes, flecked with gold, the grin—those were the same and just as alluring. The frog (beast!) sat at Cedric's feet, throat swelling and deflating as it breathed. She noted with grim satisfaction that it seemed tired. She tried to wipe the drool from her collar, only stopping when Cedric stared at her.

"Well," she said, folding her arms. "This is a fine sight. I spend all night searching for that . . . that *toad*. I grapple with it. I ruin my clothes. And here you are, all of you, not one bit of help!"

Cedric winked, then bowed. "Sorry, my lady. You were the one who told me he wasn't here."

My lady . . . Her anger washed away. There was a glow about Cedric, a vigor and lightness that touched her heart.

"Well, at least it's over," she said, looking down.

"Indeed," replied Cedric. He turned to Satchmo. "Are you and your fellows ready?"

Ready? Mary thought.

"What is going on?"

Satchmo scribbled a note, an embarrassed look on his face. The note read, WE ARE ALL LEAVING WITH CEDRIC.

"Leaving!"

Cedric nodded. "Yes. The drifters, the frog, and I. They have been waiting a long time, you know. I should have found this place much sooner."

"Leaving," she said again, shocked. "But *why*, Satchmo? This place is your home . . ." *My home.*

Scribble.

YOUR HOSPITALITY HAS BEEN WELCOME, BUT HUD-
DLING AROUND AN ELECTRIC FIREPLACE IN A LIBRARY
IS *NOT* LIKE HOME.

For a moment, Mary could think of nothing to say. They were
all leaving, taking her dreams with them. Then, from above, she
thought she heard a whisper, a slow flutter of wings. A wild hope
sprang into her mind.

"Wait," said Mary as Cedric turned toward the door. Cedric
stopped.

"What, Mary?"

"The eagle. You can't leave the eagle." *You can't leave* me.

"The eagle? What about the eagle?"

"It's alive and it's trapped," she said, hoping beyond hope that
he would stay, that she could make him stay. Or take her along,
where ever they might go. "The glass around its wings is killing it.
It won't be alive much longer." Did she sound crazy?

Cedric glanced up at the dome, produced an old-fashioned spy-
glass from a pocket, and squinted through it. Finally, he nodded.

"So it is," he said. "So it is. But if I help rescue the eagle, the
library will be destroyed. The air of reality will enter and contami-
nate it. The clocks will just be clocks. The portraits will never speak
again. I will never enter here again, Mary. You will have to leave.
Do you want to leave, even to save the eagle?"

He stared directly at her as he spoke, the gaze that told her,
I know you. I know everything about you.

She bowed her head. The eagle had pleaded with her and she,
cruelly, had not answered it. Besides, surely Cedric would take her
with him now.

"Yes," she said. "Yes, I do."

A shadow passed over Cedric's face.

"Very well," Cedric said. He faced the drifters. "Will you help?
We will need good dancers. Very good dancers."

Satchmo scribbled a note.

WHAT IS ANOTHER HOUR OR TWO?

Cedric clapped him on the shoulder.

"Thank you, Satchmo. Everyone, close your eyes. Tightly!"

The drifters closed their eyes. Mary closed her eyes. And when
Cedric said to open them —

—they were all on top of the dome and she was freezing. Her
shoes had snow on them. She almost fell in surprise. The brisk
wind sent them all whirling like tops. Cedric laughed, breath
smoking from his mouth. The drifters giggled like children.

"Stomp your feet!" Cedric shouted over the wail of the wind. "Stomp your feet and set this poor bird free!"

It was then, Cedric jumping up and down on the glass, his body silhouetted by skyscrapers, a shadow against the frozen air, Lake Shore Drive threading through him like a glittering necklace, that Mary realized how much of the Faery was in him, and how little in her.

But then Satchmo tumbled by, grabbed her arm, and all thoughts left her head. Together they danced, slowly at first: a waltz to warm up. Soon he pulled out his saxophone and, with one hand around her waist, played it to perfection, a rising cluster of notes that did not waver, that flowed to the gyrations of his hips. She jumped up and down for the joy of it, the cold air slapping her face, making her tingle all over.

Around them, the drifters jostled, pushed, crawled, and boogied. Some stood on their heads while others stomp-stomp-stomped in position. The glass began to shake. The shaking became a self-sustained tremor so that when she stopped dancing for a moment, Mary could feel it. She saw that the dome's far edge had begun to sink inward. Drifters hastily moved toward the center.

And there was Cedric, still on the damaged portion, jumping higher than all of them until his upward pumping arms seemed to embrace the moon. His frog jumped higher still until, at the top of its arch, Mary could not even see it against the stars: just the two amber eyes glowing like faraway planets.

Soon Cedric came over to take Mary's hand. Satchmo drifted away, lost in his music. Together, Cedric and Mary bounded across the dome through the scattered snow. His hands were warm, almost electric, and she held them tightly.

Some minutes later, the entire dome rumbled and roared beneath them. In mid-dance, glass crumbled under Mary's feet. She screamed, but Cedric yelled, "Don't worry! Keep dancing. Keep dancing." She believed him, believed in the warmth of his hands, the fire in his eyes. *Faery Fire.*

The rumbling intensified as the cracks grew deeper. Still they danced, dancing to their deaths without a care. It was all too much fun.

She could not pinpoint the moment she began to fall. First she weighed 112 pounds, then she was weightless, still holding Cedric's hand. Shards of glass passed them, followed by the almost-animate glass feathers of the eagle's right wing. She glimpsed the eye, the beak, the talons, and then she fell farther, faster, and actually laughed, laughed her lungs out in freefall. Something warm and bright welled up inside Mary and she wondered lazily if she had ever been so happy, falling toward the library's floor in Cedric's arms. The marble crept up on them. Around her: arms and legs, more above her. She caught sight of Satchmo's hand holding the saxophone. Everything seemed silent—the flying glass, the eagle as it rose; she could not even hear herself breathe.

At the exact moment vertigo threatened to overwhelm Mary, Cedric snapped his fingers. He released her hand. Suddenly as two-dimensional and truly weightless as a leaf, she drifted toward the floor. The wind played with her, creating new ways for her to move, running fingers through her hair, but protecting her from the glass clouds that stormed across the library's upper level.

Then: something hard against her back. The floor. The spell broke and all 112 pounds of her felt betrayed. She was so heavy, so heavy after being so light. She longed for that sensation again, to fly away. Now the glass crashed—against marble floors, against shelves and chairs, with a thousand crystalline shudders.

Soon Satchmo and Cedric, grinning ear to ear like fools, had reached her side. She ignored them, watched the other drifters—light as snowflakes, as butterflies. No weight. No sensation. Why couldn't life be like that? Simple, with no thinking to it, only motion.

Across the face of the deep, she saw the eagle gliding, gliding . . . Suddenly she was glad, so glad, that they had freed him. How light he must be.

When Mary finally got to her feet, tingling and bruised, a single glance told her the library would never be the same. Glass had threaded her hair. Glass had barricaded the elevators. Glass had infiltrated the computers' keys, smothering her files. Glass hung from the stacks like belated Christmas decorations. The emergency lights had turned on. Sadly, she realized she could not see the silence, not hear it in any form. Cedric's frog squatted nearby, but she could not sense the familiar green silence. The portraits against the wall were shrouded in darkness. Only faces. Pipes spilled water on the floor; it froze over as she watched. The fire alarm, burglar alarm, and repeat book offender alarm lights were all flashing, meaning they would not be alone for long.

She walked over to the entrance where the drifters had congregated. The frog hopped over with her, jumped onto Cedric's boots.

Cedric extricated himself, took Mary by the arm, and led her out of the drifters' earshot.

"There is no magic here anymore, Mary," he said. "We must go."

"Yes, we must," she said, smiling. She clasped his hand. Gently, he removed it.

"Not you. The drifters, the frog, and I. I'm sorry."

"But . . . but I thought . . ."

"You were wrong. I'm sorry."

"I love you," she said. "I loved being with you on the roof. I want to go with you."

Cedric sighed. "My lady, everyone loves me. It is part of my Glamour, useful when I must travel in this world. I cannot take you with me."

"Why not?" she said. "You're taking the drifters."

"I can take the drifters because where we are going, they are normal. Satchmo is not mute. The others are all themselves, not crazy, or hiding behind other people's personalities. And I can use them. You only came to this library because you hated yourself."

"But I've changed."

"Yes, you have. Satchmo tells me you yelled at the portraits. My frog tells me you almost bested him in a fight. And, just now, you told me you loved me, not caring how I might hurt you." For a moment, his face was creased with wrinkles, the eyes sunk deep into the orbitals. "Don't cry, my lady. I must take the drifters away now. Do not follow us. It would kill you."

She nodded, but avoided his gaze.

"The police will be here soon. Even my magic cannot cloak us from so many probing eyes."

"Go," she said.

"You saved the eagle, Mary."

She tried to smile. "Yes, I guess I did."

Cedric walked with her to the door. There, Satchmo kissed her hand—and pressed the saxophone into it. He scribbled a note while Mary just stared at him, too surprised to respond.

KEEP THE SAXOPHONE SAFE. I WON'T NEED IT ANY-MORE. DON'T BE SAD, MARY . . .

She nodded, squeezed his hand, then watched as the drifters followed Cedric out the door.

Halfway down the street, the city enveloped them. But what a city! For a moment, the skin of reality peeled back to reveal twinkling pagodas, streets shiny with silver, crowds of brightly clad folk; and, in the air, strange beasts roamed, not the least of which was the eagle, which glided between the pagodas with a nightingale's grace.

The vision faded. She was alone. In the cold stone library. Moonlight bled through the shattered dome. Wind blew in her face. Sirens rose over the sounds of tinkling glass. Snow had begun to fall, coating the floor. Slowly she walked back to her desk, took her purse and *Jerusalem Poker* from the drawers.

A dream. It all felt like a dream. But a hint of cinnamon flecked the air and her hair was still caked with frog spit.

At the door, she stopped, turned off the emergency lights, and looked back for the last time. There, in the gloom, she could just discern the stick-figure phantasms of her husbands, dancing slowly with each other, disintegrating as the moonlight touched them. The sight was almost funny.

It was only when Mary walked onto the street that she remembered the saxophone in her hand. She looked down at it. The hollow, smooth wood felt warm, warmer than her palm. On a whim, she raised it to her lips, unfurled her fingers to play, and blew . . .

The sound? An echo of an echo: a silence that seemed to remember the past and present simultaneously. It reminded her of panpipes, of mystery and illusion. A different silence. Not a graceful tune, surely, to prickle only the very edges of her senses, but pure.

And new.

Notes on
Greensleeves

I have great affection for this story. For one thing, in an act of serendipity after I wrote it, Gainesville, Florida, the city I lived in at the time, built a public library that could easily be the one described in "Greensleeves," sans the eagle in the roof. For another, half of this story appeared in The Book of Frog, *my first collection, self-published in 1989. I remember sending out "sponsorship letters" to my first-year college professors, my relatives, my friends: for $25 you would get two copies of my collection and a small plastic frog. My sister drew an illustration of the plastic frog on the letter—to prove authenticity, I suppose. I'm sure it sounded like quite a deal.*

My mother contributed illustrations, my best friend, Duane Bray, wrote an article about the collection for the Gainesville Sun, *and fantasy novelist Meredith Ann Pierce contributed a quote about my work. The newspaper photographer took a picture of this very thin, very serious bearded youth standing behind a display of his plastic/wooden/ceramic/metal frog collection. For a couple of weeks after the article appeared, I would be walking down the street on the way to class and someone in a car speeding by would yell out "frog boy!" It was my first taste of either fame or humiliation—I'm not sure which.*

Detectives and Cadavers

THE CREATURE'S RIBS, HALF-BURIED BY THE tides, stuck out from the sand at odd angles, leg bones trapped beneath the torso. The head—four times the size of my own and, I'd dare say, more handsome—remained connected to the neck. Flesh covered the face, but could not hide the snarl of teeth, the cold stare of the vacant eye socket. Quite a specimen from where I was standing, half up to my mug in sand and water on the East Shore. Soggy weather, with an early morning fog.

"Unique. Ugly. Dead," said my partner Devon, a tight-lipped man whose broad features suggested caricature. He stood seven feet tall. I had only worked with him a few times before, but he seemed dependable.

"All true," I said, "but none of it helpful."

We were there on the whim of a sharp-eyed wall patrolwoman. She'd spotted a "suspicious shape, a possible muttie." Never ones to skimp, the Converge had sent us.

Getting out of Veniss had been problematic, demonstrators surrounding the front portal as ever: doomsayers convinced that the city's growing isolation from other Earth enclaves and off-world colonies was directly related to the muttie expulsion and supposed "persecution" of the Funny People. Never mind that the Conserge continually changed the definition of "muttie" and "Funny" to fit their own political agenda.

"If ever there *were* a full-scale muttie invasion, why there we'd be, you and I, to shake their little paws and offer 'em tea," I'd said to Devon as we were finally flushed out of Veniss. I would have preferred a small army to deal with a possible muttie, but the Conserge had other priorities.

Devon wrapped his trench coat tighter around his frame.

"How should we go about reporting this?" he asked.

I took a quick glance back at Veniss before answering. Emulsifiers spewed green filth—the cost of our bioculture—across the walls, the fortifications, coated our poor defenseless defenders of city and Conserge. The flesh had awakened in Veniss. I could smell it even from here, the peculiar mélange of heat and frustration that said, *Too many people, too little room.*

"The Conserge is a strange lot," I said, from the strength of twenty years experience, "Sometimes they can tell you what you're going to find before you find it, so be thorough. And start simple— *what* is it?"

Devon bent mechanically to his knees, to better examine the beast. His creakiness was, so he told me, the result of an accident. Funny People had assaulted him while he worked for the bioneers below level.

He looked up, smiled through crooked teeth. "It's mostly bone. I know a bioneer who could run tests for us."

I grunted, dug my hands into my pockets. "Could we call it Funny and leave it at that?"

Devon's face tightened. Now there was a bad move—mentioning Funny People—but how else could I phrase it? No matter what the scars, the poor bastard would have to grin and bear it.

"No," he said. "Not a Funny Person."

I had been pulled from my wife, Arcadia, and a warm bed for this assignment; I had a mind to rub it in, but time pressed. Behind me, the dirigibles had sounded their horns, cast moorings, and now hovered whalelike over the city as they policed it. Some carried floating gardens to an altitude above the miasma of pollution that choked the life out of Veniss.

Besides, after a moment's reflection, Funny People hardly seemed amusing. Arcadia and I wanted a child, but the bioneers had told us there was a good chance it would turn out Funny. A chief detective with a Funny Person for a child? No future for the child, possible confinement. No promotion and "voluntary" sterilization for me.

"A muttie, then," I said. *That* word didn't raise his gander.

Devon got up. "I'll take the pictures. You decide what it is. It'll keep my mug out of the heat. Look to the horizon. My knees can't take bad weather."

Devon was right. The wind blew in bursts. Strange, crested waves of sargasso rolled in under a watery sun. If a bit of weed were the end of it, fine, but the sea had given us nasty surprises more than once. And, of course, the rain would soon be here, hindering communications and contaminated with flesh knew what. Arcadia would already be sealing the apartment, listening to the weather report on the split screen.

I had left her lying on the bed, her hair tangled in one up-turned palm, her face turned away from me as she said, "How long?"

"I don't know. Muttie. East Shore."

There was a curious lilt to her voice as she said, "Afterward, we could go out to Hospital Central for another checkup. You could . . . I mean we could . . . "

She trailed off, perhaps sensing the hurt in my rigid stance, belt taut in my hands.

"I'll be back as soon as I can," I had told her, sealing the promise with a kiss, taking the salty taste of her with me.

Devon took out the trusty v-c and started clicking stills. He carefully avoided touching the carcass. More tissue had survived on the beast than I'd thought: hair or fur clung to the ear holes, the jaw line. The underbelly appeared intact, though naturally I wasn't going to turn the stinking thing over to confirm—I'd get Devon to do it. Only, there was a problem with that description. The thing wasn't stinking. Which seemed strange. The water was full of chemicals that ordinarily broke down flesh within hours.

"Could this be another experiment gone bad?" I asked. "Some clever bioneer thought he'd violate the Prohibition and hide it in the sea."

Cases of unauthorized genetic experiments still made it into the books, even with both the bioneers and the Conserge determined to enforce regulation.

Devon shook his head. "No. Too sophisticated. They'd need at least six months in one place. Someone would have caught them at it."

"Yes, well," I said, "we'll have to call it—"

That's when my day was spoiled for good. A moan cut the air, froze the freckles on my ears, dried the spit right out of my throat.

Devon chuckled in a way I found unnerving.

"Just the wind. Through its mouth."

The wind was brisk and, yes, it whistled through the beast's mouth.

"Oh," I said.

I covered my embarrassment by pretending a profound interest in the beast's nose. Nose? I stared into the eyes—the vertical pupils, the gold irises—and found myself lost, at sea. Was I an old fug or had only *one* eye been intact minutes before? Now I truly felt the wind lash my neck, recognized that the dawn was darkening, and the salt spray stinging.

"How clever," said Devon. "Very clever."

"What do you mean?" I knew what he meant.

"The flesh is reforming. Coming back to life."

Sweat beaded my forehead. I wanted to run—run and not look back. Arcadia awaited my return. For a moment, I had an image of her pure white skin, the liquid amber of her eyes, the way she could say a word, a phrase, and give it a meaning I had never thought of, and I almost lost my balance. This *thing* was big enough to rip us both apart and clean its teeth with a thighbone.

"Does . . . Does that mean it's muttie?" Devon seemed to enjoy the fear in my voice.

He shrugged. "Not really. We should wait. See if it's a full regeneration or—"

"Or what?"

Devon smiled. "Or an involuntary reaction. The cells may grow back. The creature may then be intact but dead. We will need to observe . . . for our report."

That rattled me. Devon telling *me* the rules. Yes, he was right: we were expendable, but the city's security was not.

"Okay," I said, "but if it starts to revive . . ." I pulled out my laser-sight Diamond .38.

He nodded. "Fair enough."

We kept a strange vigil—like the parents who used to wait at Hospital Central to see if their child was normal or Funny.

I wondered if Devon had children. I had never asked, but I thought not; he was too impersonal, aloof. He click-clicked the v-c until I thought the lever would fall off.

Me, I tried not to watch as layers of flesh sprouted from the bone, as tendons and muscles began to fill in the gaps. The leer of teeth was soon covered. Organs ballooned inside the ribcage. What Arcadia would have made of it, I don't know. She might have laughed.

Devon had seen such things, of course, working as he had for the bioneers below level. He had even been to the fifteenth level.

So, I thought about mutties, about Funny People. They were, as you might expect, much on my mind. Though I'd never told Devon, I had seen Funny People before—alive, not preserved in vat jars for school field trips.

I had been on the fifth level (considered marginally safe because bioneer apprentices live there) and had just finished taking the statement of a Mrs. Jilla Collander about her missing husband. Missing! In a walled city. Surrounded by mutties and water. I wanted to say, *Where the fug can he go, Mrs. Collander?* Though there were at least two possibilities: that spies for the rogue bioneers in the wastes had taken him for the flesh—the city wasn't *that* secure—or he planned to create a new data file on himself and show up six months later, secure in a face lift, with an obedient young blonde on his arm.

A step from the elevator and the promise of an early dinner with Arcadia—I had gone out and bought lilies, mushroom wine, the works—I heard a sound: like distant bells or chimes. It made me trip, bend my head, concentrate on the source. I walked until I could hear it clearly: a chorus of reed-thin voices that reminded me of whale-song, of wind through hollow glass. The holographic operas they put on to take your mind off the city's troubles couldn't compare. I had to find the source. I had to. There are so few things of beauty in Veniss.

The voices led me through progressively worse sections until even the overhead lights sputtered and shadows cringed away from me. (Thank flesh for a glow-in-the-dark detective's badge.) Two green hand-held find flares bobbed and weaved down the corridor, but it was so dark I could not even see the faces behind the lights. Rancid water lapped at my boots. The smells of overheated plastic, machine oil, excretion, spices, liquor, and sweat all inundated me, but I clung to the sound like a drowning man. And it was difficult at times to follow the sound, to unwind it from the chugging air filters, the hissing oxygen pumps, the maniacal canned laughter of split screens in the boxed-in tenements.

Finally, trudging through refuse from higher levels, I came to a corridor between two ramshackle single roofs. A flickering light above revealed neobaroque representations of former Conserge members.

On the dusty floor, three children played coddleskatch to a nonsense rhyme. No, not just children. Funny People. Unlike most, two were flesh poor: just a head, neck, and an arm to pull them along. The third had two arms, but the welts and exposed tissue told me she (yes, she, with an angelic face) would be dead soon. All three must have required special gear. But still, there they were, playing coddleskatch after the fashion of children all over the city, moving from square to square with sidles and hops. The song? I remember only two verses. Nonsense, as I have said, but sung to perfection.

> I-wire, I-wire
> adders and ladders
> detectives cadavers
> it's really no fuss
> to simply forget us
>
> Psychewitch, psychewitch
> eat your flesh sandwich
> make us metal like you
> swallow what we chew
> flesh sandwich . . .

When they stopped singing my shoulders sagged, as if their voices had supported my weight, and they saw me. All three with their large, luminous eyes. Fearful. They must have thought I would arrest them, for they quickly gathered up their game and, hobbling along, disappeared into the gloom.

While I watched. The music gone. The corridor thick with dust and overlooked imperiously by the gargoyle likenesses of leaders long dead. Devon had lived in their world for six years—undercover, alone. I envied him.

The memory of the voices did not fade. Late at night as I lay beside Arcadia, the faces came to me in dream, the mouths like open wounds whispering, "Daddy . . ." Sometimes I recoiled in disgust and sometimes I embraced them. Embraced them all, despite my revulsion.

I think it was then, in the aftermath of these nightmares, that I truly understood the difference between Funny and muttie. The muttie had been fashioned to serve, to obey, and the master fears the servant. But the Funny was born of us and we tried to love it, no matter how staunchly we also hated it for reminding us of our own failures.

Arcadia had never once spoken of leaving me because of my deficiency. The question hung between us, never spoken, until finally it evaporated, had no power over us other than that a ghost wields, a memory that has never come to pass.

I would go to her at her ad job in the Canal District and we would walk home along the enclosed piers, amid the diaphanous glow of chemicals in the water, her hand in mine. Her grasp firm, without doubt, even when I looked into her eyes and almost pleaded to be reminded, to be accused.

"My lover," she would say, and ruffle my hair because she knew I hated that. "My lover," she would say, and I would feel proud to be with her, in the Canal District, hand in hand, just walking.

Devon had spoken.

"What?"

He pointed to the beast. "Beautiful, isn't it?"

I stared at it. From outward appearances, it had fully regenerated: fur covered it, the claws were wicked and long, and one fang peeked innocently from the mouth.

"Oh, yes, smashing," I said. "If you're a Funny Person."

Devon scowled. "This is clever bioneering. A muttie that dies before it lives. A creature born dead which then revives."

"A muttie?" My fingers tightened on the .38. My heart hammered in my chest. "I thought you said it probably was *not* a muttie?"

The creature's death rattle interrupted us: a groan of anguish that roared out, then diminished. The claws flexed. The eyes blinked. The head moved, the eyes tracking us as we backed away. I raised the Diamond .38 until the laser trace pulsed green on its forehead.

Devon knocked the .38 from my hand. I grunted in surprise. As it hit the sand, out of reach, I realized every word of his had been an attempt to stall until the beast could awaken. As I spun to face him, he kicked me in the stomach, then brought both hands down on the back of my head. There was a soft *crack* and pain seared my skull. I fell. I tried to get up, but slumped in the sand.

"You bastard!" I hissed, gulping for air. "You flesh-poor bastard!"

Now Devon was tearing the trench coat from his body, buttons popping loose in his eagerness to be free. When he had finished disrobing, I cursed myself for a fool.

Beneath the coat, a metal frame of gears and levers and wheels: living bone, tendon, sinew holding it together. A bioneer's wet dream. Within the organic wiring, the gimshaw circuitry, not Devon, not the seven-foot Devon I knew. No. Two Devons, each identical, each the same three-odd feet tall. Each with extra limbs, external lungs, sprouting from the chests. The top one sat on the lower one's massive shoulders. The lower dwarf operated the legs. Funny People. Hysterical. A carnie show. I would have laughed if my head hadn't hurt so much. A marvel of coordination. How many bribes to keep their secret? How many corrupt bioneers? And, more important, how many Funny People had they saved from the Conserge? I heard the nonsense rhyme then, the children's voices. Mocking me.

Lithely, Top jumped from the frame, followed by Bottom. I don't know which disgusted me more. As I staggered to my feet, the empty frame tottered, fell to the sand. The dirigibles hovered over the city, unaware of the danger beyond the walls.

The Devons hesitated and I saw the indecision on their faces. For a moment, I thought they might attack me, but then a grin cracked their mouths wide open, a grin that, perversely, made me grin back, it was so pure and spontaneous a reaction. Then, without a word, they began to run down the beach, away from the city, toward the wastelands.

Me, I wanted to find my Diamond .38, but something growled and swiped out at my legs. The muttie had slipped my mind in the wake of the twins' striptease. Claws locked around my left ankle. Again I fell. I scrabbled at the sand and kicked out, hoping to break a tooth or two before it swallowed me whole. My hand met something solid: the .38. I raised it. I fired. The muttie screamed as I severed its arm at the elbow. I kicked once more and was free. The severed claw-hand still clutched my ankle. I tore it loose, threw it away from me. I looked to see how far the Devon marvels had gotten.

Too far to kill, or even maim.

"You flesh-poor *bastards!*" I screamed, nothing if not original.

No answer, of course. No answer at all, just Devon times two bobbing up and down, dancing along a shore under siege of rain.

Behind me, the muttie hunched closer. I turned, fired. Blood spattered everywhere. Fired. Fired again.

The golden eyes looked up at me, still bright. "Mann . . ."

Speech? Stunned, I fired a fourth time. More blood. I had opened a major artery. I was crying now. It/he was *talking*.

"Mannn . . ." Plaintive. "Mann?"

I drilled it between the eyes. It groaned. It struggled to its feet, fell sideways, fur matted with blood. "Mann . . ." And the death rattle again.

The storm was coming in quick, the wind rising, lightning in sheets of silver. The Devons were shadows in the spreading darkness. Soon they would be beyond even the range of the dirigibles. How the lower one must have sneered, held back giggles at my stupidity.

"Mann . . ." The reverse death rattle. I turned in surprise. How to kill that which lives and lives again?

"Why?" I screamed. I kicked it. "Why?"

I will never know what the creature really said. Its mouth was full of blood, its words already garbled. I suppose I heard what I expected to hear.

"I-wire, I-wire, adders and ladders . . ."

Like a message in code, and me without the skills to solve it.

Blood sang in my arteries, the storm's electricity lifting the hairs on my arms. My job—my life—was to uphold the law of Conserge, but the Conserge had never told me that mutties could speak, could think.

The beast raised its head, eyes fixed on me.

"You killl," it stated or asked. "You killl Funnnyyy."

I thought of the three children playing coddleskatch. I thought of Arcadia's hair tangled in one up-turned palm. "*Afterward, we could go out to Hospital Central for another checkup . . .*" My hands were cold on the trigger. "*. . . you could . . . I mean we could . . .*"

"Weee makkk," it said. "Wee makkk you . . ." Struggling to speak, perhaps to explain.

This time I kept on firing, cutting the legs out from under it, quartering its head, knowing as I did so I could not kill it. As the beam sawed splinters out of the bone, its voice rose in an agonized scream to match the hysterics of the storm, a deafening wall of sound that left me trembling and weeping. I crouched to one knee, breathing hard.

A wail of sirens from Veniss warned of rough weather as the dirigibles wallowed in troughs of calm air and indifference. If the Conserge fell, the children I had seen, who came to me in sleep, would not be Funny. I would be Funny. Arcadia would be Funny. In my mind, the children sought the embrace of my arms, as if I could save them. But I could not move.

It was then, with the rain moving in, the thunder and lightning, that I realized how much I loved Arcadia. I loved her with a resolve that surprised me. I could not sacrifice her safety, not for the children singing in the alley, not for the beast on the shore. Flesh preserve me, I would have betrayed the city and its tick-silly Conserge in that moment—but only for love of her. Funny People be damned. Devons be damned. Damn the lot of them. I would return to Veniss and report this new muttie to them. And the Devons. I would not allow them to slouch closer to the city, to harm its citizens, no matter how undeserving those citizens might be.

But when I took one last look out to sea, I realized the choice was not mine to make. And I knew why the Devons had abandoned their disguise with such defiance.

There, in the surf, not waves, but corpses. Thousands of skeletons churning water to foam as they made landfall. As if every muttie we had ever mistreated, tortured, murdered, had come back from the grave. Some were huge, larger than a dirigible, others like small fish. All with one eye intact to guide them, vertical pupils amid the gold. It seemed the water had evaporated—just skeletons clattering against one another, chattering in wind-spray. Piling up.

I went a speck mad then. I laughed a dry, hacking laugh. Turning, I ran, but at my back was the terrible vision that told me the Conserge had failed, that I had failed: the corpses piling up, returning to life. The sound they made took the form of bone-thin voices in the waves, voices in my mind, "detectives cadavers, detectives cadavers."

How now to save this city for us funny people?

Notes on
Detectives and Cadavers

I *still like the deceptively simple static quality of this story. However, I honestly cannot remember the circumstances under which I wrote it, or what inspired it—although I suspect an article about tissue regeneration might have been the catalyst. I do remember that Meredith Ann Pierce, an extremely talented fantasy writer to whom I was but a wet-behind-the-ears kid, was kind enough to suggest improvements. (I owe a huge debt to Meredith for allowing me to attend her regular writers group early in my career. Not only did I receive feedback from Meredith, but also from the noted poet Enid Shomer and several other excellent wordsmiths.)*

After writing "Detectives," I wanted a better picture of the inside of the city, a wish that manifested itself through my subsequent novel, Veniss Underground.

Exhibit H:

Torn Pages Discovered in the Vest Pocket of an Unidentified Tourist

(Note the blood-red discoloration in the
lower left corner.)

An Excerpt from Hoegbotton's
*COMPREHENSIVE TRAVEL GUIDE
TO THE SOUTHERN CITY OF AMBERGRIS*
Chapter 77: An In-depth Explanation
For the City's Apparent Lack of Sanitation Workers
(And Why Tourists Should Not Be Afraid)

UPON THE TRAVELER'S FIRST VISIT TO THE LEG-
endary city of Ambergris, he will soon espy crimson,
rectangular flags, no bigger than a scrap of silk cloth, attached to
the tops of pencil-thin stakes hammered into dirt or between pavement cracks. Such a traveler, as he peruses the Religious Quarter,
the various merchant districts, or even the rundown Industrial
District, may also notice the complete absence of rotten food,
human excrement, paper refuse, flotsam, jetsam, and the like on
the streets—as well as the almost "spit-cleaned" quality of the gutters, the embankments, the front steps of public buildings—and no
doubt with a measure of puzzlement, for this sparkling condition
contrasts sharply with the disheveled state of Belezar, Stockton,
Tratnor, and the other picturesque southern cities that straddle the
silt-mad River Moth.

Such a naïve traveler (unless having had the good sense to buy this particular guidebook, available in Ambergris itself only at The Borges Bookstore [see Ch. 8, "Cultural Attractions"]) may not at first, or even on second or third glance, discern the connection between the flags, as uniform and well-positioned as surveyors' marks, and the preternaturally clean quality of the city's convoluted alleyways. The unobservant or naïve traveler, therefore, may never come to understand the city itself, for these flags mark out the territory, and are the only daylight sign, of those unique inhabitants of Ambergris known in the vernacular as "mushroom dwellers."[1]

Travelers should expect a certain tight-lipped anxiety from the locals upon any query as to (1) the red flags, often as clotted and numerous as common weeds, (2) the preternaturally clean nature of the city, or, especially, (3) "mushroom dwellers." The curious outsider should not be particularly surprised or alarmed at the stone-faced non-response, or even hostile extremity of response, engendered by such questions. (See Ch. 6, "Survival," for a list of mannerisms, sayings, and articulations that will charm or mollify angry locals.) A corollary to these questions, "When is the Festival of the Freshwater Squid?" should also be avoided if possible. (see Ch. 5, "The Festival of the Freshwater Squid: Precautions, Preferred Weapons, Hoegbotton Safe Houses")

However, given a choice between satisfying rampant curiosity on these matters through consultation with the locals or through interrogation of the mushroom dwellers themselves, it would be advisable for even the adventurous traveler to seek out the nearest local. The mushroom dwellers generally remain mute on any subject related to their close-knit clan, nor are they likely to help the disoriented or lost traveler find his way to a safer part of the city.[2] Nor are they likely to converse with the casual passerby on *any* topic, especially as their only documented language consists of equal parts clicks, grunts, and moist slapping sounds that have thus far frustrated even the most prominent linguists.

Nor should it be expected that the average visitor will actually ever set eyes upon a mushroom dweller. These shy citizens[3] of

---

[1] Please see "Exploration of a Theme," the rather inaccurate if pleasant rendering by the famous collage artist of the last century, Michael Shores. Shores has included in his montage an even earlier and more whimsical drawing of the "monkfish" by the celebrated draftsman Nablodsky. "Exploration" is currently on display at the Voss Bender Memorial Art Museum.

[2] For a list of inexpensive Hoegbotton Safe Houses, please refer to Appendix A.

[3] Sometimes referred to as "mushies" by the locals when drunk, but never when sober; indeed, if the mischievous traveler wishes to provoke a full-scale riot, he simply need shout into a crowded tavern or church, "You're all a load of stupid 'mushies'!"

Ambergris sleep from dawn until dusk, and although the red flags often do indicate the close proximity of mushroom dwellers, they are likely to be resting below ground. Such flags—always found in clumps, except when a single flag marks the doorstep to a house or building[4]—may simply indicate an opening to the network of old sewage conduits and catacombs that have existed since the First Construction Empire presided over by Trillian the Great Banker. (see Ch. 3, "Rulers, Tyrants, and Minor Merchant Barons")

It has been put forth by the noted naturalist and social scientist Loqueem Bender—cousin to the great opera composer Voss Bender (see Ch. 2, "Native Celebrities")—from the bloodstained notes discovered near the sewer duct where he was last seen (see Ch. 15, "Unsolved Mysteries of the City") that the mushroom dwellers have excellent night vision, but that as a consequence of their generations-old sleeping patterns, their eyes can no longer bear any but the weakest sunlight. If true, this intolerance would certainly explain the wide-brimmed floppy gray felt hats they wear during the day (and which, in combination with their short statures, diurnal habits, and long necks, have no doubt given them their eccentric reputation).[5] Bender's notes include fascinating physical details about the "mushroom dwellers," whom he once, during the early days of his research, described as "merry little pranksters": "I find they are remarkably strong, this strength at least partially due to a low center of gravity combined with thick, flat feet, extremely well-developed, almost rootlike leg muscles, and very large yet supple hands." Although it is not advisable to attack a mushroom dweller, or even to defend oneself from an attack (L. Bender, in his later notes, recommends standing quite still if charged by a mushroom dweller), it should be noted that their long, strangely delicate necks will break easily if the traveler can get past the clinging, flailing hands thrown up in defense (and which, coincidentally, may be groping for the traveler's own neck).

It was L. Bender who first conducted credible scientific studies[6]

---

[4] Do Not Enter any such marked house or building. Often, these dwellings will, on closer inspection, prove to contain relatives mourning a late relative still encased in a living-room casket. The mushroom dwellers seem particularly sensitive to the presence of death.

[5] Incidentally, L. Bender posthumously received the Manque Kashmir Award of Achievement from the Morrow Institute of Social Research for "his close friendship with and in-depth studies of the mushroom dwellers." The book of his notes published by the Institute is on sale at the aforementioned Borges Bookstore.

[6] Previously, there had only been such romantic renderings as a slight description

of the mushroom dwellers' two main preoccupations: mushroom harvesting and the daily cleansing of Ambergris. L. Bender discovered that the ritual cleaning of the city's streets provided them rich leavings with which to propagate their midnight crop of fungus. "Although the mushrooms are grown underground for the most part, and may reach heights of four feet, weights of 60 pounds," L. Bender wrote, "on occasion a trail of mushrooms—like a vein of rich gold or silver—will burst out from the netherworld to riot in a spray of mauve, azure, yellow ochre, violet, and dead man's gray upon the walls of a merchant's pavilion or across the ceiling of a mortician's practice."

L. Bender's studies further proved that the mushroom dwellers' nightly mastery of city refuse was due not to incredible efficiency so much as to a large population—they simply exist in greater numbers than previously thought by so-called "experts," much as a single cockroach seen implies the existence of a dozen cockroaches unseen. Second, by studying the few civil records still in existence, as well as the 30-year writings of the obsessed statistician Marmey Gort,[7] L. Bender discovered that over hundreds of years Ambergris' citizens had altered their patterns of consumption and refuse disposal to accommodate easy pickup by the mushroom dwellers

The locals' treatment of the mushroom dwellers varies drastically between valley residents and city residents (see Ch. 9, "Cultural Differences Between Valley and City, and How to Exploit These Differences to Get Better Bargains"), no doubt because the city folk have spun a complex series of legends around the mush-

---

in Voss Bender's famous opera "The Refraction of Light in a Prison" sung by the distraught, suicidal Frange when he looks out of his window to exclaim:

> What mystery fringed by dusky dawn
> has given the soul of misery form?
> Has the face of love come stumbling
> crippled and confused to mewl 'neath
> a sneering moon? No, 'tis only the elders
> of the city eager to cleanse, and pray.

More descriptive is this melodramatic passage from Dradin Kashmir's semi-autobiographical short novel *Dradin, In Love:* "Positioned as he was at the mouth of the alley, Dradin felt as though he were spying on a secret, forbidden world. Did [the mushroom dwellers] dream of giant mushrooms, gray caps agleam with the dark light of a midnight sun? Did they dream of a world lit only by the phosphorescent splendor of their charges?"

[7] Gort kept minutely detailed records of city denizens' sanitary habits, including their storage of refuse. A typical entry reads: "X—outhouse use increase: av. 7x/day (5 min. av. ea.); note: garbage output up 3x for week: connex?"

room dwellers, while the valley folk, who rarely see them, know them only from the watered-down versions of such stories.[8]

These legends run the gamut from the inspired to the inane, although the traveler will, as mentioned previously, find it hard going to pry even a word or two from the lips of locals. Some folk believe the mushroom dwellers whisper and plot among themselves in a secret language so old that no one else, even in the far, far Occident, can speak it. Others weave tales of an origin in the subterranean caves and tunnels beneath Ambergris, inferring that they are not of human stock. Still others claim they are escaped convicts who gathered in the darkness many years ago and now shun the light from guilt over their forebears' crimes. The sailors on the docks have their own stories of mushroom dwellers as defilers of priests and murderers of young women to provide nutrients for their crop of fungus. The poor and under-educated spread rumors that the mushroom dwellers have supernatural powers— that newts, golliwogs, slugs, and salamanders follow in their path while above bats, nighthawks, and whippoorwills shadow them. And, even among the literati, especially among the Shortpin Group led by the noted author Sirin, irresponsible gossip has revived the old chestnut that the mushroom dwellers can "control our minds simply by spreading certain mushroom spores throughout the city's public places, where they may be inhaled all unknowing by the general populace, this inhalation soon followed by an unnatural fascination with fungus, and, of course, an unwavering devotion to the mushroom dwellers."[9]

However, the most ridiculous version of their origin postulates that they once belonged to a guild of janitors, ordained by the Priests of the Seven-Edged Star when that order ruled the city so many centuries ago (see Ch. 21, "Conflicting Religions") and that, during the lawless Days of the Burning Sun, they became feral, seeking haven underground as a desperate remedy for unemployment and the persecution meted out to public workers as a form of protest against the government. (see Ch. 1, "A History of the City")

---

[8] As recently as three years ago, a mushroom dweller that wandered into the valley, presumably by mistake, was lynched by an angry mob of tradesmen. (Coincidentally, short travelers, defined as "under four feet six inches tall," are advised not to visit the valley without several sets of corroborating identification.)

[9] L. Bender seems to have disproved this once and for all in his final set of notes, when he writes, "Not only did I allow them to sprinkle my entire naked body with the spores, but I readily breathed them in. At no point did I lose control of my mind. At no point did I fall asleep, or come under the spell of a hypnotic trance." Thus, the spores appear to be a friendly form of ritual welcome.

While this theory provides an explanation for the mushroom dwellers' need to "cleanse" the city of refuse, it ignores the blatantly spiritual nature of their many rituals.

In any event, anecdotal evidence from rare eyewitnesses (including two of the compilers of this book) suggests that the city folk secretly worship the mushroom dwellers,[10] setting out plates of eggs and moist bread or mugs of milksop for them at night, while some young girls and boys, strangely unafraid, have been known to feed them by hand as they would pigeons or squirrels. For the traveler interested in a more scholarly pursuit of the mushroom dweller myth, the L. Bender Memorial Museum, until recently kept up by his wife, Galendrace Bender,[11] provides a good starting and ending point. The museum contains the actual bloodstained notes discovered near L. Bender's last known location. It also displays items L. Bender stole from an underground mushroom dweller religious site, including such enigmatic objects as an ancient umbrella, a duck embryo preserved in ether, a mop even more ancient than the umbrella, and the steering wheel to a now-extinct motored vehicle.

As with most attractions in Ambergris, however, the careful traveler should not visit the museum after dark. To reiterate the safety precautions set out in Ch. 13, the wise tourist should avoid the following areas after nightfall: the Religious Quarter, the Industrial District, the Majori Merchant District, the Hoegbotton Merchant District (save for the Hoegbotton Safe Houses, half-price during the monsoon season), the docks, and the old bureaucratic center. Mushroom dwellers are notoriously near-sighted despite their fabled night vision, and have been known to mistake even the best-dressed gentleman as an exotic form of refuse, fit to be processed and dragged underground.

If confronted by mushroom dwellers (they often travel in groups of fifty or more), safe places (in addition to the Hoegbotton Safe Houses) include: (1) the top floors of tall buildings, especially

---

[10] Two editors, it should be noted, preferred the phrase "secretly fear," followed by "setting out placatory plates."

[11] Sadly, Ms. Bender, a noted specialist on fungus reproduction, did not long survive her husband's death. She disappeared one month before this revised guide went to press, leaving behind a letter in which she indicated she had decided to live in the catacombs among the mushroom dwellers. A postscript to the letter which read in part, "I believe the mushroom dwellers are doomed angles [angels?] who have lost their wings, their position, and even any knowledge of their glorious past, and now consigned to a lugubrious state of semi-awareness," does not say much for her current mental state and it is only to be hoped that she will indeed someday emerge from the catacombs. [Ms. Bender was a frequent contributor to the Ambergris travel guide—she contributed greatly to this very article—and her expertise will be sorely missed.—Eds.]

buildings that do not possess dumbwaiters or air ducts; (2) the top-most branches of tall trees; mushroom dwellers are mediocre climbers at best and will, at dawn, forget their prey and return below ground, allowing the traveler ample opportunity to escape any light-sensitive sentry they might leave behind; (3) the center of large groups of fellow tourists (groups of locals may be inclined to give up the unsuspecting traveler).

The traveler planning a vacation to Ambergris this year should not be unduly alarmed by the information set out above. In fact, there have been far fewer tourist fatalities this year than in the previous three years combined, no doubt due in part to the extensive citywide bloodletting that occurred at last year's Festival of the Freshwater Squid (see Ch. 5). For this reason, it is the opinion of the editors of this guide[12] that even travelers who too closely investigate the apparent absence of sanitation workers in Ambergris will enjoy a pleasant stay.

---

[12] Six in agreement, two in abstention.

Notes on
Exhibit H

*This story predates my novella "The Hoegbotton Guide to
the Early History of Ambergris by Duncan Shriek," and
provided me with a rough blueprint for the approach I
would take in that work. In "Exhibit," I was mostly concerned with having a bit of ironic fun, and it shows in the
writing. Finally, I'd found at least one way to express my
sense of humor in my fiction.*

*Many of the themes and details first set out here made
their way into parts of "The Early History" and other
Ambergris stories. "Exhibit H" also marked the beginning
of my experimentation with using traditionally nonfiction
forms to create fiction. Several critics have speculated
that these experiments on my part come from a close
reading of Borges. Although I enjoy Borges, the true
influence here is the historian John Julius Norwich,
whose masterful Byzantine and Norman histories dazzled me not only with their ability to string fascinating
details off of a strong central storyline, but with footnotes
that are prose poems of rare vigor and wit.*

Black Duke Blues

WHEN THE BLUES IS IN YOU, THEY'S IN YOU LIKE
a muskrat always got mud under its claws. You can't never
get the blues out no how, no way . . .

I'm my Papa's son borned in 1923 as black as the devil though
my Mama's Creole: Maria an Elijah Washington. Papa, he fished
for crawdads an catfish an carpentried some for neighbors an even
made a little flatbottom boat to pole round the swamp, fast an quiet
like. Mama, she washed dishes at Belezar's Diner, a low-down
waterin hole though course "No Niggers Allowed" cept in the
kitchens. That place ain't even a memory now. They's raisin chickens o'er its bones.

Mama's black hair—I member that most of all. Black hair
shinin like the mornin light over them cypress trees. Even as a ol
woman, she always had her hair down to her waist like a live thing.
Young no one woulda thought lookin at her hows she'd brought
four lives into the world, or that the Good Lord took three back so
early it make the heart cry to think of it.

Grieves me thinkin bout it. Didn have no graveyard to call ours
—just the First Baptist down the road a mile, an us in our two-room
stilt-wood house bout thirty miles from Nawlins, so my three sisters
was buried out back the house under three wood crosses with three

names carved in em: Cassandra an Naomi an Maria (after my Mama, course). None lived long—the one lived longest might've felt the sun on her cheek no more'n three years. My Mama learned me they names when she forgot an talk bout em, then a shadow fell on her, as if she'd taken em all back in her an took that darkness too.

Fore Papa an I gone to Nawlins, I'd go out at dusk an sit in the grass an talk to my sisters. They'd talk back in they's own way an I felt close to them. Close to God, y'know?

Papa fished the Delta the whole week fore what he call his "carpentry exp'ditions" to Nawlins an he'd come wake me sometimes fore dawn put a big hand over my mouth an say, "Boy, you keep quiet now an don you wake your mama an we gonna go fishin."

I liked that more than anythin cept his stories bout Nawlins an he tol me these after polin the boat out to anchor near mud flats with big-clawed crabs pokin heads outta holes to look at us. Cold— man, it'd be so cold, but I didn mind. Papa'd sit line tight tween his fingers an tell me bout Nawlins.

What a fine sight that was those mornins, my Papa tellin me stories. Cause you know he was a big man, an I'd look at him an the power in his hands on the line an his shoulders an the simple way he be settin his weight. I'd look fresh at him an forget the times he got drunk an took to moods like Mama an me wasn't even there. I'd forget Mama cussin him for spendin her money. An I can see Mama seein what I saw those mornins, cause otherwise she'd've left him. She saw his comfort with his body an how he could be kind an gentle with his strength. Like when he tell me bout them blues clubs in Nawlins.

Why, one time Papa come trampin in on a Sunday night in dead winter shakin frost off that big ol coat of his an he sat down side me at the fire. He puts his arm round me an he says, whisperin like they's this secret he got to tell me. "Benjamin," he says, "you know where I been?" No, I don an that's the truth. "Ben," he says an breathes on me so as I'm gigglin I near fade away from the spirits an garlic. "Nawlins!" he says. "That city, son, she's just bustin out at the seams with song. You can't go a foot or more an not see for yourself some club stuck in the wall, the music spillin out the window, tween the bricks, the mortar, through the wood. You jest can't stop it, Ben," that's what he'd say. His eyes get all wide when he speaks an that's the only time I ever seen his eyes like that cept when he'd be at the bottle or times when he'd look at Mama.

Well, sir, by age twelve I want Nawlins somethin bad, the kind of bad that's a itch in your joints an the tips of your fingers. I'm workin at Belezar's peelin taters an bussin tables an I was sick hearin the other busboys talk bout that city!

Comin home from the diner, I'd pick up a stick an make it a guitar. I'd give the most rip-roarin, clean an sorrowful preformance this good Earth ever done seen—I'd blast them mockinbirds from the sky an set the dirt road aflamin.

If Mama's with me, I'd be thirty miles away, imaginin streets of gold an rich folk dressed fancy in tux n tails, an all I had to do was go there an be rich too. I must've thought poorly of Papa, for goin to Nawlins an us still bad off an soon worse still. Demon alcohol I tol myself—the Devil's work sure, an I tol myself I'd never touch a drop though I since touched much worse this side of death an got scars to show for it.

Mama was dead set again Nawlins. She didn see me havin nothin to do with "That city of devils, un barrio de tentación," as she'd say, givin Papa an evil eye, an eye full of sadness. "No place for a man neither," she'd say.

Papa didn used to cross her. When he got mad he'd just be all quiet cause she held some power over him he couldn break. Voodoo? Maybe one time I thought that. Maybe. But now I tell you this true: I know he loved her somethin painful. Like he loved my three sisters buried in the earth, God rest they souls.

So I might've run off an gone to Nawlins myself but the mornin I turn thirteen Papa wakes me early an he says, "Son, you n me, we goin to the city for your birthday, cause you almost a man now." He grin real big an I grin back an then he gives me a look an says, "But be real quiet-like, or your mama'll hear an then we's in a world o trouble. Understan?"

We slipped out onto the ol dirt road leadin to the diner an to Nawlins after that. Cold an windy but we walked that mile to the bus stop both gigglin like we'd fooled the Devil herself.

"Yessir, you gonna learn bout life, Ben," Papa said, dancin round me, his faded ol jacket dancin with him. "Now you gonna hear real music!"

Two of Papa's friends waited at the bus stop. The small one, Jon L. Jonson, had on a worn brown suit with a ripped pocket an black shoes so dusty I felt like spit shinin em. Jon L. had a face like somebody made him suck a lemon his whole life. Papa n me, we'd fish with him a time or two an come back to Mama for Sunday dinner. He worked pickin cotton an his hands was white with scars.

He'd never been friendly fore but when he saw me his ol lemon face broke a smile so's I could see his horsey yella teeth. Givin my hand a shake, he says, "Happy Birthday, Ben! Happy Birthday!"

The next man, Charlie MacIntyre, was somethin else again—the "blackest Scotsman," Papa call him. Big as Papa but walkin funny. Straight as a post so when he walked you'd look at his chest or face an think he was sittin still. He wore a rake's hat an a big overcoat so's no one could tell he was muscle or gone fat. Everythin he did an touched was slick. Had it from Papa he knew people could help you—all kinds of people with all kinds of help, if you get me.

Charlie'd seen Papa an me walkin up an he flicked the butt of his cigarette onto the road an ground it out with a turn of his heel.

"Long time, Charlie," Papa said, seemin smaller as they shook hands. "Long time." Strange now I think on it, like he wasn't saying hello at all.

But Charlie just says, "Yeah, a long time," an he grins so we'd all look at his perfect white teeth. "This your youngun?" he says.

Papa nodded so Charlie leaned over an shook my hand. Sweaty hand. He smelled like soap an breath mints.

"A pleasure," he said an all I said back was "Yessir" cause the man frightened me.

Papa an Jon L. an Charlie talked together till that bus came kickin up dirt. It stopped alright but only when Charlie an Papa stood in the road. A wreck that bus but I don care if the windows busted out an Spanish moss be hangin on the seats cause it's takin me to Nawlins.

We took seats in the back an the bus started up again wheezin like an ol man.

Papa an me, we grinned at each other an he squeezed my arm. Ain't ever gonna be able to tell you if I was more happy to be goin to Nawlins, or proud to be with my Papa, who took so much joy of it.

I held the bar on the seat in front an watched out the busted window. Thought I could smell the sea. Could've been papermill an I would've smelled the sea. I was watchin the swamps white with herons an how the land turned quick to oak trees an farms with posts n wire round em. Men was walkin to work in the early mornin light, shadow men with shovels over they shoulders an hats down low over they faces. Walked like the dead an none bothered us a look as the bus run past em. Maybe I shoulda been sorry for them poor souls goin to work on a Saturday, but all I done is laugh, cause my blood was singin an I felt powerful strong inside. Like nothin an nobody gonna touch me.

Man, but Charlie didn like that bus! Not with them smart clothes. He kept brushin his pants—maybe dust was gettin on em. Maybe. He'd look out the window, then back at Papa an Jon, not payin mind. He talked to Papa most while Jon L. sat back like me.

Charlie just couldn shut up. "Are you sure you want your youngun with you?"

"It's his birthday," Papa'd say.

"But why, why take him with you," Charlie'd say.

"Ain't gonna hurt nothin Charlie," my Papa'd argue. "Do us our business an him in the corner."

Charlie'd scowl an say, "Can't know that, Elijah. You shouldn't have done it because you can't ever know that for sure."

"It's done now. I'd best bring him fore he come on his own," Papa'd say.

The rest I don't recall. Too busy lookin out the window. Soon, they wasn't no more farms—just trees an then little grocery stores an then we was in Nawlins.

Nawlins bout ten in the mornin in 1936. Spring, but winter nough for the cold to be hangin bout.

Down street after street, dirty with people. More folks I'd never seen: white, black, cajun, creole, indian. An the smell! My eyes watered so I couldn't hardly see if them streets was gold. (They wasn't.) Such a smell! Only time worse was a day in '75 when the floods came an opened all the crypts an as they say, "Sent fayette's bones home to France."

It smelled as if every man an woman an child been smokin pissin an screwin all at a time every which way. Why, they's even lettin chickens an hogs peck an root in the garbage, like at home. Some of them chickens almost got run over by the autocars all shiny an slick an more kinds an colors than I ever fore seen. Buildings was tall an some fancied up with iron lace balconies, but they wasn't *that* tall. Didn hear music neither an Papa said, "It's early, Ben, an so maybe I made it up too big, but you jest wait till night an see if I ain't right, boy."

Maybe I shoulda tol Papa we should go back on the next bus cause Nawlins wasn't worth Mama's gettin mad. Maybe if I'd known, I'd done that thing, but dirty as Nawlins was, it was more dirt than I'd yet known. More everythin. An I didn want to let Papa down.

When we get off the bus Jon shook Papa's hand nodded to me

an took off like his ass on fire. Papa said Jon gonna meet us that night, at a club called *The Fresh Bucket O' Blood*, which don sound like no blues joint to me. Which anyways left Papa an Charlie an me at the bus depot the white clerk lookin at us like maybe we'd let them chickens an hogs on the street. Cause it ain't no mistake when I tell you them boys hated to see a black man in town an havin fun an I ain't sure it ain't still true.

So I asks Papa where we was goin an Papa said, "To Charlie's place, till the bar opens. You gonna need sleep if you're up all night."

Off we went, Papa walkin like he always did, big steps, an Charlie glidin along an me on Papa's arm. Down cobblestone streets an horse n traps folks never gettin outta the way till almost too late. That far in the city, with the crowds, they wasn't as many autocars but they sure was garbage all over. Still is; Nawlins can't never get clean. But now I'm seein vendors with loads of food, better than anythin at the diner: hot sausage, watermelon, blue-berry pie, catfish steaks. Even a few musicians singin or playin guitar for pennies. When I saw them street musicians, my heart jumped outta my chest, I tell you.

Other folks sold clothes or haircuts or horseshoes or fortunes. Sailors in from the docks was everywheres, even some men of the navy, lookin smart in white-face-on-white-uniforms with fancy caps. Ladies, too, faces painted, they dresses so low I blushed an got all excited.

"Look but don touch," Papa says when he sees me starin. "Unless'un you want it to fall off an your balls turn blue."

Charlie laughed an Papa laughed an I looked the other way.

Soon we come to Charlie's place: top floor of an ol brick flop-house in the Negro District tween two hostels with signs read "Negro Accommodations Available." Could tell it was Negroes Only without the sign cause they wasn't a white face for a mile. We'd be pushin through crowds of white an black an brown an then they'd only be black an brown an one or two white faces, lookin like fallen moons in among the rest.

You could hear a trickle of music comin from Charlie's place, but from the outside the building looked tired as the rest. Went up in a elevator almost didn get us there. Somebody cursed us as we was goin up, but quick pulled his fool head back inside his door-way. Water dripped somewheres an echoed down the hall. Charlie n Papa was real quiet an Papa shot glances round like he was guilty of somethin. Charlie looked whitish round the edges.

Charlie's digs inside was a big empty loft with a shiny wood floor, bedroom off to the left. A whole lot of folks crowded round pool tables gamblin an drinkin. An some of them folk played music. That made the place light up, through the smoke of cigars an cigarettes puffing: guitars an fiddles an instruments I didn know cause I was so young to the world.

Soon as they shut the door behind, Charlie n Papa got cool an relaxed.

"This's the life, boy," Papa said, hitchin up his pants.

"You know it, Elijah. I can agree with you there," Charlie said, takin off his hat an overcoat an settin em on a chair by the door. Under, he had on a fancy white shirt with a bow tie. He had a small gun tucked into his pants in back an the shirt pulled out to hide it.

"You wanta rest, go ahead," Papa said. "Charlie an me, we gonna try the cards. So you jest do whatever you want."

But I didn hear him—I was watchin the musicians. I come on over an sit with em. They was three an listenin to em now I'd not think they was anythin special but back then not yet a man, listenin, they smoked the joint. They's sittin in these big ol chairs an rockin up an down keepin balanced how I don't know. A cat on the bass, one on the twelve-string an a fiddler. The twelve-stringer had a wicked pick, mother o pearl an he'd toss it hind his back, see, tween riffs an catch it lefthanded. Played slow, too, real slow, drawin the notes down an out so you could hear every one an think on it. Torture an pleasure all together. The bass player was a small man with a barrel chest played everythin fast to push again the twelve-string. The fiddler, well, he was sure nough drunk but walked that line with bare-bones raw playin.

That was the first time. First time I ever heard "Last Fair Deal Gone Down," "Hellhound on My Trail" an "Cross Road Blues." They played Nawlins style mixing in the blues an gospel an cajun an the singer playin the twelve-string his voice was like the sound of wood bein sandpapered smooth.

I tell you I can still member what they played note for note. Couldn't forget it cause it woke me right up an got into my skin so's I couldn get free. They's singin bout *my life* you unnerstan but singin bout Papa's life too an everybody else.

I tell you true, I was high on that music an the smoke an the smell of spirits. I'd've called Papa to listen but Papa an Charlie was busy at that poker table an all I heard was cussin.

The music stopped an the twelve-string singer takes out a towel an wipes the sweat off his arms an face. Stubby gray beard an eyes like black marbles.

He looks down at me an says, "Name's Jimmy Barber. You like the music?"

"Yessir," I say back. "I wanta play like you do."

At that the fiddler laughed an says, "Teach em, Barber boy. Teach em to play."

Jimmy says in a quiet voice, "Don't be givin the boy ideas." An to me: "You about twelve?"

"Thirteen."

"Thirteen then," he says an laughs. He says, "Well, you gotta be a lot bigger just to hold this guitar an you gotta play it long an do it for life."

An to that I said, "I been practicin with a stick."

They all three laugh real loud an long at that. Bet they tol that one over a hundred times.

"Imagine that," Jimmy Barber said. "The boy's been practicin with a stick. An what's that you been practicin then, boy?"

So I decided that, yessir, I'd take a nap after all seein as they was makin fun. As I'm walkin into the bedroom, I hear them start up behind me again, smooth as if they never stopped.

The bed had stains on it an no sheets an springs bout to quit. I didn care. I really was gettin tired.

But, Lord, when I slept, I dreamt I was back in the First Baptist Church with its gray walls an paint peelin off the ceiling an that ol altar, smaller than the big wooden cross on the wall hind it. Dark an empty was that church, with the sunlight comin sleepy thick through the window.

I says it was empty an I mean it was empty cept right in front, ten pews up from where I was sittin, sat my three dead sisters, all in a row. They was as old as if still alive an growin an dressed in white dresses with red bows. Gigglin an carryin on while my blood near froze in my veins. Cause they dead an I know they dead but I can't wake up though I sure want to.

They must've seen me cause they stop carryin on an look round an when they turn I see they faces, which had no eyes. No eyes at all an yet they must've seen me cause the tallest the eldest Maria looks at me with them blank eye holes an says, "What you doin here, boy? You don't need to be here yet. An where's our pa?"

Scared, I can't move can't wake up an as I sit there a wave of pure mortal sorrow come washin over me like chrysanth'mum petals opening an I was asleep again an they was gone an all they'd left behind, those sisters of mine, was an emptiness inside of me that I didn know what to do with. Why didn I know it then?

Well, sir, when I woke I knew right way most everybody left.

The music wasn't playin an the windows was dark. Rubbin my eyes, hungry, I got up an walked into the poker room. Papa an Charlie still sat there an a couple other players but everybody else'd left. Charlie looked worried.

"Hey, Ben," Papa said when he saw me. "You brought your papa luck today," an he flashes me a roll of bills an a shadow hides his face an makes it skull-narrow an I thought I heard one last chord from the twelve-string guitar player but he wasn't there no more.

Then Papa gave me a hug an everythin was good again.

Papa turned to Charlie an said, "This gonna be smooth with them?"

"Yeah," Charlie said, "I'll take care of it."

But Charlie was sweatin like a condemned man at sight of the noose an there wasn't no smile, no flash of teeth.

I'd be lyin if I tell you there's anythin like night in Nawlins. Daylight puts a lid on happiness an sin an when the night comes, that lid comes right off an everythin was hidden spills out an everythin clear is muddy an everythin bad's good. An it still that way even now, but not so much. Not so much cause the world's smaller an we got our TVs an computers. It's like I say: you get all them music college grads studyin the blues an what it comes down to is this: you take away the mystery an it's just a couple chords an a old man with scars on his fingers. But if you play an play right an you don't think bout what you be doin, so it comes out of your heart, then it's spiritual. Then it's close to somethin like that night in 1936 in Nawlins when I was only thirteen an with my Papa my hand tight in his. My hand always gonna be in his hand.

We walk out onto the street an the buildings didn look so bad all lit up with lantern an candle an lectric light. Street was so crowded I was bumpin up against some folk's back. Lots of feet an lots of legs an got my share of shoves, too.

Papa let me buy a meat pie an I ate like it was goin to be my last meal. Everybody was playin music or prowlin it seems to me—if they wasn't prowlin for drugs, they's prowlin for women an if they wasn't prowlin for either then they was lookin for some kind of trouble.

Soon we was at *The Fresh Bucket*, light streamin out from the beat-up windows an turnin the sidewalk gold. Music come out too, like somethin distant closin fast. People crowded the front pushin to get in.

"Talk to him now, Elijah," Charlie said to Papa. "I do not want any accidents occurring because of your youngun."

Papa didn look happy cause of Charlie's disrespect an he turn to me an gave my hand a tug.

"Now Ben," Papa says to me, "this ain't no place for a kid, so's you got to stay by me an mind me. Or we gonna go home early."

"Yessir," I said an tol myself if I was goin to talk to musicians in there I sure as hell wasn't gonna say I been practicing with a stick!

Inside, couldn't find room to sit, not even hardly stand. Smilin men with beards an blank-eyed stares stood round the bar an watched the stage to the right. Ten, eleven tables'd been stuck between bar an stage. Men an women stood an sat around em, some white an some black—at separate tables. Just cause it was a mixed club didn mean nothin. Tables still had to be separate.

Lord, was there ladies, real ladies, in dresses: green an black an red an blue, sequined an plain, lookin so fine. The men, some of em, wore suits. The sweat an perfume an spirits was thick nough to leave a taste on your tongue.

Couldn't see no band from that doorway: just hear it. High an sexy-like—saxophone believe it was, an chilled my skin to hear it. Smooth, sweet sound. Too sweet. Stopped dead in my shoes, stood there an drank it all up. I'd still be there if Papa'd not dragged me to a table where Jon sat; he'd got there long fore we did.

Charlie says to Jon, "Elijah won the poker game an the money he didn take from me, the rest of those thieves got." Showed his teeth an made like he wasn't angry. Charlie says, "I think Elijah should pay for the first round."

"Fair enough," said Jon, cause Jon ain't goin to turn down no free drink.

Papa, he nodded an slapped me on the shoulder as he got up. Leavin me to Jon an Charlie.

Jon said, "Enjoyin your first time in New Orleans?"

Fore I can say anythin, Charlie's in my face pullin my chair toward him an I'm starin into his trickster eyes.

"Benjamin," Charlie said, bein real precise. Most precise fella I ever met, Charlie. Charlie says, "You watch out tonight. You just watch yourself. You stay close to your father and that way you can't make trouble for anybody, even by accident. You understand? And if anything happens, you run the hell away."

He said it just that way, dottin his "t's" an such.

Me, I just nodded an said, "Yessir," rememberin that gun of his an gettin scared. All I wanted was to sit with Papa an listen to the music. I didn care bout nothin else.

After Charlie's bein precise, Jon didn want no part of talkin.

Charlie, he tried to light a cigarette, but his fingers shook so much he stopped tryin.

Papa came back with the drinks an Jon, Charlie an him start talkin again as if I was a ghost. Which I didn mind. If I sat up in my chair I could see the musicians. The saxophone player had gone an now they was a vocal group, big band stuff. All five had dressed to the nines with red bow ties an looked good. An, brother, could they sing! They sang like they was on fire an tryin to take us all down with em or they lowered they's voices for a love song an all the women in the room got real quiet an turned from they husbands to watch. Voices silky an smooth, soarin an dippin. I could feel it tinglin through me, though sad thing is I couldn't never sing like that, nor could want to cause it was too happy a song.

The trouble, well, the trouble was there long fore we walked into *The Fresh Bucket,* but I didn see it till after them singers left the stage cause that was when the three men walked up to Papa an Charlie. Jon'd gone outside an now it didn look like he'd be comin back.

Those three men made me poor lookin at em, with slicked-back hair, slick suits, an gator shoes. They'd a dark look to em an spoke in harsh voices that cut the smoke an music. I didn notice em till one came up to the table an bumped into me. I come face to face with that third button on his suit, polished an dark green like his shoes. Papa put a hand on my shoulder but the one bumped into me was talkin to Charlie.

He says to Charlie, "Last month this happened. We've got no more time for it, okay?"

Charlie unbuttoned the first button on his shirt. I saw his hand move till it rest at his side, fingers tucked through his belt loop. Music faded right away for me an everythin seemed sharper than fore. I could see the crystal-clear ice glitterin in Charlie's honey glass an that yellow sweat stain cross the front of his shirt an the ragged edge of nail on his left thumb.

I looked at Papa an Papa looked at me. Lookin at him was nough to rip my heart out an his too. His eyes kept tellin me he was sorrier than I could imagine that he'd brought me here.

The one Charlie kept callin Donnie pushed Charlie down in his chair when he tried to get up.

Charlie pointed to Papa an said, "He's the problem. He's the whole problem. He wouldn't give me his share."

Now, I know this is a lie an Papa said he didn know what Charlie was talkin bout but he'd like to take his boy an leave an let Charlie figure it out with such fine gentlemen hisself.

But Donnie pushed Papa back in his seat, like he had with Charlie an I already tol you Papa's strong, so I'm scared. I didn move cause I didn dare, even if my heart was beatin in time to the chords of the twelve-string guitar player that now start strummin from up on the stage.

Donnie asked Papa if Charlie'd tol the truth an when Papa'd says nothin he kinda hisses, "I said, is this lying cheat of a nigger telling the truth? Is Charlie on the up-and-up?"

Donnie was workin hisself up into a rage like a musician workin up to a solo an Papa kinda stuttered an said, "No, sir. No. I give my share to Charlie an he know it."

Donnie, slick hair an switchblade eyes, he turned to Charlie an said, "How'm a supposed to choose? Am I gonna have to break some bones?"

But the Good Lord got different plans for him, cause Charlie took out his gun an shot Donnie in the forehead. A dot of blood no bigger than a dime an yet Donnie go fallin across the table an made folks at other tables set to screamin.

Donnie's friends pulled guns an shot Charlie. He got a shot off, but not fore they got him good. He tried to crawl, but he only got a couple feet an his head hit the floor an he was dead. Donnie's two friends took off runnin for the door an no one tried to stop em.

Papa let go his grip on my shoulder just then. Papa sat limp in his chair, his left arm danglin an his eyes rolled up in his head. Blood on his chest. Even a fool like me seen that blood.

"Papa?" I says as the music start swirlin up inside my head an the smoke risin to cover everythin an my screams risin too, to cover what I didn know. People makin a fuss an gettin the hell out, but I can't hear that. I just see my Papa dead on the chair an I'm thinkin I hate Nawlins, hate her like a mangy dog, hate her an hate Charlie an glad Charlie's dead an Mama was right, Nawlins no place for boy nor man. How I wished I'd never come to Nawlins, but it was too late. Too late.

But that wasn't the end, cause as I watched the blood drip from the bullet holes in Papa's chest an I'm wailin like a baby, a strange thing happen, a strange an terrible thing. They's the silence in my head, but then they's a sound, crashin through like a runaway train. It was the guitar player, who'd kept on singin an playin like he wasn't no part of this world. In his own space, set aside.

I looked up from my Papa's body an I saw him, eyes shut, playin his guitar like it was his lady love an the world could die in fire an ice an he'd keep on playin. He was the oldest man I'd ever seen, wrinkled as Methusalah out from the Bible an blacker than delta mud comin down the Mississippi, his eyes lookin out at me but not seein me. The light come off the shiny wood like he was playin a rainbow or a handful of stars he'd grabbed outta the sky. An the music, oh man, that music I'd loved but seemed so light an bright an full of hope at Charlie's place . . . well, I heard its underbelly then, its darkness an despair an loss. An I knew then, truly knew, sweet Jesus, what the blues was about. Finally. Forever.

I could hear my sisters' voices in that music, in the spaces tween the notes, an I knew Papa didn come to Nawlins on account of worryin bout money or to escape them graves dug out back of our house. He'd come to Nawlins to remember, cause there they was, in the music: the voices of our dead wellin up with the voices of all the other ghosts, my Papa's voice just nother chord in a painsong played by the oldest man in the world.

How could I do anythin but listen to the man play my blues? While the blood on Papa's shirt dried an I tried to hug the life back into him.

Police never found Papa's killers, but then they never looked too hard. Mama an me never did find out xactly what Papa got hisself into. But we laid him in the earth next to the graves of my three sisters. We did it cause Mama loved him though she couldn't forgive him puttin me in harm's way. But Papa didn mean harm to me, I know that. He just wanted his piece of Nawlins.

Mama an me, we moved in with Mama's family up Shreveport way. It wasn't so bad. In Shreveport I learnt to play the guitar an I did a whole lot of growin up an when I was grown I traveled the whole world singin the blues an I earned the name "Black Duke." (That's nother story, for nother day.)

An I love Nawlins. Lord help me, I wish I could say it wasn't so, but I'm old now an I been many strange places an seen many strange sights, an I don't have to lie to no one no more. Nawlins' a dirty, piss-filled, cum-smeared city who don't care much for no one, but She gave me the music an I can't leave her for no other woman. Cause when they say my music haunts em in all those magazines an such, that's on account of Nawlins. That's Papa an my dead sisters an the ol guitar player hauntin me still. I can't put them in the earth, not when I hear em every time I play my guitar on that stage.

Cause on that stage you got to tell the truth or you dies a little each night.

Notes on
Black Duke Blues

I studied dozens of interview transcripts before writing this story. Some blues musicians spoke in a rough, uneducated way, using a simple vocabulary. Others, like B. B. King, had very sophisticated speech patterns. In the first draft of the story, I imitated the King syntax . . . only to have my trusted first readers — representing a spectrum of racial and cultural identities — complain that the narrator sounded too educated for an old bluesman from the Delta. I don't usually make major story decisions by committee, but I had to admit the draft lacked something. So I retooled it, stripping it down, and worked at using a "dialect" more in keeping with bluesmen like Muddy Waters.

"Black Duke Blues" won a Florida Individual Artist Fellowship and fooled at least one member of the judging panel into believing that I was African American. Reader reaction to the story has been positive, although a few thought the dialect was too over the top. I remain conflicted on that issue. I do know that I have no doubts about the core story: a boy coming of age through a tragedy.

The Emperor's Reply

I

THE LAST INCAN EMPEROR, TUPAC AMARU, HAD neither eaten nor drunk for three days in his tower above Vilcapampa, the Spaniards neglecting him as they tightened their control over the city. But now, over the ghostly moans of the dying, Tupac heard footsteps on the stairs outside his room.

It was a large, drafty room, for the invaders had stripped it of everything except a chair and the burnished salt birch floor, which they could not carry away with them. They had bound Tupac Amaru to the chair with rough hemp, positioning him near the only window. Outside, the Sun God Inti, father of the divine messenger, the hummingbird, faded in the west. In the courtyard below, the Spaniards had begun to slaughter llamas and alpacas, their screams not unlike those of his nobles from the days and nights before.

But he remained calm, even as he had remained calm when, on the second day of his imprisonment, he had seen the likeness of his son Hualpa—whom he had sent into southern exile five days before—in the clefts of rock and shadow.

Despite, or perhaps because of, the numbness in his limbs, the burning thirst, his son's image had become sharper, etched into the land with a permanence that mocked Tupac's own failing strength.

Ichnoti and Tuectolt formed his son's eyes: turquoise lakes pooling on a hilly shelf outside the city's walls. Tupac had taken Hualpa there in the summers to swim, for the lakes remained icy cold even during drought. The sight of his son diving deep, fearless, and then surfacing, pushing effortlessly up against the cold, hard weight of water had made the Emperor flush with pride.

He heard the footsteps again, much closer, the sound coming to him through the rock and wood like a premonition of disaster.

His son's mouth was a smile formed by the union of two rivers, the Bilcapampa and the Nuexcan. At the conjoining where rapids raged they had fished for gar and trout. His nose was a slope of granite worn down by erosion. Hualpa had often smelled of sweet plums plucked without permission from his mother's orchard, his poncho stained with their juice. How fleet of foot his son had been under the towers of Vilcapampa! How quick to learn!

The footsteps paused outside his door. He closed his eyes and prayed to Inti for his son's safety.

As the door opened, twilight settled over the city.

II

Captain Gaspar de Sotelo entered the Emperor's room with a priest at his elbow, a dour Dominican carrying a crucifix and a bottle of holy water. Behind them strode two swarthy soldiers. The gleam of gold had eclipsed the pupils of the soldiers' eyes until their level gaze was the distillation and reflection of gold and everything that passed across their field of vision was sifted through a sieve of gold. They stood at attention to either side of the Emperor's chair, their swords clanging against muddy armor.

In Castilian Spanish, the Captain said, "We have established control over Vilcapampa. We have routed the armies of your allies." He paused for emphasis, his gaze darting toward the window, then continued: "I am sorry, Emperor, but we must find your son. For the safety of my men and their descendents who will settle these lands. You must tell us where he is." Gaspar de Sotelo had an ordinary face, pocked with disease, and his regret, the way his mouth pursed as his teeth worried his lower lip, was ordinary too.

Tupac Amaru said nothing.

"Can you understand me?" Gaspar cocked his head. "I was told you would understand me. I had expected a man of reason, of restraint and shrewdness. Not a savage."

The Emperor stared out the window.

"I am mistaken. I can see that now."

The priest mumbled a few words in Latin. He nodded to the Captain.

"Forgive me, Emperor," Gaspar de Sotelo said as he motioned to the soldiers.

They removed Tupac Amaru's bonds. They forced him, hobbling, to his feet. They stripped off his mantle and doublet of crimson velvet, the shoes made of wool, his crown with the mascapachu royal insignia woven into it, then lowered him to the floor.

They beat him with the flats of their swords until he screamed. They gouged his toenails and fingernails. They carved patterns in his skin, stroking him with the blades.

Blood misted the room. Blood pooled in the corners. Blood rose in the torturers' nostrils like an aphrodisiac.

Night fell with no moon.

The priest lit candles.

The soldiers removed their armor, revealing pale skin whorled with scars.

They sliced the flesh between his fingers. They chopped off his thumbs. They stabbed his testicles. They twisted his shoulders until bones popped from sockets.

Night fell.

The Emperor made noises like the weeping of a child's ghost.

Night fell.

The soldiers did not blink. Their eyes formed a surface so smooth blood and tears could not cling to it.

As Tupac Amaru trembled and groaned, spasmed and gasped, Gaspar de Sotelo said, more times than sane or necessary, "Because of who I am and who you are at this time, in this place, I must punish your silence. I do not enjoy this. I am not a savage. I would not wish this upon you if it were not forced upon me."

III

Gaspar de Sotelo, like the soldiers, filtered the world through eyes of gold, but behind the gold lay the moldering image of the rainforest. Those eyes had recorded the madness of treks into the interior: the moist rot that seeped into brain and bone and soul, trapped in armor that roasted him day after day, rooted him in place and made him an easy target for poison arrows from enemies as formless and oppressive as the ever-present humidity. Gaspar feared the rot would never leave him, that it would infect the marrow of his bones, eat him up, and then eat of itself, until even the fear left him and only the gold lust remained; afraid that he would not even feel his own death until coins, cold and slick, were placed over his eyes.

Sometimes he hoped God would show himself in the patterns left on the flayed skin of his victims, for in no act of decency or betrayal had he seen God's will at work in this strange hemisphere. Even the stars betrayed his knowledge and he whirled beneath them, ripe to fall if not propped up by his fading religion and the discipline of his military experience.

IV

After a span of time measured by the swift and slow rhythms of his torturers, the Emperor could hear only the febrile rattle of his own breathing. He lay on his stomach, splinters from the wooden floor biting into his wounds.

Above him, Gaspar de Sotelo said, his voice dry and taut, "Tell me where your son is or my men will cut out your tongue. I do not wish this. I do not enjoy this. But I will do it."

Tupac Amaru struggled to rise, coughing blood, drenched in blood. Blood clouded his eyes so that his torturers were gray, distant shapes. He lifted his face toward the window, wanting to tell Hualpa that he had not betrayed him, but his hands slipped in his own blood. He fell back against the salt birch floor—

—and immediately convulsed, cried out against a new pain. The wood against his wounds felt as if a hundred stars the size of arrowheads had exploded inside his heart. The pain seared his flesh, then dulled, replaced by a tingle, an itch. The itch gave way to a stretching sensation, his flesh expanding and contracting in the same instant. The Spaniards' voices rose in consternation, drowned out by the pumping rhythm of blood in his ears: the rainforest's pulse, the opened veins of fire beetle and freshwater porpoise, the rushing capillaries of anaconda and jacaranda; the pulse, too, of rivers and trees, valleys and slow-sighing mountains. The Empire's pulse, beating beneath his bones, leaching upward through the birch floor. His mutilated fingers began to throb and he awkwardly turned over on his back and raised his hands. Blood bubbled from the severed joints, but upward, as though seeking to replace missing flesh. His entire body began to throb and he moaned, disoriented and afraid.

Above him, Tupac heard the priest gasp as the blood swayed at his fingertips and scintillated, forming sinuous shapes. The blood danced on his chest and legs as well, tapping out a staccato beat. Pain swept across his body in waves that left numbness behind, his heartbeat swallowed by the pulse of the Amazon.

"The Devil!" the priest cried. "The Devil!"

"Do something!" Gaspar ordered, but the soldiers did nothing.

Tupac looked at his hands. Where the blood ran thickest, it separated from the host finger and floated in the air, where feathers sprouted, then wings, and from above each finger appeared a hummingbird, Inti's messenger in the world of men. Wherever the torturers' blades had touched him, feathers sprouted as scarlet as a woman's menses, followed by the birds, glistening with afterbirth, wing bones clenching and unclenching, the emerald eyes blinking once, twice, three times, as they hovered over the Emperor. Where they rose, the blood soaked into their breasts, his wounds closing puckered lips that left no scar.

Then a river of hummingbirds poured from his eyes, leaving him blind and cold. Everywhere, he heard their rustling speech, the weight of their departure lifting from him until he felt lighter than a single feather. But cold. In the whispering of the hummingbird wings, he heard the echo of his own voice, praying for his son. He smelled the wild plums his son had plucked from the orchard. He saw his son breaking the lake's surface, mouth wide with laughter.

His hands uncurled, bloodless but whole. His pulse beat weakly in his ears. He thought he heard footsteps on the stairs. He thought he heard his son's voice. *How quick to learn, how fleet of foot.*

"The Devil!" the priest screamed. "The Devil! The Devil! The Devil!" until he could scream no more.

V

Gaspar de Sotelo stood at the window, the Emperor curled up at his feet, and watched the sun rise in the sky. Against its corona, hummingbirds flew in long, dark lines. Gaspar's face was impassive as he watched them, his lips quivering only slightly. He thought—he knew—that for a moment, a flicker at the edge of his awareness, he might have—had—seen Him in the birds flying from the Emperor's wounds. His knuckles whitened as his fingernails bit into his palm.

He stared through eyes so pure a gold that even the rainforest's green had been stripped from them. The tears that lined the contours of his face dripped to the floor, mingled with the blood to form a patina of red and gold.

VI

In the Gorge of Cusac, many miles east, Hualpa struggled through the snows, clad in a cloak of white alpaca fur. The air in the Gorge was so thin that Hualpa's heartbeat slowed in his chest and his every movement was sluggish.

Lost, supplies frozen, he was treading ever closer to despair when the first hummingbird, a splash of red against the whiteness, fluttered before his eyes—and then another and another, until a flock hovered above his head. Their wings were edged with frost and their breath blew in flumes of white from their beaks. They flew up against Hualpa and in their silken touch he could feel his father dying. He knew this as surely as he could see the outline of his father's face in the mountain cliffs.

But even as he wept for his father, his legs became warmer, his breath quicker. He could sense the old Emperor's spirit all around him: in the birds' hot wing strokes against the cold; the eyes that reflected intelligence beyond the animal; the honey with which they sustained him; the iridescent arrow they formed in the sky, leading him through the Gorge of Cusac and into southern exile.

VII

It is said that Tupac Amaru survived the torture at Gaspar de Sotelo's hands long enough to return to Cuzco and be burnt at the stake.

At no time did Tupac Amaru seem aware of the jeering crowds or of the priest who begged him to embrace the European God. He did not blink as his wife was torn apart by four white horses.

His eyes, like glass, reflected nothing, and there was nothing behind them. The flames hovered over his body, those same eyes cracking, then melting. Soon after, the hollow frame tottered, fell, the spirit having long since left it.

Notes on
The Emperor's Reply

I minored in Latin American History while attending the University of Florida. We read all manner of firsthand accounts of the Conquistadores' entry into the New World. The histories always read like fiction to me, and proved to be fertile ground for a number of my stories. Marquez once said, with bemusement, that he considered himself a realist, not a magic realist, but no one believed him. He also said that if you were going to write about one hummingbird flying out of a character's mouth, you might as well make it one hundred hummingbirds.

Hummingbirds fascinate me. Why? Once, between Peace Corps stints, my family traveled to Peru. I still had attacks of asthma, and the air in Cuzco was too thin for me. They had to bring oxygen tanks into my hotel room to help me breathe. The hotel abutted a mountain. The window in my room showed the mountainside, which was covered in a thick, green moss or lichen. As I watched, two ruby-emerald hummingbirds appeared, mating on the wing. For me, in that moment, trying to breathe, they were like tiny miracles: unexpected, beautiful, unreal. I called out to my parents and sister, who were in the other room. By the time they came in, the hummingbirds had vanished. After that event, and all else I had seen on our world travels, did I need more evidence that the world was a fantastical place?

If reality were fantasy, if history were fiction, then why not reconfigure history as myth? This did not mean giving up one inch on the harsh reality, or telling detail, with which we try to define the real world. But it did mean that the semi-stylized form of the tale appealed to me. In tales, images can take on more resonance, as they better complement, and in some cases replace, more three-dimensional characterization.

Later, when I came across André Breton's statement about "beauty in the service of liberty," by way of Angela Carter, the image of those hummingbirds flashed through my mind.

The Compass of
His Bones

IN THE SUMMER OF 1615, CAPTAIN GASPAR DE
Sotelo, arm of the Viceroyalty in Peru, watches as the last Incan
Emperor, Tupac Amaru, burns to death after first accepting Christ
and renouncing all land claims. The Emperor burns slowly and his
blood turns black as it catches fire and seeps out beneath the
branches heaped around him. The Emperor does not scream as
once he screamed while being tortured in a tower high above
Vilcapampa. Instead, silent, the Emperor stares at Gaspar with a
hollow gaze. Gaspar cannot look away. The Emperor takes a long
time to die. Gaspar burns as if he were back in the rainforests waiting for the insects to devour him.

Later, after the body has faded to ash and smoke, gray plumes rising
into the Cuzco sky, Gaspar finds himself in the courtyard where
the execution took place. At his side stands a shadow wrapped in a
cloak: Manuel de las Vegas, the Dominican priest who has, since
the storming of Vilcapampa, become his companion in all things.
Beyond them both stand squat stone houses, mantles covered in
honeysuckle, the thick *sweet* of it as disturbing as the smell of
corpses. Through the archway to the street, Quichua Indians pass,
bearing fruit and vegetables on their backs, leading llamas to

market. Ladies of the Viceroyalty pass less often, looking exotic on scented divans borne by native youths. Beneath their feet, the alleys suffer under layers of dirt, garbage, and excrement.

Manuel hands Gaspar the still-warm skull of his enemy. The skull—the freedom of its eye sockets, gaping mouth, hollow nasal cavity—gives Gaspar no answers. As he stares at the skull, he imagines it talks to him. It says, "Nothing is left that can betray my will. Not eyes. Not hands. Not arms. Not legs. Nothing." Gaspar gives a little laugh. It is hard to concentrate through the layer of sweat that always coats him; never a cool breeze in Cuzco now.

"We're a long way from Madrid," Gaspar says as he stares at the skull. "I wonder if the Church knows how far?"

"The Church is not your enemy," Manuel says. For the Dominican, the laconic has become both law and religion.

"It is not my friend."

Manuel's shadow falls upon him. It is a long shadow and sometimes it seems to rustle, as if the darkness of it were composed of a thousand black moths.

"What," says Manuel, "is your desire?"

A sly smile plays across Gaspar's lips. What is his desire? To tell the present from the past. To slake his thirst. To distinguish night from day.

"Simply this," he replies. "Take this skull and have it smoothed and cured and oils applied to it. Fashion it into a compass and candle both, so that it may guide and light our way through this miserable land. Place the skull atop a standard, as you would our beloved flag, and then fasten this standard through a stirrup on my horse, that I may always carry the head of my enemy upon a pole."

Gaspar stares up at Manuel, slight and effete beneath his robes, hands more weathered than his face. Startling white hands against the black.

"As you wish," Manuel says.

Gaspar sees nothing in Manuel's countenance to mock him.

Gaspar and Manuel have never discussed what occurred in the high tower above Vilcapampa, during the Emperor's torture. From the wounds on Tupac Amaru's body, wherever he bled, black-and-crimson hummingbirds had burst forth and flown into the greater wound of the sky. Until the blood had dried and the Emperor had stopped his moaning. Gaspar and Manuel had stood there, unable to believe.

Gaspar has blocked it from memory. He knows it happened,

but at best it remains a fluttering at the edge of his vision, an event from a fever dream. The shock of it still frightens him during his sleep. He wakes now with a sharp, upward lunging motion that, as he will not or cannot admit, mimics the hummingbirds rising from the Emperor's body. Where had they gone? What had they meant? Their crimson bodies had been like flakes of blood against the mountains outside the window.

"I dreamt of nightmares within nightmares last night," he tells Manuel sometimes. To which Manuel replies, "Nothing in dream is real." Or in waking life, Gaspar thinks. Or in that place between sleep and wakefulness, the twilight he inhabits more and more. He is always sweating, the coolness of Cuzco given way to heat. And the plains below the plateau of the city have faded away into a heat-inflicting haze. And the insects are ever-present around him, reminding him of the hummingbirds.

If he saw a hummingbird now, he might not recover.

Even in letters to his wife Isabel, a beauty with raven hair that he has not seen in several years, Gaspar cannot express what he has seen. He sits in his office near the barracks and stares at her portrait on the wall—an image more real to him than her face in his memory. Behind her, a window, and through the window, a wide lawn, with a church in the background. Sometimes he wishes he could step through the portrait back into Spain. Sometimes he wonders why the scene in the portrait seems so unfamiliar to him. He searches his memory for that moment, sun-drenched and far away, but cannot find it. Maybe someday it will find him.

Gaspar reads poorly, and his writing is painful, simple. It is Manuel who takes the words from his Captain's mouth and translates them into missives Isabel might appreciate, if read to her by their son's tutor. The first time Gaspar wrote to her after the Emperor's death, it seemed like a confession. Although Gaspar could not tell her, through Manuel, what had really happened to him. The closest he came was this: "After the Emperor would not divulge his secrets, Manuel administered the last rites and we brought him to Cuzco in an ox cart." Something in this statement seems true. Something in what it denied calms him even now.

Later, when he is alone, he tries to compose his own letters to his wife, his fingers soon black with ink, raw. He does not want Manuel writing for him anymore. He knows the priest changes things, although he does not know what. He knows that he himself has changed, but he does not know how. The clues are few enough. Finally he gives up, lets the ink dry on his hands. Lets the sweat trickle down his back.

The Viceroy requested Gaspar's presence, to report on the taking of Vilcapampa, as soon as he returned to Cuzco. Gaspar has resisted the request for days, uncertain of what he might say to the man. What was the truth? What would be seen as lies? He knows what the Viceroy wants. He does not want to give it to him.

Gaspar hears a flurry of beating wings, but when he looks up, the sky is empty.

Two days later, Tupac Amaru's skull graces the top of a pole fastened through a stirrup on Gaspar's horse. Everywhere Gaspar rides through the cobblestone streets, the light of the Spanish conquest shines within the burnt skull of the Incan Emperor. As Gaspar wanders without purpose, without need, it seems for long moments that he stares through the Emperor's eye sockets.

The gleam of gold has spread across so many eyes in Cuzco that it unnerves even Gaspar. Many of his soldiers use the blankness of the Quichua stare to justify their plunder, yet have become blind to the film of gold closing over their own pupils. Sometimes Gaspar wonders if he controls his men or if they control him. Already, many of them want to be released from duty to pursue the dream of an *encomienda*. Gaspar refuses to share these concerns with Manuel. What if the priest accuses him of weakness?

At dusk, he pretends he stares through the Emperor's eyes at the torches lining the streets.

"I must take you to the Viceroy," Manuel finally tells him, on the fourth day of Gaspar's random journeys across the city with the Emperor's skull.

Gaspar laughs. The portrait of his wife is particularly distant that morning as they stand in the middle of a street, gutters filthy with the entrails of slaughtered chickens and soggy decaying tobacco leaves. His beard holds evidence of two nights haunting military barracks and their homemade wineries. The inside of his mouth feels raw and viscous. Although he does not have the staff with him, he can feel the presence of the skull, there, in the street with him.

"It's simple enough, Manuel. You can tell the Viceroy yourself. 'After the Emperor would not divulge his secrets, we administered the last rites. And although the Emperor seemed dead to the world, we hauled him back to Cuzco in an ox cart, where we burned him to death.' What more is there for me to tell?"

Manuel shrugs. "Not much, of course, but you must tell it to him in person."

Gaspar sits down on an overturned barrel to conceal a shudder. For a moment, Manuel's face had been a death's head, a leering vision of the enemy.

"Manuel, did anything else happen?"

"What do you mean?"

"Up there. Vilcapampa. While we were with Tupac."

"I still don't know what you mean," Manuel says. Gaspar can feel his frown.

Around them stagger badly hung-over soldiers who gambled away their pay the night before. Beyond, the mountains, a searing white.

The next morning, Gaspar meets with the Viceroy. The Viceroy is an expressionless man with a big belly, who has taken to consorting with prostitutes. According to the physician Gaspar and the Viceroy both share, the Viceroy is already displaying symptoms: a burning when he pisses and sores upon his member.

The Viceroy, dressed in opulent waistcoat and scented wig, seems to float behind his desk, hovering just off the floor. The staff with the Emperor's head upon it stands beside Gaspar's chair. Dust-heavy light flows from the open window. From below, Gaspar hears the sounds of slaughter that have followed him from Vilcapampa.

Patches of light and dark across the floor. Does the staff rise above the ground?

Gaspar leans forward. "I bring you the skull of our enemy."

The Viceroy smiles, ignores Gaspar's shaking, outstretched hand, ignores the skull.

Gaspar begins to shiver. "The Emperor's wounds," he says. "They seemed to . . . close . . . to heal . . . and out of them came . . . birds . . . hummingbirds . . ."

The floating Viceroy smiles but does not reply.

Outside the window, an old Quichua stands atop a crumbling watchtower, watching him. The armies of the Inca have gathered. The world is silent.

The next day, Gaspar sets out toward the heart of the cloud forests that cling to the Andean mountainsides. He has told Manuel that the Viceroy has granted his request to lead his men on another expedition. Perhaps the Viceroy did, perhaps he didn't.

The priest sits high upon his horse of sable and Gaspar rides beside him, the skull of his enemy atop its pole. In front of them, slowing their passage, fifty foot soldiers, their armor and thick leathers dull from constant use, their faces pinched from breathing in the thin air, their expressions, by necessity, grim.

They follow a dirt path fashioned by the Quichua that, like the Vilcapampa River, changes course year after year, traveling where it will or where human feet tread upon it. The dirt clings to the horses' shoes. It smells to Gaspar like the sharp bite of Spanish whiskey just opened from the flask. The branches of low trees that soon surround and then cover them brush against his forearms and leave their smell in the form of crushed leaves. The sunlight grows mottled and indistinct through the branches. The rising humidity sucks away his breath, makes him sweat more heavily beneath his leathers.

They have food for ten days; when Manuel asked him why not more, Gaspar waved off his concern, says, "We can live off the land."

When Manuel asks why Gaspar has chosen this particular path, the horses nervous under them, the men uncertain as to their mission, Gaspar tells him, "It is as good any other." His thoughts are already drifting to his wife, back to Barcelona. Fantasies of returning there drift pleasantly through his head.

The path leads through the southern Andes and into an area of intense jungle through which flows the westernmost branches of a mighty river patrolled by Amazons. He could, he thinks, have told Manuel that it is the route most likely to be used by fleeing members of Tupac's court, or of other refugees flushed out by the destruction of Vilcapampa. But that is not why he has chosen the path. He has chosen it because it provides the quickest way to leave both Cuzco and Vilcapampa behind.

As they trek, hours turn, liquid and fetid, into days. The slap of leather against armor has taken on a rhythmic quality. It mesmerizes with its certainty. Gaspar finds his gaze wandering as he ignores Manuel's increasing concern over their path. They have not encountered anyone for four days. They have been traveling for six days. How long should they continue before turning back?

But Gaspar finds his gaze drifting. Insects capture his attention. He remembers the Viceroy once telling him that Spain's greatest scientists believed decaying bodies turned into insects and beetles. If this was true, could they also turn into hummingbirds?

Gaspar's gaze becomes more precise. He cannot focus on Manuel at his side, or his complaining soldiers, but he can see a rhinoceros beetle lumbering away across the forest floor, its horned head swinging blindly, the metallic hue of its back catching glints of sunlight. Clever-quick snout beetles with long heads that become a down-curved beak with green pincers, and undulating along the trunks of trees, benchua: slugs thin as a wafer until they suck blood and become sated, their sharp mouthparts grinding away against flesh; treehoppers with the gold and black of the executioner's axe upon their heads; springtails, primitive, wingless creatures pinhead small, black and fuzzy; walking stick grasshoppers with close-set eyes, antennae concentrated on a narrow extension, wingless, mute, and deaf, with long, thin back legs; blue-green darners or "mosquito hawks" zipping in and out of swarms of midges . . .

When he wakes from this reverie, he finds himself alone on his horse and no longer on the path. Vaguely, he remembers an argument with Manuel, his soldiers' attempts to make him go home with them. Finally, when he drew his sword, they abandoned him.

He feels hollow inside, short of breath. The light around him is distant, cold. The skull of his enemy still rests atop a pole protruding from his left stirrup.

He shakes his head. He thinks of dead bodies and insects rising from them. He thinks of how the flesh has to fall away for the insects to come forth; he imagines a body falling into a hundred butterflies, a hundred thousand moths, until only the eyes remain, soon scuttling away like beetles.

And the thought brings him to . . .

The thought brings him to . . .

Later, he is walking through the night, clutching the pole with the Emperor's skull moon-white atop it. His horse is gone. He cannot remember what happened to it. He was on the verge of remembering something. Remembering something fully. He fumbles at his pockets, wondering if he has paper enough to write a letter to his wife. No paper. No ink. No plume. Where has Manuel gone? Where are his soldiers? The old Quichua won't stop staring at him from the crumbling watchtower.

Gaspar stumbles through the darkness, branches scratching his face. He crosses a river, but the water isn't cool: it's hot. He cannot stop sweating. The darkness frightens him. How did he get here? The floating body of the Viceroy hangs before him, silent. Or is it the moon through the trees?

He is choking now. Choking on words. But he holds onto the Emperor's skull.

The stars above him are so different from those above Barcelona. Around him the insects sing, but all Gaspar sees are the red-and-black hummingbirds coming out of the Emperor's wounds.

"No!" he says. "No," and moans and falls to the ground, the staff beneath him.

He stares into the eye sockets of the skull. The Emperor stares back.

When Gaspar wakes in the early morning, he is calm. Grit on his tongue, muscles aching, he feels every vein and artery in his body pumping blood. As if the insects are inside of him, as if the forest is inside of him. He still hears a river flowing somewhere behind him. The fading stars seem familiar.

Beside him lies the staff. Rising, he picks it up, follows the sounds of the river. He no longer sweats. He no longer thinks of Isabel, the Viceroy, or Manuel. The hummingbirds no longer trouble him. As he trudges toward Vilcapampa, he mutters to himself about vengeance.

Notes on
The Compass of His Bones

Few stories have been as excruciating to write as "The Compass of His Bones." I had the initial scenes written in 1991, but made the mistake of explaining what I had of a plot to a friend, whereupon any desire to write the story left me. I kept trying to write it, because I'd always been fascinated by the mindset of people who commit atrocious acts in the name of an institution or idea, even if just paying lip service to that institution or idea. I kept juggling the images, the characters, and trying to find the right mix. But, as it turned out, the real problem was that I didn't know where Gaspar de Sotelo, or the story, was going. When I finally figured that out, I was able to complete the story.

Balzac's War

I

"Time held me green and dying
Though I sang in my chains like the sea."
 —Dylan Thomas, "Fern Hill"

BALZAC AND JAMIE STUMBLED UPON THE FLESH dog on a day when the sky, seared white as bleached bone, split open the world and allowed any possibility. Sixteen and free of the crèche, two as one, they ran across the desert floor to the ruined city of Balthakazar. Balzac sucked air as he tried to match her long strides, his tunic and trousers billowing in the wind as if he were a human sail. Just ahead of him he could see Jamie's tangles of black hair snarling out behind her, her burnished mahogany thighs pumping beneath the flurry of white dress plaited at the knee and drawn up between her legs. Within hours his older brother and self-proclaimed guardian, Jeffer, would track them down and, returning them to the crèche, force them to complete their lesson with the boring old water dowser, Con Fegman. No doubt Con Fegman was, at that very moment, recounting for the thousandth time how he had discovered the oasis lakes with a mere twitch-twitch of his fingers.

Ahead, the ruins shimmered in the heat, the dark metallic glints of edges and curves beginning to resolve into cracked causeways, broken-down battlements, and crooked buildings fifty stories high. The city had in its demeanor, the sand ever in motion across its metal and concrete carapace, a sense of watchfulness, a restlessness.

At the fringe, where buildings slept like bald and eyeless old men, they found an ancient highway; it shook itself free from the sand as if from a dream of drowning. Once, it might have been eighteen lanes wide, but now, choking on sand, it could fit only four abreast.

Breathing hard, Balzac slowed to a walk. Sweat dripped down his face. A delicious nervousness pierced his stomach.

Jamie, hardly winded, turned her face out of the sun.

"Why did you stop?"

"Because," Balzac wheezed, "*this* is the city . . ."

Husks and shells, as dead as the hollowed-out, mummified corpses of tortoises and jackals after a drought: the idea of "city" stripped down to its most fundamental elements, the superfluous flourishes of paint, writing, road signs, windows, scoured away in an effort to reveal the unadorned and beautifully harsh truth. Gutted weapons embankments pointed toward the sky, but could not defend the city from the true enemy.

Jamie interrupted his reverie. "Don't just *stand* there—we've got to hurry. Your brother will find us soon."

He held out his hand.

She stared at it for a moment, then took it. Her palm felt flushed and warm.

"I'll deal with Jeffer," he said with newfound confidence, although as he led her forward he didn't dare to see if she was impressed or just amused.

Straight to the city's heart they went, the buildings encroaching on the highway, while beneath their feet four-o'clocks, cactus blossoms, and sedge weeds thrust up through cracks in the highway pavement. Scuttling through these miniature oases, anonymous gray lizards waged a war with coppery metal scorpions that pursued with mechanical implacability, their electric stingers singing static to the wind. Con Fegman had shown them one cracked open: beneath the metal exterior lay the red meat of flesh and blood.

Balzac loved even this most deadly part of the mystery that was Balthakazar. All the crèche machines—heirlooms from centuries past—broke down regularly and had to be cannibalized to repair other machines, and yet the Con members did nothing. Even practical Jeffer must realize that some day there would be no machines at all. Some day only the dormant technologies of the city would save them.

"Look at the bones," Jamie said, and pointed at the ground. Scattered across the highway were whitish-gray shards. It made Balzac shiver to think about it. Bones did not fit his pristine, cold-metal vision of Balthakazar in its prime.

"How do you know it's bone? It could be plastic or mortar, or almost anything."

"It's bone. Why else do you think the Con members don't move us back into the city. Why they don't even want us to visit?"

"Because at night, *creatures* come out of the underground levels, *things* with sharp teeth, and they *eat* you."

Jamie threw her head back and laughed; Balzac could see the smooth skin of her neck and marveled at its perfection even as he blushed and said, "It's not funny." Yet even her laughter pleased him.

"You," she said, wiping tears from her eyes. "I stopped believing in that old tale a long time ago."

Something in his expression must have given him away, because she shocked him by saying, gently, "I'm sorry about your parents—really, I am—but the only truth is this," and she bent to pick up a shard that might have been bone. "My father says no one knows what did this. If these are just old graves opened by the sands or if something killed them all off." She paused, looked at him oddly, as if weighing her options, then said, "My father brought me here when I was much younger, and I just liked the texture of the bones. I didn't know what they were. All I knew was that they felt good to touch—lightweight and with those porous grooves—and that my father was there with me after so many nights away from the crèche, showing me something that filled him with awe." She tossed the shard aside. "It's only bits of bone, anyhow. Whatever happened, happened a long time ago. There's nothing to be done for them."

True enough, and it was reassuring to know that the years had created a barrier between him and the bones, so he could look at them as curious reminders of another age. How many times had Con Fegman, or even Jeffer, retold the old legends from before the collapse of the cities, as if the mere repetition would fend off the spirits of the dead?

"Come on," Balzac said. "Let's go." This time he did not hold her hand.

The pavement became hot, cool, then hot again as the sun

sliced through the spaces between structures. The landscape had changed, become both rougher and smoother until buildings were all edges or had no edges at all. Others gleamed with an odd hint of self-repair, their skins smooth and shiny.

They encountered the hull of a rusted hovercraft over which, looking like a weathered lizard, lay the leathery, discarded skin of a dirigible. Balzac did not recognize the faded crèche insignia on the wrinkled cloth. Near the hovercraft lay a misshapen rock, as tall as two or three autodocs. The top of the rock was black and shiny.

"Let's sit down for a moment," Balzac said.

"If you must."

"I must. And besides, it's not just to rest. I've got leechee fruit."

They climbed up onto the rock and lay down on its smooth surface. He handed her a leechee and bit into his own, the juice dribbling down his chin. The fruit helped to rejuvenate him and he soon became acutely aware of her rising and falling chest, the sharp lines of her legs, the faint musk of sweat. She ate the leechee in huge bites, ignoring the juice as it trickled down her neck and stained her dress.

The rock was warm and it relaxed him to lie there with her, so close together. Confidence rising, he tried to explain why the city intrigued him so. He spoke of its rich history, how it must be considered the home of their ancestors, how it used structural designs and technologies unknown to the crèche.

Propped up on one shoulder, Jamie gave him no encouragement. He stuttered, groping for the words that might unlock a true sense of mystery, of scale.

Stymied, he started all over again, afraid that when he opened his mouth, the words would come out jumbled and senseless.

"The city is alive."

"But it isn't," she said. "It's dead."

"But you're so wrong. I mean, you *are* wrong." He squinted at the city's outline until his eyes burned. "I see these buildings and they're like dozens of individual keys, and if I can turn enough of the keys, the city resurrects itself. Take that thing there." He pointed to a rectangular patch of sand dotted with eroded stone basins and bounded by the nubs of walls. "That's not just a box of sand. That used to be a garden or a park. And take that strip." He pointed to a slab of concrete running down the middle of the highway. "That wasn't just a divider for traffic lanes—that was a plot of plants and grass."

"You mean that you see the city as if it were organic."

"Yes! Exactly! And if I can rebuild the city, you could bring back the plants and the trees, flesh out the skeleton. There's a water source here—there must be—how else could the land support a city? In the old books, if you look, you'll see they used plants for decoration."

"Plants for decoration," she said slowly. Then she lay back down against the rock.

His heart pounded against his rib cage. He had made her see it, if only for a moment.

A silence settled over them, the sun making Balzac lazy, the leechee fruit a coolness in his stomach.

After a time, Jamie said, "No rain for at least a month."

"How do you know?"

"The water dower's last lesson—don't you remember, stupid?" She punched his shoulder. "Look at the clouds. They're all thin and stretched out, and no two are grouped together."

Balzac shielded his eyes against the sun and examined the clouds. At the edge of his vision, he thought he saw a series of black slashes.

"What are those?"

Jamie sat up. "I see them. They look like zynagill."

The scavenger birds circled an area east of the highway. Balzac shivered and stood quickly.

"Maybe we should go back now. Maybe if we find Jeffer before he finds us he won't be as angry."

But a sudden intensity and narrowness had crept over Jamie's features—a stubborn look Balzac had seen many times before. It was the look she wore in class when she disagreed with her teacher. It was the look she wore with her friends when they wanted to do something she didn't want to do.

"No," she said. "No. We should go see what they've found." She shimmied down the side of the rock, folded her arms, and stared up at him. "Well?"

Balzac stood atop the rock for several seconds, his pulse rapid, the weal of sky and sun burning above while all around lay the highway, littered with bones. Only when he looked into Jamie's eyes and realized she doubted him did he move; even then he hesitated, until she said, "If you don't go, I'm going alone."

She held out her hand. Her palm was calloused from hard work. He grasped it awkwardly, leaning against her compact weight as he jumped down off the rock. As they came together, her lips brushed his cheek; where she had kissed him the skin tingled and flushed bright red. He could smell her hair, was caught between its coolness and the heat of her lips.

But she was already moving away from him and before he could react, she shouted, "Catch me if you can!" and sprinted down the highway, smiling as she looked back over her shoulder.

He stood there for a moment, drunk with the smell and feel of her. When he did begin to run, she had a lead of more than a city block. Even worse, she didn't so much thread her way through the fields of broken stone as charge through them, leaping curved girders as blithely as if playing coddleskatch back at the crèche. To see her run for the joy of it, careless of danger, made him reckless too, and as much as his nature would allow he copied her movements, forgetting the zynagill and their destination; watching only her.

Balzac had gained so much ground that he bumped into her when she finally stopped running.

A mountain of sand rose above them. Vaguely pyramid-shaped, it buttressed the sides of a massive amphitheater. Balzac could just see, at the top of the sand pile, winged phalanges curling out from the circular lip. Above, the zynagill wheeled, eyeing them suspiciously.

Jamie moved away from Balzac. She pointed at the sand and bent to one knee. Balzac knelt beside her, saw what she saw: an outline in the sand, seven times larger than his own palm, so large that at first he didn't realize it was a paw print. A greenish-purple fluid had congealed inside the paw print. Several more indentations followed the first, leading up the side of the amphitheater, gradually obscured by a huge swath of sand where a heavy body had dragged itself forward.

Jamie traced the paw's outline and sand fell inward.

"Whatever it is, it's hurt," Balzac said. "Probably dangerous. We should wait for Jeffer."

"No. Let's at least walk up to the top and see if we can find it." Jamie softened the rebuke with another dazzling smile that made his ears buzz.

Helpless, Balzac took her hand when she offered it. He let her lead him as they trudged up the slanted wall of sand, parallel to the purple trail until, his sense of balance nearly betraying him, his muscles aching, they stood at the lip, blasted by the sudden wind.

He looked out across the city. Now, finally, it revealed the mystery of its structure: a broken pattern of radial spikes piercing toward a center to the southeast, obscured by the sun and the distance. The sight confounded him, and he almost lost his balance for a second time. No longer did he have to fill in the gaps with his imagination. The buildings at the center of the spokes, those would have to be governmental or administrative in purpose; this would explain their archaic shapes, the arches and the domes. The remains of one- to three-story buildings immediately north of the center had to be the former homes of the city's leaders. Each revelation led to another until he forgot his chapped lips, the grumblings of his stomach, and the beast. He could have stood there forever, linking the city's streets in his mind, but Jamie tugged on his arm and pointed down, into the amphitheater.

"Look," she said.

The amphitheater had concentric circles of seats, most nubs of plastic and metal. Railings trailed off into open space while a series of gap-toothed entranceways spiraled down into the circle of what had at one time been a stage but now could only be called a hundred-meter-wide depression. At its center a large, black hole spiraled farther downward. Halfway between the edge of the stage and the hole lay a dark shape, onto which the zynagill, leathery wings aflap, would land and then relaunch themselves. Not a single zynagill used its double-edged beak to saw at the flesh.

"It's some kind of animal," Balzac said. "And it's dead. Satisfied?"

Jamie stared at him, then peered into the amphitheater again, as if weighing his unease against the mystery of the beast.

"Jeffer needs to see this," she said. "It might be important to the crèche."

"He'll just get mad at us."

"You worry too much," Jamie said. "Stay here—I'm going down."

"Wait," he said, but he was already climbing down into the amphitheater because he knew he couldn't stop her.

By the time they reached the stage, Balzac noted with satisfaction that Jamie was breathing hard. A thin layer of sand covered the stage, broken only by the animal's purple-tinged drag marks. Jamie ran forward. Balzac followed cautiously behind. The zynagill loitered, their leathery hooded heads bobbing nervously, then rose as one, the rasp of their wings, the sudden cry of alarm, making Balzac think he saw movement from the body itself.

The body lay on its side, heavy flanks rising to the height of Balzac's chest. A dog. Coarse, black fur covered the body and the legs, sparser only at the paws, which ended in dulled double-edged hooks. The jowly, horrific head ran into a muscular, thick neck that disappeared into the torso without delineation between the two. The head lay against the ground and from the open mouth the purple tongue lolled, running over fangs longer and more numerous than Balzac's fingers. A pool of green and purple liquid had congealed near the mouth. The dog's eyes, staring blankly into the far wall of the amphitheater, shared the purple tint of the tongue, although they were partially hidden by loose flaps of skin; these same flaps camouflaged a bulbous knot of tissue, twice as large as a clenched fist, which jutted from the forehead. The beast could not have died more than an hour previous and yet it had an unnatural, almost mechanical, stiffness. The curled, taut quality of the limbs made him wonder how it could have walked or run. He had a sudden, chilling image of the creature dragging itself across the desert floor. The thought of the creature crippled disturbed him more than the thought of it whole.

Jamie knelt beside the forepaws. She took one paw in her hands.

"It's raw."

Five pads formed the underside of the paw. The pads had been worn to redness and the sides of the paw were as smooth as wind-washed stone.

"This beast traveled a long way just to die here. I wonder where it came from—another city or maybe even from beyond the desert. How could anything with such thick fur come from the desert?"

"It looks dangerous to me."

"It's dead, Balzac."

"Even so."

Balzac's gaze traveled the length of the creature and beyond until, lightheaded with dread, he realized the beast's destination: the hole. The hole that must spiral down into level beneath level, threading its way through catacombs without number, musty and old, where lived the creatures from nightmare.

"Jamie. Jamie, we should go. We should find Jeffer."

"Too late now. He'll find us." She did not bother to look up, but held the paw gently in her hand. "Such a distance to travel."

The sun beat down, hot and withering. It stung Balzac's eyes and brought beads of sweat dripping onto the bridge of his nose. But, despite the sun, the creature had no smell, no stench of decay. This creature had padded across the desert, the mountains, perhaps, and seen things Balzac could only imagine, and it had had the singleness of purpose to head for the darkest hole it could find when its legs had begun to give out . . . and it had no smell.

He wanted to run, to finally leave Jamie behind if she insisted on being so foolish. But, foolish or not, she was right: it was too late, for at that moment Jeffer appeared above them, staring down from the lip of the amphitheater.

II

"It seems to him there are a thousand bars,
and behind the bars, no world."
— Rainer Maria Rilke, "The Panther"

Ten years after the amphitheater, on the forty-eighth night of the war for Balthakazar, Jeffer saw Jamie for the last time and his mind wobbled strangely. He stood on the third-story balcony of the crumbling, baroque building he had chosen as a resting place for his men, but seeing her he was suddenly adrift, the stone beneath his feet shockingly porous, apt to fall apart and spill him onto the street below. Seeing her, he could not help but curl inward, downward, into a spiral of memories, surfacing only much later to the implications of her existence below him. Almost in self-defense, his thoughts circled back to the one ritual that had proven impervious to change: When he slept in those years before and after the amphitheater, he would dream of the oasis lakes reflecting the stars. In his dreams, the lakes transformed themselves to light-choking, frictionless surfaces, as motionless as, as smooth as, lacquered black obsidian, the stars that fell upon the lakes screaming down like shards of broken, blue-tinted glass. Other times, the lakes became the land and the surrounding desert metamorphosed into thick, churning oceans through which swam fish flipped inside out so that their organs slithered and jiggled beside them.

Once, he had found Balzac at the oasis lakes, alone, his bony, frail body naked from a midnight swim, skin flushed blue with cold. Balzac's smile of greeting had suddenly shifted to doubt when Jeffer told him the news; and then Jeffer could see the darkness invading his brother, that luminous, expressive face blank with self-annihilation.

The images, the content, of the memory maintained a blurry constancy, across a dozen years, so that Jeffer could always conjure up the pale blue gloss of Balzac's face, lit from within, and the awful curling of his lips, through which he sucked air as if he were a deep lake fish, slow and lethargic in the cold, dying out of water.

What had he told Balzac at the time? The exact words had been erased from his memory; they lingered only as ghosts and he knew them only by their absence, the holes they left behind. The event itself he remembered with perfect clarity. He had been in a service tunnel with his parents, all three struggling to fix a clogged waste-water conduit sensitively located next to a main support beam. Polluted water streamed onto the tunnel floor. They all knew the dangers of compression, how that stream could become a flood. Their portable light flickered an intense green, staining the white tunnel walls as they toiled silently. The air, recycled too many times, tasted stale. Above them groaned the weight of five underground levels, enough rock, sand, and metal to bury them forever.

When it began to look as if the patch on the conduit would hold, Jeffer took a break, turning away to sip from a water canteen. He was sweaty and covered with grit. He faced the blinking red light that beckoned from the exit and wondered idly whether there would still be time to get in a quick drink or a game of cards before the night shift.

Behind him, like a door slamming shut, the supporting wall collapsed. Deafened, he heard nothing, *felt* the weight of sand and rock suddenly smother the tunnel.

He knew.

Before he spun around.

His parents were dead.

The foreknowledge strangled the scream rising in his throat, sent it imploding into his capillaries.

Kill the messenger, Jeffer thought. *Then maybe the message will die too.*

Seeing Jamie on the street below, Jeffer knew of no way to protect his brother from the image of her.

It was two hours before dawn, and as Jeffer stood on the third-story balcony the wind blew out of the southwest, cold and oddly comforting against his face. He hadn't showered or shaved for three weeks and there were holes in both his shoes. Sleep had become a memory, no more or less diaphanous than all the other memories, which crept in when he wasn't on his guard, because there was too much time to think.

Also from the southwest came the smell of gunpowder and the acidic stench of flesh burned by laser. Gouts of flame revealed dirigibles on fire, their barrel bodies cracking like rotten orange melons. There, amid the fiercest fighting, the crèche leaders had decided to use most of their remaining laser weapons. Spikes of light cut through the jumbled horizon of rooftops. The enemy hated light. It could not use light. Every spike of light extinguished was a human life snuffed out.

Jeffer's men, sequestered inside the building, numbered four. He could no longer lie to himself and call them a unit, or pretend they had any mission other than survival. Sixteen men had been killed in less than three nights. Of the rest, Con Fegman, wounded, had become delirious; Mindle counted as no more than a dangerous child; and Balzac . . . Balzac he could no longer read, for his brother hid beneath his handsome features and revealed himself to no one. Even their sole remaining autodoc—a portable, two-meter-high model with wheels and treads—had become increasingly eccentric, as if, deep in its circuitry, it had succumbed to battle fatigue.

Their predicament had become so dire that Jeffer found himself giggling at the most unexpected times. For over two hundred hours they had been cut off from communications with their superiors. The four of them had fought and fled from the enemy through tunnels, aqueducts, the ruins of old homes, and across the cracked asphalt of a thirty-six-lane highway.

Through it all—the deadly lulls and the frenzies of violence— Jeffer had survived by fashioning a new identity for himself and his brother; they were refugees fleeing the past, and their best strategy had proved to be the simplest: in the unraveling of their lives to forget, to disremember, to exist purely in the *now*. They had successfully eluded the past for two nights running and yet, somehow, she had found them again.

The war had extended into the heart of the desert winter, the buildings that crowded the street etched in sharp, defining lines by the cold. But how to define her? She walked in the shadow of her own skin, lit by the intermittent flash of laser fire. Was she human? She loped along the chill pavement of the street below, nimble and dainty and muscular as she navigated the long-abandoned barricades.

Jeffer stared, his body stiff. His breath caught in his throat. Centuries slow, he picked up his rifle from the balcony railing.

"Who is it?" Balzac's tired voice, muffled, came from the room at Jeffer's back. They had barricaded themselves in and had booby-trapped the stairwells. Inside the room, the autodoc produced a thin, blue-tinted light that couldn't be seen from the street.

The pale, moon-faced boy Mindle, a refugee from a northern

crèche already destroyed by the invaders, sidled along the wall until he was close enough to whisper, "Is it her again?" Mindle's voice held no fear, no surprise. Only Mindle's body registered such nerve-end pricklings; at his spiritual core he had been frozen solid for a hundred years. Jeffer had seen too many like him in recent months as the crèche sent younger and younger men into battle.

"Keep Balzac quiet," Jeffer whispered back. "If she hears him . . . get Con Fegman, if he's able, to watch the door."

Mindle nodded and, wraithlike, disappeared into the darkness.

Below, Jamie began to cry out Balzac's name in the plaintive timbre of one who is lost and alone and afraid.

Balzac muttered a few words and Jeffer heard Mindle's soft voice, calm and reasonable, coo a soothing reply.

The shape on the street below stiffened, sneezed, and said, "Balzac, my love?"

Balzac's voice in reply: "Is it—could it?"

Mindle cursed. Jeffer heard a scuffle, a strangled cry, and silence, his gaze never straying from her. Lost and afraid. How could he ever consider her someone he had known? The sounds of her aloneness, her confusion, struck him as faintly pitiable, that she should, in any manner, try to re-create her former life. Such a curious double image: to see her on the street below and yet to remember all the times when Balzac had invited him over for dinner, Balzac and Jamie both exhausted from twelve hours of overseeing their reclamation projects in Balthakazar. She had never seemed vulnerable while arguing with him over the Con's latest decisions or about how to adapt the hydroponics hangars to open-air conditions. The lack of hardness in her now, the weaning away of any but the most dependent attributes, made him wary.

The stone wall behind him bruised his back. He didn't play the statue very well; he was sweating despite the cold and he imagined his breath as a vast, unmoving field of ice particles.

Perhaps, as on the two previous nights, she would miss them, would pass by, rasping out her song.

Jeffer raised his rifle to his shoulder. *Pass by*, he wished desperately. *Pass by and be gone*. He did not want to risk the sound of a shot. Come dawn, they would move elsewhere, maybe come across another unit and cobble up enough numbers to mount a counter offensive.

Pass by. Even better, remake history. Let Balzac come to me swimming at night at the oasis. Let Balzac tell me of our parents' death. Let him be the eldest and follow me to Balthakazar.

She stopped directly beneath his balcony, at an extreme line of fire. She sniffed the air. She growled deep in her throat.

"Balzac, are you there?" Such a reedy, ghostly voice.

She paced in a circle, still sniffing.

Jeffer allowed himself to be seduced by the fluid grace, the single-minded purpose behind the strides, the preternatural balance, for she was still beautiful.

She stopped pacing. She stared right up at him with her dead violet eyes, the snarl of fangs below the mouth.

"Jeffer," she said.

His finger closed on the trigger. The red tracer light lit up the pavement. The bullet hit the pavement, sent up a rain of debris.

But she was not there.

He could already hear her—*inside* the building. Battling through their booby traps. Barricades ripped apart, flung to the side.

"She's coming up!" Jeffer shouted, running back into the room. "She's coming up!"

Mindle and Con Fegman stood against the wall farthest from the door. Balzac sobbed, curled in a corner, guarded by the auto-doc. It was clear Mindle had propped Con Fegman up and that the old man would fall down given the opportunity. Which left Mindle and him to stop her. Mindle had their last two laser weapons, a rifle and a hand-held beam. He aimed the rifle at the door. They both knew it had only two or three more charges left.

"Give me the rifle," Jeffer said. "Keep the other one—a cross-fire."

Mindle nodded, threw the weapon to him. Jeffer caught it. His heart pounded. His hands shook. He flicked the safety.

Mindle said, "Soon now. Soon now." He rocked back and forth on his heels. His eyes were dilated. He licked his lips.

They heard the scrabble of claws upon the stairs. Heard the rasping of her breath.

The terror left Jeffer in that instant, as if he had become as cold as Mindle. He wanted her to come through that door. He wanted to kill her.

The sound of claws faded. Silence settled over the room.

Jeffer looked at Mindle in puzzlement.

Mindle smiled and winked. "Just wait. Just wait."

Then she hit the door with such force that the metal shrieked with fatigue.

"*Balzac! Open the door!*"

Another blow to the door. An indentation the size of her paw.

A growl that would have ripped up Jeffer's insides a minute before.

"Go away," yelled Con Fegman, who fell, thrashing, in the fever haze of his infection.

"Balzac! Open the door!"

Balzac looked up from his corner. Jeffer could see the anguish in his eyes.

"Don't," Jeffer said.

The door tore open as if it were paper.

Metal and stone exploded into the room. Jeffer was yelling but Balzac couldn't hear the words. She stood there—huge, black, half-seen in the autodoc's blue glare. She shook herself, debris fluming out from her body. Mindle dove into Balzac's corner and caught him in the ribs with an elbow. It drove the air out of Balzac's lungs. Before he could get to his feet—to warn her? to protect Jeffer?—she leapt at Jeffer. Jeffer's laser rifle flashed and burned her hindquarters off. Jamie screamed and, trajectory altered, landed in a bloody, crumpled heap beside him, brought to a stop by the wall.

The body thrashed, the claws whipping out from the pistoning legs. Balzac ducked, covering his head with his hands. Con Fegman, struggling to his feet, was ripped by a claw and sent reeling by the impact. The front legs sought traction, flailed, and the great jaws beneath Jamie's head gnashed together, opening reflexively only inches from Balzac's throat. Fangs the size of fingers. Breath like an antiseptic wind. Blood spattered over the blunt muzzle. He could see the tiny pink tongue muscles tensing and relaxing spasmodically.

Jeffer shouted an order to the autodoc. The autodoc lurched over on its treads, extended a tube, and stuck a needle into what remained of the flesh dog's left flank. The flailing died away. The great jaws lost their rigidity and rested against the floor. Blood seeped out from beneath the body, licking at Balzac's drawn up feet. Con Fegman moaned.

Balzac sat up against the wall, unable to look at his beloved. An endless singsong ran through his head: if only, if only. If only Jeffer had let him talk to her while she was still on the street, perhaps he could have persuaded her to go away—and perhaps he didn't want her to go away. He let out a deep, shuddering sigh and stood on trembling legs.

Mindle blocked his path, so close he could smell the boy's rotten breath.

"Kill it," Mindle hissed, his face white with hatred. "Kill it now!"

Mindle's eyes had narrowed to knifepoints. Balzac looked away —toward Jeffer, toward Con Fegman.

Con Fegman, in a misty, faraway voice, said, "I can't see anymore. I can't bear to see anymore," and covered his eyes and began to weep.

Balzac pushed past Mindle, turning his shoulder into the boy so he stumbled backward. He went over to Con Fegman and knelt beside him, looked into his ancient face. Such sadness, such shame, that one of the crèche's elders should be dying here, like this.

Balzac took one of Con Fegman's hands, held it tightly in his own.

Con Fegman grinned with broken teeth and said, "I need water. I'm so thirsty."

"I'll get you water. Autodoc—Con Fegman. Full medical."

Balzac stood and allowed the autodoc to do its job. It injected tranquilizers, enveloped Con Fegman in a sterile white shield and, away from meddling eyes, went to work on him.

"Don't waste ammunition," Jeffer said. "It's dying anyhow. It can't hurt us."

"No, she can't hurt us," Balzac said.

Mindle's hand wavered on his laser. Balzac stared at him until he lowered it.

"Jeffer," Balzac said. "Please, get him out of here. The traps. Have him redo the traps."

"I'm here," Mindle said. "I'm in the room."

Mindle's hot gaze bore down on him, and he tensed, prepared to defend himself.

Jeffer nodded to Mindle. "Go downstairs and fix the barricades. Put up more traps. I'll keep watch on the balcony. At dawn, we move out."

"And will we take that thing with us?" Mindle asked, in a voice sweet as poison.

"No," Jeffer said, and stared pointedly at Balzac. "I promise you we won't take her with us."

"*Compassion!*" Mindle spat, but he headed for the door.

Balzac watched him—a man-child, both ancient and newly born, gaunt but innocent of hunger. Balzac couldn't blame him for his rage, or for the madness that came with it. He could only fear the boy. He had always feared the boy, ever since he had come to the crèche: an albino with frazzled, burnt white hair sticking up at odd angles, and eyes that made Balzac want to recoil from and embrace Mindle all at once. The eyes hardly ever blinked, and even when he talked to you, he was staring through you, to a place far away. Mindle had laughed at their reclamation project, had not seen the point in the face of war. Why did they persist when they knew what they knew? Perhaps, Balzac thought, they had simply refused to believe in the proof Mindle brought with him.

It had been Mindle, a refugee from the north, who had first given a name and a face to the enemy, fed the growing unease of the Con members. Before him, there had only been disturbing phenomena: strange, ungainly creatures lurking at the edge of campfire and oasis; dismembered human corpses not of the crèche; then little gobbets of divorced flesh with cyclopean eyes that twitched like epileptic rats as they walked and, when dissected, proved to be organic cameras, *click-click-clicking* pictures with each blink of the single liquid-blue eye.

Mindle had brought them a present, unwrapping the corpse of one of the enemy at a Con meeting. It was the only body yet recovered, badly burned and curled up into a fetal position like a dead black cricket, but still recognizably mammalian. Weasel-like. Two meters tall. Fangs snarled out from the fire-peeled muzzle.

"At first they walked around in plain view, directing their troops," Mindle had told the Con members. "Darting here and there, sometimes on four legs, sometimes on two legs. A meerkat hybrid, no doubt a leftover from biotech experiments before the Collapse, with a much bigger skull and an opposable thumb. *Made* creatures. When we captured this one, they went into hiding, and now they only send their servants, the flesh dogs . . ."

Watching the grimace of Mindle's features, the hatred embedded there, Balzac had felt a prickle of unease, as if Mindle were not the messenger, but the presence of death itself.

With Mindle gone, Balzac turned to Jamie, her face set like a jewel in a ring, nearly buried by the folds of tissue on the flesh dog's head. Clinically, he forced himself to recall the little he knew about such symbiosis: Jamie's head had been cut from her body and placed in the cavity usually reserved for the flesh dog's nutrient sac; the nutrient sac allowed the beast to run for days without food or water. Her brain stem had been hardwired into the flesh dog's nervous system and bloodstream, but motor functions remained under the flesh dog's control. She could not shut her eyes without the flesh dog's approval, and although she kept her own eyes, they had been surgically enhanced for night vision, so that now her pupils resembled tiny dead violets. Sometimes the wiring went wrong and the symbiote would fight for muscle control with the flesh dog—a condition that ended with uncontrollable thrashing and a slow death by self-disembowelment.

Jeffer stumbled over a chair and Balzac became aware that his brother still shared the room with him.

"Why don't you leave, too," Balzac said, anger rising inside him.

"You shouldn't be alone. And what if there were others? I need to watch from the balcony."

"There's no one with her."

"I'm staying. You'll hardly know I'm here."

Balzac waited until Jeffer had stepped out to the balcony. Then, thoughts a jumble of love and loathing, he forced himself to stare at his lover's face. The face registered shock in the dim light, stunned as it began to recover itself. As he watched, the eyes, pupils stained purple, blinked rapidly, the full mouth forming a puzzled smile. Balzac shuddered. She looked enough like the Jamie he remembered for love to win out over loathing. He had known it would; deep down, in places he would never reveal to anyone, he had hoped Jamie would track him here. He had assumed that once she had found him again he could bring her back from the dead.

Looking at her now, he had no idea what to do.

"Balzac? Balzac?" That voice, no longer demanding and sexy.

He was so used to her being the stronger one, the one who had an answer for everything, that he couldn't reply. He couldn't even look at her. Throat tight and dry, legs wobbly, he took a step toward Jeffer. Jeffer was only a silhouette, behind which rose the night: a ridge of black broken by faint streaks of laser fire.

"Help me, Jeffer."

"I can't help you."

"What should I do?"

"I would have shot her in the street."

"But you didn't."

"I missed."

"Balzac," Jamie said. The disorientation in her voice frightened Balzac. He ground his teeth together to stop his tears.

"She can still hurt you," Jeffer said.

"I know," Balzac said. He slumped down against the wall, his shoes almost touching Jamie's head. The floor was strewn with dirt, pieces of stone, and empty autodoc syringes. Beside Balzac, the flesh dog's entrails congealed in a sloppy pile.

"Balzac?" Jamie said a third time.

Her eyes blinked once, twice, a miracle for one who had been dead. She focused on him, the flesh dog's head moving with a crackly sound.

"I can see you," she said. "I can really see you."

You're dead, he wanted to say, as if it were her fault. *Why aren't you dead?*

"Do you know where you are?" Balzac asked. "Do you know who you are?"

"I'm with you," she said. "I'm here, and it's cold here."

The effort too much, too soon, with the flesh dying all around her, Jamie's eyes closed to slits.

Balzac wondered if what he saw was not just a carnie trick, if beneath the flesh lived nothing more than an endless spliced loop, a circuit that said his name and tried to seduce him with the lie that Jamie lived, long enough for it to drive him mad. Jamie had died. He knew that; if he saw her now, she was ghost cloaked in flesh, as dead as the city of powdering bones. The same war that had given the city a false heart—a burning, soul-consuming furnace of a heart—had resurrected Jamie. Yet he must assume that she was more than a shadowy wisp of memory, because he could not prove her ghostliness, her *otherness*. What cruelty for him to abandon her should she be aware. And trapped.

Jamie had died on the front lines a week before, *then* and *now* separated by a second and a century. His recollections were filtered through a veil of smoke and screams, the dark pulsating with frantic commands. Particular moments stood out: the irritation of sand grit in his shoes; a lone blade of grass caught *just so* between yellow and green; an ant crawling across an empty boot, its red body translucent in the laser glow; the reflection of an explosion, the burnt umber flames melting across the muzzle of his rifle; the slick feel of Jamie's grime-smeared hand in his, her pulse beating against him through the tips of her fingers.

Crowded together in long trenches, they had been only two among several thousand, waiting. They did not talk, but only touched.

The flesh dogs appeared promptly at twilight, bringing silence with them in a black wave. They wore the masks of friends, the guise of family. They jogged and cantered across the fires: fueled by a singleness of purpose, pounding on shadow muscles, ripping swathes of darkness from the night so as to reimagine themselves in night's image. Eyes like tiny dead violets. An almost-silent ballet of death.

Then, on cue, they halted, forming a solid, uniform line. They stood so still it would have been easy to think they were a row of ancient statues built on the order of a brilliantly deranged despot.

In the lull, Balzac hugged Jamie, taking comfort in the feel and scent of her body.

Above, dirigibles coughed and grunted with the effort of discharging missiles, flashes of light catching ground combatants in freeze frame.

As the flesh dogs came into range, in such numbers that the ground reverberated with the thunder of their passage, the defenders of the trench opened fire: the spitting sparks of lasers and the rhythmic *phutt-phutt* of rifles entwined in an orgasm of recoil and recharge. It took immense discipline to stand in the teeth of such a charge. The rifle in Balzac's hands seemed heavy, difficult—it wanted its head, and in the heat of battle it was all he could do to keep it aimed and firing, his finger awkward on the trigger.

In reply to the defenders' barrage: a chorus of bone-thin voices attached to alien bodies, a thousand ghosts wailing across the ruins in the timbre of old friends pleading for their lives, calling out to the living by name.

It brought madness bubbling to the surface, so that the defenders shot and recharged with incredible speed, shouting back their own hatred to block out the voices, obliterating the present that it might not obliterate the past.

As the wave broke over them, the tableau dissolved in confusion. Mostly, Balzac remembered the stench of gunpowder as he loaded and reloaded—but more slowly now, mesmerized by the carnage—and the fleeting images through the smoke . . . Huge bodies flung without reason or care . . . a dark blue-black wall of flesh . . . the swiftness of them, almost as fast as a dirigible, so that a blink could cost a life . . . Sinuous muscles, caricatures of human faces as wincing passengers . . . The bright black slickness of spilled oil . . . Throats ripped from bodies . . . bodies fallen, whirling and dancing in the jaws of the flesh dogs . . . flesh dogs toppling, sawed in half or legs cut off, crawling forward . . . others, shot in the head, falling over on their backs.

Through the black-white-black of dirigible flashes, Balzac saw Jamie fall in stop-gap motion *and his heart stopped beating* away from him into the darkness *he couldn't see her anywhere.* As he put out his hand to pull her up, she was no longer there.

"*Jamie!*"

A flesh dog galloped toward the breach in the line left by Jamie's absence. He spun, shot it, and jumped to the side, the fangs snapping inches from his throat. It slammed into the trench, dead. He got up . . . and when he looked back toward the gap in the line of defenders, she still hadn't filled it, hadn't regained her feet as he'd expected, even when the dirigibles scorched the night into day.

In his panic, he couldn't breathe, he couldn't think.

"Jamie!" he shouted over the screams and detonations. "Jamie!"

And the echo passed along the line to him: "Retreat! Fall back! Breached! Breached!"

A death sentence for Jamie. A section of the trench had been overrun and to avoid being flanked they must fall back. The retreat, a haphazard, broken-backed affair, piled confusion on confusion, some soldiers running away while others commenced a vigilant rearguard action to allow stragglers to cross back over what was now enemy territory.

A dirigible exploded directly overhead, the impact knocking Balzac to the ground. Swathes of burning canvas floated down on the combatants. Molten puddles crackled and hissed around Balzac as he got up. Mechanically, he haunted the burning ground, searching for his beloved with his infrared goggles. He dove into ditches, crawled through the most dangerous of firefights, lending his rifle only long enough to clear a path to the next embattled outpost. Each minute of failure added to the heaviness in his chest, the rising sense of helplessness.

Later, he would recall the black-and-red battlefield as if he had been aboard a dirigible; he would even remember watching himself run across the treacherous ground: a tiny figure leaping recklessly between trenches, scurrying through flames without hesitation. Other times, he would remember it only as a series of starts and stops. He would be running and then fellow soldiers or flesh dogs would be all around him like a sudden rain, and then he would be alone again, his thoughts poisoning his skull.

Only the sight of the creature saved Balzac from the endless searching, for it was only then that he realized Jamie must be dead.

He sat down heavily, as if shot, and stared at it as it bustled about its business some thirty-five meters away. It was so sleek and functional and not of this world—so much more *perfect* than anything perfect could be—that for a moment Balzac could not imagine its function: it was merely a beautiful piece of artwork, a thing to be admired for its own clockwork self. How could humankind compete with such a creature? He watched it with mounting dread and guilty fascination.

It scuttled along on cilia-like feet, almost centipedal, and yet it was clothed in dense, dark fur—long and low to the ground so that it seemed to *flow*, a species composed of the most elemental combination of flesh and bone. The head, which swiveled three hundred sixty degrees, reminded Balzac of a cross between cat and badger, the bright, luminous eyes and curious smile of muzzle conspiring to make the beast almost jolly. Thin, Balzac thought at first. Thinner than thin, the spine caved in on itself so that its back appeared to have been scooped out with a shovel, leaving a long, low compartment walled in by shoulders and flanks. The smooth-squishy sound it made with its thousand limbs he had heard before, on the battlefield, as a low, underlying counterpoint to the screams and explosions.

But although the beast stunned him with its perfect strangeness, the function it performed stunned him more.

As he watched, the beast threaded its way through the scattered corpses. Finally, at the body of a young man with open, vacant eyes, and a thin line of blood trickling from the mouth, the beast came to a halt. Then, with a discernable *pop*, spinning wildly, the expression on its face insanely cheerful, the beast's head unscrewed itself from its body and, with the aid of cilia positioned beneath its now autonomous head, lifted itself over the edge of its own shoulders. Once it had sidled up to the head of its victim, the beast grunted twice and two appendages emerged from the thick fur: a powerful blade of bone and a two-thumbed hand. The blade came down, slicing through the man's neck. Almost simultaneously, the hand grasped the dead soldier's head and placed it over the hole left by the departure of the beast's head. It waited for a moment, then pulled the man's head, which had been "capped" with a pulsing purple slab of flesh, back out of the hole. Balzac watched with horrified fascination as the hand then tossed the capped head into the scooped out cavity of the beast's body. Both blade and hand disappeared into the beast's grinning head, which then rolled and huffed its way back onto its own neck and twirled twice, before the whole nightmare contraption scuttled on, out of sight.

Leaving Balzac alone, with the dead.

After the battle, behind the lines, they assigned him to Jeffer's guerilla unit. Jeffer would watch over him as he always had in the past.

Jeffer placed his hand on Balzac's shoulder. Balzac flinched. Jeffer realized that the gesture was unappreciated, but he tried by an act of will to put all of his love and fear for Balzac into that

simple touch of hand on shoulder. Love. He might not have admit-
ted to love a few years ago, beyond the love expected by blood, but
Jeffer had seen an unlikely transformation come over Balzac.

Balzac, with his piercing green eyes and firm chin, had always
been handsome to the point of callowness. But slowly, as he and
Jamie became closer, and especially in the year after their marriage, Jeffer had seen the callowness stripped away. A certain *weight*
and *depth* had entered the perfect lines of his brother's mouth, a
seriousness and mischievousness that illuminated the eyes. It was as
if a fear had conquered Balzac simultaneous with his love for Jamie
—fear for the death of his beloved, that their love could not last
forever—and that these entangled twins of fear and love had peeled
away his shallow qualities like a molting lizard skin.

Jamie had remarked on it during a tour of the Balthakazar reclamation projects, as they sat and watched Balzac out in the sun,
badgering the engineers.

"I don't know if I would still love him," she said. "Not if he
was just handsome. I used to love him for his mouth and his eyes
and his awkwardness, and I wanted to protect him." She flashed the
smile that had driven dozens of men to despair. "Now he's grown
up and become real."

The memory haunted Jeffer as he said to Balzac, "It will be
okay. You don't have to do anything. It won't be long . . ." Jeffer
suddenly felt weary. Why must he comfort others at those times he
most needed comfort? The muscles in his throat tightened. Ever
since he had been left with an eleven-year-old boy who could never
again quite be just his little brother it had been this way.

"I should have rolled in the dirt and disguised my scent," Balzac
said. "I should have become someone else. Then she couldn't have
found me. Ever. I shouldn't have let her find me. *But where's the
kindness in that?*"

Jeffer smiled at the mimicry of Mindle's favorite phrase.

"Kindness?" Mindle said, surprising them both. Eyes bright and
reptilian, he stood in the doorway. "Kindness? How can you speak
of kindness? There's no room for it. We've no need of it."

Jeffer half-expected Mindle to crouch down and lap up the
blood pooling around the flesh dog's body. Who could predict the
actions of a child who had never been a child?

"Are you finished with the barricades, Mindle?" Jeffer asked.

"With the barricades? Yes."

"Then wait outside until dawn. Stand watch from the second-
story window."

Mindle stepped inside the room. He licked his lips. "Yes, sir. But first I thought we might interrogate the prisoner."

"The prisoner will be dead soon."

"Then we must be quick—quicker, even," he said, and took another step into the room.

"Take up your post on the second floor," Jeffer ordered.

Mindle took a third step into the room.

Before Jeffer could react, Balzac snatched up Con Fegman's rifle from the floor. He aimed it at Mindle.

Balzac said: "Go. Away."

Mindle smiled sweetly and turned to Jeffer, one eyebrow raised.

"Do as he says, Mindle," Jeffer said. "And Balzac—put down the rifle!"

Mindle shrugged and turned away.

Balzac tossed the weapon aside and hunkered over the flesh dog's body. His brother's gauntness, the way the autodoc's light seemed to shine through him, unnerved Jeffer. Such an odd tableau: his brother crouched with such love and such gentleness over the massive body of the flesh dog, as if it were his own creation.

Jeffer tottered forward under the spell of that image, his intentions masked even from himself, but Balzac waved him away.

"Please, let me be," Balzac said. "Watch the window. Watch Mindle."

Even as he nodded yes, Jeffer hesitated, wondering for the first time if he could aim a rifle at his own brother. He walked over to the balcony and watched Balzac and Jamie from the darkness. Jamie's face was pale, her lips gray. The beast's flesh surrounded her like a rubbery cowl.

He marveled at the affection in Balzac's voice as his brother touched the creature's face and asked, "How do you feel?"

"Cold. Very cold. I can't feel my legs. I think I'm dying. I think I'm already dead, Balzac. Why else should I feel so cold?"

Balzac flinched, and Jeffer thought: *Think? Feel? Can it do either?*

"It's a cold night," Balzac told her. "You need a blanket. I wish I had a blanket for you, my love."

"Cold. Very cold," she said, in a dreamy, far-off voice.

"I'll find something for you," Balzac said, his voice cracking with grief. "Jeffer, I'm going to look through the supplies downstairs—maybe there's a blanket. Watch her for me?"

"She's almost . . . I mean, I don't think we have a blanket."

"I know! I know that. Just watch her."

Balzac scrambled to his feet and fled through the ruined door-way, leaving Jeffer with the enemy. As he circled her, he wondered if he should kill her.

"Who is there?" Jamie said. "Are you cold too?"

At the sound of that voice, Jeffer stepped away from her, made sure she couldn't see him. What if she recognized him? What if she spoke his name again? What then?

In the corner, Con Fegman stirred and said, in a singsong voice, "The sand toad told the sand itself and the sand told the toads and the toads told the sand and . . . and . . . and . . ." He faded back into unconsciousness, the myth trapped between his withered lips.

Jeffer tried to ignore Con Fegman. He had so resigned himself to the old man's death that he sometimes started in surprise during Con Fegman's moments of lucidity, as if a ghost had drawn breath.

"I want to get up," Jamie said, face tightening as she strained to move the flesh dog's leg muscles. "I can't seem to get up."

Jeffer knew better than to interrogate her. If he couldn't shoot her, he would have to content himself with watching her.

In the early days, before the full-fledged invasion, he had volunteered to help capture and interrogate such surgically altered specimens. They never had much to say and, anyhow, who could tell if what the prisoners said was authentic or preprogrammed? The heads when separated from the bodies would live on unimpaired for two or three hours, and perhaps there was a hint of miracles in this delayed mortality, but surely nothing more.

Locklin, the subject of Jeffer's final interrogation, had believed in miracles, and as Jeffer stared at Jamie he could not help but see Locklin's face superimposed over hers.

Locklin had laughed at him even during those moments of the interrogation that most resembled torture. When asked a question, the creature would say its name and make a low, bubbling laugh through its flesh dog and human mouths. The violet eyes would widen, his craggy, heavily tanned and scarred face sprawled across the flesh dog's forehead. "I am Locklin today, but tomorrow? You will all be me."

Locklin claimed to come from a crèche located in the far north, nestled against a frozen sea. Cliffs four hundred meters high sheltered them from the cruel winds, and from these same cliffs came the enemy in great numbers, on a winter's day when many of the crèche were dying from cold; the heaters had failed and the crèche's leadership had wavered on whether to wait out the weather or to abandon the crèche.

"But the m'kat," Locklin offered near the end, contempt for Jeffer poisoning his voice, "they fixed us up! Ho! They surely did. Immortality in return for service—a fine, fine body that will run forever, and we said *yes!* We said *yes,* all of us shivering in that frozen place . . . as most of you will say yes in your turn."

Always it was flesh dogs fashioned from members of this particular crèche that Jeffer found least like a poorly animated holovid. If some responded like sand through a sieve to his questioning, then these hardened types were steel traps. For they had not just pledged allegiance to the "m'kat" but worshipped them, giving up their children to immortality and abandoning their old religions. This betrayal of species terrified Jeffer. Among the Con members it was the greatest of all fears: to be captured by an enemy that did not know mercy as humans knew it, an enemy unparalleled in the art of psychological warfare. To be sent back in the guise of a flesh dog, mouthing your own name or the name of your beloved as the creature fought you.

Only now did Jeffer realize he had talked to Locklin too much, for as he watched Jamie, Locklin's hypnotic words drifted in and out of his thoughts: *"You could live forever this way, if you would only submit . . ."* A great sadness welled up inside Jeffer, for he and his brother had become estranged; it was there in Balzac's words, in his face: that the love he had for Jamie had become monstrous, had taken him over and eaten him from the inside out. Did Balzac sense a truth to Locklin's words that escaped him? A chill crept into Jeffer's skin. He could already foresee an outcome monstrous beyond imagination and he told himself he would not help *in that way*—he could not—and he tried to convince himself this was because he loved his brother, not because he stood alone in the same room with a creature so familiar to him and yet so alien.

Mindle had been Balzac's hateful shadow as he rummaged through their meager cache of supplies for a blanket. The boy had said nothing, had followed almost without sound, but Balzac could feel that gaze blasting the back of his head, scorching his scalp. He didn't mind; better to know where Mindle was than not. At times on his miniquest, he even tried talking to Mindle, and took a perverse pleasure in his facade of cheeriness, knowing it must make the boy burn even brighter. Burn, then. Burn up.

But there was no blanket, and with each step back up the stairs, the facade faded a little more until he could barely walk for the weariness that pulled at him. On the third-floor landing, Balzac heard Mindle's retreating footsteps and was glad of it, not wasting time with a taunt, but ducking into the room where Jamie still lay in the autodoc's blue light. Jeffer stood to one side.

"I couldn't find a blanket. You can go back to the window."

Jeffer gave Balzac a wan smile, but Balzac only slumped down beside Jamie.

"Jamie," he said when Jeffer had gone back out onto the balcony.

"I'm cold." A voice like an echo, rich with phlegm or blood.

"Cold like the oasis lakes—do you remember the oasis lakes?"

He thought he saw her mouth curl upward. She gave a little hiccupping laugh.

"I remember. I remember the cold. It makes me sneeze." Then, doubtful: "That was a long time ago . . ."

The water had been cold. They'd dived in together, into the hardness of the water, swum through it, their muscles aching. They'd snorted water, gurgled it, luxuriating in the decadence of so much water, and surfaced to kiss, breathlessly, under the stars. Her lips had tasted of passion fruit and he had pressed her into the shallows where they could stand, then moved away from her shyly, only to find her pulling him back toward her and putting his hand between her legs; making sharp, quiet sounds of pleasure as his hands moved lightly on her.

But, faced with her in the flesh, he could not hold onto the memory of the emotion. It dissipated into the grime and darkness: a dimly glittering jewel against whose sharp edges he could only bleed.

"We made love there," he said.

Silence.

Dawn would come soon and they would have to move on while they had the chance.

Jamie whimpered and moaned and cried out in her half-death, half-sleep. He was cruel (wasn't he?) to prolong her pain.

He could feel Jeffer staring at him. If not Jeffer then Mindle. Mindle hated him. Jeffer loved him. But they both wanted the same thing.

Balzac let his gaze linger over Jamie's face, the thickness of it which had overtaken the grace, as if the architects that had put her back together could not quite re-create their source material. This was the woman who had worked side by side with him to rebuild the city, she planting trees as he excavated and drew plans. He had even grown to enjoy the planting—long hours, yes, and the work made his fingers bleed and blister, but he had liked the smell of dirt, enjoyed the rhythms of the work and the comfort of her presence at his side.

He thought of the times he had made love to her on the cool desert sand under the stars, and how they would sneak back to the crèche in the years before they were married, there to lie in bed for hours afterward, talking or telling stories. The sweet smell of her, the taste of her tongue in his mouth, these were *real*, as was the peace that came over him when he was inside her, so very close to her, as close to her as he could, to be inside her and looking into her eyes.

He owed it to her. If he loved her.

In agony, he ran to the balcony, pushing Jeffer aside, and beat his fists against the stone railing.

"Listen to me: it's better this way," Jeffer whispered. "Come morning, there's a good chance we can come under the protection of a larger unit. If we can only survive—"

"Shut up!" Balzac hissed. "Shut up or I'll yell and *they'll* all hear us."

"Should I leave?"

"Leave? No . . . but I don't want to talk. I just want to stand here for a moment."

"That's fine. That's fine. I'm your brother, Balzac, *your brother*. I don't want to hurt you."

Balzac tried to slow his breathing. He leaned on the railing and looked out across the city. Dawn soon, and still the dirigibles burned and still the darkness closed in around them. A hundred shades of darkness for a hundred different tasks—darkness to cover buildings; darkness to cover pain; darkness to cover thoughts; darkness to cover the light, and the light, when it came, only emphasized the darkness all the more. He could no longer hear the faint, ghostly shouts from the front lines; the darkness had swallowed the voices, too.

For the first time, looking out over not only the ruined city but also the ruins of his own ambition, Balzac felt the pull of that darkness, felt overpowered by it. He was tired. He was so tired. He began to weep. He could not bear it. He must bear it. He could not. He must.

Where into that darkness had she been taken? Where had the scuttling creature dragged her? Had it dragged her into the hole at the center of the amphitheater? Some place underground where the darkness grew thick and unfettered—in the tunnels under the city, wherever *they* had their headquarters, where the creatures from nightmare used to live before the enemy displaced them. It hurt to think of such places. They scared him more than anything. All he could imagine was suffocating dirt, the tunnel imploding and burying him alive.

What sort of immortality had she found there? When they'd reawakened her, had she pleaded with them? Did she know, even now, exactly what had been done to her?

And if he took her back there, could they live together, in the darkness, all alone with only one another for company amongst the ghouls and ghosts . . .

"Help me to imagine it, Jeffer."

"Imagine what?"

"Never mind."

A red wound bled across the horizon. Balzac stared at Jeffer. Jeffer looked away.

"I know I have to do it," Balzac said.

"You don't. I'll do it for you."

"No. I have to do it."

"Then do it."

Balzac nodded and walked back to Jamie. He leaned over her, touched her face once again, smoothed back a strand of hair. Strange, the calm that settled over him.

"Balzac?" she said in such a questioning tone that he almost laughed with grief.

"Jamie. Jamie, I have to ask you something. Do you hurt, Jamie? Jamie, do you hurt a lot?"

"I'm so cold," she said. Then something clicked behind her eyes and he thought he saw the old confidence.

"Close your eyes then, Jamie. I swear, Jamie. This won't hurt. Jamie, it won't hurt. I wouldn't lie. Not to you, Jamie."

"I know, my love."

He exchanged weapons with Jeffer: his rifle for Jeffer's laser. Then, hugging the flesh dog's head to him, he adjusted the setting on the laser for a needle-thin, ten-centimeter-long blade. If he cut the throat, she might last for a few minutes, in pain. But if he could spear her through the head . . . his hand wavered and for a moment every atom, every particle, that made him Balzac streaked in opposite, splintered directions. If only she wouldn't stare at him . . .

His hand steadied, and with it his resolve. Two smooth strokes and he had separated the node of tissue that contained Jamie. There was no blood; the laser cauterized the wound instantly. Her eyes still stared up at him though her lips did not move. He held her against him, closed her eyes, kept the rifle in his right hand, reactivated the normal settings.

He looked up at Jeffer, who was staring at him in horror.

Balzac's shoulders sagged, the weight of darkness too great, and then he righted himself, found his legs.

Jeffer took a step forward, as if to block the door.

"Don't. Don't do that," Balzac said.

"Balzac! Leave her be."

Tears blurred Balzac's vision; he wiped them away viciously with his forearm. Seconds were as precious as water now; he could not waste them.

"I can't do it, Jeffer. I. Just. Can't."

"You can! You know you can. You remember how I was after . . . after our parents died? You remember how I was? You brought me back. *You did that.* I can do that for you. I know I can."

"And if you do? I couldn't bear it. I couldn't bear it. *I can't lose her too.*"

"It's too late. You'll lose her anyway."

"Not if I find them in time. I've got an hour. Two, maybe."

Silent as an executioner, Mindle appeared at the door, his hand-held laser aimed at Balzac.

"*Mindle, get out of here!*" Jeffer screamed, raising his own rifle. The barrel wavered between Balzac and Mindle.

Mindle's eyes had the fatal density of dead stars.

"Shut up, Jeffer," he said. "If he moves, I'll shoot him."

Into the deadly silence crept the first light of the sun. Grainy yellow rays revealed them all as tired, grime-smeared, gaunt figures frozen in time, while Con Fegman stared with sightless eyes directly into the sun. Balzac could hear his brother's muttered prayers, could sense the tension in Mindle's trigger finger. He looked first at one and then the other, their shadows flung against the far wall.

Looking down into her sleeping face, Balzac knew he was impervious to the other voices, the voices that were not hers. For her sake, he had to get past Mindle, make it to the doorway, and onto the street below. The odds were bad, and yet he felt at peace: the darkness was still with him, cloaking and protecting him.

Vaguely, he heard Jeffer tell him to put down his rifle and Mindle scream that if he took a single step he was a dead man, but their words came from very far away. They could not touch him —not Mindle, not his brother. No one but Jamie. The darkness covered his face like a veil. He caressed Jamie's cold cheek with one trembling hand.

"Goodbye," he said. He threw his rifle in Mindle's face. He ran toward the door. Behind him he heard Jeffer's slow, drawn-out shriek of loss, and then the ice-heat of Mindle's star exploded against his back. The force drove him forward, knocked the breath from his body, and he was falling through the doorway, falling into the darkness of the stairwell—and kept falling, a numbness enveloping his body, until the darkness was complete and it was no longer the stairwell but the black oasis lakes, and he was diving into and through them, the wet wave and wash licking blackly at his limbs, and just when he thought he might fall forever, he caught himself.

Sand, bright sand, beneath his feet, the grains like glittering jewels. He looked up—into the glare of late afternoon—and saw Jeffer staring down at him from the lip of the amphitheater. Jamie saw Jeffer a moment later and gasped in surprise.

Jeffer stalked down to them, cold-shouldered and stiff, sand spraying out around his boots. Balzac had risen from his position near the beast, thinking Jeffer would give them both a thrashing.

But instead, Jeffer became very quiet and asked them if they were all right. Balzac said yes and Jamie asked how he had found them.

"The zynagill," Jeffer said, still staring at the beast. "I thought you might be dead."

Before Balzac could speak, Jamie laughed and said, "No. It is. What do you think of it?"

"I think you should get away from it." Jeffer walked closer.

"It came from underground," Balzac said.

"It came from far away," Jamie said. "Look at its paws."

"It's like something from the old books," Jeffer whispered, skirting the edge of the beast as if it were poison. "We should burn it."

"Burn it?" Balzac said. "It's dead."

"Burn it," Jeffer said.

But it was too late. They heard a leathery, cracking sound and the flesh dog's bulbous forehead split open and out struggled a creature the size of a man's heart. It glistened with moisture and, seeming to grow larger, spread its blue-black wings over the ruins of the flesh. It had all the delicate and alien allure of a damselfly.

"It's beautiful," Jamie said.

The creature gazed at them from one red-ringed eye (luminous amber, with a vertical black slit). The bone-thin legs ended in razor claws. The wings rose and fell with its breathing, which was steady and unruffled. The wings were those of a fallen angel, miraculous in that the black, shiny surface reflected greens and purples and blues. They were monstrously oversized for the body and the beast flapped them to keep its balance.

Jeffer moved first, fumbling for his gun. The creature, alarmed by the motion, moved its wings more vigorously.

Balzac put himself between Jamie and the creature, his swift embrace so tight she could not move, though she struggled against him.

Before Jeffer could aim, the creature launched itself into the air and spiraled up through the flock of hovering zynagill, scattering them in all directions. It made a swift pass over the amphitheater, still gaining altitude, then veered abruptly toward the west and began to pick up speed, soon out of sight.

Jamie wrenched herself from his grasp. "Why did you do that?"

"I didn't want it to hurt you."

"I don't need your help," she said, but when he looked into her eyes, he saw a sudden awareness of him that had not been there before. It sent a shiver through his body.

"What does it mean?" Balzac asked Jeffer, whose face was still clouded with thought.

"I don't know. We will have to tell the Con members."

"Where do you think it went?" Jamie asked.

"I think . . . I think it was a messenger. A beacon. I don't know."

"It was incredible," Jamie said.

The afternoon shadows so emphasized the brazen lines of her eyes, nose, cheekbones, that her image burned its way into Balzac's heart. He would have willingly lost himself in her, if only for the mystery he could not unravel—that her beauty was as luminous and sharp-edged as that of the winged creature. He experienced a rush of vertigo, fought for his balance on the edge of a darkly glittering future that would bind her to him beyond any hope of untangling.

Then he was falling again, willingly, gripped by sudden happiness, laughing as he saw the adventure of their lives together spreading out before him.

Jeffer and Mindle stood side by side at the top of the stairs, looking down through the early morning gloom of dust motes. Mindle shook with spasms of tears, undoing all the savagery of his face. Below, on the landing, Balzac's body lay sprawled, a wide, black hole burned through his back. His hands were tightly clasped around the flame-distorted head of Jamie, whose lidless eyes stared sightless at them. Even in the shadows, Jeffer could see the thin, pale line of his brother's mouth fixed in a smile.

An emptiness Jeffer could not quantify or describe opened up inside of him. For a moment, he could not contain it, and he looked over at Mindle, intending to kill the boy should he discern even a trace of mockery upon that ancient face. But the tears had washed away the predatory sarcasm, the bloodlust, and he was almost vulnerable again, almost boyish again.

Jeffer slung the laser rifle over his shoulder and motioned to Mindle.

"Come on—if it's safe, we can bury them in the amphitheater," he said.

Horror, yes, and pain, and sadness—and yet, this relief: *It was over.* It was finished. And this final thought, which overcame the guilt: *I'm alive. I survived it.*

Mindle looked disoriented for a moment, as if he had been dreaming or listening to a distant and terrible music. Then the mask slid back over his face and he sneered, muttered a hollow "Yes," and followed as Jeffer walked down the steps to the body of his brother, the sun warm on his back.

Notes on
Balzac's War

This novella may be my most structurally complicated story, but it comes from the most direct and visceral of images. When I first saw the 1970s movie version of Invasion of the Body Snatchers, *starring Donald Sutherland, it really frightened me. The worst scene showed a dog—a mastiff or other large breed—with a human face. Images carry weight, they carry resonance and subtext. An image, if it is the right image, can tell you as much about a character as any amount of exposition.*

Because I couldn't shake the image from the movie, it eventually manifested itself in my far future stories as the flesh dogs. Although the flesh dogs appear in my novel Veniss Underground *as well as "A Heart for Lucretia" in this volume, they only reach their full, terrifying potential in "Balzac's War."*

A Heart for Lucretia

This is the story of a brother, a sister, and a flesh dog, and how two found a heart for the third. The story has both oral and written traditions, with no two versions the same. It begins, for our purposes, with the city . . .

"THE CITY, SHE HAS PARTS. THE CITY, SHE IS dead, but people live there, underground. They have parts . . ."

Gerard Mkumbi cared little for what Con Newman said, despite the man's seniority and standing in the crèche. But, finally, the moans as the wheezing autodoc worked on his sister persuaded him. The autodoc said Lucretia needed a new heart. A strong heart, one that would allow her to spring up from their sandy burrows hale and willowy, to dance again under the harvest moon. Gerard had hoped to trade places so that the tubes would stick out from his chest, his nose, his arms, the bellows compression pumping in out, in out. But no. He had the same defect, though latent, the autodoc told him. A successful transplant would only begin the cycle anew.

In Lucretia's room, at twilight, he read to her from old books: *Bellafonte's Quadraphelix*, *The Metal Dragon and Jessible*, others of their kind. A dread would possess him as he watched his sister, the words dry and uncomforting on his lips. Lucretia had high cheekbones, smoky-green eyes, and mocha skin which had made all the young men of the crèche flock to her dance.

But wrinkles crowded the corners of those eyes and Gerard could detect a slackness to the skin, the flesh beneath, which hinted at decay. The resolve for health had faltered, the usually clenched chin now sliding into the neck; surely a trick of shadow. Anyone but Gerard would have thought her forty-five. He knew she was twenty-seven. They had been born minutes apart, had shared the same womb. Watching her deterioration was to watch his own. Would he look this way at forty-five?

"Gerard," she would call out, her hand curling into his . . .

It had become a plea. He forced himself to hold her hand for hours, though the thought of such decay made him ill. The auto-doc insisted on keeping her drugged so she could not feel the pain. Could she even recognize him anymore, caught as she was be-tween wakefulness and sleep, sleep and death?

Flesh Dog, eyes hidden beneath the rolls of raw tissue that were its namesake, stayed always by his side. Flesh Dog shared few words with Gerard, but every twitch of its muzzle toward Lucretia or the squat metal autodoc reminded Gerard she would die soon—too soon, like their mother before her. Unless a miracle arose from the desert.

"The city, she has parts . . ."

And, finally, he had gone, taking Flesh Dog with him.

Thus it begins. The ending is another matter, a creature of fragments and glimpses that pieced together only tease . . .

That summer, as the stars watched overhead, an angel descended to the desert floor. And, when it departed, Lucretia arose from the dead and danced like a will-o'-the-wisp over the shifting sands; a fit-ful dance, for she often dreamed of Gerard at night, and they were unpleasant dreams.

That winter, Flesh Dog and Gerard limped back to the crèche. He did not speak now. Always, he looked toward the south, toward the great sea and the city with no name, as though expecting strangers.

And the middle, finally, in which meat is placed upon the bone.

For twenty days and twenty nights, Gerard trudged the sands, sub-sisting on the dry toads that Flesh Dog dug up for them. They encountered no one on their journey, listened only to the dry winds of the desert.

Finally, at dusk of the twenty-first day, they climbed a dune and stared down upon the city. The sun lent the city a crimson glare, silhouettes burnt into the sand. Gerard saw that the walls had crumbled in places and the buildings within, what could be glimpsed of them, had fallen into disrepair. Although Gerard looked for many minutes, he could discover no sign of life. The only movement came from the west, where a vast ocean glittered and rippled, red as the dunes which abutted it.

Though tired and disappointed at the city's abandoned appearance, Gerard would have plunged forward under cover of darkness. But Flesh Dog sniffed the air, sneezed, and counseled against it.

"Strange smells," it ruminated, "strange smells indeed . . ."

Gerard, fatigue creeping into his bones, could not find the strength to argue. He fell asleep against Flesh Dog's side, sand on his lips and the wind in his hair.

During the night, he woke in a cold sweat, convinced his sister had been leaning over him the moment before, her hair back in the ponytail she had lovingly braided at age nine, giggling and warning him to stay away from the city, the city that lay at the edge of his vision: a dark and ominous block of shadow.

As he drifted back to sleep, Gerard imagined he felt his sister's pulse weaken, back in her crèche bed.

In the morning, Gerard and Flesh Dog found that the city was nearly eclipsed by the cusp of the ocean, its waves a blinding green. Flesh Dog wished to bathe, but Gerard said no. The waves echoed his sister's voice in their constant rush and withdrawal: hurry, hurry . . .

Flesh Dog scouted ahead as Gerard entered the city. The walls had been breached in a dozen places and overhead zynagill hovered, waiting for carrion. The smell as Gerard passed under the shadow of walls made him bite back nausea. A subtle smell of plastic and leather and unwashed drains.

The interior was littered with corpses: a valley of corpses. Flesh Dog, whimpering, retreated to stand by Gerard. Gerard stared at the spectacle before him.

Dead people had been stacked in rectangular pits until they spilled over the edges. Nothing stirred. No flies tended the dead. No zynagill touched them. Plague, Gerard thought, putting a hand over his mouth and nose.

But the bright, festival clothes, the perfection of flesh without hint of boil or scab, mocked his intuition.

Gerard stepped forward, Flesh Dog shadowing him. The clothing upon the dead remained limp, lacking even the secret life of the wind. Eyes stared glassily and the jaws beneath were stiff, locked against giving up their mystery. Gerard would rather they sprang up in parody of human form than lie there, staring . . . A chill entered Gerard's bones. Watching. Bloodless. Cold. A vast tableau of the unburied and unburnt.

"So many dead," Gerard muttered. Once, he had been told of the legend of the Oliphaunt's graveyard. Was this the human equivalent? Would his Lucretia soon find her way to this city, against her will, because he had failed?

Flesh Dog sniffed the air as they skirted the nearest pit.

"Dead?" it said. "They smell as if they never lived . . ."

"Hush," replied Gerard, respectful of the silence.

And so they shuffled forward through the army of bodies, some appealing with outstretched arms, but all quiet as rundown clockwork mice. The eyes seemed to have lost the hope of blinking away deep sleep, the skin of feeling dappled sunlight upon it.

Beyond the pits lay the city proper: a maze of half-buried fortifications and jumbled buildings. In places, it appeared wars had been fought among the ruins, for the ground was burnt and some walls had melted into slag. All Gerard could do was remind himself of what Con Newman had said: "People live there, underground." It was obvious none lived above. Not even grass grew in the pavement cracks. They trudged on, to the sound of their own belabored breathing.

Finally, they came upon a strange sight amongst the wreckage: the top of an exposed elevator shaft some fifty meters ahead; the tower which had once housed the device had fallen away entirely, leaving only a rough rectangle of regular stone embedded in the ground. The shaft, which had all the looks of a bony arm, veinlike girders naked to the sky, the mortar peeled away, revealed a compact glass box, intact, which was the elevator. Gerard recognized it from *The Metal Dragon*. Jessible had escaped using an elevator. That something so fragile could have survived for so long amazed him.

Standing by the shaft were three creatures, each larger than Gerard by a third. They resembled giant weasels but no fur grew upon their clawed hands and they stood upright as though it was their birthright rather than some carnie show trick.

"What are they?" he hissed to Flesh Dog. "I have never seen them before."

"Meerkats," it replied. "Distilled somewhat with other species, but still meerkats. Your father used to read you tales of the meerkats and the dances they did for the men who created them."

Meerkats! This was indeed magical, and it created out of the torn and wasted landscape some small scrap of hope. Meerkats! He had killed meerkats for the meat before, but they rarely reached two feet in height. For a moment, he considered the possibility that Flesh Dog lied, but dismissed it: Flesh Dog had taught his father how to read and write. Flesh Dog never lied.

"Are they . . . they are intelligent?"

"Yes," replied Flesh Dog flatly.

Intelligent. He almost laughed. Was he to believe an intelligent toad next? His heartbeat quickened and with it he could feel his sister's heart, uneven and diseased, slowly winding down. He sobered.

"Flesh Dog, are these the folk who live underground?"

"Almost certainly," replied Flesh Dog.

When they came before the meerkats, the leader spoke to Gerard, ignoring Flesh Dog. The leader was a sleek, jet specimen with amber eyes and the language it spoke was all trills and clicks. The meerkat soon switched to *gish* when it interpreted the confused look on Gerard's face.

"State your business," it said in a bored voice.

"I need a human heart," Gerard said. "I am willing to trade for it."

A huffing rose from the leader, followed by similar noises from the other two.

"Parts," the leader ruminated, his tone bordering on contempt. "Fifteenth level." He barked a phrase to his followers and they stepped forward and passed a glittering rod in front of first Gerard and then Flesh Dog.

The leader nodded and escorted them to the elevator.

Gerard had seen elevators in books before, but never dreamed he would one day ride in one and so, when the doors closed, he bent to his knees and whispered to Flesh Dog, "Are elevators safe?"

Flesh Dog, sensing the tremor in Gerard's voice, replied, "Hold on to me if the motion makes you sick."

And so Gerard did hug Flesh Dog as they descended into the city's belly. He clung also to the rucksack full of precious stones and old autodoc parts with which he hoped to woo a human heart.

The levels seemed to crawl by, each more wondrous than the last, more terrible, more strange. Many of the things they saw, Gerard did not understand. They saw winged men with no eyes and vats of flesh and monstrous war engines belching, spitting sparks, and tubes and gears grinding and metal frames for ships in enormous caverns and stockpiles of small arms and old-style lasers and meerkats walking on ceilings and ghosts, images which reflected from the floor, that could not be real and more meerkats —meerkats in every size and color, crawling all over the engines of war, the tubes, the metal frames.

Fires burned everywhere—in rods and in canisters, on walls and floors; yellow fires, orange fires, blue fires, tended by meerkats more sinister than their fellows. Meerkats with frozen smiles and cruel claws and mouths that like traps, shut. The acrid smell of fire came to Gerard through the elevator walls, a bitter taste on his tongue. Around some fires meerkats threw squirming creatures the size of mice into the flames and, once or twice, larger metallic objects, their alloys running together and melting like butter to grease a pan.

Gerard turned away and ignored the cruelty of the meerkats, tore it from his mind. Lucretia needed a heart. Lucretia needed a heart.

The weight of earth and rock above him and to all sides made him dizzy and nauseous, but still deeper they went, silent and fearful, into the blackness beneath their feet.

At the fifteenth floor, they were greeted by a man who resembled the people in the pits: the same lifeless eyes and fixed jaw. But this man was alive and he indicated that Gerard was to follow him down the corridor. The corridor led into a maze of tunnels, all lit by a series of soft, reddish panels set into the ceiling. The smell was dank—a sharp, musty scent as of close quarters and many residents over many generations. The original reliefs carved into the walls had been defaced or done over, so that meerkat heads jutted from human bodies and *gish* became a weird series of sharp, harsh lines. Unease crept up on Gerard as they walked and, when he looked down, he saw that Flesh Dog's hackles were raised and its fangs bared: a startling white against the black-blue of his muzzle.

By the time they reached their destination, Gerard was thoroughly lost and could no more have retraced his steps than conjured a heart out of thin air. He clung to his rucksack, and to the thought that Lucretia still needed him.

The man led them into a large room. It had partitions that hid other sections from them. A chair had been provided, and the silent man gestured to it. Then he left, locking the doors behind him. Gerard sat down and Flesh Dog flopped to rest at his feet.

"That man smelled of the pits," Flesh Dog muttered. "Everything smells of the pits."

A whirring sound made Gerard sit straighter in his seat and a brace of meerkats appeared from behind a partition. One was tall and white, the other short and yellow. Flesh Dog growled, but they ignored the beast.

"My name is—" said Whitey, pronouncing a series of high-pitched trills.

"And I am—" said Yellow. "Together, we are the Duelists of Trade. I assume that is why you are here?"

Gerard nodded eagerly.

"First," said Whitey, "you must be thirsty."

He clapped his paws together and the lifeless man reentered, holding a glass of clear liquid. He offered it to Gerard, who took it with nodded thanks.

"Do not drink!" Flesh Dog hissed. "Do not drink!"

"Hush," Gerard said. "Hush."

The liquid smelled of berries and the first tentative sip rewarded him with a tangy, smooth taste. He took one more sip to be polite, and then heeded Flesh Dog's warning and set the glass by his chair.

"And now," said Yellow, "what precisely do you wish to trade for?"

"A heart," replied Gerard. "A human heart." He reached for his rucksack.

Whitey looked at Yellow, made a huffing sound. They both had fangs which poked out from the muzzle. Red dye designs had been carved into the whiteness, designs like scythes and slender knives in their sharpness. The eyes were slightly slanted and they devoured Gerard with a kind of hunger.

"What do you have to trade?" asked Yellow.

The hairs on Gerard's neck rose. The question had been asked with quiet authority and now, and only now, did he think that perhaps these meerkats were not as simple as the ones he had caught in the desert. That they might be dangerous in their own way. But the drink had created a sharp warmth in his stomach and it made him careless. Besides, Lucretia still needed a heart. He reached into the sack.

"I have gems," he said, pulling out a huge orange stone he had found at an oasis.

Whitey took the stone from Gerard's hand. He examined it for a moment, held it up to the light. Then he dashed it to the floor. It shattered. Flesh Dog growled.

"Gems?" Whitey hissed. "Gems! For a human heart?"

Gerard shrank back into his chair.

"But I—"

"Do you mean to insult me?" His tail twitched and twitched.

"No! My sister Lucretia is dying! Her heart is bad. I have brought the richest stones I could find . . ."

Flesh Dog rose onto his haunches, fur bristling, teeth bared.

Yellow patted Gerard's shoulder.

"There, there. No need to shock our guest. What else do you have?"

Here was a warm-hearted fellow, a generous fellow. Perhaps Yellow could be satisfied. Gerard scrabbled in his pack, pulled out an autodoc part.

"There. It is almost new."

Yellow's claws bit into his shoulder. Strangely, Gerard felt no pain, though the shock made him bite back a scream.

"No," said Yellow, voice like ice. "No, I'm sorry, but this won't do . . . this won't do at all. You come here, down all fifteen levels, spy on us, and offer us used parts?"

Flesh Dog growled and Gerard shook off Yellow's grasp. Why did he feel so numb? He was a fool, he realized, to have come here. In his ignorance he might well have come into the clutches of villains.

Gerard felt Flesh Dog against his feet, a position from which to guard him, and an unworthy thought crept into his head.

"What about Flesh Dog?" he asked Whitey. "I will trade Flesh Dog's talents for a heart . . ." An unfair trade considering the multitude of services Flesh Dog performed, but it was after all a beast. Surely a human life outweighed ownership of a talking beast? He tried to ignore the animal's whining.

Yellow nodded. "Very good. Very good indeed. However," and he pushed a button, "not good enough."

One of the partitions slid back. Behind it: one hundred Flesh Dogs, their parts not yet assembled, so that the heads sat upon one shelf while the bodies sagged in rows below. Two men, like the ones in the pit, lay sprawled in a corner.

Gerard gaped at the sight. So many Flesh Dogs. Dead? Decapitated? It made no sense. But then, neither did the numbness spreading through his body.

Flesh Dog shuddered, shook its head, and moaned.

One hundred heads, connected by one hundred wires to one hundred nutrient vats, turned to stare at him, with their globby folds of tissue dangling.

"We are," said Yellow, pausing, "overstocked on Flesh Dogs at the moment. Human hearts, now, those are rare. We have only one or two."

"However," said Whitey, "there is one way in which we might be persuaded to part with such a heart . . ."

"Yes?" said Gerard, afraid of the answer. He had volunteered his own heart before, but that had been with the assurance of care, faulty though it might have been, from the autodoc.

"It would involve both you and Flesh Dog," said Yellow slyly.

"It would take six months," said Whitey.

The delightful warmth had crept up his chest, the cold following behind.

"Afterward we would let you go . . ." Whitey held his hands while Yellow caressed his neck. "And in return, we give Lucretia a heart . . ."

"How soon?" Gerard asked. "How soon?" He shivered under Yellow's touch.

"Immediately," whispered Yellow in his ear. "Flesh for flesh. You must simply show us on a map where your crèche lies—you do know what a map is?—and we will send it by hovercraft. We do not break our word."

"So what of it, friend Gerard," said Whitey. "Do you agree?"

Gerard turned to Flesh Dog.

"What do you think, Flesh Dog?"

Flesh Dog peered at him through its fleshy folds. It turned to the Flesh Dog heads on the shelf—and howled. And howled, as though its heart had been broken. Then, with a sideways stutter, it leaned into the floor and was still, trembling around the mouth.

"Poor, poor machine," hummed Whitey. "It has forgotten it is a machine. So many years in service. Poor, poor machine . . ."

"Rip their throats," growled Flesh Dog from the floor. "Rip their throats?" The growl became a moan, and then incoherent. Gerard would have comforted it as it had comforted him in the elevator, but he was too numb.

"Do you agree?" Yellow asked, one eye on Flesh Dog.

"Yes," Gerard said, immobile in the chair now, able only to swivel his head. He imagined he could feel his sister's heartbeat become more regular, could feel a glow of health return to her cheeks. This, and this alone, kept him from panic, from giving over to the fear which ached in his bones. "Yes!" he said with a drunken recklessness, at the same time knowing he had no choice.

"You will leave with a smile upon your face," Whitey promised.

"Oh yes, you will," sang Yellow gleefully, taking out the knives.

As for the ending, there are many. Perhaps the next day, the next month, a new face stared up from the pits, the arms of the body reaching out but frozen, the eyes blank. Perhaps the meerkats never honored their agreement. Or . . .

That summer, as the stars watched overhead, an angel descended to the desert floor. And, when it departed, Lucretia arose from the dead and danced like a will-o'-the-wisp over the shifting sands. She danced fitfully, anger and sadness throbbing in her new heart.

That winter, Flesh Dog and Gerard limped back to the crèche. He did not speak now. Always, he looked toward the south, toward the great sea and the city with no name, as though expecting strangers. Always, as he sat by the fire and sucked his food with toothless gums, Gerard-Flesh Dog looked at Lucretia, the Lucretia who saw only that Flesh Dog had returned a mute, and smiled his permanent smile. Beneath the folds of tissue, Gerard's smoky-green eyes stared, silently begging for rescue. But Lucretia never dared pull back the folds to see for herself, perhaps afraid of what she might find there. Sometimes she would dream of the city, of what had happened there, but the vision would desert her upon waking, the only mark the tears she had wept while asleep.

After a year, the men of the crèche held a funeral for Gerard. After two years, Lucretia married a wealthy water dower and, though she treated Flesh Dog tenderly, he was never more than an animal to her.

Notes on
A Heart for Lucretia

With "A Heart for Lucretia," I wanted to write a story set in the far future that is actually written about the distant past. As I wrote the story, I imagined myself as a story-teller in the year 12,000 A.D. writing a story about the year 11,500 A.D. Thus can the mythic coexist with the science fictional, with no harm done to either.

One thing I like to do in stories is present the reader with a situation that seems clear and self-evident, but by the end of the story invert the meaning of the scene or situation that began the story. This process of transformation, if executed correctly, doesn't just dislocate the reader. It makes the reader question the assumptions he or she makes in processing what we call "reality." It's a reminder that the world is more complex than the limited ways in which we encounter it on a daily basis.

My sister Elizabeth had heart problems at the time I wrote this story. I started out writing "A Heart for Lucretia" to comfort her, but the narrative soon became dark and twisted and strange. I doubt it provided much comfort in its final form.

London Burning

CAROLINE BANCROFT WALKED PAST THE MANY cots in the children's ward on St. Bartholomew Hospital's third floor, stopping at the last cot, the one that faced the wall, the one that held Rebecca.

Rebecca, a five-year-old girl who had lost her arms and legs to the German bombs, existed in the ever-widening no man's land between the quick and the dead; she had neither the precious breakability of a porcelain doll, nor the ruddy toughness that distinguished so many of London's survivors. No, the child's skin seemed translucent and Caroline had the irrational fear that, were she to touch the child, under the harsh glare of hospital lamps, her hand might well slide *through* the body.

The only anchors, the only hints of solidity beyond the fixtures of flesh and blood, were the eyes, which stared at the far wall, at a point between ceiling and floor. A frigid gaze, the pupils the color of deep water, frozen over and motionless.

"Rebecca, won't you please say something?" she asked the girl, as she did every morning. "Just so we know you're all right?"

Caroline had a hundred more important duties than making a child speak, but the eyes—cold and dead and blank—hypnotized her.

Rebecca kept her silence. Caroline sighed and went about

cleaning the child's body: disposing of waste from the catheter, washing the pale skin with wet cloths, and massaging the memory of arms and legs, the seamless stitched-up places that reminded Caroline of stocking dolls she had made when she was young.

"Come *on*, Rebecca," she said, after having fed the child. "Just one word . . ."

No response.

According to the doctors, Rebecca hadn't suffered any brain damage, but there she lay, unmoving, alive in a straitjacket of flesh.

Caroline pulled the sheets up to Rebecca's neck.

"When I was your age, my dad used to take me for walks through Hyde Park on Saturday afternoons. Did you ever feed the ducks at Hyde Park, Rebecca? When we got back, my mum would have rice pudding waiting for our tea."

Caroline pushed back Rebecca's hair, used a pin to fix it in place, then tucked it behind the child's head.

Rice pudding, yes, and more recently, before he'd been called up, George had come by her parents' house, the smile that passed between them conveying knowledge of secret meetings at his flat. After tea, they'd go over to a pub and drink gin and lime, see a movie with George's pals.

The theatre was empty now, one wall having fallen in during a *Luftwaffe* attack, and most of George's friends were also in the army, or dead.

Strange, she thought, straightening the sheets, how one vision could lead to another, until it was like the pack of cards in *Alice in Wonderland*. She became conscious of the warm, humming sounds of the hospital, the quiet tread of feet in the hall, the fan blades swishing above her head.

"I have to go, Rebecca."

Was the child even now turning over memories in her mind, examining them like dolls within dolls?

"I really must go," Caroline said as she rose. "Please try tomorrow, dear. I know you can hear me."

A quick, forced smile and then she was through the door, sweating, breathing heavily, as though she had run up to the eighth floor and back.

No one understood her helplessness, the helplessness that became irritation, that became fear, because she could not reach a little girl. (And the fear beneath the fear: if she could not heal Rebecca, then . . . No, it was too terrible to think of.)

Once, she had tried to tell her mother. She described men

screaming, chunks torn from their legs, their groins, the smell of rotting flesh thick and cloying. The spray of arterial blood from a man with glass in his throat. The nakedness, the flash of white belly, sodden with ash and mud; hopeless burn cases she wanted desperately to save.

Her mother had wrapped her in a smothering hug, said, "It's all right, dear," and hadn't understood. Couldn't connect.

George would have understood, in a darkly luminous way, but his hopelessly dated postcards with their mandated cheeriness never responded to the weave and warp of her letters, in which she told the truth—about how alone she felt, about conditions at the hospital.

Finally, at dusk, uniform still flecked with blood and grime, Caroline found herself out on the streets, walking toward home. The undamaged blocks closest to the hospital reminded her of a time before war, when houses boasted sparkling clean porches, the greens, browns, and yellows bright, the paint not peeled away by fire. Then it was just London again, Hyde Park and Piccadilly and *home*. London fading into autumn.

The farther she walked, the more blackened the houses, until she could no longer pretend anything was the same. Crows strutted about on bowlegs, eager for flesh, while gangs of ragged boys ran from house to house, turning up treasures in the smoking ruins: a brass candlestick, a girdle, a toothbrush.

But more than the boys, the fires, or the dazed look on people's faces, there were the cats: tabbies, calicos, and mixed breeds. Many had survived the bombings and lived in the foundations of buildings reduced to caricatures of ash, cement, and glass. Now the streets crawled with mewling strays, driven off by the occasional lorry. Some strays were rumored to have feasted on their dead owners and, even after the war, Caroline would remember the sensation of being watched by a hundred feline eyes, cats carrying still other eyes daintily in their mouths.

In her nightmares, George's eyes stared out at her across the miles and she was unable to help him.

For a moment she lost control and memories of George before the war spilled out like unframed family portraits. She found it difficult to breathe or move, but she stifled her panic, forced it down.

She took a wrong turn. Then another, and another, until, thoroughly lost, bumping into people like a lost child, she stopped walking, almost sank to her knees.

The deserted street ahead had opened up onto what had once been, in happier times, an outdoor marketplace. Now the wooden tables were splintered and upended. A lukewarm breeze blew scraps of cloth and newspaper across the pavement and made her mouth water with a last teasing scent of fresh fried fish and vegetables.

A *clap-clap* of shoes to her left caught her attention and, turning, she saw a woman in a remarkable robe walking away from her. Patchwork scenes had been woven into the robe, rendered in bright blues, reds, and yellows that should have been garish but lent the woman a fevered elegance.

"Excuse me," Caroline said to the woman's back.

No response. No break of stride.

"Excuse me," Caroline said, louder this time, hurrying to catch up.

The woman walked faster.

"Do you know the way to Fordham Street from here?" she shouted when the gap had widened to forty feet, thinking that perhaps the woman was hard of hearing.

The woman broke into a run.

"Wait!"

The woman ducked into an alley.

Caroline ran to the alley mouth, saw nothing ahead but leveled buildings and a rat snuffling through rubbish beneath a rotted chair. She hesitated for a moment, debated turning back, realized she had no hope of retracing her path, and, with a suspicious glance at the rat, continued forward into the alley.

Alert for the slightest movement, Caroline's steps soon grew heavy. She began to sweat. The sky glimmered slate-gray and a heady smell, like petrol, hung in the air. Everything was too dark, too hot. A cat brushed against her ankles, begging for food. Caroline's movements began to mimic the frantic fluttering of moths around two shop lights that should have been turned off, the frenetic clawing of cats as they tried to catch the moths. How stupid she had been.

Sirens wailed. The scream, rising and falling, forced calm upon her. The all-too-familiar searchlights of ground-to-air defenses eclipsed the sky, followed by the indifferent hum of bombers.

The whistling, tumbling song of the bombs as they fell unfroze her legs. She ran forward, looking for shelter. Beside a pile of rubble, she saw a tobacconist's shop, but its sidewall had collapsed.

The steps of a nearby clock tower were blocked by wood and stone. Panicked, she dived beneath two girders that had fallen at an angle to each other, bruising her legs. She covered her head with her arms, snuggling as deep into the concrete as possible. She waited, trembling.

The ground bucked beneath her, set her down roughly. The aftershock bruised her spine and wrenched the breath from her mouth. But the ground did not break beneath her. Thunder rolled over Caroline, dust coating her as debris sprayed up around the sanctuary. Fires roared and flared, their hot breath gushing over the girders. Wood splintered not ten feet away, slivers of flame sent flying like shooting stars.

When the aftershocks faded and the fires had calmed to a low crackle, she slowly unbent and touched her feet, her legs—then head, shoulders, belly. No injuries, only the dust, which she brushed from her uniform without success.

She rose slowly and looked around her. To her surprise, buildings still stood, ragged as curtains, draperies of facades that glowered with fires or with shadow, propped up by no discernable means. The clock tower caught her eye. The hands were dark and twisted, but the bricks remained in place.

Then she saw the woman in the patchwork robe.

At first, Caroline just stared, her skin prickling. She wanted to pinch herself, to make sure she was awake, alive, watching.

Beneath the clock tower, the woman danced on a raised slab of brick and mortar, lit by flame and the tracers of antiaircraft fire. Her hair was streaked with dust, but beyond the hair and the outlined nose, mouth, chin, Caroline could see only the silhouette and the dance.

The dance began as a formal waltz, in step with an invisible partner, so much in step, so cohesive, that Caroline squinted, wondering if she had missed some dark-clothed suitor in the haze, perhaps hugging the clock-tower wall.

But no, the woman was alone. And her dance soon changed, became angry and solitary, fast and flickering as the flames, choreographed for warfare. Her hands cut the air like those of a flamenco dancer, but faster, so much faster that her body appeared to move in several directions at once, the legs with their own purpose, the arms and torso separate creatures twisting, twisting, almost twisting free.

The sirens' wail brought Caroline from her trance. A louder, insistent hum began to drown the sound of the sirens, and she realized a second raid was two minutes, one minute, away. She hesitated, turned to her sanctuary, then reversed herself and ran toward the woman.

"Take cover!" she shouted, stumbling over rubble.

The woman continued to dance, more fiercely than before, using the robe as a weapon, with a snap and curl that warned, *stay away!*

Caroline cleared the slab edge with one jump. Her momentum carried her into the dancer and as they fell together against the brick, the woman punched her in the stomach. Caroline cried out in pain and by the time the surprise wore off, the dancer had followed up with two stiff kicks. Furious with fear and pain, Caroline smacked the woman hard across the face. She forced the woman's arms down, turned her around so her face was against the bricks. Maintaining her grasp on the woman, Caroline pulled her up and dragged her, wriggling, kicking, and biting, back to the shelter. There she dumped her burden without kindness or ceremony.

The bombs hit, closer, and both women shook with the tremors. Caroline's stomach lifted and fell, her body jolted off the ground so that for a moment she felt as if she were floating.

The shaking subsided again. The fires provided intermittent illumination and Caroline, breathing in fishlike gasps, watched the dancer cough as she propped herself into a sitting position. The dancer crossed her legs. The robe had fallen open revealing her breasts, and she wrapped it tightly about herself. Where before she had seemed an expanding multi-limbed demon, now she had folded into herself, small and defenseless.

"You hurt me," Caroline said, her voice dry with dust.

A dazed expression widened the dancer's face. A rough face in the fire's light, as if a talented sculptor had done a hurried clay sketch of a striking woman. The jaw was too set, the cheekbones too unyielding. Her lipstick had smeared, the red slashing across the chin and, above, to the lower part of her nose.

"Stupid, stupid girl. Why?"

The voice, deep and husky, conjured up images of gypsy caravans, tarot cards, and thick Mediterranean stews. The incomprehension in the question made Caroline stumble over her reply.

"You would have died. You heard the sirens."

The woman laughed, a hacking sound, as she tried to clear her lungs of dust.

"Let them come. I danced for them."

"What do you mean?"

The woman shrugged. She leaned toward Caroline, who flinched.

"Don't be scared. What's your name? I can't read your tag."

"Caroline Bancroft," she said, blood rising to her face. She wanted to hit the woman for her rudeness. "You've a strange idea about suicide." Caroline's voice cracked and she swallowed, then continued in what she hoped was a calm tone: "Why not just take some pills or cut your throat? It's much more precise than doing a striptease for the *Luftwaffe*."

A chuckle, followed by high-strung laughter, as if some internal cog had come loose.

"Why are you laughing?" Caroline demanded. A flurry of giggles. She kicked out at the dancer. "*Stop it!* It's not funny."

"Oh, but it *is* funny, child," the woman said when she had recovered. "Much funnier than what others have said."

"Others? Air raid wardens?"

The dancer took a cigarette from a pocket in her robe, used a lighter on the tip, blew smoke toward Caroline's face.

"Not polite, are we? Not bred on politeness. You ask my name. Ask my name first."

Caroline sighed, settled back against a girder.

"What's your name?"

"My name is Moriah, Moriah Wisenman." She proffered a cigarette. "You want one? No? Then I have two." She stuck the second in her mouth, lit it. "As for dying, when I was very young, Rabbi Spevack took me aside and said, 'Moriah, always put yourself in God's path and he will reward you. If you make your own path, you risk great unhappiness.' He must have been drunk." She took a long drag. "I found these on a dead man. Hah! Imagine that! A dead man with smokes. As if he needed them."

"I've heard about people like you," Caroline said.

"What sorts of things?" The dancer's voice trembled with uncertainty or eagerness.

"That you're a crazy old woman!"

The savagery of her response surprised her. She was shaking, actually shaking with rage, she observed from a part of her self that had escaped the war, escaped the deaths, or been numbed beyond feeling by them. Her thoughts darkened as she thought once more of George.

Moriah slapped her across the face. It stung. It brought the anger out onto the surface, contorting her features.

"I want to die, child," hissed Moriah. "Can you understand

that? Isn't that my right?" She looked out at the raging fires, the fountains of flame spraying up the sides of buildings. "I used to dance in West End theaters. I used to have a husband."

Caroline looked at the ground, her eyes wet. This, she realized (*breathe deeply, try to relax*), was shell shock. This was post-bomb trauma. The emptiness. The helplessness. The anger. Had Rebecca gone through this?

Moriah plucked the cigarettes from her mouth, extinguished them in one fluid, cruel scrape against concrete.

"Let me tell you why I want to die. Perhaps then you'll understand."

"You're crazy," Caroline said, putting her hands over her ears. "I don't want to listen."

Moriah wrenched Caroline's hands away. "But you *will* listen, stupid girl. At least let me give you a *reason* to call me crazy: I have visions. Do you understand what I mean by visions?"

Caroline shook her head.

"Visions, Miss Caroline Bancroft, *visions!* At night I dream of true events. I fly above the Earth, looking down on all the people. The wind blows like glass through my robe and the trees are needles in my skin . . ."

. . . But I cannot control my flight. I can only follow the path set for me. I always dive lower. Too low. Too near, the world no longer so clear, clean, or undivided.

In my vision, I fly over a work camp somewhere in Europe. The snow is four feet deep, yet naked men and women stand out in the cold. Soldiers, too, with swastikas on their helmets, wearing thick coats. They chat about the war, the Russian front. It is so cold I can feel it in my joints.

Beyond the soldiers: the barbed wire and bonfires of the camp. The camp is never more than wire and smoke in the dream. I cannot taste it, hear it, smell it . . . as though it has already faded from the senses into memory.

"I would have gone ice skating today," one soldier says to another, in German.

The men and women have formed two lines, their lips blue, their eyes dull and staring straight ahead. I could draw for you from memory every detail of those faces, each wrinkle, each flinching glance across the snow.

An officer trudges over, begins to shoot the first line. The second line of workers stands behind the first, forced to watch.

The officer doesn't always shoot them in the head. Sometimes the stomach. Sometimes the legs. Until, finally, the whole line is dead or dying. Quietly. In the blood-clotted snow.

In the dream, I am now among them, shot in the stomach so I die slowly.

I watch as the soldiers round up the workers from the second line, bring them back to camp. The bodies, our bodies, remain behind, sprawled and orderly, eyes staring into nothing and nowhere.

And so the few of us who are still dying and not dead have this cold comfort: beneath us are others from the days, the weeks, before—frozen, the fingers reaching through the layers of snow, perhaps touching the arms of the newly dead. The roots of this field are fingers, their touch the only eyes for the blinded. I am a corpse. I am a corpse among many corpses, my hands moving slowly toward the light, searching for the brittle fingers of another . . .

Caroline, glancing over at Moriah, saw that she had drawn herself up into a fetal position, the eyes locked on a field of the dead. She reminded Caroline of Rebecca, looking so small, with the gaze so focused and mature.

Moriah's hands shook as she relit a cigarette.

"I've had these visions since the bombs killed my husband and leveled our house. I was unconscious for five days. When I woke, I could see into the minds of the dying. I've died a hundred times."

"They can't be true," Caroline managed to say. "They're nightmares. Not real."

"They *are* real."

"And so you try to kill yourself each night."

She shrugged. "One more death? It's not so bad. The bombs gave me this gift—" *gift* with a hiss, like a curse "—and they will take it away from me."

In the dark, in the flames, they stared at one another.

Finally, Moriah whispered, "Listen. I can hear the bombers again."

They waited as the hum came closer, coupled with the familiar whistle. Caroline watched the religious intensity on Moriah's face, the tight jaw and cocked head.

Then the clock tower exploded. The sky blossomed orange. Caroline shrieked from the heat. Under the roar and weight of impact, her skin seemed on fire.

Somehow, she pinned Moriah to the ground as the woman

tried to wriggle past her. Debris rained down on their shelter, gouts of flame shooting up. The acrid smell of bombs stabbed her nostrils. Moriah kicked. Moriah bit. Caroline held on until the body beneath her went limp. The bombs fell, fell, fell, shaking Caroline until all sensation or memory of sensation was gone. She lost hold of Moriah at one point, but it didn't matter: no one could have moved more than a few feet under the onslaught. The rain of rocks and wood made her deaf.

All she could do was make believe that houses still stood, that people would be bustling about happily in the streets when she opened her eyes, that they would not be pulling corpses from the rubble in the morning.

Later, after the all-clear, the sun was coming up and, incredibly, a light rain had begun to fall. Fires sizzled in the ruins and cats blinked, shook themselves, and went about their business with an air of mild reproach.

Caroline raised herself from the wreckage, every muscle, every bone, aching. Her face was black with soot. She bled from shrapnel cuts on her arms and legs. Slowly, she began to stumble over the debris, not sure where she was going, and not caring.

Moriah had vanished.

A postman who reminded Caroline of George came with the photograph six days later. He came in the evening, grunted greetings from beneath his raincoat hood, handed her the envelope, and disappeared into darkness.

There seemed no urgency in opening the envelope, so she put it on the mantelpiece. She was so tired from her rounds—a sour ache she could feel in her bones when she walked—that she simply took off her dirty uniform and curled up in bed. Let the bombs come.

The next morning she opened the envelope as she sat in the kitchen eating cold porridge. Light from the kitchen window blurred the features and Caroline had to stare at the photograph for several seconds before she recognized George. He stood in front of a vast stone paw, his hair disheveled. Dunes curved off into the distance.

George smiled, but his eyes had been reduced to pinpricks by the black-and-white photo.

The image had a sharpness, a neatness of composition, that confounded her. On the back George had scrawled, *Hope you are safe and well. An American reporter friend took this. Home soon. I hope. Love, George.* The date was four months stale.

When the message began to sound like gibberish, she stopped rereading it and put it in a box with all the other letters. Someday soon they had to stop coming. They had to.

At the very bottom of the stack was an official letter from the army, dated three months earlier. It related the circumstances of George Harrington's death in combat, body irretrievable. George's mother had forwarded it to her.

At 11:00 P.M. that night, Caroline pulled back the sheets on two more of the dead. One was a pilot, his face a welter of bone and eyeball and gray matter. A sickly sweet smell rose from his corpse, diluted only by the sterility of the sheets.

The body he escorted was Moriah, her eyes closed, the robe of many colors wrapped tightly around her. The lighting made the body paler than alabaster.

Caroline's throat tightened. For the first time in six days her features constricted in a display of emotion: an ache, a scream, a laugh? She did not know which, but she clenched her jaw against the impulse.

She opened the robe to reveal pristine flesh beneath, from neck to breasts to thighs. Not a scratch. Caroline ran her hands over the body, searching for a wound, an indentation, anything that might hint at a cause of death; she found nothing but unbroken skin. Surely she was only asleep, not dead, *not looking so perfect.* Caroline's stomach almost betrayed her. She swallowed several times.

But her hands, superbly trained, had continued their interrogation. She discovered a sliver of metal, no thicker than a needle, lodged in Moriah's neck.

Later, in a stolen moment of solitude, Caroline found herself again mouthing a litany to a child who seemed not to hear her. This time tears scalded her cheek as she sat with Rebecca.

"What are you looking at?" She shook Rebecca's shoulder. "Say something, damn you!"

Rebecca stared at the wall.

She released Rebecca, shuddered, and bowed her head. She looked up at the wall through her tears—and a shock ran through her body. The convulsion surprised her with its intensity, in the way her nerve ends caught fire.

For she did see now, finally, as Rebecca saw, as Moriah had

seen, that the wall was not made of plaster, but of bones, skeletons stacked atop each other, the skulls crushed and compressed, the legs fragile as bird wings. A layered field of the dead. She saw George and Moriah, and many others, so many she did not recognize, but who had surely passed through her hands at the hospital.

She let out a sharp, barking laugh. Even as she watched, with the new eyes the bombs had given her, even as she thought herself mad or damned with the Sight, her shoulders slumped, a score of muscles relaxing with relief. Here were dozens who could not be saved, already beyond any salvation she could give them. It would take all her strength just to save herself.

Notes on
London Burning

A character with a bit part in a television adaptation of a Dennis Potter novel inspired me to write "London Burning." I remember wondering why her character had been introduced, only to be taken off stage. Who was she? Where was she going in the middle of the Blitz?

This story had a very rough beginning—a now-deleted subplot that then-Omni editor Ellen Datlow wisely questioned led to a frenzied rewrite. A first reader from the magazine Interzone suggested that some of the historical details weren't accurate, which spurred another round of revisions. Really, the story itself got beaten down much the way the characters in it get beaten down by life. Over time, as a result, I became very distant from the story. I had encountered it from too many different perspectives for it ever to be new for me again. I do like that the story has no major male characters, and I do appreciate how much I learned from tackling "London Burning" so many times.

Corpse Mouth and Spore Nose

NEAR DAWN, THE DETECTIVE PULLED HIMSELF sodden and dripping from the River Moth. Dry land felt hard and unyielding to him. His muscles ached. The water had made him wrinkled and old. The stench of mud and silt clung to him. All around him, light strained to break through the darkness, found fault lines, and pierced the black with threads of gray and orange. To the west, from between the twinned towers the gray caps had erected when they had reconquered the city, the sky shone an unsettling shade of blue. Strange birds flew there, winking out when they reached the boundary formed by the towers.

The detective lay against the smooth stones of the jetty and realized he had never been so tired in all his life. He would have fallen asleep right there, but it did not feel safe. With a lurch and a groan, the detective stood, stretched his legs, took off his trench coat, and tried to wring the water from it. After a while, he gave up. Suddenly aware that the gray caps could already be coming for him, alerted by microscopic fungal cameras, he spun around, stared inland.

No one walked the narrow streets ahead of him. No sound broke through the crazy and upended buildings. A mist coated the spaces between dwellings. Everything was fuzzy, indistinct. A chill seeped through the detective's wet clothing and into his skin. In the half-light, Ambergris did not appear to be a city but instead a blank slate waiting for his imagination to transform it, to re-create it.

Out of the mist, as the mist withdrew and circled back like some solemn, autumnal tide, a great head loomed suddenly: a product of his dreams, the unexpected prow of a ship. But no: only a statue when finally revealed, and the detective exhaled the breath he had held. His legs shook, for the mist's withdrawal had resembled the advance of some death-pale giant.

He recognized the features now. Who would not? Voss Bender had been dead five hundred years, but no one who had ever heard his music played could forget that face. The statue's features suffered from fissures, pocks from bullet holes, infiltrations of mold, and the spurious introduction of a large purple mushroom upon its head. Yet even this did not detract from the grace of the rendering. Even the sliver of stone missing from his left eyebrow only served to make the statue appear more imperious.

Now the detective heard the sound of breathing. A quiet sound, neither labored nor erratic. At first, the detective fancied the sound came from the statue itself, but after listening carefully discarded this theory. In truth, he could not tell where it came from. Perhaps Ambergris itself breathed, the breezes and updrafts that drove the mist before them the even, comfortable breath of stone.

Automatically, the detective followed the gaze of Voss Bender's statue: down, and to the left. It was an old habit of his—he always must know where people were looking, for fear they stared at something more interesting, more profound, more alive . . .

And so he came upon a most remarkable signpost, shaded by the largest mushroom he had ever seen.

The mushroom stood taller than a palm tree, its trunk of lacy white flesh six feet in circumference. Its half-moon hood was stained purple and blue, with yellow streaks. The fragile grid work underneath the hood, from which the inevitable spores would one day float forth, had a lacquered, unreal appearance. Rootlike tendrils gripped the pavement, cracked and speared it.

As the detective walked toward the signpost and the mushroom, the breathing sound became louder. Could it emanate from the mushroom itself? Could the mushroom be breathing?

The signpost rose almost to his height of six feet. It had originally been composed of a gray stone, but a viscous white substance had gradually seduced the cracks and other imperfections until now the detective could hardly read the words. The sign did not include the name of the city, but simply a giant "A". Beneath the A, in letters sick with flourishes, a short inscription:

> Holy city, majestic, banish your fears.
> Arise, emerge from your sleeping years.
> Too long have you dwelt in the valley of tears.
> We shall restore you with mercy and grace.

Many elements of this inscription disturbed the detective, but certainly no more so than the quiet breathing. First, he wondered who had written the words. Second, he could not connect the words to Ambergris. Third, he had no clue who "We" were or how "We" would restore the city with mercy and grace.

The detective left off such questions in favor of solving the more perplexing problem of the breather. He took out his gun, then stood motionless for a long moment, listening.

Finally, he decided the sound must be coming from *behind* the mushroom. Nimbly, he walked around the mushroom's left flank, disgusted by the stickiness under his feet.

On the opposite side, he discovered a tendril that was not a tendril. And a statue that was not a statue. Such conclusions would have been neat, safe, rational. Unfortunately, the mystery to the breathing, the detective now knew, had no rational solution. A man lay beneath the mushroom. If he had not seen that the feet merged with the root-tendril, the detective might have thought the man was just taking a nap.

The man's paleness astounded the detective—he glowed in the shadowy dawn light. His head had been stripped of all hair, including eyebrows, and so had the rest of his body. His eyes were closed. His genitals had been replaced by some frozen-blue bulb of a fungus. Tiny tentacles had sprouted from his fingernails and now searched the earth around them restlessly. From the sudden fibrous hardness around the man's kneecaps, the detective could tell that the man became mushroom much farther up the leg than the foot, but despite this intrusion, this invasion, he saw by the gently rising chest and, yes, the quiet, steady breathing, that the man was alive.

The detective stood over the sleeping man, this living corpse, his gun hanging from the end of his arm, dangling from one finger. He had come to Ambergris to solve a case, The Case, and he had come to Ambergris to find a missing person. But not this person. And not this mystery. He began to see, with a frisson of dread, that to solve the Case, he might have to solve a dozen other cases before it. Or else they might conspire to obscure the True Case. The True Crime.

He considered the man's face. The thickness of the white mask reminded him of rubber. Everywhere, any delicacies of cheekbone, of nose, of ear, had given way to an over-ripe fullness. The breath issued from the slightest gap between the thick lips. The bulbous eyelids fluttered, the eyelashes miniatures of the tentacles that had colonized the man's fingers.

Against his own better judgment, the detective knelt beside the man. He had room for neither disgust nor fascination within him. He was simply tired, and eager to explode this lesser mystery by any means possible. He tapped the side of the man's head with his gun. No response. He tapped again—harder.

The man's eyes shot open. The detective caught a swift glimpse of limitless black, across which tiny insects glided and fell, an entire world trapped on the surface of the man's eyes. The detective rose with a cry of horror, stood back, gun aimed at the man.

The mushroom-man opened his mouth—and his mouth was filled with corpses. Not a tooth remained in that mouth, that it might be more thickly packed with corpses. Lean corpses. Fat corpses. Headless corpses. Corpses with gills. Corpses with wings. Corpses with single eyes. Corpses with multiple eyes. Corpses that mumbled through their dead mouths. Corpses that tried to dance in their stumbling decay. Grinning corpses. Weeping corpses. And all of them no taller than three inches high.

The man's mouth continued to open long after it should have stopped, while the detective continued to stare at this mystery he was not sure he would ever fully understand. His finger trembled on the trigger, and he held the gun so tight the imprint of the grip burned into his palm.

The man began to cough up the corpses—they slid up out of his mouth at odd angles, all of them coated in mucus. They spilled across his belly and out onto the ground. Hundreds of them. They reached the detective's legs and he recoiled in disgust. And fear. But he couldn't stop staring at the tiny corpses, so like naked dolls or children. And he couldn't stop staring at the man's mouth as it continued to expand. Or at the dead eyes brimming with life.

If not for the Case, the detective would have stood there for a long time. He might have let his trench coat fall softly to the ground. He might have taken off all of his clothes and laid down beside the mushroom-man. He might have waited for the tendrils to stealthily crawl and slide and coil across his arms and legs. He might have acquired tentacles and strange dreams to keep him from thinking about what he had become . . . but something in the awful complexity of the mushroom-man's face made him think of Alison, the missing girl, and with that thought the mist began to clear, the morning light became brighter, and the trance broke. He bent low, next to the mushroom-man's head.

"This isn't right," he said. "This isn't right. There is no mystery here. You are as transparent as your skin. Your case is as old as this city, and no older. The solution is simple. We both know this."

The detective held the gun against the mushroom-man's head, the mushroom-man's gaze slowly drifted to the left, to take in the gun and the gun wielder.

Through the glut of corpses, the mushroom-man mouthed "No," in as soft a whisper as its breath.

"I. Do. Not. Believe. In. You," the detective said.

He stood. He aimed. He fired. The bullet entered the mushroom man's head—which exploded into a hundred thousand snow-white spores that lifted themselves into the air like chained explorers suddenly set free. They floated down upon the hundreds of tiny corpses. They floated down upon the remains of the mushroom-man's body. They floated down upon the detective, caught in the detective's hair while he waved his hands to avoid them.

Not even the mushroom-man's eyes remained—just his jutting torso, his spindly legs, the feet that were not really feet.

No one came running to investigate, despite the echoing recoil of the gunshot. No one came to arrest him. The looming mushroom did not rear back in pain. The spores rose, carried by the breeze, destined to explore the city well in advance of the detective.

As for the detective, he just stood there, surrounded by the spores, and marveled at what he had wrought. He had killed a man who was not a man. Out of the shattered head had poured a hundred thousand lives, scattered by the explosion. How did one stick to just one case in this city?

Slowly, reluctantly, the detective put away his gun. The dawn had truly arrived, a second sun beginning to blaze in the space between the gray caps' two towers. He could hear voices in the city behind him. The mist had begun to evaporate. He could see clearly now. He had a Case. He had a Client. His shoulders fell, his muscles relaxed. He breathed in deeply, through his nose . . .

A spore entered his nose.

He felt it wriggling in his nasal cavity. He sneezed, but the spore hooked itself into the soft flesh inside his left nostril. The pain made him jerk upright, and he howled in anguish.

Abandoning all pretense, he drove his left index finger up into his nostril in search of the spore—only to be stung (he could only think of it as a bee sting) by the spore, which proceeded to advance up his nostril. The detective withdrew his finger. The tip was bleeding. In desperation, he put both hands up to the bridge of his nose, cursing as he tried to prevent the spore from going any farther.

To no effect—except that now he felt the spore slide down into the back of his throat and begin to crawl back up into his mouth. He flailed about as he tried to loop his tongue back over itself to deliver a knockout blow.

The detective was still cursing, but the words came out all garbled and blurbering.

The spore, despite the best efforts of his tongue, stuck defiantly to the roof of his mouth. He began to feel as if he were suffocating. He again tried to dislodge the spore with his tongue. His tongue became numb, then a dead weight lolling in his mouth. He put three fingers of his left hand into his mouth, pushing aside his tongue, and tried to pull the spore out, but it began to burrow into his palate to get away from his hand. Hopping on one leg, the detective dropped his gun into his trench coat pocket. He dug into his mouth with as many fingers as he could fit. The burrowing sensation became more intense. His fingers, getting in each other's way, caught at the tail end of the spore. Pulled, but only succeeded in breaking off a tuft.

He withdrew his fingers, panicked. As if they had been waiting for the right time, another dozen milk-white spores floated into his mouth. He made a gurgling sound. He clutched his throat. It felt as if he were choking to death on feathers. He began to feel faint. He gargled. Tried to scream. Fell to his knees. Beside the tiny corpses. There was a humming in his ears. He could sense a breath, like the breath of the world, and a distant laughter. The spores were laughing at him. *We shall restore you with mercy and grace* . . .

Anger rose within him. As he continued to be deprived of oxygen, the sensation of mocking laughter from the spores intensified. He rose to one knee, tried to insist that he would not become a home for corpses. But all that came out was a whimper. He fell back against the ground.

For a moment—a horrible, gnawing millisecond—as the detective hunched over on his knees among the corpses, there was a great Nothing in his head. Not a thought. Not a memory or even Memory. There was only the relentless squirming of the spores as they raced through his body.

Then, like a King Squid exploding to the surface, the detective wrenched himself to his feet. He muttered to himself. He leaned to the side. Cocked his head like a monkey as he looked around. He licked his lips. He stared down at the shattered head, the corpse mouth that had once been him.

"Haw haw haw." The great, looping syllables came out of the detective's mouth as if he had always spoken that way. The detective's body danced a thuggish dance around the husked-out corpse. "Haw haw haw. Odessa Bliss. I am Odessa Bliss!" bellowed the detective. And scratched an armpit absentmindedly.

Then, with a frightening burst of speed, the detective's hijacked body ran into the city of Ambergris, legs pumping, face contorted in an expression of sheer and unrelieved stupidity, sometimes abandoning the straight arrow of its lumbering path to jump for joy at freedom.

The detective no longer heard the giggling of the spores. The detective heard only the vacuous mumbles and half-formed thoughts of Odessa Bliss. The Case had been subsumed by this new situation. He had no case now. He did not even have his own mind. A phrase curled through his proto-thoughts like a length of razor-sharp wire: *"We shall restore you with mercy and grace . . ."*

Soon he had a new perspective on everything.

Notes on
Corpse Mouth and Spore Nose

I plan to write three novels set in my imaginary city of Ambergris, the site of so much of my most recent novella-length fiction. The third novel, Fragments from a Drowned City, *is far from completion but so exciting to me that sometimes pieces of it spill out as vignettes and self-contained scenes. One even graces the cover of my* City of Saints and Madmen *collection. "Corpse Mouth and Spore Nose" is another. In it, readers can see the first glimmer of an idea I hope to carry through to completion in the next few years: the combining of the dark fantasy and detective genres, with a touch of narrative dislocation.*

The Machine

ONE NIGHT, BECAUSE YOU WERE DISTRAUGHT, because you took a wrong turn, because you wanted to, you find yourself deep below the City, spiraling through labyrinths. In the cold and the damp, with echoes and with the dead weight of your own thoughts. Rumors from the underground flit through your mind—about a door, about a mirror, about a machine.

You feel it and hear it before you see it: a throbbly hum, a grindful pulse, a sorrowing bellow. The passageway rumbles and crackles with the force of it. A hot wind flares out before it. The only entrance leads, after much hard work, to the back of the machine, where you can only see its innards. You are struck by the fact of its awful carnality, for they feed it lives as well as fuel. Flesh and metal bond, married by fruiting bodies, joined by a latticework of polyps and filaments and lazy strands. Wisps and converted moonlight. Sparks and gears. The whole is at first obscured by its own detail, by those elements directly at eye level: a row of white sluglike bodies curled within the cogs and gears, eyes shut, apparently asleep. Wrinkled and luminous. Lacking all but the most rudimentary stubs of limbs.

You cannot help but look closer. You cannot help but notice two things: that they dream, twitching reflexively in their repose, eyelids flickering with subconscious thought, and that they are not truly curled within the machine—they are curled *into* the machine, meshed with it at a hundred points of contact. The blue-red veins in their arms flowing into milk-white fingers, and at the border between skin and air, transformed from vein into silvery wire. Tendrils of wire meet tendrils of flesh, broken up by sections of cruel-looking wheels, sharp as knives, clotted with scraps of flesh, and whining almost soundlessly as they whir in the darkness.

As you stare at the nearest white wrinkled body, you begin to smell the thickness of oil and blood mixed together. As the taste bites into your mouth, you take a step back, and suddenly you feel as if you are falling, the sense of vertigo so intense your arms flail out though you stand on solid ground. Because you realize it isn't one pale dreamer, or even a row of them, or even five rows of five hundred, but more than five thousand rows of five thousand milk-white dreamers, running on up into the distance—as far as you can dare to see—millions of them, caught and transfixed in the back of the machine. And they are all dreaming their pale dreams, and all their eyelids flicker in unison, and all their blood flows into all the wires while a hundred thousand knife-sharp wheels spin soundlessly.

The hum you hear, that low hum you hear, does not come from the machinery. It does not come from the wheels, the cogs, the wires. The hum emanates from the white bodies. They are humming in their sleep, a slow, even hum as peaceful as they are not, while the machine itself is silent. Silent.

The rows blur as you tilt your head to look up, up, up, not because the rows are too far away, but because either your sight or your brain has decided that this is too much, this is too much to take in without going mad, that you *do not* want to comprehend this crushing immensity of vision, that if comprehended completely, it will haunt not just your nightmares for the rest of your life—it will form a permanent overlay upon your waking sight, and you will stumble through your days like a blind man, the ghost-vision in your head stronger than reality.

So you return to details—the details right in front of you. The latticework of wires and tubes, where you see a thrush has been placed, intertwined, its broken wings flapping painfully. There, a dragonfly, already dead, brittle and glassy. Bits and pieces of red flesh still writhing with the memory of interconnection. Skulls. Yellowing bones. Glossy black vines. Pieces of earth. And holding it all together, like glue, dull red fungus.

But now the detail becomes too detailed, and again your eyes blur, and you decide maybe movement will save you—that perhaps if you move to the other side of the machine, you will find something different, something that does not call out so incessantly for your surrender. Because if you stand there, if you stand there for another minute, you will enmesh yourself in the machine. You will climb up into the flesh and metal. You will curl up to something pale and sticky and embrace it. You will relax your body into the space allowed it, your legs released from you in a spray of blood and wire, you smiling as it happens, your eyes already dead, dead and dreaming some communal dream, your tongue the tongue of the machine, your mouth humming in another language, your arms weighed down with tendrils of metal, your torso split in half to let out the things that must be let out.

You stand on the fissure between sweet acceptance of dissolution and the responsibility of movement for a long, long time, the enticing smell of decay, the ultimate inertia, reaching out to you . . . but eventually you move, you move away with an audible shudder that shakes you to your bones, almost pulls you apart anyway.

As you hobble around to the side of the machine, you feel the million eyes of the crumpled, huddled white shapes snap open, for a single second drawn out of their dream of you . . .

There is no history. There is no present. There is no future. There is no past. There is no surface to the world. There are only the sides of the machine. Sick, slick memory of metal, mad with its own brightness, mad with the memory of what it contains. You cling to those sides for support, but make your way past them as quickly as possible. The sides are like the middle of a book—necessary, but quickly read through to get to the end. Already you try in vain to forget the beginning.

The front of the machine has a comforting translucent or reflective quality. You will never be able to decide which quality it possesses, although you stand there staring at it for days, ensnared by your own foolish hope for something to negate the horrible negation of the machine's innards. Ghosts of images cloud the surface of the machine and are wiped clean as if by a careless, a meticulous, an impatient painter. A great windswept desert, sluggish with the weight of its own dunes. An ocean, waveless, the tension of its surface broken only by the shadow of clouds above, the water such a perfect blue-green that it hurts your eyes. A mountain range at sunset, distant, ruined towers propped up by the foothills at its flanks. Images of jungles and swamps riddled with strange birds, strange beasts. Always flickering into perfection and back into oblivion. Places that if they exist in this world you have never seen them or heard mention of their existence. Ever.

You slide into the calm of these scenes after a while, although you cannot forget the white dreaming shapes behind the machine, the eyelids that flickered as these images flicker. Do dreamers dream this world? Only the machine knows, and the machine is damaged. These thoughts run liquid-slow through your brain, even though you wish they would stop.

After several days, your eyes finally stray and unfocus and blink slowly. You notice, at the very bottom of the mirror, the glass, a door. The door is as big as the machine. The door is as small as your fingernail. The distance between you and the door is infinite. The distance between you and the door is so small that you could reach out and touch it. The door is translucent—the images that flow across the front of the machine sweep across the door as well, so that it is only by the barely perceived hairline fracture of its outline that it can be distinguished beneath the desert, the ocean, the mountains, that glide across its surface. The door is a mirror too, you realize, and after not focusing on anything for so long, letting images run through you, you find yourself concentrating on the door and the door alone. In many ways, it is an ordinary door, almost a non-existent door. And yet, staring at it, a wave of fear passes over you. A fear so blinding it paralyzes you. It holds you in place. You can feel the pressure of all that meat, all that flesh, all the metal inside the machine amassed behind that door. It is an unbearable weight at your throat. You are buried in it, in a small box, under an eternity of rock and earth. The worms are singing to you through the rubble. You cannot think. You cannot breathe. You dare not breathe. Your head is full of blood.
    There is something behind the door.
    There is something behind the door.
    There is something behind the door.
    The door begins to open inward, and *something* fluid and slow, no longer dreaming, begins to come out from inside, lurching around the edge of the door. You run as far from that place as you possibly can, screaming until your throat fills with the blood in your head, your head now an empty globe while you drown in blood. And still it makes no difference, because you are back in that place with the slugs and the skulls and the pale dreamers and the machine that doesn't work that doesn't work that doesn't work that-doesn'twork hatdoesnwor atdoeswor tdoeswor doeswor doewor dowor door . . .

Notes on
The Machine

At a certain point in my development as a writer, I stopped using dream sequences in my fiction, for the simple reason that much of my fiction reads like a dream, or nightmare. Adding a real dream to a story that already feels dreamlike destabilizes the story. It unmoors it so totally from reality that the reader has no anchor.

"The Machine" reads like undiluted nightmare. One day, I was thinking about the subterranean inhabitants of my imaginary city of Ambergris, called "gray caps" or "mushroom dwellers." What was it really like under the city? The next morning, when I woke up, I had a line in my head: "A door that isn't a door. A window that isn't a window." I sat down and wrote "The Machine."

"The Machine" is a stand-alone selection from my novel-in-progress Shriek: An Afterword. *It forms the central mystery of the novel, in a sense. I like "The Machine" because it doesn't try to explain itself. You're free to reach your own conclusions, based on whatever other Ambergris stories you've read.*

Mahout

MARY: THE LARGEST LIVING LAND ANIMAL ON EARTH. 3 INCHES LARGER THAN JUMBO AND WEIGHING OVER 5 TONS . . .
—Billboard for the Sparks Circus, 1916

YOU WATCH THE BRUISED SKY AS THE SUN SETS outside Dan's Eatery. Dan's lies off County Road 12 in Tennessee. The farms and paint-peeled houses surrounding it form the town of Erwin.

Flocks of starlings mimic the dance of leaves on the dirt road outside. Rust-red leaves. Your hands are brown. People stare at you from other tables, someone whispering, ". . . East Indian darky . . ." 1916: you are sixty-seven years old and thousands of miles from home.

You arrived with the circus early this morning, south about a mile, where the railroad tracks crisscross a small station, amphitheater, and coal tipple: a staggering troupe of stiltmen, clowns wielding saws, and high-wire women so stiff they cannot bend at the waist, at least until the next show. The trains don't even bother passing through Erwin, but this is your day off and you wanted to escape the swelter of people. Tomorrow your elephants, the ones you have trained for fifteen years, will perform for the Ringmaster. After the elephant show, you will perform again: *Come see the*

*amazing psychic! He can read your mind! Come see the Brahmin
holy man!*

You are not truly psychic. Neither are you of the Brahmin caste.
You wear a Sikh turban. They expect it, even though you are
Hindu and the weather hot. But at least you can be near the ele-
phants.

> "I have been with the shows for three years and have never
> known the elephant to lose her temper before."
> —Mr. Heron, press agent, *Johnson City Comet*,
> September 14, 1916, page 1

> " 'Murderous Mary,' as she was termed by spectators, has been
> in the circus for fifteen years and this is the first time anyone
> has come to harm."
> —*Nashville Banner*, September 13, 1916, page 9

The light fades from the windows until the starlings are blurs of
shadow and bar lamps reflect on the glass. You sweat despite the
chill; the nervous tic under your right eye where the blood vessel
has burst works in and out. Your hands become clenched claws.

The lady to the left with the matted hair and distant stare—she
thinks about her next trick, the dull slap of flesh on flesh . . . the
ache in her body, her heart. *Tease, you tease too much*, she thinks.
The man at the bar who deliberately combs his few hairs and sips
his whiskey—he fears for his bloodhound. It used to run for miles
across his farm, but now the farm is smaller, eaten away at the
edges by bankers. His wife has left him. The dog has tumors, weak
back legs, and cannot hold its bladder. It lies at home by the furnace and dreams of better days. The man hates the dog. He loves
the dog. If he goes home, he might find it dead, and then he will be
waiting to die. Alone.

The claws bite into your palms, draw blood.

The waitress smiles as she leans over to take your plate. You
smile back, her face blank to you. You can only sense the pain,
enter minds through agony. Sometimes you block it by concentrating on dust motes or the pattern of raindrops on a blade of grass.
You can escape it.

When you are with the solid shadows of your elephants, all the
sharp edges fade away. Your clenched hands relax.

> "Suddenly, Mary collided its trunk vice-like about his body,
> lifted him ten feet in the air, then dashed him with fury to the

ground. Before Eldridge had a chance to reach his feet, the elephant had him pinioned to the ground, and with the full force of her biestly fury is said to have sunk her giant tusks entirely through his body. The animal then trampled the dying form of Eldridge as if seeking a murderous triumph, then with a sudden . . . swing of her massive foot hurled his body into the crowd."

—*Johnson City Staff*, September 13, 1916, page 3

You grew up in Jaipur, under the maharajah's benevolent neglect—a man who employed your parents as servants. Twenty years later, the maharajah would sell his elephants, and your services, to the Americans to pay his debts.

Every day you suffered headaches or crying spells. The leper woman with her bag of shriveled flowers would ask you for coins, and you saw the young woman inside her, the pretty one who would have married, laughed many days by the washing stones. If not for the decaying flesh. You ran from her, not understanding *how* or *why* you had these visions.

The merchant at the market would say, "Nice boy: have a sweet," smiling at your parents and you would hear, from deep inside his coiled thoughts: *Ugly child. Scrawny. No good for lifting sacks.* The headaches would pick away your skull. You wondered why people lied so much.

Then, when you were seven, you met the elephant and its mahout. You went with your parents on holiday to see the Amber Palace, a tilted terrace of fortifications and tile buildings and minarets atop a mountain ridge. The snake of road circled higher and higher. Below: fields and a lake.

You gnawed your lip bloody listening to the desperation beneath beggars' prayers and your father's impatience with them as you trudged along. Your mother you could not read. Never could.

Then, sweaty, halfway up:

The elephant. Straddling the road, one front foot alone larger than you and your parents. Trunk curled, tusks capped in gold, a gilded carriage upon its back. You gasped, stumbled. And looked into its eyes.

Long-lashed, black, with no hint of reflected light. Age wrinkles spiraled down into the eye. The elephant stared at you, measured you. You shivered. *Ganesha*, you thought. The elephant-headed god of luck and wisdom.

You wanted a ride. You begged your father, clutched at your mother's sari. Tired of walking, they smiled, said yes.

That was when the mahout stepped out from behind his elephant: a shriveled man with no flesh on his bones so that his head, small on another man, seemed large. A holy man. A wise man.

You stared at your future teacher unabashedly and he bowed, pressed his palms together.

"I am Arjun, mahout of the Amber Palace."

You, solemn, bowing also: "Gautam, boy of Jaipur."

He laughed. "And someday mahout, perhaps?"

You nodded, watching the elephant.

Only after your father shoved you up onto the side ladder and you climbed into the carriage did you realize that the mendicant's pain was gone. From the dizzying height, lurching forward, touching the prickly black hairs, you could not feel the world's agonies spread out below you: the farmers on the plate-sized fields, the swimmers in the lake. Nothing. You laughed. You laughed and snuggled into your mother's arms.

You remember that moment as if it happened yesterday. You felt like a god, free of pain. Though that is impossible. The elephant was the god and the mahout its keeper.

> "There was a big ditch at that time put there for the purpose of draining . . . and they'd sent these boys to ride the elephants. They went down to water them and on the way back each boy had a little stick-like that was a spear or hook in the end of it . . . And this big old elephant, Mary, reached over to get her a watermelon rind, about a half a watermelon somebody eat and just laid it down there; 'n she did, the boy Eldridge give her a jerk. He pulled her away from 'em and he just bowed real big; and when he did, she took him right around the waist . . . and throwed him against the side of the drink stand and just knocked the whole side out o' it. I guess it killed him, but when he hit the ground the elephant just walked over and set her foot on his head . . . and the blood and brains and stuff just squirted all over."
> —W. H. Coleman, eyewitness

Only one woman's face haunts you. You have been with many women, trying to block the pain. It never works; even in the throes of orgasm there is always a larger ache than before.

But you did not know this woman. Not even a name.

Four years ago—almost to the day you sit and eat at Dan's—she came to you as the shadows began to shut down your booth.

Exhausted, half in trance, you had peered into the pains of a dozen men and women, lied for the contented ones who hid their disappointments deep.

The woman cleared your thoughts. She had an elegance beyond her simple cotton dress, which reminded you of the leper woman as she might have been. Around her, the circus folk melted away. The Scaled Man and the Bearded Lady, the Man with Two Spears Through His Cheeks and the Lady Who Drank Blood: they enhanced her beauty all the more. She smelled of jasmine and treacle. You imagined her skin smooth beneath your touch.

You bowed to her, recited the routine the other performers had taught you, in the despised pidgin English. You speak the language with only a hint of accent.

She listened patiently, gave the drunken crowd gathered at her back a single glance, but did not wave them away. A large crowd, enlivened by an entire day of merrymaking.

"Is my husband cheating on me?" A harsher voice than you imagined . . .

She had been biting back her pain and now it flooded out, embraced you. You looked into her eyes (such pretty eyes: long-lashed and black, with no reflection) and winced. The answer was wrapped around her doubts. The lies she had told herself, the imagined explanations for late-night forays.

You hesitated, glanced around at the litter of bottles and cartons, the mud and filth.

"Come on!" It was a plea.

"Yes."

The crowd roared. The circus folk chuckled, quietly mocking: the Scaled Man and the Bearded Lady and the Man with Two Spears and the Lady Who Drank Blood. A low mumble of "Fool!" and "Slut!" swept through the crowd. The wide, happy wave of amusement muffled her pain, numbed you.

You smiled. You almost laughed.

The smile left your lips when you looked up at her. You have never seen that expression before or since, the betrayal that bled from her eyes, the perfect mouth.

The woman pulled a knife from her purse. She plunged it into your chest, above the heart. Out it came, trailing red. She raised it to strike again—and on the downward stroke the Man with Two Spears caught the blade in his palm, wrenched it from her. The Scaled Man and the Bearded Lady dragged her away, she snarling and fighting them.

You stared stupidly at the wound, at the blood smeared across your costume. The crowd had broken down into its thousand parts, some screaming, some backing quietly away, a few calling for a doctor. You just stared. Time, urgency—these things were unimportant.

You daubed your finger in the bright, bright blood. *This is me?* you thought. *I am bleeding?* No pain. Like the leper in Jaipur. No pain. And, for one glorious moment, looking up into the clowns' faces, you believed you were free. But:

The clowns radiated pity. The Lady Who Drank Blood clasped your arm, aching over your wound, licking it. Your face became a mask, then crumbled. You had only become numb to your own pain. Like the old men in the Jaipur market who sucked and sucked on their opium pipes.

You are old now and the elephants have robbed you of your pain.

The cooking of crayfish brings your attention away from the window of Dan's Eatery. You know the sensation of death now (brittle, withering), have experienced it in many forms. Arjun eventually taught you to bear it, to sit still while life slipped away, though even he could never fully understand the pain.

The crayfish are lowered into the pot, their chitin turning red, dozens of eyes popping. Tiny slivers. Then: silence. Or an echo. The ghost of another, more distant pain. You cannot tell. Your hand cannot feel the heat as it clutches a cup of coffee.

You are homesick.

> "The crowd kept hollerin' and sayin', 'Let's kill the elephant, let's kill 'er . . .'"
> —Mr. Coleman

> "Sheriff Gallahan thought he could shoot her, but he couldn't with a .45. It just knocked chips out of her hide a little."
> —Mr. Treadwell, eyewitness

> ". . . [the owner] said 'People, I'd be perfectly willin' to kill her, but there's no way to kill her. There ain't gun enough in this country that she could be killed; there's no way to kill her.'"
> —Mrs. E. H. Griffith, in a letter to Bert Vincent

Last night you shared the crowded freight compartment with your elephants; the *chump chump* of wheels on the track lulled you to sleep. You were so tired you slept standing up, leaning against Mary, your largest.

You dreamt.

Mary grew until her feet touched the four corners of the earth, so large that you measured less than the height of her toenails. Absurdly, the trinity—Brahma, Siva, Vishnu—whirled above her head on their appointed vehicles. She took you with her trunk, grasping you so gently that the tiniest twitch and you would have fallen to your death. She brought you up, up through the clouds until you were in the cold dark of the cosmos, looking into her eye. It seemed to question you.

You wept. In Hindi, you said, "Please, Ganesh. I am so old. Take away their pain. Give me back my own pain . . ." You wept and Mary stared at you. There was no answer. It was only Mary, not Ganesha at all. The stars whispered in Sanskrit, wrote messages across the dark you could not decipher.

When you woke, you brushed her and fed her cabbage heads, watermelon rinds, cooed softly in her ear when the shivering of boxcar metal disturbed her.

> "Everybody was excited about it, you know—'n' come down there to watch them hang the elephant. They had a coal tipple down there; I guess the coal tipple was three hundred, four hundred feet long from the ground to the top of the tipple; and it was covered up with people just as thick as they could stand on that tipple, you know, besides what was on the ground. I'd say they 'as three thousand people there . . ."
>
> —Bud Jones, eyewitness

Your stomach is queasy as you walk out of Dan's Eatery into the humidity of main street Erwin. You stare up at the moon. Tonight, it is Ganesha's tusk, thin and bright through tree branches. A lucky moon.

> "They brought those elephants down there, four or five of them together. And they had this here Mary bringing up the rear. It was just like they was havin' a parade, holdin' one another's tail . . . These other ones come up . . . and they stopped. Well, she just cut loose right there and the showmen, they went and put a chain, a small chain, around her foot, and chained her to the rail. Then they backed the wrecker up to her and throwed the big 7/8 inch chain around her neck and hoisted her, and she got up about, oh, I'll say five or six feet off the ground, and the chain around her neck broke. See, they had to pull this chain loose; it broke the smaller chain, and that weakened the other chain. And so, when they got her up about five or six feet from the ground, why it broke . . ."
>
> —Mont Tilly, railroad crew

". . . And it kind o' addled her when it fell, you know. And we
quick 'n' got another chain and put it around her neck then
and hooked it before she could get up."
— Bud Jones, fireman on the 100-ton derrick car

You are running out of Erwin the moment the chain first bites into
Mary's neck—down the dirt road, into the darkness of trees. The
circus is a mile away. *The trains don't even bother passing through
Erwin* . . . How will you save her now? Your teeth bite through your
lower lip, blood trickling onto your shirt. You feel nothing.

The scene flickers across your mind, brought to you by clowns'
eyes: bonfires lick across train tracks, the coal tipple engorged
with people, the crowd below noisy and whiskey-slicked. Mary
trumpets as she rises. The derrick strains. The other elephants,
already packed onto the train, trumpet too, butt their heads against
the steel doors. You choke on tears as you run, the air tightening in
your throat.

Soon you can see the fires for yourself, the tops of tipple and
derrick, twin towers. Mary trumpets, *mahout!*

The derrick (in the clowns' eyes) trembles, chain breaking, and
Mary falls with a soft thud onto the grass, onto her lungs. You cry
out, fall with her, tumble, and lie sprawled on the ground. Blind,
images superimposed over your sight, you scramble to your feet.

The chain is brought twice around Mary's neck. You cannot
breathe. A branch whips across your face, stings, but you see only
Mary's shadow, lit by fires, rising again into the air. You choke on
the crowd's fascination as they watch. The hooker and the man from
the bar are both there, forgetting their own pain. *Tease, you tease too
much.* You cannot go home to a dog which may be dead . . .

Mary against the fire sky, against the tusk of moon.

Now you sprint, sure you will die of the exertion, but not caring.
You can smell the smoke, hear the crowd for yourself. So close. So
close.

Mary jerks and you jerk, brought up short. Blood trickles from
both your mouths. "Ere—look at the beast!" The crowd laughs.
Clowns sob. The Bearded Lady rips out her hair. Mary's struggles
weaken. Your legs dangle.

For a moment, you gaze out from Mary's eyes as you gently
swing, look down upon the crowd, the dancing fires, across the tipple and its human cargo.

*Juicy leaves; muddy waterholes; a lazy trunk across the backs
of other elephants; hoopoe birds pecking lice from wrinkled skin;*

shadows of elephants at twilight, under the saffron sky; and then danger, danger orange and bright; fangs and tusks. Tiger.

You cry out, convulse at the moment of death, the reluctant *crack* of neck, and as Mary's eyes roll back into her head, so do yours. Your neck snaps to the side and you fall, hands clenched so tightly a knuckle pops. Your nerve ends are on fire. Everything around you shrieks with pain; every blade of grass, every tree.

The pain is an elephant eye with a corona in amber. *Ganesh.* Then you lose yourself in the reflectionless black.

> "She kicked a bit and that was all; see, that thing choked her to death right quick."
> —Sam Harvey, train engineer

1857. The smell of attar, the humid, moist taste of death, surrounded Jaipur. A bad year for you when you could not be near elephants. You had nightmares. The Sepoy Revolt, starting outside Mekut, spread until even the maharajahs seized at chances for independence.

One summer day you glanced up from the lake below the Amber Palace and saw elephants trudging across the ridge, fitted out in full battle dress. Arjun, your teacher now, rode the lead elephant, and he too was dressed for war.

Your parents had told you the plans last night, but you hadn't believed them. A show of strength, your father said. They would not fight, only bring luck to the maharajah. Your mother frowned, shook her head. Regardless, to send elephants against the British was madness. How could elephants match rifles and cannon?

You watched for a long time, while trumpets sounded and peacocks gave their mating calls. To the west: smoke and vultures. The battle. All day, after the elephants had faded from sight, you watched the trail of smoke, the circling vultures. So many vultures. So much smoke. Sometimes you imagined you heard cannon recoil, a tremor beneath your feet.

The lake waters turned a darker and darker blue, shadows long and distorted. You fell asleep. When you woke, the smoke was closer, the vultures identifiable by species. Along the ridge, the sun's rays driving like spikes into their backs: the mahouts and their elephants. Some mahouts upon litters, bodies stretched out, others slumped across their elephants. You counted. Thirty elephants had gone out. Twenty had returned. You could hear their moans, could feel their pain, even from the lake. Your heartbeat quickened. Disaster . . .

Breathless, you ran up the road to the Amber Palace. Through the quiet courtyard, the gardens, to the stables, there to meet a tired, wounded Arjun, death reflected in his eyes. He reeked of smoke and gunpowder, had burns on his face and arms. All around, elephants screamed, some with shrapnel wounds, veins laid open; others on their knees, their mahouts pleading with them to get up.

Your jaw dropped and the pain twisted your joints. Not real. A nightmare. Where was Arjun's elephant?

"Lakshmi, master?" Your voice shook.

For the first time, Arjun was an old man to you, back bent, movements slow.

"Lakshmi is dead."

"Dead?"

"Yes! Please. Go away."

And you left, too shocked to cry.

Ganesha dead? How could a god be dead?

> "We did not sit in judgment on her fate and I don't believe any of those who witnessed the event felt it was inhumane under the circumstances. She paid for her crimes as anyone else would."
> —Mrs. Griffith, eyewitness

Blood drips onto the grass; the Lady Who Drank Blood laps at the widening pool. They have hoisted Mary upside down from the derrick. Her head hangs three feet from the ground, her shadow small in the early morning light.

You crouch beside her, the clowns behind you. Mary's eye is open again, the wrinkles and long lashes and the reflectionless black. You wave the flies away. You are crying. You cannot help yourself. Your throat aches. *Ganesh . . .* You touch the bristly hair, the rough skin. Cold. Much too cold.

You will not work the booth today. Or ever again. The clowns weep but you feel nothing. Just your own grief. Just the chill wind blowing through you, and you so light and heavy at the same time. Burnt out. Now what will you do? *Take away their pain*, you said.

But, like your old mahout, you know you will never be whole again.

[Quotes adapted with permission from the *Tennessee Folklore Society Bulletin*, Vol. XXXVII, March 1971.]

Notes on
Mahout

The idea for "Mahout" came from a story someone told me about Mary, an elephant that was hanged for killing a person. The idea that an elephant would be hanged for a crime struck me as both absurd and sad simultaneously. When I thought about it, hanging an elephant also said something about human beings in general. So I researched the story, not even sure it was true, and I came across an article in the Tennessee Folklore Society Bulletin *about the incident.*

The more I read, the more it haunted me. But I couldn't think of a way to approach the subject that wouldn't be melodramatic or sentimental. Then, one day, I was staring at a photograph of myself as a child on an elephant outside the Amber Palace in Jaipur, India. Standing by the elephant was the elephant's mahout. Instantly, a synergy occurred. The story wasn't just about the elephant—what about its trainer? The mahout suffered the most from the animal's death. This was the person I had to write about.

But when I sat down and started to write the story, it just didn't work. Everything I wrote about the elephant was sentimental and insanely melodramatic. Everything about the mahout seemed remote and disconnected to reality. So I thought about it for a while and came up with a solution. The story of the elephant's hanging would be told using the newspaper quotes to provide some distance from the events and to provide irony. The story of the mahout would be told in second person, to make the reader almost be the mahout, thus removing the distance. The problem, of course, is that second person is rarely used in fiction, so some readers might react in the opposite way—they might feel more removed from the character than if I had used third person. (First person wasn't even an option—how could I possibly use first person for a sixty-seven-year-old Hindu man and get away with it?) But I didn't feel like I had any choice, so I stuck with second person. And then I decided that the flash-backs should not necessarily be chronological but instead thematic. Finally, I used my own memories of visiting Jaipur, and riding atop an elephant there, to create the flashback scenes. (I remember Jaipur because the run-down palace-hotel we stayed at served mutton curry for dinner every day for seven straight days, and because a piece of ceiling tile almost killed my sister when it fell near her bed.) I also used my further studies in Indian/ Southeast Asian religion and culture to frame the beliefs and viewpoint of the mahout in his maturity.

The result was the most complex story I'd yet written, and at the same time, I hoped, the most involving emo-tionally and intellectually. All of the elements with regard to chronology, structure, and voice that I used in "Mahout" I've since used in my more recent work, which is one reason I'm so fond of the story.

The Mansions of the Moon

(A Cautionary Tale)

ONCE UPON A TIME, IN THE CITY OF BLACK in the midst of the Great Desert, there lived a man named Murak Ubu. Murak bred, sold, and butchered goats for a living. He was so good at breeding, selling, and butchering goats, and acquired so many acres of land to do so that he eventually amassed a fortune with far-flung tendrils in a dozen lands.

For the first forty-five years of his life, Murak survived through a mixture of shrewdness, market leverage, and an unflinching sense of when to take risks. But, on the night of Murak's forty-fifth birthday, according to legend, Murak Ubu lost his mind.

It happened this way: Desperate for fresh air to clear his head of wine drunk at his birthday party, Murak fled the crowded, smoke-filled hall of his palatial home—left behind the noise and friends and the many presents heaped across the dining hall—and walked out into the spacious grounds of his estate. Studded with poplar trees and irrigated by ornamental ponds, his estate pressed up against the outskirts of Black and faced the low ridge of hills where he had first found fortune and fame as a goatherd.

Murak staggered to the ten-foot-tall statue of himself built in the central courtyard and pissed in the fountain that formed a moat around the statue. He stood there, giggling, as he contemplated the pompous image of himself. The night wind lay chill against his cheek, for it was the heart of midwinter and the stars above sparkled in the cold like the scales of a huge silver fish rippling through dark water. A long rectangular pool, lined with elderberry bushes, led from the courtyard to the edge of Murak's property. Murak had an unimpeded view of the hills beyond.

After a minute or two of watching the hills, Murak performed his first inexplicable act. Instead of returning to the party with its red-and-emerald lanterns, its lilting music, its musk of drugs, Murak climbed the statue until he clung precariously to his own stone head, his hands around his own stone eyes, blindfolded by the flesh.

Settling into his new position, perhaps even finding it comfortable, Murak hummed an old goatherd song to himself and looked out fondly across his beloved, goat-grazed hills . . . and nearly fainted from shock, brought back to consciousness by the intense vertigo that came over him as his hands began to slip. Or, as he put it in an account, dictated to a scribe, that eventually wound up in a text of famous quotations, still in print these five centuries later: "My being fought between the utter destruction of beauty beyond imagining and the utter inability of the flesh to be destructed." (Although some scholars believe an articulate scribe embellished Murak's utterance, for the man had a limited formal education.)

What had Murak seen so fleetingly, between one blink and the next? "I saw the mansions of the afterlife—ghostly gilded palaces and filigreed balconies, and pale tall towers with winding staircases, all of such intense beauty, and built at—twisted into—such odd and gravity-defying angles that my heart quickens even now to think upon it."

According to legend, Murak shouted so loudly that his wife Nepenthe and manservant Pook ran out into the courtyard, there to gasp at the sight of Murak gamely hanging onto the slippery brow of his own stone likeness.

Murak shouted at Nepenthe to look—"look at the hills, *look at the hills!*"—but when he looked again the vision had faded to ashes. The hills were just hills. The sky was black and whole, not nudged by the upward thrusting spires of impossible buildings. The wind brought the unsanctified smell of dust and goats.

Nepenthe and Pook, in their own highly individual ways, suggested to Murak that perhaps he had had too much to drink and it might be best to return to the party and forget this unfortunate hallucination, this eclipse of the common senses.

Murak, faced with barren hills, fertile wife, and perplexed manservant, giggled, shrugged, climbed down from the statue, and rejoined the party, no damage apparently done.

But the vision Murak had seen now inverted itself and, imprinted behind his eyes, became an obsession—a dream from which he would never really wake, despite all manner of begging and pleading from Nepenthe. His wife came from true aristocracy and she was not amused by the suddenly whimsical nature of her lowborn husband. Lowborners were not allowed eccentricity—that was reserved for proper, inbred folk.

Nevertheless, within the year Murak had assembled a sampling of the best architects, artisans, and stoneworkers the city of Black had ever seen—brought from the farthest reaches of his business empire. Once gathered, they listened as Murak described his vision: Mansions that seemed to float; palisades that swooped and swooned from the weight of their own transient beauty; gargoyles as heavenly as cherubim and cherubim as devilish as gargoyles. Plans were drawn up, scrapped, and drawn up again, until finally approved by Murak. Laborers were hired from Black to lay the foundations. But even as they lined their pockets with Murak's gold, the men and women of Black laughed behind their hands. Such a project could never be completed! It was ludicrous! Maybe Murak had lost his mind sniffing the fumes that rose from goat turds.

Yet, slowly, despite the doubters, the Mansions of the Moon took shape over the next thirty years, with all the ponderous beauty of a reluctant-to-open rosebud made of white marble.

No mere buildings, these: Murak saw the Mansions of the Moon as the fullest expression of his own being, the one true mark he would leave upon the world; a humble goatherd become the architect of a wonder that would last a thousand years. His wife, however, believed it would mark Murak as "a feeble-dreamed eccentric whose destiny, if destiny smiles upon him, will be to be laughed at throughout the ages." (A quote that appears in an obscure tome on etiquette in which the Lady Ubu would not stick to or expand upon her topic.) Early on, Nepenthe abandoned Murak for the comforts of a seaside villa in the port of Green. Murak hardly noticed, caught in the throes of his fever dream. (In fact, his journal from three months after her departure notes, "It has been at least a week since I last saw Neppy—doubtless she is being considerate and trying to keep out of the way.")

As the Mansions began to rise above the city, those who

laughed grew fewer. The merchants and members of the city's ruling oligarchy still laughed—but with greed, ensconced as they were in splendid new villas among the hills. Murak welcomed the steady flow of rich businessmen, landlords, and politicians—glad of their money and oblivious to their backstabbing, two-faced compliments. Where he saw dreams made stone, they saw profits and real estate.

In the thirtieth year of the project, Murak declared that he could now rest in his labors and that the Mansions of the Moon could be considered "as completed as is likely to occur in my lifetime." After all, he was already seventy-six.

More and more rich townsfolk left Black for the hills above. Tourists traveled from distant lands. Murak himself led triumphant tours through the catacombs, the bedeviling twists and turns, the false exits, the secret entrances, the hollow walls: the thousands of architectural innovations intended to lend the Mansions a sense of mystery and wonder.

Murak shone from within despite his age—his steps were light, his demeanor ever gracious. He would lecture on the Mansions for hours, continually walking through his creation at all hours of the day or night.

But, within the year, even the most casual observer often sensed an abnormal restlessness in Murak. He would spend long hours staring up at the enameled columns, the frescoed ceilings, the detail work on the gilded stairs—so immersed in what he had wrought that he might have been his own statue in the courtyard of his former home, long abandoned for the Mansions. Like a wraith possessed (but possessed of what?), he would glide from room to room in his long, dark robes, his weathered face inscrutable except to his loyal but aging manservant, who must have known the anguish that lay behind the razor-gray eyes, the concealing beard.

The extent of that anguish was not known until, on the first anniversary of the Mansions' "completion," Murak climbed to the top of the tallest tower overlooking his beloved hills. He waved to a young shepherdess tending to her flock on a nearby hill. Then, as she would recount later, he stood balanced on the edge of the window, looking out across his lands. After a moment, he took a quick step forward, arms at his sides, and plummeted to his death on the rocks below: an old sack of bones and blood used up by the years.

He left only the sparest, most enigmatic of notes, which his estranged wife would eventually read: *It can never be the same as in my vision.*

Murak's death served as a dark christening for the Mansions, as if those elegant houses had not existed until Murak's blood brought them to completion. A malaise spread over the hills and into the city, an invisible but palpable tension building between those who lived above and those who lived below. This poison seeped into the foundations of social discourse so that beneath the facade of normal trade and dialogue lay an immeasurable distance. Even so, trade did continue, and it might even be said that the two groups understood that, at heart, their similarities meant more than their differences.

All would have been well, if not for the Awakening of the Beast (as the priests called it): an earthquake that rippled through the desert in the fifth year after Murak's death. Unfortunately, it became apparent that Murak Ubu's experts had built their masterwork atop a deep natural reservoir of water—useful during drought, but the root of disaster, for many mansions crumpled inward like toy paper houses, swallowed by the treacherous earth, the undulating hills. Smashed, rent, torn asunder, the Mansions of the Moon collapsed.

In the years of lawlessness that followed, the remnants of the city and the remnants of the Mansions withdrew into themselves like two mortally wounded pain-maddened jackals whose only hope of survival was to retreat to separate burrows. But if the city had the outlet of the wastes to drain off the madness, the Mansions had only the stifling silence of the marble halls, the haughty sterility of a dream come to dust. Many were the tales of incest and cannibalism and desperate rites that trickled down to the city folk in a constant stream of rumor. Many were the nights that the wild lights of the Mansions revealed bone-thin apparitions dancing to fast, unspeakably alien music while laughter wafted down like the language of the damned.

And, when the troubles ended, the tenuous link between the Mansions and Black had snapped like rotted hemp, and they were separate ships adrift, with no ties between them. No one from the city ever again visited the Mansions by choice, although on occasion youths pale as the deep-water fish the merchants brought from the coast would descend to buy food and supplies with old gold coins that many claimed had been pilfered from the houses of the dead. When the city folk imagined the mansion dwellers, they saw fey, hidden people ruling from on high, but ruling over nothing. Literal ghosts, come back out of death to abide awhile in the realm of the living. At night, the twisted, broken Mansions soaked up the moonlight and transformed themselves into a vision out of dream or nightmare, the white marble as ethereal and alien as the moon itself, forever suspended in the sky like a blind, ravaged face.

For, as Murak could have seen had he lived, it had taken a cataclysmic event for the Mansions to reveal their true, intended form. Surely Murak, gazing up at these Mansions—the palisades, the balconies, the columns all hopelessly askew—would have seen again the Mansions of his vision, in the form he had rhapsodized over that night when he had perched upon his own likeness and, drunk, stared up at his beloved hills.

Notes on
The Mansions of the Moon

"Mansions" is a tale set in the city of Black, the milieu for at least one other short story and a novel in progress. I think the Mansions of the Moon, in their ruined form, may well become my Gormenghast—over time, a peculiar society has sprung up within its broken walls. I like the idea in "Mansions" that perfection can only be achieved through ruination—that in the destruction or reconfiguration of "perfection," a different kind of beauty reveals itself.

The City

I

The Detective

T HE RABBIT WAS DEAD. WAS WHITE. WAS DEAD. Was six feet long. Supine on the ground. A trace of red against its mouth. A pocket watch half-buried in the sand. Rubbery and indistinct, a blackish waistcoat curled across its midriff. While above us the mountain rose like a threat or a throat.

I could smell the death in its matted fur. I could feel its death in the complete, the utter stillness of the body. The eyes stared out into a great nothing, a vast nowhere.

I was supposed to solve this.

Brown eyes, flecked with green. Fur around the mouth, stained green with grass. There was no grass anywhere around here. Bitter winds. Desiccated. Husk.

I stood up, fought the urge to struggle against the gentle pressure on the nape of my neck.

Hush. Dusk. I had spent an hour staring at this *apparition*, with no insight forthcoming.

What makes death solvable or soluble? What might be considered a clue? The red hissing from the mouth like a sleek ribbon of snake? The wound to the belly, spilling out like sawdust? The ticktock of the watch on my wrist, telling me to hurry. Should I solve the crime, I'd be much lauded. Should I fail, none would care but me.

Behind me somewhere lay the city of teeth and blood and exhaustion and skies full of smoke and streets at night lighted like strands of emeralds, the towers set to rise like knives cutting the underbelly of the blank sky.

Here, in the desert, the sky was a deep blue shot through with deeper cloud, masked by the mountain rearing out of the sand.

Out here, I had my familiar. In the city, my familiar could not always manifest himself, make himself known to me. No one could manifest in the city all the time. Out here, he could stretch, uncurl, spread his wings of manta-ray black to their fullest extent. The desert glinted off of them, melting into a relaxation that seemed earned.

"Rabbit," I said. To hear myself say it. It sounded just like I wanted to hear myself talk.

"Rabbit," my familiar agreed.

I had no name for my familiar. I felt no need for names, even for myself. How could anyone mistake him for another? His shape formed a shadow across me, his breath a black spurling of memory, cloves, desire, and cinnamon. With the desert's red dust around us, the mountain rising, it seemed I could be his familiar. His voice like a smooth rasp of cloud across a night sky. His flickering appearance like the glimmer of a coin at the bottom of a pool of still water. In a courtyard in the city. Where a hundred thousand familiars . . .

"It's not from here."

My familiar rippled and coalesced behind me, over me.

"Not from there, either."

Where a hundred thousand familiars gathered, the motion of their passage a mighty wave across a parched land . . .

Helplessness and shame overtook me, the emotions I always feel at the scene of a crime. The death that cannot be catalogued except by time. The death that cannot be avenged except by the deceased, the only person who cannot avenge . . . anything.

What could my familiar and I do? The taste of continuous failure was like sand on my tongue. I could not remember any of my other cases.

What I cannot solve may kill me.

Sunset. Reds peeling off across the reds of the corpse, the fur flush with dust and dirt and sand.

I felt the tickle in my throat caused by the umbilical that hung between me and my familiar—this cloak, this being that spread out behind me through the celestial air. My familiar was feeding me, and I did not want to be fed.

I saw a children's book. I saw a large white rabbit. I saw a girl in a dress. I saw a talking caterpillar. The familiar was feeding me what was not familiar. But the *story* seemed familiar somehow. As if I had pressed my face against a fogged up pane of glass, just barely able to see inside a house of marvels. I shuddered. Stop feeding me.

"You don't recognize it."

If a familiar could ever feel disappointment, I felt that emotion course through its undulating body and into mine. The itchiness in my throat became severe.

"This is not a real murder," my familiar told me. "This is a dream of murder. It will fade, if you do not recognize it."

I began to panic. I began to have memories from before the city. I really was a detective once. I knew this; it had not been fed to me. All the blood cells, the flesh, the skin, the nerves crawled with this knowledge.

What I cannot solve may kill me.

The red desert dust, the clot of dust in the air, like a stroke about to claim me. I could feel the tube from its body to mine in the back of my head, my neck. I could feel it there, coiled like a question mark. The taste of lime on my tongue.

He should have had a real waistcoat. He should have been somewhere else, this rabbit. Not here.

"You will see," my familiar said. And then said again, in another way: You will see. And you will be amazed.

For that was when the white rabbit shuddered. That's when the white rabbit shivered. Shook, coughed, wiggled its ears. Shook. Sat up. Wiped the blood from its mouth.

"I thought you were broken," I said to it. "I thought you were dead. I thought you did not know what you were."

The creature turned to me, its eyes brown and deep: as deep as hazelnut in winter, by a fireplace, in a city, but not *the* city, except I should not have that memory. Was it fed to me? Was it *me*?

It turned to me, this creature, and said, "You are the broken one. I've been sent to solve you."

"Solve me? But I'm not dead?"

"How do you know?"

II

The Accounts of Others

"Get out of my brain!" he shouted while at some far-flung trading post. Dirty shanty town without enough water. Faded grass. A couple of horses looking close to gone. This place would not be here much longer.

"Get out of my brain!" he shouted again.

I didn't know if he meant the city, or the familiar rising half-invisible above him.

The familiar was dead white—it was just drifting in the breeze, in the pale sunlight. The umbilical was like a dry reed. The man could have pulled himself free at any time.

Was I the only one among them who could see it?

I met his wild stare.

"I've come to take you back to the city," I said.

He ignored me. He was already there.

There was nothing to stop me from getting there. I had been walking for a long time, but there was still nothing to stop me. Why should there be? I could either walk or stop walking. There's no real decision in that, is there?

The desert spread out ahead of me, the city where it had always been: in front of me. It never changed. It always seemed to be in the same place: a dark glitter, a black speck in the corner of my eye. A hint of a scent, taken by the wind. I never made any progress toward it. It never made any progress toward me. You could say we were equals in a way.

Sometimes I passed other people, most of them dead, their flesh flapping off them like little flags. Sometimes I passed no one but the ever-wheeling hawks against the blue disease that was the sky. It did not matter. Walking mattered. Finding water mattered. Finding food mattered. Eventually reaching the city mattered. Not minding the mirages mattered.

The mirages could become intense. A mirage could kill you if you let it. You had to want to let it. You had to want to let it inhabit you. It could take any shape, any form.

Like a familiar. I had heard tales about the familiars. The city blossomed with them, all manifesting in different ways. Manta rays. White rabbits. I heard about a detective once. Just once. But never again.

People in the city had lost the thread of living without familiars. People there had just lost the thread, period. Deep wired into the spinal cord. Sucking into them. Sucking out of them. A city of spines. A city of familiars. A city of people. A city of not-people. Had it created them or had they created it?

Sometimes, as I walked, I didn't think I ever wanted to reach it, though the blisters on my feet yearn for it. Sometimes, it seemed the promise of bliss.

Walking is good, but walking can change you. Endless walking. When it first occurred to me that the city wasn't getting closer, I wondered if perhaps I didn't deserve the city. Sometimes, I thought it didn't deserve me. Perhaps both were true. But, regardless, there was nothing else to see on the horizon. Nowhere else to head for. It really was the last. The only.

And sometimes I would drop to my knees in a wordless rage. How could it keep evading me? How could it make me keep on walking?

And it's true. I admit it. Eventually, I begged the city to accept me. I stood there and begged for this dot at the corner of my vision to let me get close.

But by then it was too late. By then its absence had become too familiar.

The tube of flesh is quite prophetic. The tube of flesh, the umbilical, is inserted at the base of the neck, although sometimes inserted by mistake toward the top of the head, which can result in unexpected visions. The umbilical feeds into the central nervous system. The nerves of the familiar's umbilical wind around the nerves in the person's neck. Above the recipient, the manta ray, the familiar, rises and grows full with the knowledge of the host. It makes itself larger. It elongates. The subject goes into shock, convulses, and becomes limp. Motor control passes over to the familiar, creating a moving yet utilitarian symbiosis. The neck becomes numb. A tingling of lime forms on the tongue. There is no release from this. There should be no release from this. Broken out from their slumber, hundreds are initiated at a time, the tubes glistening and churling in the elision of the steam, the communal need. Thus fitted, all go forth in their splendid ranks. Thus filled, all go forth in their splendid ranks. The eye of the city opens and continues to open, wider and wider, until the eye is the world.

This is what I have been told. I never witnessed it myself. I heard it from a walker. A man who told me that the city is a mote in

his eye. I suppose it might not be true. I cannot verify it. I cannot
deny it.

A city in her head that could not be true made her wince. A city
that she had been searching for her entire life—all across the wastelands that often revealed more of their past than made her
comfortable. A city that pulled her out of herself. Something that
was more than a thought but less than an idea. A city that became
so real to her, in its scraps and tatters, that her own life became the
abstraction. She saw glistening spires and sudden terror, and an
illumination that nearly blinded her. She saw great black shapes
passing through the sky, attaching themselves to more mundane
shapes. She saw causeways made of air that bore weight. A thousand images that could not be real, that would never be enough to
sustain her in that vision, that delectation, forever on the tip of her
tongue, the word she could not say: the name of the city.

I left my lover in the city because I found the city too immense.
Now all I had of her were memories. Rosebuds. Rose petals. Dried
roses. Flowers found in parks and more dangerous places. The
thought of the forests in the south of the city where you could
always find the blood-soaked remains of a person for whom the
familiar had become strange. The visitations in the north. The long
palatial glide down the ramp above which gather the umbilicals.
The music of the city that permeates the air, reaches into the
stones, the trees, the rich dirt. The fragrance as of a thousand per-
fumes, the air jagged with the musk of familiars. The clean, strong
lines of buildings. The way everything is planned, one can hardly
contain it in one's mind. It's like sunlight shining on marble that
turns to water that ripples with light as seen through a mirror.

I had broken from the city as she could not. I proved stronger
than my familiar, and feasted on his memories. Now, in exile, I lie
in her arms every night and make love to her. Although she is not
here, in these tiny rooms in forgotten towns, she stares at me from
the bed, and this comforts me. She has become my familiar.

The city? I remember little of it now. It is like a long caravan
disappearing into distance and time. Day by day, my lover conquers
more and more of my memory. Perhaps one day, it will seem as if I
never lived in the city at all.

A story, passed along in the wastelands as a warning:
Two men are fighting in the dust, in the sand, in the shadow of

a mountain. One says the city exists. The other denies this truth. Neither has ever been there. They fight until they both die of exhaustion and thirst. Their bodies decay. Their bones reveal themselves. These bones fall in on each other until each man is the other.

One day, the city rises over them like a new sun. But it is too late.

III

The Detective

"You are the broken one. I've been sent to solve you."

It's dusk now, when the rabbit tells me this. It's dusk and there's no light except the lights of the city at our back. An unimaginable sorrow comes over me. I cannot help it, even with my familiar pumping good thoughts, good images, into me through the umbilical, the cord, the chord, the knot, the fence, the gate, the conduit that reaches him into me.

"No, you're not dead," the rabbit says. "And there lies part of the problem."

"Familiar?" I say. "Familiar?"

But there is no answer. Just the rabbit. Staring me in the eyes. Trying to tell me something.

"Do you want to return to the city?" he asks me.

I turn away to look back at the city. It is as a mote in the corner of my eye.

I tell him, "No. Not really."

"Then don't be afraid to leave this behind."

The rabbit stands over me. His fur is rough, his scent thick. He brings his arms around my head as if in an embrace. There is a slight sound, indescribable, as he detaches my familiar. My familiar detaches. The weight lifts. The tickle in my throat is gone. I cough, cough again.

Above me, in the dark, with no moon, just the afterglow of sunset, my familiar floats, his voice no longer in my head, my mouth, my guts, my guilt. He is taken on the breeze. He is taken from me. Away. Toward the city. I crane my neck to watch him go. I watch him go: a black manta ray drawn to the lights.

I am alone with the rabbit. I am alone. I was sure the rabbit had been created by my familiar, but now I am not so sure. I am frantically searching my memory for some prior experience, some glimmer, some fragment that will help me.

The rabbit's hand is surprisingly human. He takes my hand in his. He whispers in my ear. And the black waistcoat unwraps itself from his torso and rises, whole and glistening, above his head, plugged into his neck. His familiar's tube is bifurcated. As he whispers, part of it coils around my own head. It connects. And there is no city. And there is no sand, no thirst. And I am weeping. I can see the girl and the rabbit and the caterpillar and the rest of it. It is no comfort. I am nowhere again, like the first time, walking with the rabbit into the desert, the familiar's familiar.

By what right should I have achieved this state? By what right should I never solve my case, only to have it solve me?

Notes on
The City

I ruined a PS Publishing trade paperback edition of China Miéville's The Tain *to write "The City." I didn't do it out of spite, but I was at an Aimee Mann concert and hadn't brought enough paper with me, probably because I thought it unlikely I'd write a story there. For years, I'd been struggling with a White Rabbit image — of a detective being brought to the scene of the murder of a huge, dead white rabbit eerily reminiscent of a certain children's book character. I tried a novel. I tried a short story.*

Then, suddenly, in the middle of an Aimee Mann song, something clicked and I just started writing furiously — using up every bit of white space in China's book. I didn't think about what I was writing; it wasn't that kind of story. It was the kind of story that you have to write without thinking about it. So that's what I did. Then came the shaping, the crafting, to get it right without ruining the subconscious elements that gave it intensity. (Alan DeNiro provided some great line edits.) The result is surreal and disturbing and yet, somehow, right. I see it as the ultimate far-far future story, possibly the end result of the Veniss Underground *milieu. But, in a sense, it hardly matters whether the setting is fantastical or futuristic.*

Experiment #25 from the Book of Winter: The Croc and You

YOU WATCH THE CROCODILE AND THE CROCO-
dile watches you. Under a slate-gray sky. Dusk over the midway. Clowns and jugglers. Stiltmen and acrobats. Cotton candy and rancid buttered popcorn. Your father's hand in your hand, his palm still sweaty from the calfskin gloves that were a present from your mother. A strip of masking tape on the side of the reptile's tank reads "Greed." Who had named him Greed, and why?

You watch the crocodile. It watches you. A waiting game you can never win. It is an expert at waiting. With no room to move, it wallows in five inches of brackish water, awash in coils of its own feces. Algae have turned the sides of the tank a corroded green that reflects your face back at you. The ridges of Greed's spine are dried out and cracked, with a revelation of pink sensitive flesh beneath, fly-circled and fly-settled. Greed spasms but cannot dislodge the flies. The claws on the strangely delicate front and back legs clack at the glass like a dog's paws on linoleum.

The permanent grin of Greed's mouth opens and closes on packed rows of greenish teeth. Atop the narrow snout, ornate nostrils spiral close together, the eyes far apart as if to compensate. The eye nearest you regards you oddly, the vertical black pupil set against bright speckled gold. The filmy nictating membrane licks the eye, withdraws. No photograph in a school science book could convey the mystery of even that single eye.

The barkers, standing larger-than-life against the snow-threatening sky, goad spectators to throw pennies and nickels into the tank. Greed thrashes and hisses, tormented by people who will read the evening paper and weep over reports of drowned puppies and tortured kittens. While you live inside a tunnel with the croc in the tank, your gaze open and unblinking. Your face reveals nothing, but inside something bends; something could be said to break.

Your father squeezes your hand and his voice descends to you through layers of cold and wind. "That's enough, don't you think. I think we've seen enough. Let's go see the rest of the circus."

When you do not respond, your father kneels, takes both of your hands in his, and looks you up and down with his flinty gray eyes.

"Let's go," he says with a gentleness that surprises you. He is such a large man, with shoulders hewn from stone. "Let's go," he says, and you see in his gaze not a reflection of Greed, but an image of your dead mother.

You allow yourself to be led away from Greed to the other attractions. But you do not remember them later except as glimpses, fragments, through a film of cold. The elephants have snowflakes in their long, dark eyelashes and red welts along their flanks. The jugglers wander aimless and forlorn, mouths cruel and unsmiling. The trained monkeys look like motley convicts in their red-and-black-striped shirts.

Your third-story apartment stands only four blocks from the circus grounds. The red brick building has dirty black balconies and laundry lines strung across the meager front lawn. Inside, the dark wooden staircase wheezes like a chronic asthmatic when stepped on.

Your apartment opens onto the kitchen where once your mother cooked dinner and washed the dishes. From the kitchen window, the familiar spreads out before you at the speed of boredom: the running lights of railroad cars like a crude necklace at the farthest extreme, near the dark spackle of liquid that marks what you can see of the river, shackled by bridges and overpasses; then the dark, rectangular factory buildings where your father works as a foreman; the smokestacks that drip black fire; the blinking red lights atop the smokestacks that make the darkness even more complete. On a good day, you catch only a tinge of pulped paper smell in the air. Most of the smell is brought home on your father's clothes.

Your father heats up cabbage and beef stew on the oven burners, under the dull kitchen light bulb, surrounded by the shelves of cans that form most of your meals.

"Did you like the circus?" your father asks.

On the walk home you had said nothing to him and he, for whatever reason, had said nothing to you. The circus hadn't come to town for years, but as you left under the peeling fake gold of the rotting front gate, you did not beg to return.

Now you nod and smile, playing with the salt and pepper shakers shaped like snowmen. "It was fun."

"What did you like best?"

The crocodile.

"I dunno. What did you like best?"

"The clowns. Maybe. But maybe the elephants. I always liked the elephants when I was a kid."

"The elephants were neat." But all you see is an image of Greed, watching you watching it.

Your father does not know this about you. Your father likes to hunt deer on the hills and slopes beyond the factory. He took you once but you just stood there, the rifle slack in your hand. Sometimes his eyes search your face for something that is not there.

He smiles at you as he pours stew into a bowl. You smile back, but your mind is elsewhere.

After dinner, in your room, beneath the airplane mobiles and the dormant ceiling fan, tucked into bed because tomorrow is a school day, the image of Greed eats away at you. Your gaze flickers from desk to drawers to bookcase to baseball bat to neatly stacked toys in the corner near the closet. The cold has crept into your bones and inside you can feel the infections eating away at your back; can feel the cool, slick coins strike the pink flesh; can feel a helpless animal rage.

Greed is coiled inside your chest and you cannot sleep. Sheep jump over fences only to turn into smiling crocodiles burrowing under fences.

You turn on the light, leave the bed, and dig a book out of the pile on top of the bookcase: *The Big Golden Book of Nature*. A crocodile photograph on page six stops your random flipping. You frown. The shape is familiar. The eyes hold your attention for a moment. But it is just a photograph. It conveys nothing real to you. On the mantel there is a photograph of your mother at the beach, holding you, her gaze serious yet serene. That photograph conveys nothing real to you either.

Later still, when the pressure becomes too intense, you sneak out with your baseball bat to save the crocodile.

Later still, when the pressure becomes too intense, you sneak out with your baseball bat to save the crocodile, the writer reads with smoldering disgust.

"Enough!" he shouts. Loud enough to hear himself through the Mozart rumbling from the speakers of his stereo system. Erupting from his seat by the window. Rips the sheet of paper from the anachronistic typewriter. Crumples it up and tosses it in the general direction of the wastebasket.

He stands in front of the window, breathing heavily, face flushed. Then sits back in his chair. Notes the precision with which the whorled black branches of the oak trees vein out against the sky. Stares at the misplaced immigrant pecking at the bird feeder: a lone robin. Wonders what went wrong.

A boy and his crocodile. A boy and his croc. A croc and his boy. The croc and you. Old stupid croc. Which the boy went to free with a baseball bat, of all things. In the middle of a frozen night. And the town had no name. And the boy had a room as generic as a manila envelope. And the dad is some kind of silent-but-noble blue-collar worker who goes hunting in the I-forget hills above the what's-it-called city. And the mother is dead because of laziness— because he hadn't wanted to write yet another character into the story. Poor mom. Dead of sloth.

It makes him nauseous—almost as nauseous as the proofs for his latest, *The Book of Winter,* which lies in a box on the desk, each page tattooed with red copy-editing marks from failed writers given a second chance by publishing companies as grammar-and-spelling champions. Inflicting a thousand trifling wounds in the flesh of the Beast. The Beast would not be killed—no, not by them.

The writer pulls a cigar from his rosewood humidor and lights it with a silver embossed lighter. The robin still roots around the bird feeder while fat nut-nourished squirrels squabble over husks on the frozen ground.

The thing was—he reflected as he took a puff and exhaled with a sigh of satisfaction, no longer in the present tense of anger—the thing was, the only element of the story he really knew anything about was *snow,* and although you could achieve some nice effects with snow, perhaps even impact the plot, snow could never be an effective character. Snow could not watch a crocodile watching it —and even if it could, it certainly could not attempt a rescue, except perhaps in some half-assed Buñuel film where the writers all took daily doses of LSD.

Of course, he had once *been* a child of a sort, even if some of his girlfriends claimed he'd been born eighty years old, and he *had* had a traumatic animal experience when he fed his constipated rabbit so many food pellets it burst open. (Technically the rabbit's fault for not refusing the pellets.)

The writer tapped his cigar into a glass ashtray and stroked his beard (what had once been a conscious decision to cultivate an image had become an unconscious affectation, a continual posing for an author's photograph). He wondered if the story would be more real for him if he substituted a rabbit for the croc. It might even build more reader sympathy for the situation.

> You watch the bunny. The bunny watches you. A waiting game you can never win. It is an expert at waiting. With no room to move, the bunny wallows in five inches of brackish wood chips, awash in coils of its own feces. Algae have turned the sides of the tank a corroded brown that reflects your face back at you. The fur on Bunny's back is dried out and mottled, with a revelation of pink sensitive skin beneath, fly-circled and fly-settled. The permanent grin of Bunny's mouth opens and closes on packed rows of cute greenish teeth. Atop the soft head, ornate nostrils spiral close together, the eyes far apart as if to compensate. The eye nearest you regards you oddly, the vertical black pupil set against bright speckled gold.

Yes, well—*no*—the writer decided, setting the cigar in the ash tray, *that* did not present a, uh, viable option, since it seemed he couldn't make stick the metamorphosis from croc to what's-up-doc (had Kafka had similar problems?) . . . especially since, Mozart's *Requiem* swelling behind him, his restless thoughts had touched upon a bunny tangent, sparked by the memory of a pair of delightful bunny-print underwear worn by . . . Carla? Stephanie?

A procession of carnal pleasures enjoyed with Carla and Stephanie (alas, separately)—the old Latin tricks that had withstood time and the Internet; the slow and the fast tumescence of the flesh, the truly religious revelation of the newly naked and the nakedly new —ran through his brain. Which put the lie to the overriding theme of his croc story: that a ten-year-old boy could have an experience that would alter his whole life. Unless it was seeing your whole family offed by a serial killer while peering out of the closet. Or a freak tornado that lifted the whole house up and wind-blendered everyone to death but you. (That neither Carla nor Stephanie would be talking to him again in the near or far future made no difference to his theory.)

He reread the beginning of the end from the yellow longleaf sheets he had been massaging into typed sheets:

This happened thirty years ago. I was ten. So was she. I never saw her again and the croc was gone when I checked the sewer the next day. I don't know if it survived for long. For almost a year, the image of the girl possessed me: the sudden appearance of her at Greed's tank that night, the sudden disappearance of her.

I am not old yet, but I have been through two failed marriages. I have no children. I am good at my job with a sales company, but I will never be famous or very rich. I find myself coming back to the memory of that night again and again. How she said almost nothing and yet I understood her perfectly. In the photographs of my ex-wives I now see the shadow of her in their black hair, the high cheekbones.

The memory of that night is like a beacon to me now as I seek to make my life more meaningful. It is a moment fraught with mystery. It is the kind of moment that may never come again. Where the elements and your companion join together in a way that makes you feel as if you have become one with the world once and for all. To be so very light against the heaviness of flesh.

Boy, the writer thought as he stopped short two paragraphs from the end, like a horse drawing up lame in the final stretch, that was beautiful. Except it wasn't particularly true, which made it a lie, and therefore as ugly. If you lived in the moment—for the moment, of the moment—that could never be true. Each moment layered on the next and in each you could find something or someone unique, beautiful, irreplaceable. How could anyone exist in the world without continually dying from the irredeemable beauty of it?

The writer picked up his cigar and breathed in its thickness. Take winter—such a bracing time of year, he thought, addressing the glowing red tip as if it were a good friend. Every detail on the sidewalk, from a rage of red-orange leaves to a green meandering crack in the concrete, took on a binocular significance. It was a forethought of the awareness that overtook him when he wrote: the premonition of something moving through him and onto the page, the pen in hand become a blur and the heart so full, limbs aflame, body with fever. Like sparks burrowing into you until, finally conquered, you become vessel, container not contained—trapped and free—and all the little hairs on your arms rise, and you feel as if your own skin has been painlessly flayed back to reveal, beneath the perfect diagram of veins and arteries, the beauty and horror of the world—the words like tiny mysteries and the combinations of words solutions to those mysteries, and yet more mysterious for the revelation . . . and you're crying silently because, after all, these words are your life, even in distilled form, even brought forth by an unknown will . . . and you know this is the closest you will personally ever come to an awareness of what God might mean—this feeling that so encompasses the whole of your being that you are unimaginable strength and weakness intertwined . . . and in the aftermath, the writer often found, as the madness left him, that he would observe, say, the reflected worlds within a perfect drop of water as it lazed in the sudden sunlight across the yard, and was spent, exhausted, by even that simple image.

Yet another lie—*a lie!*—he realized as, shivering though it was eighty degrees in the house, he turned off Mozart and returned to his desk, to stare at the sheets of paper. A lie because he had felt that madness, that high, when he had been writing what he had come to think of as "Experiment #25—The Croc and You Story," and "Experiment #25" had turned out to be a steaming heap of dung, despite having originated in "inspiration."

He put out the cigar for good and rummaged through the papers until he came to what he now believed had been the fault point—the introduction of the girl once the boy had snuck back to the circus at night:

> *A girl stared at him from the other side of the tank. He came to the realization slowly—the lighting dim, the tank corroded with algae—but as he turned inward, into his thoughts, he stopped focusing on the crocodile and his gaze fled into the glass, where he saw his own face and, as if superimposed over it, the girl's face opposite him. She stood very still. He thought her an apparition*

and then, with a start of dread, something far worse: a
circus hand who had discovered his trespass.

    Taking hold of his fear, the boy slowly walked to the
far edge of the tank and peered around the corner . . . just
as the girl peered around her corner of the tank. The
white of their breath mingled. Warmth leaked into him
through his pores. Black hair shot through with the white
of snowflakes. Cheeks flushed with cold. Eyes soft and
blue and lined with long lashes. She gave him such a
searching look that he shivered from something other
than the cold. The words she spoke came out with a melo-
dious tingle: "He's Sorrow, not Greed. They named him
wrong. We will call him Sorrow."

The writer had originally added her not as some inspiration or
epiphany, but because the boy's plan—the baseball bat—had been
so bad and he saw no way to dissuade the boy from it. Except perhaps through an accomplice—someone who *did* have a plan. He
had chosen a girl who had snuck into the circus at the exact same
time. How very convenient, and depressing. It meant some sentimental echo of a Hollywood formula film haunted the story.
Mass media should be gut shot and left out in the desert to die, he
decided, looking again at the page proofs on his desk.

    The writer leaned back in his chair. The robin had left the
feeder because the robber baron squirrels had found a way up the
greased pole—good for them. He should have left the girl out. After
all, Hemingway hadn't written *The Old Man, the Sea, and the
Coincidental Girl.* Nor had Nabokov, for that matter, written *Lolita
and the Boy with the Baseball Bat.*

    Women. Carla and Stephanie in his case. He loved them both
—whichever he was with he found himself sincerely devoted to, in
that moment – but had hurt them both. It had become a theme in
his family, a tradition carried forward by his grandfather and father,
a curse that you could resist, like encroaching vampirism, but to
which you finally succumbed, faltering into a life of frank debauch-
ery. At least, unlike his recent ancestors, he had never married.
Still, worse fates than the guilt of adultery awaited him. Last
Thanksgiving, brought to the dinner table by the smell of turkey,
his grandfather, defiant in the mid-to-late throes of Alzheimer's,
had suddenly stood up and, before the assembled mob of two-score
relatives, recited in pornographic detail—like an erotic sergeant at
arms barking out name, rank, and serial number to the capturing

enemy—the particulars of every romantic roll-in-the-hay he had had over a sixty-year career of philanthropic philandering. While the family sat aghast, unable to stop him, and every man in the family under the age of fifty smirked behind his mashed potatoes. It had been, in an odd way, his grandfather's finest hour.

If truly generous, he should write a story about two beautiful, intelligent women in which they did *not* meet a visiting writer at the sales office where they both worked. They might appreciate that. They might even thank him for it. Alas, he doubted either would ever talk to him again. He had deliberately hearticulated his love for Carla in glistening glissando at her office, in front of a green-card Bangladeshi who, at last glance, had known little English. But the intern had, in the interim, empowered himself by colonizing the language via correspondence course and, giddy with self-improvement, shared the discussion with one of Stephanie's friends.

At the time, the writer had thought his idea cleverly erotic: to reveal a secret while a third party who could not possibly understand sat within earshot, oblivious. Instead, it had simply been hysterical. The next day a wildly comical farce had played out when the woman he was sleeping with met the woman he was sleeping with when he came by to pick up one of them for lunch (he had forgotten which one).

Maybe the croc story was just an attempt to keep his mind off of these things.

Just visible from the window, icicles hung from the golden wind chimes by the front door. Though frozen, the chimes moved in the wind and made a sound somewhere between bells and the crack of an ice cube tray. It was definitely winter—the winter of a nonterminal discontent. He could feel change coming in his bones: they shifted and shook in contemplation of it. The truth of it would be revealed soon, as it had finally been revealed to his father that autumn, in the form of inoperable colon cancer, no doubt brought on by his abandonment of his wife, the writer's mother (for the aforementioned reasons of philandering, as before stated, in this court of law, your honor, sir, and therefore the monies released to my client should be quite substantial and should include such properties as . . .). Neither of them was happy: Dad was dead and Mom spent her days re-wallpapering a house littered with mail-ordered commemorative plates. One day, the writer knew, the re-wallpapering would become so frenzied the rooms would shrink to well-insulated postage stamps in size. These were the kinds of revelations he could do without.

As for the boy in the story, nothing would ever be revealed to him. He could not be rescued from the story. Not that it was much of a story anymore. It consisted of a lone snow-encrusted crocodile. No boy. No girl. No father. No real setting. The writer felt a grim satisfaction. Let none of them get away alive. Not a single soul. Not on his watch.

> A million snowflakes had fallen across Greed's back during the night—so many that the crocodile shone more white than green. Frost had stolen over the ridges above its eyes and formed shimmering ice bridges. A delicate layer of ice coated the water that imprisoned its feet. Greed would die if left out here much longer. He might die anyway.

Crocsicle, Popsicle. The writer set down the papers for good. Yes, he might die anyway. But of all the story elements, Greed/Sorrow had been best described. A very good facsimile of a crocodile in pain. Maybe he could rescue the old croc—airlift him out of "Experiment #25" and into another story. Perhaps even into a poem. After all, it was the Age of Free Verse. He could just put in some lazy line breaks and sell it to a pretentious little poetry journal.

So, save the croc, briefly mourn the rest, and pray that Carla and Stephanie (her eyes so blue and her double entendres, *her* golden legs and fractured stories) would forgive him as he did not forgive himself. Meanwhile, the cigar had awakened in him a need for scotch—amber, calm, and deep—so there was nothing for it but a trip to the local bar.

On went the coat, the gloves, the scarf. He walked to the door, the cold-encrusted croc already lumbering attentively behind him in his imagination. The city in winter spread out before him: austere and bitterly clear in the cold fading light. The glow of houses and buildings floated against the horizon, half-concealed by trees. A flash of gold, shot through with early dusk, so that a corona of shadow spread across the sidewalk. The cold he loved. Better if not alone, but still he loved it. Into the glissade of snow. Into the glister of ice.

At the door, a sudden image struck him: of the boy, watching the girl walk away through the snow, not knowing he would never see her again, and he hesitated—almost bumped into the image of

Sorrow, who had already begun nestling into another story. With the smell of pine in his nostrils, the brisk burn of the cold, the glints and glimmers of "Experiment #25" that rose in his mind seemed genuine. The childhood memory that holds true when all else is ruin. The desire, in times of need, to sublimate yourself to a quest, a mission, to anything that will allow you to forget your situation. To—sweet bliss!—disengage from thinking altogether.

The last paragraphs of the story stole into his mind like the silent tread of snow across a distant rooftop.

> *Ever since then, in bad times and in good, thinking back to that night, I have wondered if I am searching for something that does not exist, something that even saving Sorrow cannot salvage, something that—like a cell or a fingerprint or even love—is so individual yet ephemeral that it never appears in exactly the same way, though you spend your whole life.*
>
> *Despite this, I can see the girl, even now, walking off into the silence of the slow snowfall, in the dark glowing with street lamps, while I just watched her, certain I would see her again, certain that Sorrow would live—and I just kept watching until the dark and the snow covered her up.*

A puzzled look appeared on the writer's face. He turned back into the doorway, where the crocodile waited. The writer watched Sorrow and Sorrow watched the writer. The bright, gold-speckled eyes regarded the writer with an odd and ancient gaze. It was just him and the crocodile, in a tunnel of cold. Shaken, he put a hand out to support himself against the doorway. A thought had overtaken him and something inside had bent; something could be said to have broken: *What if his gift knew more than he did?*

Then and only then did I relax, stretch my arms, take a puff of my cigar, and set down my pen, well satisfied with the book of winter.

Notes on
Experiment #25 from the Book of Winter:
The Croc and You

"Experiment #25" was an inspired accident, created because I found myself writing a story that didn't seem to be going anywhere. I had airlifted the image of the crocodile out of a Sinead O'Connor song about the Dublin Zoo and into an unfinished novel called Moot & the Mad Preacher, *but hated to leave the creature there: it had so much promise. So I'd tried to construct a story around it, only to lose faith in the plot.*

Rather than abandon the story, I used my frustration and anger at not being able to complete it as the catalyst to redirect the narrative. In so doing, I freed myself up to finish the original story within the frame of the new, more autobiographical direction. The crocodile had become so real in my mind that even at the end of "Experiment #25," I was reluctant to set it free. I really loved that crocodile.

"Experiment #25," "Learning to Leave the Flesh," and "The Bone Carver's Tale" form a kind of loose trilogy. I'm always curious about how the imagination manifests itself, how it leads us to disaster and to happiness. These three stories explore that theme.

Three thousand copies of this book have been printed by the Maple-Vail Book Manufacturing Group, Binghamton, NY, for Golden Gryphon Press, Urbana, IL. The typeset is Electra with Veljovic Bold display, printed on 55# Sebago. Typesetting by The Composing Room, Inc., Kimberly, WI.